First . . .
LABYRINTH
in which Jon Land drew a terrifyingly real picture
of a nuclear age gone mad.

Then . . .
THE OMEGA COMMAND
in which this enormously talented young writer
shattered the nerves of readers everywhere with a
vision of technological disaster.

Now . . .
THE COUNCIL OF TEN
in which all the enemies of freedom unite to destroy
the world forever

Fawcett Gold Medal Books
by Jon Land:

THE COUNCIL OF TEN

LABYRINTH

THE OMEGA COMMAND

THE
COUNCIL OF TEN

JON LAND

FAWCETT GOLD MEDAL • NEW YORK

A Fawcett Gold Medal Book
Published by Ballantine Books
Copyright © 1987 by Jon Land

Library of Congress Catalog Card Number: 86-91817

ISBN 0-449-13117-3

Manufactured in the United States of America

First Edition: May 1987

IN MEMORY OF MY GRANDFATHER
A PART OF THIS, THE ONES THAT CAME BEFORE,
AND ALL THAT WILL COME AFTER

PROLOGUE

DARKNESS FELL LIKE A BLACK SHROUD TOSSED OVER THE JUNGLE.

Drew ran. The rain had turned the ground to mud and his feet sloshed noisily through it. He was forgetting stealth, the first lesson. Pursuit was inevitable now. He had to make it work for him.

How many remained he could only guess. He knew Mace was one of them and Mace was the best. Drew clutched his Uzi tighter and squeezed himself against a tree. Its branches were a partial shield against the torrents.

Lightning flashed, providing a confusing moment of illumination. Drew stepped softly away from the tree, back onto the path. The rain pounded him again, but he had quickly become used to it. His uniform was soaked through to the skin, his small backpack waterlogged and sagging. Five days in the jungle now and there had been rain during all of them. But the end was coming.

A branch cracked in the mud behind him. Drew swung. His finger found the Uzi's trigger. The dark figure covered with mud sprang forward. Drew fired a burst into its stomach. The figure crumbled to the ground, invisible in the blackness.

Drew stepped backward, his Uzi fixed on the still figure. Thunder rumbled. Trees loomed on both sides of him. Drew started to turn.

It was the turn that saved him. The man snaking an arm over from behind was forced to alter his action enough for Drew to

1

sense it. *Yank the opponent backward at the throat while driving your blade into his spine*—the move was as potent as it was classic. But Drew knew it was coming now and twisted away, deflecting the blade as it came up, then ramming the barrel of his Uzi into the attacker's gut. The man grunted and Drew slammed a knee into his solar plexus. The man went down.

Drew was behind him instantly, his knife against the man's throat.

"How many? How many left?" he demanded in a whisper. Silence was paramount now.

"Just three," the man rasped.

"Who?"

"You, me . . . Mace."

Drew's lips twitched at that. It was down to just the two of them, then. . . . Wasting no time, he stripped the cord from his backpack and tied the man up, lacing his hands and feet together and stringing both to his throat, so any attempt at freedom tightened the makeshift noose. Drew dragged the man into the brush and made sure his face was tilted away from the pooling water. Then he was on his way once more.

Incredibly, the rain seemed to intensify. He could see no more than a few feet ahead, but using a flashlight here would be like serving himself up to Mace on a silver platter. Perhaps, though, that was the answer. Do something stupid to draw Mace to him. Bait a trap. No, Mace was too clever for such a ploy to work. Drew's best hope was to keep moving with obedience to the first lesson, his steps sure and Uzi always at the ready. In close, where it would surely end now, Mace's skills might be less dominant. And the rain might be an equalizer, too. Thunder lashed again and Drew's heart lurched with it. Back on the path now, he cleared his eyes with a swipe of his forearm.

His next step felt all wrong. He struck a hard spot in the soft ground. What came next his mind recorded like individual frames from a movie.

First, Mace's hands grasping his boot and tripping him up, then Mace rising over him from the gulley where he had waited, and, finally, Mace's blade angling down for his throat.

For an instant Drew thought he could stop the thrust. But when his arms came up, Mace's incredible quickness darted the blade past them and whipped it sideways in a narrow arc. Drew felt the twitch and his hands rushed desperately for this throat. He fell backward in defeat.

Mace rose to his feet and wiped the mud from his arms and face. His smile turned to a laugh and he extended a hand to Drew.

"Come on, kid, let an old man help you up."

Drew grasped it and let Mace pull him to his feet. "You win. Again."

Mace was working the knife over his pant legs to strip the mud. "But you're getting closer. How many this time?"

"One captured. Four killed."

"I think I got seven. Not sure. Hey, you're getting better each session."

"You don't get any prizes for coming in second."

"You can have my free tuition to the next session, kid. Who knows, maybe that'll be the time you get lucky."

Drew looked into Mace's eyes, which were the color of mud. He wondered if that was camouflage, too. "Only if you go back to . . . where? Angola? Chile? Where will it be next?"

"Nicaragua probably. Lots of demand down there. They don't pay for shit, though."

"Okay, so I'll spring for your tuition when you get back."

"Deal," said Mace. "Come on, let's fill the high command in on the final results."

They started walking through the rain.

"First round's on me," Mace added.

"Nope. Loser pays."

"Hell, eighteen others went down before you. Stand in line."

"I still bought it. Number nineteen or not."

Mace stopped. His face turned somber. "It was just a game, kid. Don't forget that. Reality sucks. Trust me, I've been there."

"Yeah," said Drew. "I suppose it does."

PART ONE:

THE GRANDMOTHERS

CHAPTER 1

"So, Sophie, you gonna kill him or what?"

Doris Kaplan grasped her friend's bony shoulder and squeezed it lightly.

"Huh? What?"

"The fly," Doris said, eyes aiming at the insect creeping up Sophie Guttenberg's sleeve. "You've been watching him long enough. Swat him before he bites."

When Sophie shrugged lamely and returned to shuffling her tarot cards, Doris reached across the airline seat and struck out at the fly still meandering about her friend's liver-spotted arm. The insect avoided the strike easily and flew away.

"There," Doris said, "that's all you had to do."

Sophie Guttenberg shrugged again and began laying the tarot cards out in neat rows.

The No Smoking—Fasten Seatbelts sign flashed on, and a stewardess announced that they had begun their descent into Palm Beach International. At last, thought Doris Kaplan. The flight had been an hour late leaving Nassau and she had stupidly packed her heart medication—"life pills" she called them—in her suitcase. Not that she really needed the red capsules. She was sure the old ticker was fitter than ever despite what Dr. Morris Kornbloom wanted her to believe. Damn cardiologists had to say something that got you back into their office once a month. Still, the bottle of life pills would have made a reassuring bulge in her handbag, as opposed to sitting in her toiletry case deep within the airplane's cargo hold.

"Gin!" Fannie Karp screeched from across the aisle, plunging her final discard face down atop the pile resting on a tray table. "How many points, Sylvie? Come on, how many points?"

Sylvia Mehlman frowned in displeasure. "I don't know. Let me count."

"Count? You don't have to count," accused Fannie. "You keep a running tab all the time. Who do you think you're talking to here?"

Sylvia feigned adding up the point total of her cards. "Thirty-eight. And I'm finished for today."

"Finished? You can't be finished. You still have me by at least a hundred."

"We're landing, for God's sake."

"One more hand," Fannie insisted, her arthritic, knobby hands gathering up the cards to be shuffled again.

Amazing, Doris Kaplan reflected, simply amazing. The Business had made both women rich beyond the measure of most, but death had been threatened more than once as a result of this quarter-cent-per-point gin game. Of course, the gin game had been part of their lives longer than the Business. But old habits die hard once you reach the mystical seventies, where feeling good seems a memory to be catalogued with all the others. Doris supposed that their thrice-yearly Business trips to the Bahamas were as much for distraction as anything else. You could look at only so many condo developments sprouting up along the beach and moving trucks negotiating the narrow coastal roadways before you realized that more than life was passing you by.

Doris Kaplan felt the plane's wheels lowering beneath her. Then she heard Sophie gasp.

"There it is," Sophie muttered, thrusting a trembling skeletal finger down at her arrangement of tarot cards. "Just like I thought." Her face was milk-white when she turned to Doris. "Something terrible's going to happen. The cards say so."

"Right," Doris returned softly, passing her off. "And you've been playing with the damn things since we left Nassau. How long did it take you to come up with that combination?"

"It's fate, I tell you, fate. We're being warned."

"More like the law of averages."

Sophie huffed and turned her attention back to her neat array of cards, focusing on the one marked Death in the upper right. Across the aisle from them, the final gin game was being interrupted by a stewardess insisting that all tray tables had to be placed in their upright, locked position.

"But I'm only one card away," pleaded Fannie. "One card!"

The stewardess smiled as politely as she could manage. "I'm sorry."

Sylvia had already seized the opportunity to gather up the cards and snap the tray table home. Fannie let her sure winning hand flutter to the aircraft carpeting, turning away and unhitching her seatbelt in an act of feeble defiance. If a sudden stop sent her lurching forward, it would serve the damn airline right.

Doris could only marvel at how a woman like Fannie had lasted so long in the Business, where secrecy and discretion were valued above all else. She guessed Fannie would have blurted out everything to her friends long ago, except the only friends she had were her three companions in this plane right now. It was no different for the rest. All the grandmothers had were each other, and mostly that was enough.

They had first met eight years before at the run-down apartment house that each tried to call home in Miami's South Beach. Never mind the terrors of being near seventy, widowed, and living on fixed incomes, which never left them enough money to get anything fixed except their teeth. Before long the Cubans had arrived and turned them into prisoners of rickety chaise longues set before a pool with perpetually green water that smelled of too much chlorine. It just wasn't fair. They had lived long enough to deserve better. At least that was what Doris had told herself constantly over the past five years, and up until very recently, the justification had held fast.

For the rest of the time Doris had done her best to feel no remorse over the thrice-yearly trips she and the other grandmothers made to the Bahamas. They had the rewards coming to them, didn't they? Even God Himself would understand that if He spent enough time trapped between stucco walls with Spanish music rising over Collins Avenue.

Doris's husband Sam had dropped dead of a heart attack at the tender age of fifty-two. It happened on the sixteenth hole of the members' course at the Westchester, New York, Country Club ten minutes after he complained of gas and two minutes after he kicked his ball twenty feet closer to the green. Doris took over his manufacturing business, and in a few short months had it running better than Sam had ever dreamed of, only to have a fire destroy everything but a safe containing the insurance policy he had let lapse.

The fates weren't finished with Doris yet, though. They sent a drunk driver into her son-in-law's station wagon on a rain-slicked night two years later. Her son-in-law died instantly, but it was two more days before the doctors could convince her that her daughter's brain was showing a permanent test pattern and the machines could be shut off.

So, at the age of fifty-four, Doris found herself raising her beloved five-year-old grandson, making the payments from various life insurance policies last until Andy hit college age. Then she tearfully sold the house she loved and headed south for what she hoped would be a simpler life in the sunshine. Even then, however, there were Andy's college payments to consider, and after that her insistence on supporting him until his career got off the ground. Doris had promised herself all those years ago that her grandson would never want for anything. The money was just about gone when the Business had started, but now even all the money she had made and good she had done could do nothing to ease the guilt.

Still, Doris figured that when you came right down to it, it was Andy who gave her an edge on her three friends. They, too, had grandchildren and families of varying sizes scattered across the country. But besides an occasional holiday card, sometimes a call, they were estranged and isolated; forgotten in the great South, which for all of them had once been little more than a mall-filled graveyard they hadn't known enough to lie down in. They had forsaken the repressed fear of South Beach for various locales throughout the Palm Beaches. The Business required that they spend summers as well as winters in the South, a condition that irked Doris because the summer convention trade spoiled the ambiance of the famed Breakers, where she had taken up permanent residence.

"Doris, are you all right?" Sophie was asking, all ninety shriveled pounds of her.

Doris blinked and realized that the plane had finished its taxi and people were crowding into the aisle. They were home.

"Just daydreaming," she said. "That's all."

Fannie had plowed a path forward and Doris followed her up the aisle, wondering what Sophie's tarot cards might have said if placed out five years before.

The grandmothers made their way slowly through Palm Beach International Airport. Doris would have opted for a quicker gait, except that Sophie seemed forever in slow motion these days and Fannie's size eighteen bulk had her winded between water fountains. Doris could tell that the early fall day was hot, and she longed for the quiet cool of her air-conditioned Breakers rooms.

At last they reached the baggage claim area, where the conveyor belt had only just started its rolling display of bags. A number of travelers pushed forward to better their positions. The grandmothers hung back.

Four nondescript men stood apart from the scene, each with a large suitcase by his side. The casual observer would assume that their bags had been the first off the plane. Only the men hadn't been on the plane and neither had these particular suitcases.

"There's mine!" Fannie screamed. "Doris, see if you can grab it for me."

Doris excused herself forward into the mass and grasped the handle of Fannie's plaid monstrosity of a suitcase. One of hers emerged swiftly after, and she saw Sophie and Sylvie lifting one of theirs together from the conveyor.

The grandmothers set these bags back a bit and waited for the rest.

One of the four men started forward, sliding along a huge plaid suitcase. He feigned deep attention on the conveyor while he shoved his bag up next to Fannie's. Grabbing the handle of her suitcase instead of his own, he began to back up again.

Another of the four men approached, this one carrying a perfect replica of Doris's American Tourister.

The grandmothers kept their eyes fixed on the conveyor, searching for the rest of their bags. By the time all were accounted for, the nondescript men had melted into the crowd outside the terminal, each with a large suitcase dangling from his hand.

Doris went for a porter.

CHAPTER 2

LANTOS HELD THE BRIEFCASE TIGHTER AS HE APPROACHED THE ALLEY. Not that he sensed danger, but one had to be prepared for it nonetheless, especially because of what his briefcase contained. The Miami drop had been his domain for years, and Lantos had been happy with it. Only as of late—say, the last few years—had the city degenerated into the crime capital of the country. Foreigners were to blame if you asked Lantos; spics, Colombians, Cubans, and combinations thereof. Take them out of the picture and Miami might regain its old splendor and glamour.

Lantos had often considered requesting a transfer, but he always came up short of making it because he knew Miami and a new territory, even with all his experience, would be difficult to master. He knew every street, side street, and back road in Miami, and he had never used the same one twice. Never a pattern that might allow someone to turn him into a mark. And if they tried—well, Lantos was ready for that, too.

The problem with holstered or sheathed weapons was drawing them. For a weapon to be effective, you had to have it out at all times. But how? Lantos smiled at the memory of posing that precise question to himself years before. The answer was to rig three razor-sharp, four-inch blades into his briefcase—not at the front or back, but at the *side,* where maneuverability was at a maximum. When pressed, a button on the latch just beneath the handle forced the daggers to spring out. Assailants never knew what hit them. The very object they were after was turned into

12

the instrument of their death. Lantos liked the justice in that. He had used the case often as a weapon, and always with success.

He heard the footsteps to his rear an instant before they were upon him. Lantos felt the hair on the back of his neck rise as he pressed the button. The three daggers, spaced inches apart, leaped out. From there he wasted no time, turning and swinging the now deadly weapon up in the same motion, the object being to take the assailant utterly by surprise.

But the assailant was already gone, a blur whirling by with something shiny in his hand, a shape more than a person. Lantos swung his deadly briefcase in a wide arc. It swished through the air, again finding nothing as a big arm grasped him from behind and yanked backward. The knife bit into his back and made a neat slice straight into his heart. Lantos was dead instantly, even his grip on the cherished briefcase relinquished in the end.

The shape stooped to retrieve it and walked away into the night.

Doris Kaplan felt that Wednesday was going to be a bad day even before the phone call came. She had retired early Tuesday night, but by three A.M. had given up fighting to sleep and switched on the cable news channel. She watched it mindlessly until the sky showed its first brightness beyond the blinds, finally drifting off into an uneasy slumber with the words of the anchorman forming her dreams.

Awakening alone, in the darkness of her bedroom, was far more frightening than not being able to sleep at all, and it had been Sophie, of all people, who had advised her in this regard: *Always sleep with a glass of water on your night table.* Drinking water, Sophie said, was the best way to settle yourself down once coming awake in the black loneliness. Doris had found that the water worked exactly as Sophie had promised. She stored her red life pills next to the glass on the distant chance that they might be needed some night as well.

The phone's chiming shook her awake, stiff and cold in her chair, just after nine. Joints rebelling, she stumbled to the phone at her bedside.

"Hello?"

"Doris." The voice was soft between what sounded like sobs.

"Who—Sylvia, is that you? What's wrong?"

"She's dead, Doris," Sylvia moaned. "Sophie's dead. . . ."

The police were already there when Doris arrived at Sophie's home on Embassy Drive in West Palm. Sylvia, seated in the living room, was being comforted by a police officer. Didn't she remember that Sophie never used the living room? When company came over, they sat in the kitchen or den, never here. Otherwise there'd just be another room for Sophie to clean.

"Oh, Doris!" Sylvia shrieked and Doris hugged her, smelling the too sweet perfume she had loaded on even at this early hour. She and Sophie went for a walk every morning at nine sharp. It must have been then that she . . .

"Mrs. Kaplan?"

Doris turned to her left and saw an overweight man wearing a sports jacket with a badge pinned to his lapel.

"I'm Sergeant Nickerson, Mrs. Kaplan. Mrs. Mehlman informed us you'd be coming."

Doris eased Sylvia away from her. When Sylvia tried to cling, Doris grasped her shoulders firmly. "I'll be right back." She moved to Sergeant Nickerson, not caring about the makeup she had neglected to put on, and sighed. "How did it happen?"

"The doctors are with her now," Nickerson reported. "We think it was a heart attack. We're almost certain. Did she have a history of heart trouble?"

"Can you name me a seventy-six-year-old woman who doesn't? I'm sorry, Sergeant. Yes, she had a slight history. Nothing to speak of, though."

"It happened in her sleep, Mrs. Kaplan. She went quickly."

"Where is she?"

"Well, Mrs.—"

"I want to see her."

Sergeant Nickerson had started to object, but he silenced himself and nodded. "In the bedroom. Just as we found her."

There were no ropes or uniformed police anywhere on the stairs or on the way into Sophie's bedroom. This was not a crime scene, after all. It was a simple investigation of a natural death. Doris reached the doorway of Sophie's overly large bedroom and gazed in. The drapes were still drawn. Two men were hovering over the raised shape of her friend, who such a short time ago had claimed that the tarot cards predicted something terrible was going to happen. One man was taking notes while the other seemed to be performing some sort of perfunctory examination. Doris entered without announcing herself and moved to the foot of the bed where she could view her friend clearly.

The sight made her grasp her own heart fearfully and realize that her life pills were back in her room next to her water glass. There was never anything pretty about death. Sophie's eyes and mouth hung open in a twisted mask of frozen agony, her last instant of pain captured forever. Her eyes looked more sunken than Doris had ever seen them before. She had died lying on her back, most of her body under the covers. Doris caught the soft whirl of the air conditioner humming and smelled the sweet lavender that Sophie oversprayed throughout the room.

"Was it a heart attack?" Doris asked.

The men at Sophie's bedside seemed to notice her for the first time.

"Yes," one of them said flatly, retrieving his medical bag from her night table.

"Aren't you going to close her eyes?"

"I'm sorry?" said the other.

"Her eyes. Aren't you going to close them?"

The two doctors looked at each other and shrugged. One of them leaned over and shut Sophie's eyelids.

Doris was embarrassed with herself for meddling, for insisting that her friend not be left there with her eyes open. As if it mattered. It just seemed wrong. Everything seemed wrong, but it wasn't until a few minutes after a pair of ambulance drivers covered Sophie atop a dolly and wheeled her from the house that Doris realized what was most wrong of all.

There had been no glass of water on Sophie's night table.

Doris spent most of the drive to Fannie's house in North Palm Beach in a daze. She was a slow driver to begin with, at her age unable to fathom having to replace her ancient Mercedes due to accident, and today only the honking of horns behind her kept her speed near thirty.

No glass of water on Sophie's night table . . .

So what? Doris had never actually seen one there before, now had she? All she was going on were Sophie's assertions that she never slept without such a glass within reach. Maybe one of the cops had clumsily spilled it and then returned the glass to the bathroom. He wasn't exactly disturbing evidence since this was hardly a murder investigation.

It had been just three days before on the plane that Sophie had looked into the tarot cards and had seen death. Doris felt awful for having brushed her off without a word, not that it would have changed things.

She had called Sylvia's doctor before leaving for Fannie's. She could have also used the phone to break the news to Fannie, but that wasn't the way friends treated each other, especially friends who had grown to depend on each other for so much.

Fannie lived in North Palm in yet another booming residential district of the famed Palm Beaches. Houses had been constructed virtually on top of each other, and all Fannie's neighbors were young, uniformly hated by her for their loud parties, pain-in-the-ass kids, and wild dogs who, according to Fannie, "shit up a storm" on her lawn.

By the time Doris swung onto Fannie's street, she was calmer, almost composed. The signs had been there. Sophie had given up, had seen what was coming and done nothing to avoid it, playing with the tarot cards long enough to hear what she expected them to say. Doris felt herself relax.

The police cars lining Fannie's street with their lights still flashing changed all that.

"I'm sorry, you can't go in there, ma'am. Ma'am!" said the uniformed officer blocking the entrance to Fannie's house.

Doris tried to shoulder past him. "She's my friend. Get out of my way."

Beyond the policeman, Doris could see a horde of men in Fannie's living room snapping pictures, taking notes, and dropping a powdery substance all over her furniture. In the center of it all lay a huge shape on the rug covered by a sheet. Fannie.

"Let her in," came the voice of a man from the hallway, and the policeman permitted her to pass.

Doris charged forward only to be cut off by a tall man wearing a too-warm tweed sport coat.

"I'm Lieutenant Melrose," he said, holding her back. "You said you're—you were a friend of Mrs. Karp?"

Doris struggled to see beyond his shoulder. "Yes. What . . . what happened?"

"As near as we can tell, early this morning she must have surprised a burglar in the act and he panicked."

Melrose moved to the side enough for Doris to see clearly into the living room. The dreaded pounding returned to her chest with a vengeance. The room was a shambles. Nothing was where it should have been. Pieces of furniture were scattered everywhere, the chairs overturned, bookcases spilled over. Shattered porcelain from Fannie's prized collection lay randomly on the rug and a stiff wind poured in through a gaping hole in the bay window. The mess alone would have been enough to kill Fannie, a woman who once vowed to stay up all night long to stake out her lawn in vain pursuit of the pooch who'd been leaving piles everywhere. Doris remembered that Fannie had ended up falling asleep in the flower bed.

"This is just the way we found the room," Melrose was saying.

A pair of detectives brushed by Doris holding clear plastic bags packed with evidence. Evidence of what? Something was wrong here. Yes, Fannie would have used every last inch of her bulk to defend herself if necessary. But why would she have come downstairs to face the burglar instead of calling the police? Even given that she had chosen not to, Doris knew Fannie well enough to be sure she could never have mustered the kind of strength required for such a violent, prolonged struggle. It made no sense. . . . that is, unless the real damage had been done after Fannie was already dead, to create the *illusion* that a struggle had occurred. In which case there had been no burglar, just a murderer.

And there was no water glass at Sophie's bedside.

"They killed them," Doris muttered, her words almost swallowed by the trembling that seized her.

The next thing she knew she was being led from the house by a patrolman, who helped her into the backseat of his car. Doris wanted to ask him what they were going to do about her beloved Mercedes, wanted to tell him not to bother calling Dr. Morris Kornbloom because today was Wednesday and God only knew what golf course he could be found on. But the words lagged hopelessly behind her thoughts to a point where Doris wondered if she would ever be able to speak again.

* * *

Much to Doris's surprise, Morris Kornbloom arrived twenty minutes after the police located him at his health club.

"My God, what a day you've had," he said with a sigh. "All this shock. It's a wonder you've held up this well, my girl."

He always called her that and she hated it, she admitted, because more than once she had wondered hopefully if Kornbloom, a fifty-seven-year-old widower, might not have considered asking her out. The difference in their ages was offset by the fact that his sunken face and thin white hair made him appear older than he was.

Now Kornbloom the doctor went about checking her blood pressure and pulse, then probed his stethoscope all around her chest.

"Everything seems fine," he reported. "But I'm going to leave you these pills to be on the safe side. Take one every four hours and two before bed." And he set down a small bottle of white pills on her night table next to her red life ones.

"What about Sylvia?" Doris asked hesitantly.

Kornbloom returned his instruments to his black bag. "She's been hospitalized just as a precaution. The shock of finding her friend—your friend—was very hard on her. She's under observation. Just overnight, you understand. Give it a few hours and you can visit her. Late this afternoon would be my suggestion." He paused. "I'm not leaving until I see you take one of those pills. They'll help you relax."

Morris Kornbloom gazed at her with honest feeling, and in that moment Doris longed to tell him about the missing glass of water and the struggle at Fannie's that hadn't been a struggle at all. But to draw a link between these apparently random occurrences would mean having to tell him about the Business, because that was the only possible connection, and to accept that was to accept responsibility for the death of her friends, thanks to a conscience that after five years had decided to make itself heard. Help for her might have been a phone call away, but it hurt too much to admit that the circumstances indicated she should place it.

"Well, Morris," she began, fighting to hide her fear, "get me a glass of water so I can swallow all the pills you want me to."

* * *

18

Doris took a cab to the hospital, arriving at four o'clock. She had called ahead at three, so Sylvia would be expecting her. Nothing would be mentioned about Fannie until tomorrow; nothing, either, about the possible connection to the Business.

Sylvie had a private room on the third floor of Good Samaritan Hospital, which was located in West Palm. The menu featured an international fare and the luxurious private rooms overlooked the ocean. If you had to get sick, it was probably the best place of any to come to, but Doris hated it, as she hated all hospitals. Hated the smell of them, the feel—everything. Other than the tests she'd taken, which resulted in a prescription for her red life pills, she had never spent a night in one and wasn't about to start now. Unless Sylvie wanted her to. Sylvie came first, and if she didn't want to be alone, Doris would have a cot wheeled in, would even pay the daily rate if necessary.

The elevator opened directly before the third floor nurse's station and Doris was surprised to see Morris Kornbloom standing there next to a man she recognized as Sylvia's doctor.

"Morris, what are you—"

His face was a mask of stone, providing her answer before the question was even completed.

"No, Morris, no!" she wailed above her own faintness.

"Respiratory failure, Doris," he said, exchanging a glance with Sylvie's doctor. "It happened very suddenly. There was nothing—"

"Oh, God," Doris heard herself break in. "They killed her, too. *Right here in the hospital and they still found a way!*"

"Doris—"

But it was too late. She was already sliding down the wall her shoulders had found, never feeling the floor when she struck it.

19

CHAPTER 3

SABRINA COULDN'T REALLY REMEMBER WHEN SHE HAD FIRST CON-
sidered killing the courier. It probably went all the way back to
the first time she had noticed him undressing her with his eyes
while hers were locked just as seductively on the briefcase
gripped in his right hand. She thought of the stacks of crisp bills
hidden inside. She was just a courier as well, passing on nothing
but an envelope containing his drop point instructions. The pay
was fine, but nothing compared to the contents of the briefcase
during a single run. Kill him and it was hers.

She had killed before. The first time had been ten years ago,
when she was barely halfway through her teens. Her victim had
purchased her from a white slavery ring when she was twelve
and brought her to America to make money for him. Sabrina
hadn't found it hard to live with that. What was impossible to
live with was his own vile body being forced on her every night,
big and smelly. He would thrust himself into her until she ached,
sometimes bled, and one night Sabrina jabbed a steak knife into
his belly just when he was ready to come. His blood drenched
her and his foul-smelling frame pinned her to the bed as he
wretched and spasmed. By the time Sabrina pulled herself free,
he was dead.

There had been others since, always set up over a long period
of time and always judiciously. Men were weak creatures, her
huge breasts and sultry features a greater weapon than even the
Ring. She'd had a jeweler fashion it for her personally—a knuckle-

20

size imitation emerald tapered into razor sharpness along its raised center. A simple swipe across the throat was all it took. Sabrina would look at the eyes then: always the same, bulging first with confusion followed swiftly by terror. It was her favorite moment, even better than the instant with the swipe of the Ring itself.

Tonight, though, the best moment of all would come when she opened the briefcase.

The bell rang at the front door of her Sansucci Boulevard home in North Miami. Right on time. Sabrina excitedly threw the door open without checking the peephole, saw the briefcase first.

Then the stranger who was holding it.

"I didn't mean to startle you," he apologized.

"You're not the usual . . ."

"A change. I have the proper papers."

Sabrina fought down her disappointment and eyed the man. Much younger than the other courier and big. She could feel him looking at her as well. The hope in her rekindled just as quickly as it had been snuffed out. She had planned this night for too long to pull back now. The man's youth would work to her advantage, her beauty the means that would free her to use the Ring against him.

"Come in," she told the courier.

He stepped forward clutching the briefcase with rigid unease. She closed the door behind him.

"I need my instructions," he told her, eyes running all over her frame.

"Upstairs," came her practiced response. "It's the way this is always done," she added softly as she slid against him on her way to the circular stairwell. "This way," she beckoned.

Sabrina waited until they were near the bedroom on the second floor before draping her arms around the man's back. His muscles arched and she could feel his power, certain now of his strength and aware she would have to choose the perfect moment to strike with the Ring. She eased him toward the bed. The briefcase fell to the rug.

He was over her instantly, fighting with her zipper. She worked his pants free, feeling him harden in her hands as she stroked him, matching his moans with her own.

21

The man had gotten her tight black jeans past her hips and was hovering into position. Just like the first victim had done all those years ago. . . . Sabrina drew the courier close and nibbled at his ear. Only after he entered her did she pull the hand wearing the Ring away to prepare her swipe. She maneuvered so she was over him, taking the lead, joining the rhythmic thrusting of his hips.

Her hands raised toward his throat, the Ring ready, wrist arching for the slice. Then she was in motion, just a flick of the hand was all it would take.

In her mind it was over. Only when the spurt of blood didn't come did she realize that something was very wrong. By that time she had already felt her hand forced up and back in a queer motion by the man who had suddenly become a snake beneath her. His action made no sense.

Until she saw the blood. She realized it was hers at the same time her fingers clutched for the narrow slit across her neck. She felt her eyes bulge and thought at the last how strange it felt not to be able to close them as the world beneath her changed from red to black and then to nothing.

When Doris awoke, Morris Kornbloom was seated by her bed.

"You gave me quite a scare there, my girl," he said, feeling for her pulse.

Doris's eyes gazed around her. "'Where am I?"

"The hospital."

"*Sylvie's* hospital? Good Samaritan?" She started to sit up and had almost made it when Kornbloom's hands restrained her.

"Easy. You're not going anywhere."

Doris looked toward the window. Night had obviously fallen some time ago.

"You've been with me the whole time?"

Kornbloom nodded. "You made me promise. Don't you remember?"

"Has anyone . . . tried to come in?"

"No one who shouldn't have. Say, what's gotten into you, my girl?"

Her eyes dug into his. "Do you trust me, Morris?"

His face squeezed together in puzzlement. "What kind of question is that?"

"Just answer it."

"Of course I trust you!"

"Then get me out of here. Take me home. Tomorrow I'll check in somewhere else. Tomorrow I'll explain everything," Doris promised, wondering how she might go about keeping it. "You said that you trusted me. Then believe me when I say I'm not safe. Not here. Not now. Say you'll do it, Morris, *please*!"

Morris Kornbloom nodded slowly.

Selinas sat at the Miami Airport bar watching a college football game. He had forgotten who the teams were, but he didn't care because he was a fan of neither. It was the airport that was the key, preferred by him for its anonymity, bars within airports in particular. Of course, the problem was that weary travelers, cursed by missed connections or delays, often crowded into them for refuge and bartenders were thus firm with any patron looking for just a chair and a game to watch instead of a drink. Since Selinas never drank, this could have been a problem for him. So he had devised a simple system whereby he would slip the bartender a ten upon arriving in return for a bar seat, a single glass of club soda with a twist, and no questions.

Selinas enjoyed drinking, but it simply wasn't feasible in his profession. Booze slowed you down, made you sluggish. Even a single drink with lots of water and ice could steal a half second away from you, and too often that was all you had.

His latest assignments had certainly illustrated that.

On the television screen, the defense was bringing in its special third-down-and-long personnel. Selinas watched, amazed by the degree of specialization in sports and life in general. It was thought to be the same in his profession, but that was due largely to myth. One man might be great with his hands, another with a knife, a third with a gun, or so went the popular teaching. All bullshit. You could have a favorite, that was natural. But for tenure you had to be almost an expert with any weapon placed in your hand—as well as with the hand itself. Assignments often called for specific means of elimination to be employed, and even then you didn't know what kind of weapon might be around if an opponent appeared unannounced, even if his footsteps did give him away.

Selinas heard a familiar gait now and felt his neck muscles tense. The steps turned into the bar and approached him.

The third-and-long pass fell incomplete.

"Let's get a table, shall we?" a voice told him.

"It's almost the half anyway," Selinas responded, turning for the first time. The man at his side was considerably smaller than Selinas and very gaunt. His face had a sunken, angular look and he had virtually no distinguishing marks other than an excess strip of fatty flesh sprouting from his chin. Selinas had many contacts, all nameless, so for fun he gave names to each one based on outstanding physical features, this one's being "Giblet," thanks to that excess chin flesh that looked strangely like the withered crop of a turkey.

Selinas lowered himself from the bar stool and grasped a leather briefcase at his feet. The contact led him to a booth in the corner.

"You've got to order something," Selinas told him after they sat down. "They get pissed off here if you don't drink." He sipped his club soda.

Almost immediately a waitress came by with pad and pen ready.

"Scotch on the rocks," Giblet said and Selinas smiled inwardly. The waitress departed.

Selinas slid the briefcase under the table toward Giblet's side.

"Did you open it?" he wanted to know.

"It may be booby-trapped. I'll leave the finding out to you. Be careful with it, though, it bites."

"Any problems?"

"Lantos was better than I was led to believe."

"He was old."

"Age means little in his profession."

"And the woman?"

"Your information was precise," Selinas said because it was all he needed to, not bothering to add that he probably would have let her live if she hadn't tried for him with that pretty little ring which had become the instrument of her own death.

The waitress came with Giblet's scotch and the two men stayed silent until she was well out of earshot.

"Got another for you," Giblet said finally. "Plural this time, two to be exact. The Rivero brothers, Miguel and Marco." He pulled a standard office-size envelope from his jacket pocket. "Details and doubled retainer fee inside."

Selinas raised his eyebrows. "Drug runners . . ."

"You've heard of them?"

"They tried to retain me once."

"And you refused, of course, because they didn't meet your exacting standard of values for a potential employer. I assume, then, that you'll accept."

"I find the Riveros to be pleasant objectives," Selinas said.

"It won't be easy. They're well-buffered and almost impossible to find. The barons of South Beach, some call them."

"Scum," said Selinas. "River rats it will be my pleasure to drown."

"You must be done by the end of the weekend. Use the usual number to call in the details."

"Finish your scotch," said Selinas.

The rain started past midnight, pelting the windows of the Breakers with a force that threatened to shatter glass. Thunder rumbled regularly, intermixed with occasional lightning. Doris had all four locks on her door in place and felt reasonably safe. There would be no getting to her that way. The old, elegant hotel was built like a fortress.

She was still groggy from the extra Demerols Morris had given her at the hospital and knew sleep would come no matter how hard she fought against it. Kornbloom had dropped her off two hours before, with an assurance that he'd be back at nine the next morning and that everything would be all right. Doris wasn't so sure.

She turned the television to the cable news channel and left it on even as she lay face-up in bed staring at the ceiling. The shows meant nothing to her, but a possible intruder might take the volume as a sign that she was still awake. If nothing else, the droll monotone of voices served to make her feel less alone.

But she *was* alone. Sophie and Fannie were dead. Now Sylvie, too. All her fault.

She had tried the phone number a dozen times already since returning to her room.

No answer.

No hope.

It would be passed off as coincidental tragedy. Old people in their seventies. It happens.

But coincidental tragedy had nothing to do with it. The Business had held them together and now it was killing them, one at a time.

And there was nothing she could do.

No, stop it! You've got to fight. If not for yourself, then for Andy.

Doris Kaplan had never been the kind to give up. The grandmothers were perishing from apparently natural causes or similarly explicable tragedies. All she had to do was stay alive long enough to plan a strategy. Killing the others had been easier because they didn't know what was coming.

Scratch, scratch, scratch . . .

Doris lurched upward in her bed, holding the covers tight to her chest. She had heard a noise. She was certain of it. But from where had it come?

Scratch, scratch, scratch . . .

Again. Doris fought to focus her ears. She cursed herself for rejecting the hearing aids that Morris Kornbloom had been suggesting for months.

The sound came again, and she gazed at the drawn drapes hopefully on the chance that it might stem simply from the rain whipping patterns upon the glass.

Scratch, scratch, scratch . . .

No, it was coming from outside the door! Feet shuffling against the carpet, something toying with the locks.

Doris felt her heart thumps intensify dangerously and she clutched her chest with both hands. Her life pills were within easy reach along with the ever-present glass of water, but clearly the intruder had to be dealt with first. The phone caught her eye and she grasped it quickly, hitting the number for the front desk.

"This is Mrs. Kaplan," she whispered. "Someone's trying to break through my door. Please send someone. Hurry!"

"Right away," the desk clerk responded and outside the door the scratching got louder. "Would you like me to stay on the line?" the clerk asked, but Doris had already dropped the receiver and slid quietly from her bed. If security failed to arrive on time, she couldn't expect bedcovers to save her. She had to fight. Surprise would be on her side and that might prove to be enough.

Slowly, with the gleam of the television providing her only light, she crept toward her desk in the left corner of the room. Lightning flashed as she reached it, stunning her and sending her hands clutching again for her chest.

Atop the desk rested a gold-plated letter opener, an antique heirloom she had cherished for years. Not sharp at the end, but heavy and a reasonable weapon for sure. She grasped it tight within a trembling hand and started for the door, bare feet clinging lightly to the carpeting.

The thunder stung her ears and masked whatever sounds might have been coming from beyond the door. The scratching sound was gone. Doris thought she heard jimmying around the area of the deadbolt, but she wasn't sure. She snailed on, right eye aiming for the peephole.

The hard knocks shook her backward, seeming louder than the thunder.

"Security, Mrs. Kaplan." More knocks. "Are you all right? Can you hear me?"

Doris steadied herself and peered into the peephole. A uniformed guard stood just outside the door, tall and broad. He was wearing a gun. She saw him fumbling for a set of keys on his belt.

"Mrs. Kaplan, are you all right?"

"Yes, yes. I'm just a bit shaken. Hold on and I'll open up."

Doris started to raise her hand to the chain, then pulled it back. She had never seen this guard before, but then how many opportunities had she had to become acquainted with graveyard shift security personnel?

"Mrs. Kaplan?"

On impulse, she threw back the chain, twisted the bolt, and swung open the door. The guard wasn't as big as she had thought. He made no move to enter the room.

"Someone tried to jimmy your door," he reported. "No question about it. I can see the scratches."

"Did you see him?"

"No, but the exit's just four doors down. He could have headed for it as soon as he heard the elevator doors open." He

tried to throw her a reassuring smile, the way television cops do.
"I doubt he'll be back. Not tonight anyway."

"No," Doris said, thinking fast. "It's not like that, you see.
I've been threatened. Phone calls, a letter. The police haven't
been able to help."

The security guard's face showed concern. "Well . . ."

"Could you stay up here? Outside the door, I mean."

"I'm on duty, Mrs. Kaplan."

"What's your name?"

"Mark."

"Mark, I'll pay you a hundred dollars to be on duty outside
my room."

Doris wasn't sure what woke her or when she had dropped off
to sleep in the first place. The storm had intensified and tides of
water cascaded against her window. She eased herself from the
bed and switched on her night lamp, then moved to the door.

A glance in the peephole showed nothing. Mark was gone.

She strained her eye to widen her angle of the door sides. Still
nothing. But if Mark were seated in the desk chair she had given
him, that would explain it.

"Mark," she called softly. "Mark?"

No answer.

She opened the door slowly, leaving the chain hinged.

The chair from her desk was right there. Unoccupied.

Doris slammed the door again and threw the bolt. Breathing
heavily, she hurried to the phone and pressed the receiver to her
ear.

There was no dial tone. The phone was dead.

They had her, her line to the outside severed.

Her mind sharpened. There had been a bump, a crash of some
kind from somewhere. That's what had woken her. If it had
come from the corridor, Mark's absence would be accounted for.
But it also provided an opening, a few more seconds in which
she might flee before the killers of her three friends returned.

Doris jammed her feet into her slippers, threw on her house-
coat, and rushed back to the door. Stripping off all the locks, she
lunged into the corridor and bolted at her top speed for the two
elevators twelve rooms down. The short sprint had her lungs
burning when she got there, and she realized with fear as she hit

the down arrow repeatedly that her life pills were sitting use-lessly back on her night table as usual.

She heard the elevator gears grinding upward. The Breakers was an old building, its elevators of the old-fashioned, slow-moving variety manned twenty-four hours a day by attendants.

Footsteps started from down the hall, just around the corner from her room. Reflexively, she jammed the down arrow again and again.

Finally, the brown doors slid open. The attendant pulled back the cage and looked at Doris with no small degree of shock.

"The lobby," she said breathlessly, not bothering to explain further. "Please hurry."

Nonetheless, it seemed to take forever for the attendant to get both the doors and the cage closed. At last the car was in motion downward. At the lobby Doris was out of the compartment before the attendant had the cage all the way open again. Clearly she had to flee. The killers could be everywhere by now.

The lobby of the Breakers was an ornate example of classical construction more befitting an Italian villa than a hotel. It was as long as a football field and fairly wide with plush furniture and marble tables placed regularly about. Doris hurried along the twenty-yard walk to the front desk beneath the vaulted, carved ceiling she had so often gone dizzy staring at. Her heart had begun to thump with dangerous irregularity and she distracted herself with thoughts of safety once the front desk came into view.

She had just passed her favorite wall ornament, a fifteenth-century Flemish tapestry, when she saw the two men walking directly for her. Doris froze. They seemed to take no notice of her presence and just kept coming.

And that was why she ran for the first exit she saw on the left. An old woman standing in the lobby in her nightclothes at four A.M. *should* have been noticed. Doris rushed outside into the pouring rain.

She began to run, as fast and as hard as her wind and slippers would allow. Her plan was to circle back to the main entrance and find a cab. But she saw none when she cleared the building, so she kept running toward the nearest road, a frantic glance stolen over her shoulder at regular intervals.

The rain soaked through her thin gown. Her hair was matted

and no joint was spared the agony of her first real sprint since giving up tennis twelve years before. She felt the monster in her chest rebelling, begging for letup with a thunderous lurching against the sinews holding it in place.

The Breakers was fronted by a grassy park lined by trees, and Doris struggled across it toward South Country Road. Her motions felt slow, almost dreamlike, an eternity to pass from one tree to the next. The rain pooled in the grass and her feet sloshed through it. But the only sound she could focus on was that of her own labored breathing. It felt to her as if a piece of food had gone down the wrong way so only tiny bursts of air were able to squeeze through.

Suddenly she didn't know where she was. The shapes and sights were familiar, but she couldn't place them in the context of the building she knew so well. There were footsteps mirroring hers and she turned back to look as her slipper wedged on a string sectioning off some freshly planted grass and sent her sprawling. Her hands dug into the ground and her face mashed against something soft. Her heart fluttered, seeming to stammer, and when she tried to rise there was no feeling in her legs.

She felt the cold muddy water soaking through her night-clothes and thought, quite inappropriately, how uncomfortable it was to be so dirty. The sound of footsteps nearby had stopped, making her think perhaps she had eluded the men for the time being. If she could drag herself behind those trees just up ahead, she might just fool them and make it. Her right hand pulled, followed by her left. Breath was precious and she savored every bit she was able to catch.

Up ahead, the trees were blurry, indistinct in the pelting, windswept rain.

For an instant it seemed that the awful fluttering in her chest had subsided and Doris sighed gratefully. Then the agony came, like a huge bursting blade being jammed into her chest and held there. She tried to scream, but it seemed that the horror had trapped her between breaths. She was aware of her mouth hanging open and of muddy water rushing in unobstructed. I should cough, she thought, feeling that choking was a very real possibility until she realized that she had no air left to be choked off.

There was one last tremor before the darkness of the mud enveloped her, and Doris let herself sink deeply into it.

PART TWO:

DREW

CHAPTER 4

DREW JORDAN HADN'T BEEN LOOKING FOR A FIGHT, ESPECIALLY WITH the Ryker brothers on a Wednesday night at Clyde's in the middle of his second VO and soda. To begin with, the Rykers were a feared force in Georgetown, in spite of the fact that no one knew what they did for a living. Some of the Clyde's crowd insisted they were hit men for the CIA, or Secret Service fielders responsible for keeping committed crazies off the president's tail. They certainly *looked* formidable, both big and heavyset with shoulders barely confined by their expensive suits.

It had been Drew who'd given the two men the title of the Ryker brothers, named after the villainous clan from Drew's all-time favorite movie, *Shane*. Forget Clint Eastwood and the bunch. Nobody could deliver a line like Alan Ladd with his lips squeezed together seeming to take in air through only one side of his mouth.

As it was, the fight had actually been precipitated by Jabba the infamous Hutt. Named for the slobbering sluglike beast of the third *Star Wars* film, to whom he bore more than a passing resemblance, Jabba was another enigma within the Georgetown community. The best sources said he was a former Georgetown University professor who had been released after several losing bouts with the bottle, although a dead wife was rumored to be to blame as well, along with a homosexual affair. In any case, Jabba frequently settled his obese bulk in a corner booth at Clyde's, buying drinks for anyone who tossed him a kind word,

33

holding court over those thankful or drunk enough to listen to his dissertations on the state of the world. Drew felt genuinely bad for Jabba, a lost soul who attempted to find himself at Clyde's among all the grad students and yuppies.

Drew wasn't sure where the fat man's problem with the Rykers had begun. Apparently one of them had told him to shut up so they could eat in peace. Jabba had apologized profusely, which didn't amount to "shutting up" at all, and by the time Drew got back from the bar the brothers were dragging Jabba by either arm in the direction of the front door. The fat man tried to resist, staggered, and ended up face-down in some patron's Caesar salad.

The Ryker brothers laughed and kept dragging.

Drew was in motion by then, taking the Rykers from behind and totally by surprise. It was over very fast, much faster than he had expected considering the Rykers' reputation in Georgetown.

He grasped one of the brothers at the shoulder and spun him around. Nothing fancy next, just a straight punch square into his jaw that sent him reeling backward. He crashed into a table and toppled over its side, conscious long enough to consider the loosened teeth in his mouth.

The second brother came in fast and swung for Drew's face. But Drew turned in time to block the strike and smash his free arm into the brother's gut. When the expected *whooooosh* of air didn't come, Drew knew the man was well muscled, although not much of a fighter because his next move was to try and grasp Drew in some sort of lock. Drew stepped inside the motion, immediately behind the brother, grasping his head and bringing his face down in the same Caesar salad Jabba had ended up in, only much harder. The brother stiffened and slumped to the floor, unconscious.

When he was sure both of the Rykers were down and out of the way for good, Drew turned to check on Jabba. The fat man was already enclosed by three others and seemed to be adoring the attention.

"Welcome home, Drew my boy," Jabba greeted him. "Let me buy you a drink."

It was late when Drew and the fat man finally had the booth to themselves.

"My tab is yours for a week," Jabba told him gratefully. "A modest payment for a great debt owed. But use it sparingly, please. The pension check's a bit late this month."

Drew shook him off. "No need."

"Need has little to do with it. A man who has committed such a *locratious* nonself-serving act deserves payment of a sort, even one this slight."

"Aren't you the man who claims every act is self-serving?"

The fat man's bulging jowls puckered. "Exceptions exist for everything, my boy, even the rigid dogma it has been my toil to teach for these long years. Sometimes you must use near *vicivious* insistencies to gain the attention of your audience."

Drew smiled. Jabba's pompousness made him a treat to be around, especially after a few drinks. First "locratious," then "vicivious." When he couldn't find the right word to fit a situation, he'd make one up that sounded right, never hesitating or questioning his own choice. Drew found this more sad than funny, though, as if Jabba's once brilliant mind could recall only part of the word and had to invent the rest. Drew wondered what he had been like before the alcohol set in.

"And how went things at your Georgia assassin's camp, pray tell?"

"*Mercenary* camp, Jabba."

"Semantics, my boy, semantics."

"I came in second this time. Mace killed me." Then, as an afterthought, "He's the best."

"Quite good with plastic paint bullets and rubber knives, is he?"

"He's a real professional, Jabba. Makes his living off his skills and comes back to the camp regularly to make sure they stay sharp. He even worked with the Timber Wolf once."

"Ah, the best of them all . . ."

"He told me all about him, at least as much as he knew. He said that if the Timber Wolf came to camp, the other twenty of us wouldn't last a day, even Mace himself."

"I thought you had given up plans for a story on the famed Wolf."

"I did. Years ago. But I still think of him."

They lapsed into silence and Jabba sipped his brandy.

"You know, Jabba, thinking back on it, I never felt more alive than when Mace killed me."

The fat man rolled his eyes. "Your words, my boy, are enough to make a man reconsider his drinking."

"No, hear me out. I came in second. All those pros and vet mercs and I came in second. Everything considered, I don't think I've ever felt more sense of accomplishment in my life."

"Excuse me for not embracing such a *dicdactium*, but my mind still recalls a country torn by lads not much younger than you over something called Vietnam and war in general—games or not." Jabba shrugged. "But I suppose I should be grateful for your skills for they are, after all, what saved me from the dreaded Rykers. And if I can't make it up to you in *renumical* thanks, let me make it up to you in trade. There must be something . . ."

"A question," Drew told him.

"Ah," Jabba breathed, leaning forward, "the universe, Georgetown, politics—for you, anything."

"Who are the Ryker brothers, really?"

Jabba patted Drew's shoulder with a huge, flabby hand. "What you know of them is all you need to know. Hired killers, contract assassins, men who dabble in a world of sterile exchanges—"

"I mean the truth," Drew broke in.

"Because it is all you know, you must regard it as the truth. Man is indeed a special creature, my boy. So much of what he postulates is made up of inadvertent and *closiquil* lies because his knowledge is insufficient to speak the total truth. But is he lying? Not consciously and thus not at all."

"But you're avoiding my question consciously, aren't you? Come on, Jabba, there's not a man or woman regularly between these walls you haven't got a bead on. Now tell me about the Rykers."

Jabba's eyebrows flickered. "Worried about possible vengeance, are you? Beware. They might give you the long form to fill out in 1993. They work for the census department." And when Drew's features fell, he added, "I suppose that lowers your appraisal of what you did."

"It doesn't exactly make me heavyweight champ."

"A diminishing of the heroic self-image." Jabba sipped his Hennessy, savoring his last glass of the night. "The Ryker brothers being professional killers would have let you feel what you want to feel: being a true hero. But it is not the determination of the act that matters as much as acceptance of it. When you moved to save me, your perception of the Rykers was based on the myth I helped foster. Therefore, in that context it was truth."

"Stop twisting words around."

"They seem quite clear to my brandy-soaked brain. It's turned to mush I tell you, my boy. When I die, they'll take it out and find tiny Hennessy labels etched all over it."

"You're changing the subject."

"Was I?"

"As usual. We were talking about heroes."

"I thought we were talking about you."

"Come on, Jabba, we've both had too many drinks for this."

The Hutt smiled at him. "There are two things a man can never get enough of." He tapped his stomach. "The rather *prodine* endowment I've been given renders me incapable of the first since it requires a willing partner. But the second is drinking and that requires simply a bottle and glass."

"You take a long time making a point."

"Points are made in the minds of the people listening, not speaking. An important lesson, my boy. Remember it."

"Your answer to my first question was not satisfactory."

"Then pose another."

"It's about you."

Jabba tried to laugh. "So unworthy a subject. . . ."

"What did you really do before you settled here at your table in Clyde's?"

"Obviously, my tales of spending years in not altogether unpleasant academia have not satisfied you."

"No, they haven't."

"You would prefer me to be a retired spymaster, or better yet an *active* spymaster who runs his agents from a corner booth in this very establishment."

"The terminology, you know it all."

"The vernacular of the spy world is due mostly to myth, specifically thriller novels available to everyone for under four dollars apiece. Hardly classified information. As a writer yourself, you should know." And Jabba's eyes sharpened. "Ah, now I see. Perhaps you fathom a story in the old Hutt, a piece that will demand front-page attention in all major dailies, perhaps a *Newsweek* cover. Well, fear not, my boy, the Hutt will tell all as he always does . . . but as always don't expect too many people to listen.''

Drew sank back in his chair, feeling deeply sorry for the old man and even sorrier for having pestered him so. He was hiding out here, comfortable holding court for patrons who had enough drinks to listen and on slow nights offering his endless tab just so people would sit close and pass a kind word over.

"But I haven't answered your question," Jabba was saying.

"You don't have—"

"Ah, but I do. I promised. The status of enigma suits me, don't you think, my boy? I prefer shadow to substance. Nothing concrete people can hold me to. I repeat my earlier statement to you that truth lies only in context. As the context changes, so does the truth. I can be whatever people want me to be—a drunk, a bum, a closet genuis, embattled teacher, spymaster— anything. And because I allow each context its own freedom, the people around me are comfortable, certain they have everything all figured out, even if no one else does.''

Drew smiled softly. He'd heard all the stories and rumors and supposed that none of them were true in total but at least a portion of each held some merit. The Hutt himself had often said there were no myths from which some truth could not emerge.

"Leave me my table and my court, Drew," he said, shocking Jordan with the use of his first name. "And leave yourself room. Most people want simply to be more; you want to be most.''

Drew rose and shoved his chair back. "I've got to get going. See you . . . next time.''

"I'll be here," said Jabba the Hutt.

The drive home was difficult, Drew's concentration waning and wavering. The VO was partially to blame, although Drew figured more of it was due to the lingering excitement of the fight and Jabba's vague reflections on life and all things related. They shouldn't have been unsettling, but tonight Drew found them to be.

Yes, the Hutt was hiding at Clyde's, but when you came right down to it Drew had to admit that he himself was, too. He had graduated from Georgetown four years before, after a decent academic career with a grim determination to become a writer. Writing meant freedom, being your own boss, not having to take orders or work overtime at the office. His writing was competent enough to land in several major magazines. But magazine editors quickly became bosses after you had written a few articles for them, so Drew soon fathomed that the way to go was books. He had an idea all prepared and was ready to plunge in.

In fact, he should have been working further on the research angle tonight instead of wasting time at Clyde's. He had stayed in the Georgetown area after graduation because he was comfortable there. Drew could walk M Street and still feel young, still feel he was a part of the college life-style he had refused to abandon. Clubs and social events had landed him plenty of underclass friends during his senior year, but now even the freshmen from back then had graduated and Drew felt older than he wanted to.

Accordingly, he continued to wear his dark, wavy hair overlong in more of a college style, fretting over that inevitable day when the line would show its first signs of receding. He worked out at Nautilus and jogged regularly to keep his frame youthfully toned. Only recently had he found the first slight wrinkle lines beneath his eyes, an event greeted with no small degree of paranoia.

Fortunately, through it all there was the Clyde's crowd to refresh him, providing a new and welcome outlet. They were mostly about his age, a group of lawyers and politicos who gathered regularly to wile away the night hours, many coming straight from work without even stopping at the apartments or condominiums they called home but seemed forever inclined to avoid. For his part, Drew adored his condo on 33rd and O Streets, a layered brick townhouse complete with garage. It did not bother him that there were fifty or so just like it within a three-block radius. In fact, he liked it better that way. For Drew, Clyde's offered a place he could go and be assured there would be plenty of people he knew. He supposed that maybe the success of Jabba's court lay in providing people with a secure place to loiter while they waited for others to arrive.

Of course, there was also Pam, and Drew blessed his luck there. They had been going out for six months now, Drew's longest stretch ever, and their relationship was remarkably unstrained and comfortable. It was all new for Drew, who had never been much good at relationships, thanks to partners who demanded too much or not enough. With Pam he had found the happy medium. She was a grad student in biochemistry across the city at George Washington University. She had her own apartment and insisted even after their relationship turned serious that they not share his. She slept over regularly, mostly on weekends. But she had her own life and left Drew to his. People were far better together when they were more comfortable with themselves, Pam reasoned, and Drew couldn't have agreed more.

They had met, ironically, at Clyde's through a friend of Drew's who wanted to show off his new girl friend to the gang. Apparently he showed her off too much. Drew may have lost a friend, but Pam was well worth it. Only because of her did he at long last feel comfortable not being in college anymore, the crutch of M Street no longer as sorely needed, although Drew was not yet ready to let go cold turkey.

He pulled his 325e into the driveway of his condo and noticed Pam's Escort parked by the curb. She said she might be coming over to run some material through his computer, and Drew was all too happy to oblige. The only thing he was using it for was the compilation of research on his latest and only book, which was presently suffering from an acute case of procrastination.

Stepping through the door of his condominium, he noticed the bare minimum of lights on. Pam was an energy stickler, a detail-oriented person all the way. The condo was composed of two floors with a full kitchen, dining, and living room on the first and a pair of bedrooms on the second. Drew had first planned to convert the second bedroom into an office, but working on the second floor depressed him so he moved his work area down into the living room/den.

His Apple IIe held a sacred corner position and he saw Pam hunched over it. At first he thought she was working intensely. Then he realized she had dozed off. He walked over and squeezed her shoulder with firm tenderness.

"Ah," she sighed, coming awake, "my landlord returns. Hell of a machine you've got here, boss."

"The work must have been boring."

"Just tiring. What time is it?" She stretched her arms out.

"After one."

"Late."

"I got talking to Jabba."

She gazed at him closely. "Your face has looked better."

"See, there was these two guys and one of them must've got in a lucky shot. . . ."

She looked at him disapprovingly. "Yeah, I think I've heard this one before."

"You don't sound too pleased about it."

"Why should I be? You go out with your friends, get shitfaced—"

"I wasn't shitfaced."

"Fine. Just don't expect me to be impressed with your macho bullshit."

"What was I supposed to do? Let Jabba get his head kicked in?"

"You didn't have to enjoy it."

"Who said I—"

"You did," Pam blared at him. "It's written all over your face. You look like a fucking dog who's just turned back an intruder into his territory. Come on, love, look me in the eye and tell me you weren't glad when the opportunity arose for you to use your fists."

Drew didn't bother. Lying was pointless. Pam knew him better than he knew himself.

"You go off in the woods and play Rambo," she continued, "and now you can't get it out of your system. The games aren't enough anymore. You want to play hero for real."

"They were mixing a friend of mine's face in Caesar salad."

"So it was Drew Jordan to the rescue. No white horse and six-shooter, just a pair of fists the punching bags aren't enough for anymore. And instead of leaving a silver bullet behind, you left with a smile."

She started to stand up. Drew restrained her gently at the shoulders, her resolve more than equal to his strength.

"You're too tired to drive," he said with curt seriousness.

"And if I disagree, what are you gonna do, punch my lights out, too?"

"Nope, I'm hopeless without Tonto. Besides, if I knock you out, taking advantage of you wouldn't be nearly as much fun."

She started to pull away from him, then sighed with a weak

smile. "You know why I can't stay mad at you for more than thirty seconds? Because you won't argue with me. You stand there and nod at everything I say."

"Not all the time. Tonight it happened to be the truth."

"Know thyself . . ."

"Doesn't mean I can change or even that I want to. I keep going to that camp mostly because it makes me feel alive, and tonight I felt even more alive because what I did *mattered*. I helped someone who was in trouble. What you don't realize is that when it comes to some people, you can throw all your values clarification and moderating skills out the window. Approach them with a 'come on, fellas' and you'll be lucky to get the 'on' out before a quick fist has you talking with a permanent lisp. I did what I had to tonight. How I felt about it is irrelevant."

"Savage to savage, right?"

Drew winked and squeezed her shoulders tenderly. "Speaking of savage . . ."

"There you go again."

"Me Tarzan, you Jane. What you say we go make boy?"

"Sometimes I wish I didn't love you so damn much." And they kissed.

"My place or yours?" he asked her.

"Whichever's closer."

Drew had made love with many other girls and women, but seldom did he have the desire to do anything but go through the motions once the act was over. With Pam, the act itself was just the beginning. He loved simply sleeping with her, their arms interwoven and chests pressed tight together. He loved waking in the early morning hours and just seeing her there next to him. He would hug her tight and somehow in her sleep she would hug him back. She loved him without accepting all his actions, and this constant give-and-take had brought them even closer together. Drew liked criticism, saw it in a sense as one of the greatest ways someone could show they cared. Tolerance or passive acceptance had never worked with him, nor could he involve himself with a woman who treated him with too much deference. Pam's strength was not physical, but, undeniably, it was there and in many ways far greater than the force that had allowed him to effortlessly put down the Ryker brothers in Clyde's.

Thing of it was, no matter what she might have said about him being a savage, in bed that onus fell willingly upon her. She knew when to take command and when not to, and tonight was no exception. Her hands probed, rubbed, guided. Drew never ceased to be amazed at how she could arouse him no matter his mood. Tonight he was ready and that served to increase his pleasure. He rose over her and moved patiently, trying to time every move, but after a few seconds instinct took over and he lost himself within her. Minutes later it was over and he felt full and warm.

They tried again not long after, this time reversing the positions so Pam might have a turn in the lead. They broke off after that, collapsing in exhaustion with Pam falling almost immediately off to sleep. Drew lingered awake for some time and it seemed as though he had barely fallen asleep at last when the phone ringing on his night table jarred him. He fumbled for the receiver in the darkness, grasping it finally and remembering how much he feared late night phone calls.

"Yes? Hello."

"Is Mr. Jordan there, please?"

"Speaking."

"Andrew Jordan, this is Dr. Morris Kornbloom. I'm afraid I have some bad news for you. . . ."

CHAPTER 5

"THE LIFE OF A PERSON IS JUDGED ON . . ."

The rabbi's voice droned on through the heat of Doris Kaplan's gravesite in West Palm Beach. The memorial service at Temple Beth El had been attended by perhaps two hundred people, and about half that number had formed the procession to the cemetery. According to Dr. Kornbloom, Drew's grandmother had died in the early morning hours on Thursday of a massive heart attack. Now, Friday afternoon, he watched as they buried her.

He had made it through the day thus far in a daze. He accepted polite, sincere condolences from dozens of people, few of whom he had ever met. It was all very eerie and unnerving and Drew had never felt more alone. Pam had desperately wanted to accompany him down here, but he refused to let her, aware of her work load and how far back she'd be set if she lost even three days. So, he would go it alone as he had gone so often through his life.

Of course, tragedy was nothing new for him. It had struck once before, twenty-one years ago to be exact, on a rainy night back in Westchester when news of his parents' deaths was brought to the door by a state trooper. His grandmother had handled everything. At their funeral he hadn't felt alone because she was with him. Now it was her funeral and he had cried more than he had back then.

She was a strong woman and Drew had always thought her to be a physical giant. Only when he began his growth spurt at the

44

age of eleven did he realize that his grandmother was barely five-four and that he had fallen into the syndrome children often do of making adults they respect or love mammoth in size. She had been everything to him for so long, but Drew had pulled away from her this last year and now the pangs of guilt felt like stray marbles in his stomach.

His reaction, actually, had been normal. Supported through college and beyond, he at last resolved himself to make it on his own. It was time to grow up, or at least, to try. He was too old for college and too old to be supported by his grandmother. So for the past year he had driven himself madly, pounding out article after article. Half were rejected. But half were published and he saved enough to put the articles aside for a while and start work on his book.

Saved enough . . . who was he kidding? Only the fact that his grandmother handled the payments on his car and condo allowed him even the semblance of a writing career. When he had begun refusing her regular checks, her response had been that Drew would never have to worry about money. She had taken care of everything.

Doris Kaplan had been a feisty woman who never took crap from anyone. Now, as the rabbi's voice droned on, Drew found himself sadly recalling incidents that typified her spirit. Like the time she had settled a strike at the manufacturing plant by threatening to run all the machines herself and actually doing it for an hour before the workers tossed down their picket signs and went back in. Or when a teacher gave Drew a poor quarterly grade for no good reason and his grandmother had staged a one-person sit-in in the principal's office until she received a fair hearing with all parties involved. The stories went on and on. Drew realized only now how much they meant to him, and that made the last year even harder to accept. He couldn't help but think that his insistence on turning away her checks had been tantamount to turning away her love. It was difficult to draw the line and in the process of not trying to, he had made himself a stranger to her.

In fact, she had visited Washington only once since his graduation, in spite of his constant urgings to come up. She always had an excuse ready, but Drew was certain that the truth was she didn't want to impose on whatever life he was building. For his part, Drew visited Palm Beach at least twice a year for a week or so, always staying at the exclusive Breakers where his first realization that adulthood had officially set in came when he was told he had to don a jacket in the lobby after six.

Andy (she never would call him Drew, which he much preferred), *this is your grandmother. I hope I'm not bothering you.* . . . All her phone calls started that way and they never did bother him.

The rabbi was reading from a prayer book now, words as simple as the gravesite itself. Drew shared the chairs placed at the front with two aunts he knew barely at all and whom Doris Kaplan had never had much good to say about. The only person he had really come to know here was Morris Kornbloom, who had been supportive and caring right from the awful phone call in the early morning hours on Thursday. Kornbloom had mentioned something about the will when he arrived, and Drew guessed he would have to stay around for the reading although it was the last thing he would have preferred.

Drew shifted uneasily in his chair. It was unusually hot for this time of year in Florida and the only suits he owned were made of wool. His shirt was already soaked all the way through and he could feel the warm sweat reaching for his vest.

At last it was over, and Drew did his best to separate himself from his never seen and now last remaining relatives. The rabbi came over to offer his final condolences and Drew thanked him for everything, which wasn't really much. Then he melted away, escaping all except Dr. Morris Kornbloom.

"We have to talk," Kornbloom said softly.

Drew shrugged, the doctor gauging his reaction.

"This is different," he continued, extracting an envelope from his jacket pocket. "This was among your grandmother's effects. As executor of her estate, it was given to me along with a note from her saying that I should deliver it to you personally in the event that her death was unnatural."

"Does a heart attack qualify as unnatural?"

"The circumstances do. Delirium's a convenient enough explanation, but it doesn't wash, not for me. Then there are the deaths of the other three women to consider. All explainable as well, and I might be able to accept them if your grandmother hadn't been found outside the Breakers, perhaps trying to escape something.''

"Doctor—''

Kornbloom jammed the letter into Drew's hand. "I haven't read this and I want you to take it now so I won't be able to." His voice trailed off. "I'm here if you need me, though. I . . . just want you to know that."

Drew started to open the envelope. A rigid hand from Kornbloom stopped him before he was halfway through the tear.

"Not here," he advised. "My impression is that the letter's contents are personal." He paused, eyes mournful. "You've got my number. I know you have no reason to trust me, but if—''

"My grandmother trusted you," Drew interrupted. "That's plenty reason enough."

Drew finished opening the envelope in the backseat of the limousine as it wound its way back to the Hyatt Palm Beaches. The glass divider was in place and the window typically dark, making him feel as though he were inside a coffin himself. The letter was neatly typed. Drew absorbed each word, with his grandmother's voice whispering softly into his ear.

Andy—

I've been working on this letter for days now. So many times I've crumpled it up and started over. Even now I'm not satisfied with what I'm writing. Maybe I should destroy this draft as well and spare you the truth.

But you *deserve* the truth. You must have the truth because I fear what I have become involved in might reach out somehow and destroy you as it has destroyed me. I am at this instant an extremely wealthy woman, which makes you an extremely wealthy young man. I lied to you about your grandfather's trust fund; there never was any. Sam was never much of a businessman and never would have had the foresight even if he'd had the money. But none of this is important to you. What is important is that I sought whatever means were available to secure your future.

How I would love not to tell you this . . . Andy, for the last five years, I and the other grandmothers whom you know have served as cocaine smugglers. All those trips to

Nassau were just fronts for us to pick up shipments and
deliver them back to the States. I would never say I
approved of what I did, but I believed in it because I
wanted to have the money.

Then, recently, the guilt set in. I guess it happened over
a long period of time, but I only truly felt it these past few
months. All those children's lives ruined by the substance
I was helping to make rampant. I was just a small part, but
a part all the same. I felt each tragic story related over the
news personally. It started to eat me up. I *had* to make
amends.

I went to the DEA, Andy, to an agent named Sam
Masterson. My only condition for helping him was that the
other grandmothers would be left out of it. The plan was
for him to follow the cocaine from the time we brought it
in all the way up the ladder. He assured me everything was
routine, promised me protection.

If you are reading this, it means that protection was not
enough and that the people I worked for have taken their
revenge. But this letter is more than a confession; it is also
a warning. I fear your life is in danger, too. Those behind
my employ will have no choice but to believe you were in
on everything and thus could hurt them as much as I
could. Contact Masterson. His private number is on the
back of this letter. Tell him who you are. There are ways
he can help you. God knows he owes it to me. . . .

Ending letters has always been hard for me. I feel that so
long as I sit here typing, you are with me. Remember,
then, that I will always be with you.

My love always . . .

Drew read the letter for the fifth time while seated in his hotel
room chair. His breathing stayed rapid, more tears choked off by
the shock contained in what he could not allow himself to
believe. *Doris Kaplan a drug smuggler?* Within that bizarre
proposition lay a shred of credibility, enough truth for whatever
self-denials Drew might have been able to mount to be futile. It
was all there in black-and-white, a confession, a warning. Yes, it
was something she would do. His grandmother, a woman without fear, strong in a way others could only dream of. Life could

snap out at her, but she would snap back just as hard; no, harder.

. . . *protection was not enough and the people I worked for have taken their revenge.*

Drew's eyes kept coming back to that sentence, reason unclear and thoughts jumbled. All that was clear was that he had to call this man Masterson. His eyes looked toward his hotel room door. Were people waiting outside to arrange an accident for him? Or would their approach in this instance be more direct, a bullet in the head or a blade thrust from beneath a newspaper in a crowded airport?

Drew's hand trembled as he pressed out Masterson's private number at DEA headquarters. He gripped the receiver in a sweat-drenched hand hot against his ear.

"Agent Masterson's office," came a receptionist's polished response.

"Agent Masterson please."

"Who may I say is calling, please?"

Drew started to give his name, then stopped. "I wouldn't have his private number if he didn't know me."

She didn't hesitate long. "One moment."

A pause, then a man's voice.

"This is Sam Masterson."

"This is Drew Jordan. I assume you know me."

Drew could feel the agent's breath leave him from across the line. "Who gave you this num—"

"My grandmother. In a letter. We've got to talk."

"No! Not now. Not . . . this way."

"How? When?"

"It can't be for a while. Too many—"

"Never mind that crap. Maybe I should read you the letter. We've got to talk, and quick."

The agent paused. Drew could hear him breathing.

"Give me two hours. Brown Ford sedan. Be waiting outside— Where are you by the way?"

"Hyatt Palm Beaches."

"Okay. I know it. Just be waiting in two hours at the front."

"What if they're watching? They'll see us together."

"They don't have to watch. They already know where you are."

*   *   *

The brown Ford sedan pulled up before the Hyatt five minutes past the stated two hours.

"Get in," Masterson said, throwing the door open for Drew before the doorman had a chance to move. "Quick."

He pulled away before Drew had the door fully closed. Masterson looked to be near forty with close-cropped dark hair showing the marks of recession and blue eyes that never stopped shifting about. He spoke rapidly.

"I shouldn't be doing this."

"Doing what?"

"Meeting with you. It's wrong, all wrong."

"What happened to my grandmother is what's all wrong."

The nervous eyes locked briefly on Drew. "It wasn't my fault. She knew the risks."

"All she knew was that she wanted to do something to make up for her mistakes and it ended up costing her her life."

Masterson swung right onto the freeway in the direction of Palm Beach International Airport. "So what am I doing here?"

"I'm not really sure. First off, I figure you owe me some answers. Like what exactly was my grandmother involved in?"

"You must know that, if you know everything else."

"But I don't know why. Why would someone use old ladies to smuggle drugs?"

"Lots of reasons," Masterson answered, screeching into a left-hand lane-change with nervous eyes fixed on the rearview mirror. "To begin with, we're starting to make a dent in the drug lords' business by disrupting or destroying major cocaine distribution chains. The supplies we've seized amount to barely twenty percent of what eventually reaches the street, but for *their* tastes that's too much. Add to this the pressure Washington has been placing on South American governments to cut down their export of the stuff and you're left with a scenario in which the drug lords have been forced to find alternative means to get their product into the country." Eyes back on Drew. "Like the grandmothers. Think about it."

"That's what I'm doing."

"Their vacations in the Bahamas were just a front. The women would always take an extra suitcase along. Somewhere in Nassau they would leave the suitcases and before they left for home the same suitcases would be returned to them. Full of cocaine. You can see we're not talking about minor amounts here. Each vacation saw the grandmothers return with upwards of two hundred pounds of pure, uncut cocaine, street valued at up to thirty million dollars. Multiply that by the number of trips they made and the dollar amount exceeds three hundred million. Who would have ever suspected?''

"Not you apparently; that is, until my grandmother made the mistake of putting in a call to the ever brilliant DEA.''

"What happened wasn't our fault.''

"Then tell me whose it was.''

"What's it matter?''

"It does, that's all.''

Masterson sighed heavily. "A drug lord named Arthur Trelana. We've got a file on him an inch thick, but all it adds up to are insinuations we can't prove. He's a goddamn model citizen who gives to all the right charities and joins all the right civic organizations.''

"Must have added up enough for you to use my grandmother.''

"I told you I had nothing to—''

"I'm not finished with my questions yet, Agent Masterson. I think I'm square on why Trelana used my grandmother. Now I want to know why you did.''

Masterson's tired face showed pain, drooping slowly. "It was her idea. She insisted on it. I thought I could keep her alive, I really did. I don't know what went wrong, how it went wrong. You want me to say I'm sorry I used her the way I did, but I won't. I can't.'' The agent's hands squeezed the wheel until the blood fled from his knuckles. His eyes twitched as the car came to a halt at a red light. "These people own everything. Me, you, the DEA. No one realizes the true scope of their power. How much do you really know about this drug agency? Do you know we're hopelessly outmanned by the kind of power we're up against? Do you know we lost twenty-four agents to contracts and shoot-outs last year alone? One worked with me in Miami. He had a wife and three kids.'' Masterson paused and held his eyes closed. "When we found him his guts were cut out and his balls were stuck in his mouth.''

Drew cringed. The light turned green. A horn behind them got Masterson moving again.

"We can't win, Drew," resumed the agent softly. "Sure, we can take a few battles, but you can forget about the war. Trelana was a real break for us—for me—a legitimate head honcho we had a genuine crack at."

"Thanks to my grandmother."

"She was a lead. It's what she wanted to be."

"But now she's dead while Trelana's still out there and there's not a damn thing you or I or anyone else can do about it?"

"We could arrest him, but it wouldn't stick."

Drew hesitated. "He'll try and kill me now, too, won't he?" And when the agent stayed silent, Drew repeated louder, "*Won't* he?"

"Yes," Masterson said softly, but then his tone heightened. "You had a chance until you insisted on this meeting. They'll find out about it. Maybe they know already. Now that you've seen me, they've got to figure you can hurt them, and *nobody* hurts them. Take off. Run. Go as far as you can and then keep running. If you want to stay alive, it's your only chance."

"Not necessarily." Drew's face twisted into a snarl. "I'm not really sure which of you I loathe more. It's pretty much of a toss-up. Trelana killed my grandmother and you got her killed. Only thing you got going for you, Agent Masterson, is that I'm starting to figure you can help me."

"Help you what?"

"Kill Trelana."

CHAPTER 6

ON THE SURFACE IT WAS JUST A HOUSE ON AN ORDINARY SIDE STREET of Tel Aviv. Its macadam steps were chipped and sagged with wear, its exterior much in need of a paint job thanks to the hot dusty winds that blew in over the summer months. A vendor stood lazily beneath a canopy in front of a cart full of oranges and vegetables. An Arab beggar knelt in the shade of an alleyway, shaking his cup at all those passing by.

Of course, none of the passers-by, not even the ones who stopped to slip a coin into his cup, noticed that his baggy, soiled rags concealed the black steel frame of a baby Uzi machine gun. Nor did anyone notice the Eagle pistol beneath the vendor's black jacket or the full-sized Uzi stored in a compartment beneath his oranges. The job of the two men was to protect the run-down building they fronted from any possible intruders.

Unlike other international intelligence services, the Israeli Mossad did not maintain regular headquarters. A headquarters was kept up in Jerusalem as a front for the press and foreign inspection, but a front was all it was. Instead, the Mossad chose a number of substations scattered strategically all over the country. Many of these changed locations regularly for reasons of security and to flush out possible infiltrators. Even after a move was made, the old locations continued to be watched for a time. Agents who nonetheless showed up could thus be viewed and treated as spies. True Mossad agents were disciplined to the point of being fanatical. Codes were never missed, signals never failing to be relayed. In Israel's world of the one against the many, such practice was mandated for survival.

The woman who walked out of the shadows onto the side street was not dressed for the unusually long summer that was presently intruding on the start of fall. Her slacks and sweater were too dark, too heavy. Her waist-length jacket seemed unnecessary. The heels of her boots clicked against the sidewalk in rhythm with her step. In response, the beggar eased himself a little forward and showed his cup. The vendor straightened for a possible sale.

The woman passed the beggar and dropped two coins into his cup, one at a time. The beggar glanced at them and nodded to the vendor as he pressed a button concealed within the nearby wall. The woman would now be permitted access to the building. Those inside would be ready for her.

She strode up the macadam steps without hesitating, as if the house was hers. She knocked the way a home-at-last relative might, and the door opened swiftly to her Mossad control station.

"We've been expecting you, Elliana," a small, mustachioed man greeted her inside. Although short, his chest was framed like a barrel and his hairy forearms were knotted with muscle.

Elliana Hirsch let Moshe close the door behind her and allowed herself a sigh. It felt good to be home after all these months. Yet, the circumstances of her recall disturbed her. It was too sudden, too unexplained. Such did not bode well.

"We?" Elliana questioned, recalling her control Moshe's use of the plural.

Moshe hesitated before responding. His mustache seemed to twitch. At last he nodded. "Isser is upstairs," he said.

Elliana felt her stomach flutter. Isser was the name of the very first Mossad director, and since then the name had been taken by all who succeeded him as a sort of code. To think that the head of the entire organization had come to see her. Elliana could not even guess why. Such things were not done every day. She was an ordinary field agent. Suddenly the prospects of her recall seemed even more foreboding.

"He wants to see you immediately," Moshe told her.

Elliana started up and felt her long, muscular legs go wobbly. In her own mind, she was much too tall for a woman and her steps often appeared gangly, but in much the same way that a large cat's might.

"Aren't you coming?" she called to Moshe.

"He wants to see you alone," he returned, and Elliana tried to pass off the dread in his voice.

She began to climb the rest of the flight. Her auburn hair was probably too long and dangled freely past her shoulders. She was pale and had neglected to don makeup for this recall meeting because she hadn't seen any point in it. Of course, then she hadn't known she'd be meeting with Isser himself. Listen to me, she thought, eleven years as a Mossad operative and I still can't get foolish thoughts of appearance out of my head. . . .

Elliana reached the second floor and turned right. Isser would be in the second room down. It was the way such things were done. She reached the doorway but didn't knock. Isser saw her and rose immediately to his feet.

"Ellie . . ."

She moved tentatively forward, looking at his face for a reaction.

It broke into a smile and he opened his arms. "It's been much too long," Isser said and hugged her close.

In fact, it had been over five years now. They had last met shortly after her husband's funeral when Isser had approved the operation she had worked on off and on ever since and lately all the time.

Isser was a short man, so Elliana virtually absorbed him as they embraced. Unlike Moshe, the older Isser possessed little obvious muscle, but Elliana knew many men had perished from his hand. One did not get to be Mossad chief and remain there without first proving himself in the field.

"You look tired," Isser said, pulling back.

"It was a long trip."

"The fatigue I see has little to do with the trip. Come, let's sit."

He beckoned to a pair of chairs set against a side wall of the room safely away from the window. Men in Isser's position learned fast to avoid windows. The room itself was simply furnished. A pair of desks, assorted chairs, two computer terminals presently switched off—just the necessities.

Isser spoke as soon as they were both seated. "You've been irregular with filing of reports."

"It's been difficult," Ellie told him. "I've been undercover much of the time, watched constantly. Going to a drop point would have proven too dangerous."

He hesitated. "You know why I called you here, don't you?"

"I . . . suspect."

"I must recall you, Ellie," he said with regret in his voice. "Your current operation can no longer be sanctioned."

"But why?"

"Because we have seen no results, no evidence that merits continuation."

"We had an agreement, Isser."

"Yes, five years ago I gave you permission to do whatever was necessary to find the murderers of your husband. And now five years of time and wasted expense have yielded nothing."

"Not five years, Isser. The first four I worked on this only off and on. Just during the past year have I devoted myself fully, and at last I'm getting close. I'm certain of it this time."

"Ellie—"

"No, wait, just listen. I've met with people. There's finally evidence of stirring. I have a meet set up in Prague that—"

"Ellie," Isser broke in patiently, "you are one of our finest field agents and certainly our most valuable woman. Your exploits are legend at the academy. No one is more respected for outstanding work in the field. We can no longer afford to spare you on such a wild goose chase. You are needed far more elsewhere. Israel's very existence is at stake. Qaddaffi has lost what little mind he once possessed. The peace process has broken down, leading Jordan and Syria closer together. We need your expertise at work on projects more directly related to state security."

"Precisely why you should allow me to remain on my present assignment. The Council of Ten poses a greater threat to state security than any of those posed by the crumbling peace process."

"The Council of Ten," Isser muttered. "Five years of pursuit and all you have gained is the shadowy title that you started with."

"More than just a title, also an aim. Global hegemony, Isser. That's what the Council's after and they won't stop until they've got it. David must have found out about them. That's why they killed him.''

Isser's eyes scolded her. "Time tends to make the memory selective, Ellie. David had just resigned from the cabinet to save face. He was not a man with many friends, within Israel or without. The list of suspects, well . . .'' Isser finished his remarks with a shrug.

"But his papers mention the Council.''

"In a code only you have been able to break.''

"Based on an ancient language from the time of Alexander. The Council was Alexander's concept, a manifest plan to conquer the world and divide it into ten separate regions, each ruled by a district governor. All together they would determine policy under Alexander as a council of ten.''

Isser shook his head slowly. "Five years of field work and all you can give me is a history lesson.''

Ellie had never felt more helpless. How could she convince Isser that the Council of Ten had been reborn in the modern day, that her husband David had caught on to them and been killed in a fiery plane crash as a result? She had no proof. In truth, years of pursuit had gained only leads that went nowhere and connections that were severed at every turn. David had gotten close to them and had been executed as a result. She believed firmly that the Council had arranged his disgrace in the government as well. Their reach was everywhere.

She had started her pursuit of the Council originally for David, but now she realized that she was doing it mostly for herself. Her marriage to him seven years before was a hectic affair squeezed in between assignments, seen by Ellie as a last chance at a normal life once her days in the field were over. His murder had forced her to face the realities of her chosen profession. There would be no peaceful retirement, and now at thirty-two she was almost certain to remain childless as well. The Council had stolen whatever chance she had at both away from her, and her obsessive quest for them had been as much for distraction as vengeance. The pursuit was simply all she had.

Isser pushed his chair closer to hers. "Listen to me, Ellie. Look at you, you're beaten and exhausted and what have you gained from it? Nothing.''

"That's not true!''

"Then report to me your findings now."

"It's not that simple. All I have are random occurrences. There's never any firm proof or connections. But something's going on."

"Open to interpretation, of course, and mine seems to be distinctly different from yours in this case."

"Don't you see, Isser?" Elliana pleaded. "Everything the Council does is based around total secrecy. It's the only way they can function. If all the intelligence services in the world fail to pursue them, they can flourish unhindered."

"Then tell me what you know about the Council. Who are its members?"

"I don't know."

"Where are the members from?"

"I don't know."

"You are convinced they are after some unholy *end*, so tell me the *means*."

"That's the point!" Ellie nearly shouted at him. "They were never in possession of the means until recently, so they couldn't surface. That's changed."

"And now they have this means?"

"The indications are there."

"Tell me these indications."

"They're vague, understated. I'll know better after Prague in two days."

Isser hesitated only slightly. "You're not going."

"What?"

"We haven't a safe house anywhere *near* Prague, you know that. I can't let you go illegal without shelter, backups or no. You're too valuable."

"I've gone illegal plenty of times without backups *or* shelter!"

"This is different. You've been formally recalled for reassignment," Isser said, his patience gone, his words cold and flat. "Moshe has all the details for you downstairs."

Elliana stood up angrily and stormed for the door. Suddenly she stopped, shoulders squaring.

"I can't accept this," she said, still facing the hallway.

"The choice is no longer yours."

"They killed David."

"We don't know that."

She turned around. "I'm requesting a leave of absence."

"Denied."

"A vacation, then. I've got plenty of time coming."

"All personnel are on Priority Counter-terrorist Alert. All vacations have been suspended."

Elliana tensed. "That only leaves me one choice."

Isser stood up and moved toward her. "You'd do this, you'd throw away everything you've accomplished, everything you are, just like that?"

Ellie nodded, not sure if she meant to. It was all right, though, because now Isser would understand the gravity of this operation for her. She had proven her commitment to it and he would okay her continuing on with sanction. He had to.

But he didn't.

"Your resignation will be accepted with grave disappointment," was all he said, his expression blank. He drew a little closer to her with his arms folded. "You were the best, Ellie, but you're not anymore. Obsession is the last thing an operative in your position can afford if you are going to survive. Obsession is a weakness and no weaknesses can be tolerated in the field. Death results or, worse, the compromising of others and the nation itself. The threads we hold onto are too thin to take chances. There is no place for personal vendettas once a professional attitude has been sacrificed. There's too much at stake."

"There was no new assignment for me, was there?" Ellie said with sudden realization.

"There might have been."

"A desk job," Ellie said softly, "eventually a section chief if I'm lucky. . . ."

Isser held his hands by his hips now. "Still yours if you want. My memory can be quite selective."

Elliana shook her head. "I belong in the field."

"Not on your own, Ellie," Isser told her. "Not without us behind you."

"I've got to do this for David, Isser. You understand that, don't you?"

The Mossad chief ignored the question. "Once you walk out of here, there's no coming back. You know that."

She nodded grimly and started to swing back for the door.

"Ellie . . ."

59

"Please, Isser, don't."

He spoke as she moved into the hallway, tone wholly professional. "Your last checks will be forwarded to the usual drop."

She looked at him one last time. "Sealed with a postage stamp, Isser, or a bullet?"

PART THREE:

TOO-JAY'S

CHAPTER 7

"YOU'RE CRAZY."

Drew played Sam Masterson's initial response over and over again in his mind as Sunday came closer.

"It's a state of mind that comes over me when I find out my life is in danger. My grandmother helped you and now you're going to help me. Consider it poetic justice."

Masterson was heading his Ford back for the Hyatt. "Except she volunteered and I'm not about to.'

"I think you will, Agent Masterson. You see, I had this feeling right from when you picked me up that it was more than just Trelana you were scared of, it was me. I know all about the game you guys played with an old lady. Would make for great press, wouldn't it? And I've got the letter to back up what I say. Agency wouldn't come out looking too good and you'd come out looking worst of all. That's how I see it."

Masterson fought to keep his eyes on the road. Even so, Drew could see his face had flushed first with rage, then frustration, and, finally, hopeless resignation.

"Who the hell do you think you are?"

"Someone who wants to stay alive and who's willing to do you a favor in the process. Willing and able."

"Able?"

"I'll get to that later. It gets a little complicated. I don't need much. You'll hardly have to implicate your innocent little self."

"I can't do this!"

"You couldn't have used an old lady to do your dirty work for you either."

Masterson pulled into a parking lot. "Assuming I go along with this, what would you want?"

"Your inch-thick file on Trelana and a gun, preferably a magnum."

"You mean you plan to just go up to Trelana and—"

"Let me finish. I assume someone at the DEA is doing what they're supposed to be doing. You must have virtually a constant tail on Trelana, and since you admitted he's a community figure, I've got to think he spends plenty of time in public. It's just a question of finding the right time. Chore number two."

Masterson's mouth dropped in shock. "You don't expect me to—"

"I expect you to find me a way to get close to him. I expect you to get me a gun to do the job and I expect you to help get me out afterward. I'll take care of the rest. And, of course, if you decide to leave me holding the bag, well, there's always the press."

"You're asking too much. Too much!"

"It's for my grandmother, Agent Masterson, and that makes it not even close to too much. Better head back to the Hyatt now and drop me off. You've got plenty of work to do."

When you came right down to it, Drew figured Mace was to blame for his decision to kill Trelana.

His early sessions in the mercenary camp were marked by mistakes and fears typical of the amateur. He remembered freezing on a catwalk suspended forty feet over the ground while being marked by machine-gun tracer fire. He remembered his first two forays into the jungle on individual wargames maneuvers, comic adventures in which he had "died" first on each occasion.

Mace took him aside after the second.

"You're thinking too much, son," the death machine advised. "Thinking about living, dying, and what your goddamn next move is supposed to be. What you gotta do, you gotta learn to hate. . . ."

Mace had gone on to explain that this hate was for no one individual, but just for the idea of defeat, of failure. Refined, the hate could become a weapon that could help you achieve the impossible, overcome any odds. The hate taught you to accept nothing and stop at nothing. It was the great equalizer.

"Take the Timber Wolf that time in Corsica," Mace had related. "Ambushed by twenty shiteaters with automatic weapons, and he stayed alive. Killed most and the rest ran for the hills with fudge stains in their undies. He couldn't have done it without the hate."

"But he's a professional, *you're* a professional," Drew returned. "I thought professionals weren't supposed to feel anything."

"That's crap mostly. When you're out there alone, on your own, with shiteaters ready to rip your gut out, you've got to feel something. I've known men who were like ice, but they're few and far between. So, you find something to hate and you don't stop hating until you've won, which in this case means at the end you're still alive and the shiteaters are dead. Stop hating and you got no edge. No man, not me or even the Timber Wolf, can be better than everyone else. It's the hate that makes you better."

Drew took Mace's words to heart. He had been looking at mercenary camp as merely a violent extension of his own life, had tried to apply the same rules. It hadn't worked because different rules applied. In the next session, the same obstacles remained to be overcome, but Drew's hesitance and desperation were gone. The hate had replaced them, hate for anything that threatened to trip him up. The hate gave him focus when he took to the woods, a singular purpose of survival, which made him feel more alive than ever. He slept in trees or buried under layers of dirt or squeezed between two large rocks. His concentration never wavered. The mere consideration of failure had been stricken, of success as well. There was only the moment immediately before him. Survive that one and he could move on to the next. The short term was the key. One step at a time. He was among the last surviving five two sessions previous, and in the most recent it had come down to just him and Mace. The hate had served him well.

Now it had returned. His state of mind was that of the woods. A man had murdered his grandmother and would try to kill him. That man had to die. The hate required it. Mace always said you came into the world kicking, screaming, and alone, and that was the way it might as well stay with everyone else being shiteaters anyway.

Masterson had called him back early Saturday evening.

"There's a disco in Palm Beach called Chauncey's. Meet me there at ten."

Chauncey's was located on the first floor of the NCNB Building on Palm Beach Lakes Boulevard. It was packed by ten o'clock and featured a marble dance floor and striking art deco design. Masterson had a table off to the side within sight of the door. He was working on a drink that had a soggy lemon peel floating on its surface when Drew took the chair across from him.

"Forget it, kid," were his first words. "It can't be done."

"We wouldn't be meeting here if that's all you had to say."

"Just trying to do you a favor, that's all."

"Just tell me what you found out."

"You wanna whack Trelana? No sweat. He eats lunch every Sunday at a Palm Beach deli called Too-Jay's—him and a pair of bodyguards who could pass for the Incredible Hulk's brothers."

"Six bullets can go a long way."

"You're fucking crazy."

"Yeah. Keep talking."

"Same table all the time. Rear corner. Trelana sits between the two monsters. Couple others wait in a car outside. Sure, no problem. . . ."

"Can you get me in there?"

"It's a public restaurant."

"That's not what I mean and you know it, Agent Masterson. I'll need to be close to Trelana to be sure. His bodyguards gotta have a reason to let me do that."

"Like if you were a waiter? Sure, I can handle that. We place people in restaurants all the time. Just remember, if you're closer to them, it'll mean they'll be closer to you."

"Yup."

"I've got a gun for you in my pocket. How you get it into Too-Jay's is your problem. Giving you a reason to be there in the first place I guess is mine. Call you later on that one."

"Not bad. Now what about getting me out of there?"

Masterson resisted, his mind changing tracks. "Kid, I wouldn't be doing this if in the long run it wasn't going to make my own

66

life easier. We can't touch Trelana. You're going to be making lots of people happy.''

"Just tell me about the escape.''

"It's like this. Frustration is a by-law at the agency these days. A couple other lifers feel like I do. It wasn't hard to secure their help.'' Masterson thought briefly. "I'll have a man, a spotter, watching Too-Jay's from outside at a point from where he can see the interior of the dining area. As soon as you approach Trelana's table ready to use the gun, lean over and pretend to tie your shoe. That will be his signal to call for the getaway car. When the hit's finished, hightail it out of the restaurant. The car will be waiting.''

"If it's not . . .''

"Look, kid, if I get you that far, I'm not gonna screw you. You'll have enough to feed me to both my own people and Trelana's. We'll get you out of Too-Jay's, then out of the city and back home. Do this right and nobody'll even get a look at you. If something fucks up, you've got my private number, which rings wherever I am. I'm not a hard man to find.''

"Let's hope I don't have to look.''

Masterson hesitated again. "I'd have done something like this, or hired someone to do it, a long time ago, except I never learned how not to be scared.''

"Or how to hate,'' Drew told him.

"Ordering! One turkey club with extra mayo, one liverwurst on rye with onions. . . .''

Drew's head pounded from the constant sound of plates clapping against steel. He stepped to the raised counter; behind it two men were busy with a never-ending array of breads and contents to be stuffed between slices. Quickly he clipped his order in the first vacant slot. Across from the sandwich area, the activity was similarly hectic inside the kitchen where hot orders were being prepared. A continuous stream of khaki-clad waiters passed in and out through the swinging door. A collision seemed unavoidable. The Sunday lunchtime rush at Too-Jay's deli had begun. The popular eating spot promised to be swarming with people for the next hour or so. Then things would quiet down considerably and Arthur Trelana would make his appearance.

"Ordering! One BLT, one tongue special with melted swiss . . .''

One of Drew's orders came up and he loaded the four plates onto a tray, carting them carefully back into the dining area. He felt nearly as nervous about botching things in his cover as a waiter as he did about the more pressing task soon at hand. So far he had held his own, but the rush hour would sorely test him. Stand out too much and someone might make a point of mentioning him to Trelana upon the drug lord's arrival.

Masterson had arranged the cover of a substitute waiter. Drew was told to be at the deli by six A.M. He was expected. Masterson told him the restaurant would furnish him with a uniform. He had the cab leave him off on Coconut Row at the head of Royal Poinciana Plaza, a nest of shops and stores in Palm Beach where the famous deli was located. Not only did this spare him the attention that might have been drawn by a waiter arriving in a taxi, but it also provided him with a chance to study the layout. Small access roads wound through the plaza, criss-crossing parking lots and providing easy access to the labyrinth of stores. Too-Jay's was situated in the center of one of several mall-style buildings. Drew entered and announced himself.

He hung his windbreaker on a coat rack in the kitchen, careful to make sure that the right pocket containing a bulge was concealed. There he had stowed the snub-nosed magnum revolver, checked and loaded and now waiting for him to retrieve it.

Minutes after that he had donned a pair of khaki slacks, blue Too-Jay's shirt, and white apron. He took advantage of the moderately slow first hours to study the restaurant's layout in detail. A huge dessert counter was on the left of the entrance just before the start of the sandwich counter. The cash register station lay on the right along with the entrance to the full kitchen where his jacket hung with the hidden pistol. The tables were straight ahead in an informal dining area, about twenty of various sizes. The far wall was all windows and looked out over a spacious courtyard across which lay still more shops. Masterson's men would probably be watching from one of these for Drew to lean over and feign tying his shoe at the proper time—the signal that he was about to initiate the hit. The side and rear walls of the dining area, meanwhile, were mirrored, and as Drew delivered order after order he found his eyes focusing on himself more and more.

Is it me that's really about to do this?

The mirrors told him that it was. For real. No game in mercenary camp.

By one o'clock the lunchtime rush had subsided and Drew anxiously began to wonder if Trelana was going to show. He didn't know if he could stand this kind of pressure another day, didn't know if he could maintain the mental state he had put himself into in order to accomplish the task before him. The pay phone on the wall kept grabbing his eye, tempting him to call Masterson and tell him the whole thing was off.

A little past one o'clock, two large, menacing-looking men came through the doors and spoke briefly with the manager. Dressed in light cotton suits, they made a careful walk through the deli and kitchen, checking faces but not speaking to anyone. Drew went about his business as if he didn't notice them. And since the men's eyes never regarded him a second time, he figured he must have done a pretty good acting job.

Less than a minute later, one of the big men held the door open for Arthur Trelana. Drew recognized him immediately from the file Masterson had provided. He stepped inside slowly, smiling, looking dapper and elegant in a finely cut three-piece white suit. He greeted Too-Jay's manager and shook hands with him warmly. They exchanged pleasantries.

Drew's heart picked up its pace and he felt along his chest involuntarily. Shaking himself alert so as not to draw attention, he returned to the dining area to take the order of a couple who had just been seated in his section, making eight tables occupied in all. He was distracted now and had to concentrate on appearing at ease.

Drew moved toward the kitchen to put in the order. On the way, Trelana and his bodyguards walked right by him. The man reeked of sweet, expensive cologne. Everything about him seemed perfect, his naturally bronze skin making him look healthy and fit for a man of sixty.

Drew hated Trelana's guts.

But the reality of what he was about to do suddenly struck him. Every part of him starting shaking until he clung to the hate once again. This was the man who'd had his grandmother murdered, the man who would soon order him killed as well.

Unless he struck first.

More of the lessons of the mercenary camp returned to him.

How to melt into a scene and seem simply a part of it, anything to influence those around you to keep their defenses low.

He could hear Trelana and his bodyguards chuckling in the dining area. That gave him the last fuel he needed.

His order was up on the raised counter in the sandwich area and he delivered it to the other table active in his section, mixing up the orders and having to change the plates around. He cursed himself for the oversight, for it had drawn attention to him. But returning to the dining area did afford him the opportunity to chart the position of Trelana's table and the drug lord himself. He was indeed seated between his two bodyguards at a table against the far wall of mirrors.

As expected. Perfect.

It was time.

Drew's mind was working fast now, but his motions seemed slow. His back tensed in anticipation of a scream from his rear, an accusation tossed at him by one of Trelana's bodyguards, perhaps a gun drawn to accompany it.

But none of that happened. He passed into the kitchen through the swinging door and moved unobtrusively to the coat rack. Without hesitating he extracted the gun from the right pocket of his windbreaker and pressed it quickly against his body before sliding it under his apron into his belt.

Drew was trembling when he emerged through the swinging door. This wasn't a game being played out in the woods this time. It was real. But the same rules apply, he tried to tell himself. *Hate, don't let go of the hate.* . . .

His mind sharpened. He realized he could not simply walk straight up to Trelana's table and start shooting. He'd be watched through the entire course of an apparently uncalled for approach. When he went for his gun, he'd be finished. He needed a distraction, better yet something that looked completely normal.

A tray of sandwiches appeared atop the steel counter before him. Drew had his answer.

He grasped the tray and, without hesitating, made a slow but direct path to the dining area. When he reached it, he gazed out through the windowed rear wall and leaned over to retie his shoe, placing the tray for a moment on an empty stand. The signal had now been given. The getaway car would be on its way to the front of Too-Jay's. He gazed over at Trelana's table.

One of his bodyguards had changed chairs! He was now sitting on the *opposite* side of the table across from Trelana. Drew had gone over the hit a thousand times in his mind but never with this scenario.

Improvise . . .

Yes, that was the key!

Drew retrieved the tray of sandwiches meant for another table and stood up. His hands weren't shaking anymore. They felt cold and clammy, yet steady. Even the sweat had dried up. He felt surprisingly calm.

He walked directly to Trelana's table with the sandwich tray balanced carefully in his left hand. His right was within easy drawing range of the pistol.

Just a little closer now. . . .

He stopped to the right of the bodyguard sitting opposite of Trelana, halting directly over him. All three men became silent and looked up as Drew set his tray down on the stand nearby.

"Now who had . . ."

The words were used merely for distraction as Drew yanked his pistol up and out in a single motion, in line and ready to fire. But in the last instant, even as his finger found the trigger, Drew knew he wouldn't be able to pull it. This was no game in the woods. His bullets were live and he had been a fool for believing himself capable of actually using them for real.

Drew froze and the instant unwound in slow motion as, in the movies, the last moments do before a car crash. He saw the guards lurching from their seats as their hands disappeared inside their jackets only to emerge with cold steel pistols. He saw Trelana cowering low, saw his own certain death, and remembered that he was about to close his eyes when they recorded the impossible.

The head of the guard closest to him ruptured like a melon, spraying blood and brains everywhere. The man crashed across the table as a pair of red splotches appeared on the chest of the guard who had been seated next to Trelana. The drug lord was pushing the body aside when his head snapped back and blood leaped from his throat. Drew heard two more spits. Behind Trelana a section of the mirrored wall shattered, lined with scarlet grooves. Trelana slid dead to the floor.

Drew was swinging around then and saw a tall man standing

by one of the rear tables with a gun still smoking in his hand and the barrel rotating slightly. Toward him.

"No!" Drew screamed.

He plunged to the flooor, and more of the mirrored glass exploded behind him. What was happening here?

Drew realized that he still held the magnum in his hand, and he tilted it upward as the other man changed into combat position and sighted on him. There was no time to think; that was what saved him. He brought the magnum up and fired in the same motion. He thought he pulled the trigger twice, although it could have been three times. One of the bullets found the killer's chest and the second his head. He pitched backward into a table and then over it.

Drew's ears rang with the vibrations of the magnum blasts so close. Around him everyone was screaming.

I have just killed a man.

He found himself back on his feet. His eyes locked on the bloodied mirror, on himself with the gun still clutched in his hand and fresh blood sprayed all over his apron and part of his shirt. The blood was everywhere, the death. The screaming had started to subside. Drew tried to steady his thoughts.

Stick with the plan! Something had gone wrong, but that didn't mean all. Get to the car.

Now!

Drew broke his trance and rushed from the dining area. All the patrons and workers had dived for the nearest cover. He saw nothing but their legs and covered heads as he ran for the door. He rushed from Too-Jay's out into the plaza, prepared to leap into the backseat of a waiting car.

But there was no car.

Drew felt a fear like he had never known pass through him. The bitter, coppery smell of blood seemed to have followed him from the restaurant. His heart thundered.

Where was the car?

Something had obviously gone wrong. He couldn't wait any longer. If it wasn't here now, it wasn't coming.

He ran through Royal Poinciana Plaza in the direction of Coconut Row. Trelana's car would have at least two more men in it. They would have already been alerted by the gunshots and the panic. Drew had to flee the area before they had time to put everything together.

He stripped off and discarded the bloody apron as he ran, oblivious to the stares of pedestrians and those glaring at him from cars. He realized the gun was still tight in his hand and tossed that away as well. He slowed as he approached the traffic-filled Coconut Row. Rushing had made him stand out. If he moved at a leisurely pace, he would stand a better chance of going unnoticed. Except for the damn waiter's uniform . . .

Holding his breath, Drew bounded across Coconut Row, skirting traffic. Horns honked. Brakes squealed. Threats were hurled through sunroofs and windows. Drew ignored them all. He reached the opposite side of the road and began running parallel to a row of bushes that bordered the Breakers golf course. He stole a glance behind him, checking for possible pursuit. There was none, at least none he could see. Nonetheless, as soon as the bushes were low enough, he hurdled over onto the back nine of the course.

The thought that his grandmother had been murdered on these very grounds was lost on him as he ran down the neatly manicured fairways. Again there were screams and shouts directed at him and again he simply outran them. His mind had begun to work logically now. From the golf course he would emerge on South County Road, which would lead him straight to Worth Avenue. Plenty of people, activity, and lots of stores. He'd be able to lose himself easily.

He was walking when he reached South County and kept the same pace when Worth Avenue finally appeared. The long street was lined with luxurious shops displaying their easily recognizable names. This was the Palm Beach version of Rodeo Drive in Beverly Hills, a rich version of Georgetown's M Street. Thinking of that calmed him as he approached the Esplanade arcade of shops and stores, layered one after the other on two levels. Drew turned into the Esplanade, realizing he needed a phone most of all.

He heard the sirens clearly now, screaming close by. He imagined an endless parade of vehicles screeching to a halt outside Too-Jay's from all directions. Royal Poinciana Plaza would be three-deep with police. Drew passed into the Esplanade through the parking entrance. Arrows noting Phone directed him to the right. He expected the standard pay variety, but instead he found a newer brand of pay phone with a touchtone resting on a table containing the pay slots and guts built into the front.

Drew sat down in a chair next to one of the phones, able at last to collect his thoughts. He had come to Too-Jay's to kill Trelana. But someone else had killed the drug lord and then tried to kill him.

A man he had shot. *Oh God* . . .

Everything about Masterson's plan had gone wrong. Either the agent had set him up . . . or had been set up himself. Only one way to find out which.

Drew inserted a quarter and dialed Masterson's private number. The number rang and rang.

And went unanswered.

He was alone.

CHAPTER 8

SUNDAY HAD BEEN AN ALL-AROUND SHITTY DAY FOR THE RIVERO brothers. Never mind that their six-month-old custom Cadillac seemed already to be pleading for a tune-up, backfiring and stumbling about the South Beach streets like a dying dog. Never mind that. The car they could get fixed, buy a brand new one maybe. But their other problems wouldn't be nearly as simple to solve.

To begin with, they hadn't received payment and shipping instructions on their newest shipment of powder. This particular cocaine channel had been by far their most reliable and lucrative, and the brothers didn't want to make any move that might threaten it. But something must have fucked up somewhere. They had taken delivery of the powder on time and everything was set up for the meet. Then the courier never showed. The Riveros were stuck with two hundred pounds of uncut powder they didn't dare move on their own. They had to stick to the agreement, after all. Shit, some things were sacred.

Then there was the problem of a new pusher in South Beach who had forced out their top street man over the weekend and was opening up shop for himself. The man obviously didn't know who he was fucking with. But the Riveros caught onto him plenty fast and were ready to set up a meet for him with the angels.

Problem number three was a bit more complicated. The three Anglo kids who were pushing powder and pills for them in the

Miami schools weren't returning the greens they should have
been. The Riveros knew skimming was to blame and a few years
ago would have jumped at the chance to shove hot pokers up the
boys' tight white asses. But they were businessmen now and had
to think like businessmen, like maybe using problem number two
to help solve problem number three. It would be like killing two
fish with one stone, ventured Marco, who had never quite mas-
tered American idioms.

Miguel headed the stumbling Caddy down Route 95, screeching onto the exit ramp closest to a private school with the
colorful name of Ransom-Everglades, while his brother toked on
a fat joint in the passenger seat. Miguel knew Marco was the
better looking of the two, but Miguel was undeniably the smarter.
He didn't look smart because his face was square and flat, his
skin and hair perpetually oily. Acne had cursed him as a youth
and he had torn at the blotches in frustration, leaving his face
pitted and marked. As if this wasn't enough, a pair of knife
fights in Cuban jails had partially closed his left eye and left a
long scar on his right cheek. He hated mirrors and gazed in them
only in dim bathrooms.

His brother Marco's real name was Julian, but he had changed
it on coming to the States in the great Mariel Harbor boat lift
because Julian figured he looked more like a Marco. Anglos said
he looked a lot like a dead spic comic named Freddie Prinze,
especially with his mustache. How'd he die, Marco wanted to
know? He blew his brains out, they told him. What a way to
go. . . .

Miguel pulled the Caddy up to the entrance of Ransom-
Everglades and pushed a button, which automatically flicked all
the door locks open. A long-haired Anglo boy wearing a crisp
leather jacket climbed in the backseat. Two more schools, and
two more boys joined the first in the Caddy's backseat. One
wore oyster-colored corduroys and a high school letterman's
jacket. The other wore jeans and a light windbreaker.

"Hey, man," said Marco, "let's party."

Miguel headed the Caddy back to South Beach, specifically
the southern end of Collins Avenue, which was their prime turf.
A small Cuban diner had been headquarters of their man Ramon
until the dude, soon-to-be-a-dead-fuck, moved in. The Riveros

figured he was part of somebody bigger, so an example was called for. It was Miguel who stepped inside, glad to see the diner was deserted except for a big dark man standing behind the counter wearing an apron.

"Can I help you?" the fucker asked in Spanish.

"Yeah," Miguel came back. "I'd like a take-out order." Right across the counter from him now. "For Ramon."

His fist came up fast. The fucker never had time to react. The blow bashed into his solar plexus and doubled him over the counter. The guy was big, but he was slow. Miguel cracked him once on the back of the head just for fun and then half-led, half-dragged him out of the diner and had him squeezed in the Caddy's backseat with the Anglo dudes before anyone in South Beach was the wiser. Then he was back behind the Caddy's wheel, gunning the engine.

"Let's party, man," said Marco.

Miguel drove the Caddy north toward the Orange Bowl and an abandoned warehouse, which doubled as the brothers' home and headquarters. They didn't care about bringing the Anglos down here because they wouldn't be in condition to tell anyone about it. The boys sat all squeezed together in the backseat, the effects of Marco's pot lessening in them enough for the fear to come through. The stranger next to them was only semiconscious, eyes glassy. He was moaning and he didn't smell too good.

It was Miguel who dragged him through the warehouse front door while the cooler Marco led the way for the rest of them.

"Come on in, man, it's party time!" he announced as if he genuinely meant it.

He closed and locked the door behind the boys. They were in what looked like a huge living room partitioned off with old and broken furniture scattered over a dust-coated floor.

Miguel tossed the stranger to the floor, then kicked him once in the head and twice in the gut. A *whoooosssssh* of air sped through the guy's mouth. Miguel kicked him in the gut again. He rolled over.

Marco slapped his arm around the shoulder of the boy in the leather jacket. He squeezed it tenderly.

"I like you, man," he said. "You're my favorite."

But then his hand was in motion, incredibly quick like a cat after a ball of yarn, switching from the shoulder to the throat. The boy reeled backward as he felt his air being choked off. His eyes bulged when he saw the gun in Marco's hand coming straight for his mouth.

The other boys were too shocked to move and by the time they looked to the door, Miguel was on them from behind, grasping them by the scruffs of the neck and shaking viciously. They felt like puppets in his fleshy hands.

Marco tilted the barrel of his monstrous revolver down the throat of the boy in the leather jacket. He cocked the hammer, all the soft prettiness gone from his face, rage replacing it.

"You fuck with us, man? You fuck with us?"

The boy's eyes bulged with fear. He tried to mumble something.

"I'm gonna blow your brains out! You like that idea, man?"

The boy wet his pants.

Marco heard the dripping sound, looked down, and snickered.

"You fucking baby! You gonna shit next, stink up our house? You fucking baby gringo pisspants!"

Marco shoved him against the wall, holding his hair in one hand and the gun in the other.

One of the boys Miguel was holding started to sob. Miguel slammed him into a table.

"You boys think you can fuck with us!" Miguel charged. "You think we're stupid spics who can't read or nothing? Well, we're smarter than you asswipes. When you playin' our game, you don't make up your own. You want to work for us, we give you your cut, you don't take it."

"I'm sorry, I'm sorry," said the boy with one side of his face swollen.

Miguel patted the bruise tenderly. "It's good you don't lie, gringo." He slammed the boy's head against the table again. "But bein' sorry, it ain't good enough for us." He was speaking to all three of them now. "You boys worked good for us in the beginning, but if we let you out of this, word would get out that you can fuck with the Riveros, and we can't have that. So we gotta do all three of ya. We'll make it look like the creep on the floor over there did it. Nobody'll know the difference. You boys should have stuck to the deal."

When Miguel had shifted toward the still prone stranger to make his point, he had noted something was wrong, but it didn't seem important enough to be bothered with. The stranger's position had perhaps shifted. Maybe his breathing had steadied.

No matter.

The rest happened very fast. His new position allowed an easy draw of the pistol from his armpit holster for Selinas. He had packed numerous other weapons on the chance that the Riveros would have searched him and found the gun. But the gun was what he needed now if he was going to get the boys out of this. Their presence had been unexpected and had necessitated him keeping up the ruse longer than he would have preferred.

He went for Miguel first, not because he was charging as Selinas lurched to his feet gun in hand, but because shooting Marco now would almost assure the involuntary pulling of his trigger and the splattering of the boy's brains across the wall. It took two bullets to halt the powerful Miguel and by that time Marco had the gun out of the boy's mouth and was bringing it around.

Selinas dove to the floor and rolled. Behind him a bullet from Marco blew a lamp apart. A measure of the room's light faded. Another round exploded in front of him as he snapped to a halt. Marco was about to fire again when Selinas let go a round. The glazer bullet, composed of hundreds of tiny pellets, blasted into his shoulder and tore his arm halfway from its socket. Marco pitched backward screaming.

Selinas rose to his feet.

"Get up!" he ordered the three boys who had all collapsed tight to the floor. "Get up!"

Finally, they did, slowly until Selinas lifted one bodily to his toes.

"Get up and get out of here!"

The one who'd wet his pants stood shaking with arms wrapped around himself against the wall.

"Help your friend," Selinas told the other two. Of course, his employer's instructions would have been to kill the boys. They had seen much too much here tonight, but so long as no one else found out no complications could result. "Take their Cadillac to get home," he continued. "Ditch it a few miles from where you all live. You can use the walk." One of them started to speak. "No questions. Move!"

They were gone seconds later.

Selinas walked over to Marco and leaned over him. Marco's eyes had gone glassy and the shock had forced his teeth to slice right through his lip. The glazer bullet had done quite a job on his shoulder. Selinas could see the sinews of ruined ligaments, cartilage, and muscle intermixed with the blood. Marco spit up at him.

"You set us up, man. . . ."

Selinas didn't bother to nod. He had quickly determined days before that finding the Riveros would be impossible, so he elected to have them find him and they had cooperated brilliantly.

"What you waitin' for, man?" Marco rasped. "Come on, do me and get it over with."

"Tell me where the suitcases are."

Marco grimaced in pain. "You get the powder and I get to live. Is that it, man?"

Selinas's expression was noncommittal.

"You did my brother. I got to get you for that. What the fuck, man, I don't need the powder anyway. I'll give it to you just to get my chance. Upstairs. Second room down. Wall on the right side of the window is false. Smart man like you, you'll spot it right away." Marco looked up at the gun and squeezed his ruined shoulder with his other hand. "You're gonna be dead, man," he spat angrily. "You're gonna be dead quick."

"You already are."

And Selinas pulled the trigger over Marco's face.

CHAPTER 9

SUNDAY TURNED INTO THE LONGEST DAY OF DREW JORDAN'S LIFE. His useless phone call at the Esplanade left him with two choices. One was to throw himself on the mercy of the Palm Beach police, the other to get out fast for a safe port—DEA regional headquarters in Miami. The first option was appealing only in that he was guilty of, at worst, a self-defense killing. But explaining the circumstances of his presence at Too-Jay's and his possession of a gun promised to lead to questions he couldn't answer. Option number two, then, was his best bet. The DEA was involved in this through Masterson regardless of the agent's fate. They would have to help him, learn who the assassin was, and who had sent him.

Drew had no idea if the police were looking for him, so he decided to play it safe. He was not crazy over the prospects of returning to the Hyatt under the circumstances, but he liked less the prospects of remaining in his waiter's garb. He needed clothes and money. He could be at the Hyatt and gone before news of Trelana's murder even reached television or radio.

But how to get to Miami? A rental car seemed the simplest and safest means. The key was to move fast and keep moving. He called a cab from the Esplanade pay phone, and it deposited him back at the Hyatt where he packed quickly, checked out, and took the hotel jitney bus to an airport car rental agency. With surprising ease he was heading down Route 95 for Miami not even ninety minutes after blood and brains had splattered all over Too-Jay's.

Drew kept his speed in check throughout the drive to Miami, not wanting to attract the attention of any radar-equipped troopers. He arrived in the city limits a little past four o'clock and got off 95 at the Biscayne Boulevard exit. From there he drove to Collins Avenue, cruising it from one end to the other to maintain the security the car provided. Finally, he opted for a hotel toward the northern end billed as the Ocean Palm, which boasted an olympic-size swimming pool on its marquee. He paid for the night in advance and was relieved to learn that the hotel featured room service as well as the pool. He didn't plan to spend any time outside of his room, especially in restaurants or coffee shops where he would have to linger for too long at a time.

Sunday night in the room wore on forever, Drew keeping one eye on the fuzzy television and the other on the door, expecting Miami Vice to come crashing through at any second. He tried to force himself to sleep but couldn't even though his body felt exhausted. After a few hours of uneasy slumber in the rock-hard bed, he rose, figuring he might spend a few hours after dawn by the pool where the fresh air might recharge him. But the rain came before the sun had a chance to and Drew resigned himself to watching the patterns it swept on the windows.

By nine o'clock he had eaten breakfast and tried Masterson's private number a dozen times without results. Something was clearly wrong. The only way to find out what was to pay a visit to DEA headquarters. If Masterson had betrayed him, there were plenty of avenues open. But if Masterson had himself been betrayed . . .

Drew chose not to complete the thought. He had returned the rental car the day before some miles from the hotel and had come back in a cab to avoid possible connections. The police might somehow be able to trace the car to Miami and the rental agency, but Miami was a big city and by the time they got a line on him, Drew would hopefully be long gone one way or another. He called a cab from his room to take him to the Miami headquarters of the DEA.

The building was located on Northwest Fifty-third Street. It was a modern, three-story design, nestled comfortably amid at least two dozen virtually identical structures, all enclosed by neatly cropped hedges in a Koger Executive Center row. There was little to tell him it was the offices of the Drug Enforcement Agency, and he might easily have tried a few of the other buildings first, had not the driver left him off right at the door.

He had little trouble learning where Masterson's office could be found and only slightly more in sliding past building security into the elevator. The compartment was crowded and Drew was among the first to exit on the second floor. The door to Masterson's office up the hall was open, with his full name printed clearly in bold black letters.

Inside, a secretary was packing materials into boxes. She looked up, startled.

"Is Agent Masterson in?" Drew asked her.

Her face showed first shock and then sadness. Her words emerged flatly. "Agent Masterson was killed."

Drew felt a thud to his stomach, but he wasn't surprised at all. "When?" he managed.

Of course, the answer would be Sunday—yesterday—which would explain why the plan had gone so wrong, why he had been set up and then abandoned at Too-Jay's.

But that's not what she said at all.

"Wednesday," came the secretary's almost tearful response. "It happened last Wednesday."

The rest was a blur. Drew backed out of the office without further words.

Agent Masterson was killed last Wednesday and I met him on Friday.

Confusion tore through him. Outside the headquarters, he managed to find a cab that had just dropped off someone else. He spent the ride back to the hotel with his head pressed low and his breathing rapid, an all-encompassing fear battering his senses. Somewhere in all this lay a perverted sense of order.

Masterson was not Masterson, which meant . . .

Which meant what?

Drew shivered. Everything had been a setup. No, not everything. The fact that Masterson had been murdered seemed to indicate that his grandmother had indeed contacted the real agent. Both had been killed as a result, the other grandmothers, too, and who knew how many others.

And drugs were somehow to blame; drugs, the only common denominator.

But what of the letter? All the facts contained in it might have been true, yet that didn't mean his grandmother had written it. Yes, the letter must have been a plant, a plant used to make him contact the fake Masterson at the conveniently provided number. He should have known that his grandmother never would have written such a letter, never would have risked involving him in something like this. But he had fallen for it, and the rest had fallen into place naturally. Out of fear for his own life and desire to avenge his grandmother's death, Drew had done exactly what had been expected of him.

But how could they have known he would blackmail the fake Masterson into helping him? And if Trelana's eventual killer was theirs, why had they needed Drew in the first place? So much left for chance, so much that didn't make sense no matter how hard he tried to think.

Stop! Block it out for awhile. Let it come on its own.

But the thoughts kept coming at him, smashing against each other and driving him to the brink of madness. The fake Masterson wanted the drug lord dead and, more, wanted Drew to do it and then, yes, be killed for his efforts. A dead pigeon made the perfect pigeon. But Drew had crossed them up by failing to complete the hit, necessitating a contingency plan that had allowed him to survive. But why again was it so important to involve him in Trelana's—

Wait. What if Trelana hadn't been responsible for Doris Kaplan's death at all? What if she had died instead at the hands of whoever or whatever was behind the fake Masterson? Trelana could have been as much of a pawn as the grandmothers themselves . . . and now Drew. Morris Kornbloom had reason to believe that the women were involved in *something*, but he had no idea what.

Morris Kornbloom! He had told Drew to call him if he needed him. Well, he certainly needed someone now, someone he could trust to help him out of this.

The taxi deposited Drew outside the motel. Mindlessly, he paid the driver and went straight to his room. He switched on the noon news on a local Miami television station while he searched his wallet for Kornbloom's number. So far, the murder of Arthur

Trelana was receiving plenty of mention, but the primary focus was the lack of leads. Drew could help them. Legally, after all, he was guilty of nothing more than a self-defense killing. He had nothing to hide now. He would call Kornbloom, and the doctor would help him make the right contacts.

He located the doctor's number and dialed it.

"Dr. Kornbloom's office."

"Dr. Kornbloom, please."

There was a pause.

"All his patients are being referred to Dr. Feinstein," the woman said faintly.

"No, you don't understand. I'm just a friend and I need to *speak* to him."

Another pause. "Sir, I'm sorry to tell you, but there was an accident last night. Dr. Kornbloom was struck by a hit-and-run driver. He died this morning."

The receiver slid from Drew's hand. Morris Kornbloom was dead, killed in what appeared to be yet another tragic accident. Kornbloom had met him, knew him, *delivered* the letter they had somehow planted. That made Kornbloom an unwitting part of the setup and thus a potential trace back to them. So, they had erased him.

Just like they had erased Trelana and the grandmothers.

Just like they would try to erase Drew.

Drew ran his hands over his face. He had fooled them all by surviving at Too-Jay's, but they wouldn't be giving up the chase so quickly. They could have been waiting for him to show up at DEA headquarters, could have followed him back here!

Drew's attention was drawn all at once to the television screen. The picture displayed on it was of him! He jumped up and turned the volume louder.

". . . TWENTY-SIX-YEAR-OLD ANDREW JORDAN OF WASHINGTON, D.C., BEING SOUGHT AS A SUSPECT IN THE MURDER OF PALM BEACH DEVELOPER ARTHUR TRELANA AND TWO ASSOCIATES. ACCORDING TO POLICE . . ."

No! Drew wanted to scream at the screen. *It's not like that!*

But he knew it would do no good. The enemy had played their next card. The police knew him. They thought he was a killer.

There was no place to run.

* * *

Selinas had been waiting at the Miami Airport bar, this time in the Eastern terminal, for thirty-five minutes when his contact finally arrived. All the booths were occupied, so Giblet was forced to take a seat at the bar.

"I saved you a stool," Selinas told him, motioning to the one next to his. "It wasn't easy. Morning rain must have delayed a lot of flights."

"The weather's been better." Giblet settled himself down and maneuvered his stool closer to Selinas. "We have another matter requiring your attention."

"Four in such a short period of time. That's quite unusual, almost unheard of."

"The circumstances call for it."

"So must the objective. Who is it?"

"We have no location for him except the general Miami area, and time is crucial."

"Isn't it always? Just tell me who the target is."

"A young man named Andrew Jordan, but he goes by the name of Drew. . . ."

CHAPTER 10

THE LIGHTS ON HOYSTER STREET IN PRAGUE SEEMED INVITING AS Elliana Hirsch walked slowly through the most active nighttime section of the city. Her trips to Prague in the past had left her with a romantic feeling for the city. Perhaps it was the strange juxtaposition of vitality and repression that Prague was able to manage. Communist by force rather than choice, Prague had nonetheless been able to maintain the flavor and feel, although subdued, of a western city. Take away an occasional patrolling military policeman serving Czechoslovakia more than the Soviet Union and a stranger might never have known that this was a Communist stronghold.

Tonight people walked with faces tilted down to shield them from the weather. An arctic blast of winter had made its presence felt early, with winds whipping up through the streets and whirling about the first true snowfall of the season.

Elliana trudged through it thinking how little she liked the cold and winter in general. It had not been hard for her to get into Prague. The Mossad could cut off her contacts, but she still maintained her covers and papers. Perhaps these could be voided as well, but she knew that Isser, Moshe, and the others would not want her falling into enemy hands. So, leaving open the various avenues of transit she had developed over the years was a kind of compromise. But no help would be coming from her superiors if she landed in trouble. And, worse, whatever fear of retribution did to keep possible enemies from making bold moves against her would now be lifted. No matter. She did not plan to stay in Prague long.

The city's cleanliness impressed her as always. Not a single scrap of litter, not even a cigarette butt to be found on the streets. Well, Communism must have its advantages, too. She continued to walk warily en route to a bar that in English translated into Friends and More. Its owner was known only as Annatoly, a genuine character, one of the most colorful sorts in the entire city.

Little was known of the mysterious Annatoly. Even gender was a mystery. The best information had it that Annatoly was a woman trying very hard to be a man. Ellie had met him/her only once before and had been unable to make up her mind on that occasion. Nor did she care. What mattered was that, man or woman, Annatoly was a storehouse of information, using it in trade whenever the need arose. Friends and More was one of the few aboveboard locations in Prague where prostitutes, drugs, and just about anything else could be obtained for the right price. Officials mostly turned a deaf ear and blind eye to the establishment. Annatoly was too outrageous to be accepted but too popular not to be tolerated.

Elliana had helped "Annie," as Annatoly was called by friends, out of an especially tough spot once when a pair of assassins Annie had turned in managed to escape and return in search of revenge. Ellie interceded. The assassins were tried in a higher court, their bodies, to the best of Ellie's knowledge, never recovered.

Elliana maintained a chain of people like Annatoly all over the world who owed her such favors. Mostly these were returned with the passing of vital information when it surfaced. Annie was one of several Ellie had put on the trail of the Council of Ten specifically, telling them the kind of things to look for. Annatoly's call that she had found something had reached Elliana just before Moshe had.

Ellie held the top of her coat together to shield her neck from the cold as the wind whipped up again. Thankfully, Annie's bar was just one more block away and Ellie turned off Hoyster Street onto a narrow avenue where Friends and More was located. Communist restrictions prohibited even Annatoly from posting a large sign or marquee, but the soft sound of music and the mixed garble of voices told Ellie that her sense of direction had been accurate. The entrance was made of solid wood, windowless, and formed a door to an altogether different world.

There was no doorman and Ellie was able to slip inside unhindered and unnoticed. The room was smaller than she remembered, most of the patrons crowding in small groups around circular tables. Others stood packed into the aisles, men conversing uneasily with women maybe to make a deal, while more lined up for drinks at the bar. The lighting was typically dim. Smoke pooled in clouds at the ceiling. It was much like an American or Israeli bar, except for the restrained voices and low-tipped eyes. Many patrons clearly didn't want to advertise their presence.

Elliana eased her way through the crowd, smiling politely and saying "excuse me" in Czech when required. She was aware of the eyes of numerous men checking her out as if to guess her price, but she met the eyes of none as she pushed forward toward the bar. It was warmer up there and she pulled one of her arms from its sleeve when she finally gained the bartender's attention.

"A triple vodka with no ice," she told him.

The man eyed her quickly and nodded. That had been the signal Annatoly had instructed her to use. The bartender finished the drinks he was already working on and then poured hers. Ellie never saw him press a button concealed beneath the rows of glasses.

It was a minute after her drink had been set down before her that she glimpsed the figure in white gliding around the bar toward her.

"Ellie dear, how good to see you!"

Annatoly hadn't changed, at least not much. She wore a loose-fitting man's white suit with a black-rimmed hat swung low over her eyebrows. A fake mustache was pasted over her upper lip and a cigarette complete with gold filter dangled from her right hand. Her entire outfit was perfectly coordinated right down to the shirt and striped silk tie.

Elliana moved away from the bar and fought against uneasiness when the smaller Annatoly grasped her in a firm hug.

"It's good to see you, too, Annie."

Annatoly eased away and held Ellie by the shoulders at arms length. "Tell me, dear, how do I look?"

"Sensational."

"Older?"

"The same."

Annatoly hugged her again. "You are a comfort, Ellie. If only there were more like you around. . . ."

Ellie's eyes circled the room. "You seem to be doing quite well."

"Only in business, dear. Friends are at a severe premium. Trust, you understand, doesn't exist in this part of the world. But it's the only world I know." Her eyes grew somber. "No older, you're sure?"

"Positively."

Annatoly smiled and for a moment Elliana feared her thick mask of makeup might crack.

"Then let us talk," Annie said, and they moved under one of the lights. Only then did Ellie realize just how sunken her friend's eyes had become. Annatoly must have been near fifty now with all the lines to show for it, more and more makeup needed to cover them. Ellie wasn't sure where the dressing like a man came in. She had heard all the stories: transvestite, lesbian, sadist, pervert. But, even if true, none of them mattered. Annatoly was basically a gentle soul who had never felt comfortable moving in the mainstream. The outrageous had become a way of life for her, the many fetishes she had gone through more distractions than anything else. "I'll find us a table," she continued.

"Out here?" Ellie resisted.

"You wish to avoid attention or receive it? If I take you into my office, eyes will follow us. This way, people will think I'm just interviewing another prospective . . . hostess." Annie looked her over, the tips of her fake mustache rising. "Which might not be a bad idea. . . ."

Ellie followed her toward a just-vacated table against the wall near the front door. A half-full pitcher contained warming beer. The empty glasses still had suds running down their sides.

"Let us speak in English," Annatoly said after they sat down. "It will make our business considerably more private."

"Fine by me," Elliana said, switching over. "I've never been able to grasp your idioms and idiosyncrasies anyway."

Annie ran a pair of fingers along the rim of her hat. "Idiosyncrasies have little to do with language."

"That's not what I meant. . . ."

Annie smiled. "Relax. Just my sense of humor acting up again. I enjoy being different. It keeps people from knowing who I really am. You should know all about that."

"I suppose I do."

"But you haven't come here for comparisons. You are after information and I believe I have some for you." Annatoly leaned forward, close enough for Ellie to see the edges of her close-cropped dark hair beneath her floppy hat. "I have received word about a man in the market for some unusual merchandise."

"Im listening."

"He is a Frenchman, but all correspondence seems to originate from a Spanish town called Getaria. It's on the Basque coast, in Vizcaya province. The man is after transport planes."

"Transport planes?"

Annie nodded. "Yes. Huge ones. The bigger the better. Price is of no consequence."

"Price is always of consequence."

"Not for this man apparently. Supply is far more crucial. By my estimations he has already obtained a hundred or more planes capable of airlifting thousands from one continent to another."

"I've never heard anything like it," Ellie responded, her spine prickling a bit. "But where does the Council come in?"

Annatoly smiled. "Like one of my girls' customers, you see only the surface. Go beneath it, dear."

"All right. Where are these planes, once obtained, being stockpiled?"

"No one city or country. Spain, Italy, West Germany, the Middle East, South Africa. The choices are obviously more strategic than random."

"Toward what end?"

"Use your imagination."

Ellie thought briefly. "Some sort of armed invasion, I'd guess, but of what?"

Annatoly hesitated. "The transports are required to have long flying ranges."

Ellie felt chilled. "America? Someone's planning to attack America?"

"Not just someone, dear."

"The Council! You have evidence of their existence, don't you, Annie?"

"Nothing concrete, dear, only the threads I have given you. The entire operation has been handled with a degree of tact the likes of which I have never seen before. Additional information doesn't seem to exist. All dead ends."

Ellie nodded. "That would figure. It's the way the Council has always operated. Even this much of a lead is unique." Then something occurred to her. "But it can only mean one thing."

"What?"

"A paradox, Annie, and not a pleasant one. The transports, if the Council's behind them, indicate they're surfacing. But I've always been certain that they wouldn't surface until they have the means to implement their master plan."

"The transports?"

"A part of the plan surely. The Council is like a hydra: many heads working as one, but in separate directions at the same time. The transports are a place to start, though. This Frenchman, who is he?"

Annie pulled a piece of paper from her suit jacket and slid it across the table. "His name is Lefleur. I've written down his address in Getaria. If he's part of the Council, of course, you don't expect him to talk or to know enough to help you even if he does."

"No," Ellie said. "But there'll be another level he can pass me onto. Sooner or later I'll reach the body of the hydra itself."

Annie was about to speak, but she stopped when a gush of cold wind poured through the bar's entrance along with a pair of uniformed Czech security police dressed in gray-green ankle-length overcoats. The two men flicked snow from their shoulders and closed the door behind them. Their breath was still misting. It was as though the cold of the night was draped about them.

Annatoly immediately switched her speech to Czech and changed the tenor of the conversation to small talk. It took only seconds for the security police to pick her out and approach. She saw Ellie stiffen.

"Be still," Annie warned. "Just a routine visit. I know these two. They come by occasionally so that I can remind them that all the benefits of the house are free. Just follow my lead."

The two officers reached the table. The taller one pulled off his gloves and glanced briefly at Elliana.

"Good evening, Comrade Annatoly," he greeted her.

"Good evening, Colonel dear," Annie returned, stroking the man's ego and smiling in a way that promised a more passionate stroking from the hostess of his choice if he played his cards right.

"I see business is good tonight."

"Not especially."

"Pity, though there are those in the establishment who feel your operation borders too much on capitalistic exploitation."

"Yes, and many of them are my best customers, including some of your fellows, Colonel dear. The right product for the right price has nothing to do with capitalism. Demand must be met. It's good for the soul." She followed the lead soldier's eyes toward Elliana. "I was just interviewing this one for a possible position. After all, the demands of the holiday season are almost upon us. What do you think, Comrade Colonel dear?"

The soldier grasped Ellie's chin and tilted her face toward his. She felt bile rise in her throat.

"Interesting," the soldier said, evaluating her. "Perhaps too worn, too tired, but you know what they say about experience."

"Yes," Annatoly replied. "I'm a believer in experience myself. Is there any particular one that would interest you gentlemen this evening?"

The soldier's attention was still riveted on Ellie. "Your papers, may I see them, please?"

Without hesitating, Elliana produced them from her purse. The lead soldier looked them over quickly.

"Yes," he said, folding them and sticking the sheets into his pocket. "I'm afraid you must come with me."

Ellie's eyes turned to Annatoly and saw the feigned rage in them immediately. "You bitch!" Annatoly cried. "I knew you were hiding something!"

Suddenly Annatoly was across the table shaking Ellie at the shoulders. Ellie played along, cowering and shrinking back in her chair. One of Annie's hands slipped lower and slid what felt like a pistol into the pocket of Ellie's overcoat. Its weight was reassuring and she saw Annatoly's eyes meet hers, warning her.

Obviously she had picked up something and now Ellie's lack of a gun had been taken care of.

The lead soldier eased Annie away from the table. The mock struggle had forced half of her fake mustache down her lip.

"You can have her back when we're finished with her, comrade," the soldier said.

"Keep her for all I care," shot back Annie, spitting at Ellie.

The one called colonel beckoned Ellie to rise. "Please do not make a fuss." He held her shoulder and she stood up without protest.

In fact, she had no intention of resisting. It seemed logical that the soldier wanted her only for the services that Annatoly indicated she could render. But Annie's eyes had told her something when they met hers. Obviously Annie had noted something about the soldiers' demeanor that suggested this visit was not routine.

Ellie's hand crept into her jacket pocket and felt for the reassuring steel of the gun. She recognized its shape as a Beretta .25 caliber. A woman's gun. Not much stopping power. She would have to be accurate if she was forced to use it.

"Which station?" Annie asked, as the soldiers walked on either side of Ellie toward the door.

"K Square, of course," said the lead soldier. "As usual."

They turned toward the door again. The crowd that had been viewing the proceedings with restrained interest turned back to their glasses or companions, the excitement apparently over. Annatoly, meanwhile, held her ground, knowing that Ellie could deal with these men quite easily. There was no reason to protest further.

She had started to say good-bye when the lead soldier stiffened and swung, hands tearing under his own jacket and coming out with a machine pistol. Ellie didn't notice the second soldier as she dove to the ground, but she was certain that he, too, had a similar gun ready and the sound of two rapid spurts confirmed this.

Annie dropped as well, or tried to, but the fire tore into her head and torso. She screamed, a scream that died horribly in mid-breath as death claimed her and she lay still on the floor, her white suit a mass of blood and her mustache now all the way off along with her hat to reveal a slicked-down man's hairstyle.

The soldiers had gone for her first because Annatoly was known to carry a gun while in the bar and was thus more of a threat. Of course, they hadn't known she had slipped the gun to Ellie.

By the time they turned their guns Ellie had the Beretta out and was squeezing the trigger. It had an easy catch and the shots flowed swiftly. She put two into the chest of the lead guard, then two into the chest of the second, finishing each with a single bullet to the head, as she lunged back to her feet.

Her ears burned with the wailing sound of screams. Those patrons who had not rushed for cover now rushed for the exits. A random smattering lay twisted and bloodied, several dead from the first wild bursts fired from the soldiers' guns.

Ellie kept her calm as the bodies charged for the door around her, and she leaned over the lead guard to retrieve her papers. They were wrinkled but fortunately free of blood, and, grateful for the crowd, she fled with it into the street.

People made the best cover, according to the popular teaching, and they would have this time as well if the men across the street hadn't had their eyes trained especially for her. Their bullets cut an indiscriminate path through the crowd as everyone emerged from the bar. All around her bodies toppled. Ellie dove with them to the snow, the only difference in her case being that no blood pooled under her onto the white powder.

Even in that short moment, she was able to consider what she was facing. The men had fired from across the street, from behind cover. They hadn't entered the building at the first shots, and this patience indicated professionalism, as did the fact that they had not revealed themselves now even after their target was apparently killed. They were waiting, which meant that Ellie could do nothing but remain prone with the cold numbing her face. She was facing the street but could see nothing, no means of judging their numbers or positions. She felt for the Beretta, which was clutched in her left hand by her body and was cooling in the snow. It was an eight-shot weapon. Just two left to use.

Of course, the enemy across the street, however many there were, would not know that. If she had a full clip and they exposed themselves, they'd be gunned down and they knew it. So they waited. Stalemate.

Yes, they were pros and obviously they knew she was one as

well. Behind her, no one attempted to use the front door to the bar as an exit any longer. The distant wail of sirens found her ears and Ellie knew that only minutes remained before the Czech police swarmed over the area. The shooters would have to make their move before then.

Ellie considered their options, tried to put herself in their places. One would venture out at the last instant, a potential sacrifice. To kill him, she would have to reveal her position, and then the others would have her.

The sirens screamed closer. Ellie fought not to let her rhythmic breathing give her away.

She heard the man coming before she actually saw him. Snow crunched in the street. She listened to his heavy shoes sliding through slush. Still, she didn't see him. To move her head or even her eyes would be too much of a giveaway. Patiently she waited for him to pass before her line of vision.

Ellie saw him at last as one does a character on a movie screen, limited by the screen's confines and the director's mind. He was coming straight for her holding some sort of automatic weapon. Who are you, she wanted to ask? How did you know I was here? Who sent you?

He drew within twelve yards, easily her killing range. As she acted, it was with the knowledge that she would have to move and keep moving. The others would be waiting just for this.

Ellie fired from the ground, using the motion as distraction as well as defense. There was no sense saving a bullet, so she pumped her remaining two into the approaching figure. The gun slid from his hands and he crumbled to the snow.

She was already on her feet starting to run when the powder broke his fall. There was motion across the street and then snow kicked up to the sides and before her. Ellie kept running, doing her best to avoid the machine gun's spray. She stopped suddenly and dropped behind a set of garbage cans. Bullets clanged against them. Then the shooting abruptly ceased.

Only one shooter remained now, she realized, and his clip had been exhausted.

Ellie was running again, putting distance between her and the second man while remaining as close to the buildings as possible. To get her now, he would have to expose himself. The advantage swung at least partly to her.

The machine gun bursts started up again, and between them Ellie could hear his heavy shoes crunching snow. A bullet smacked into a brick wall just ahead of her and fragments burned Ellie's face and pounded her shoulder. The shooter was good. He wasn't rushing. He knew he still had her.

Ellie ducked into an alley. It was the logical move, the expected one. Reach the next street ahead of her pursuer and go for cover. Just what he would have expected her to do.

But Ellie stopped ten yards into the alley and reversed her path. Then she pressed herself against a building and waited. An instant later his shadow preceded him across the front of the alley. He tried to slow up at the last instant, as if sensing the trap, but it was too late.

As his shadow crossed fully in front of the alley entrance, Ellie threw herself into motion. She slid against the ice for an instant, but her charge was still committed. She hurled herself forward toward the spot where he would first appear.

He saw her too late to fire and by the time his finger squeezed the trigger, Ellie's hand had locked on the barrel and forced it downward. A short burst coughed up snow at their feet. The man tried to pull his machine gun up, and Ellie let him. In fact, she joined his motion, angling the butt so that it struck him under the chin hard and snapped his head back.

The blow crunched teeth but didn't slow him down. When Ellie tried to use the butt a second time, he darted inside her strike and cracked an elbow against her sternum. The padding of her heavy jacket kept her from losing her wind, and she tilted her grip on the rifle to allow a clear shot at the man's groin with one of her legs.

The man seemed to sense her action, and when she snapped her knee upward he grabbed it and lifted, throwing her off balance backward to the street.

He fights like me, she thought. *A shadow of my every move!*

Now he had complete control of the rifle as well as position. But instead of firing, he brought the weapon down butt first in the direction of Ellie's head. She twisted quickly to the left and the butt sank into the snow. Wasting no time, she latched onto the stock and lashed upward with a pair of violent kicks to his midsection and head.

The man recoiled and smashed back against a small dumpster.

Ellie rose to her knees and brought the gun up toward him. He rushed her, and with no choice she squeezed the trigger.

Nothing happened. The gun had jammed. No wonder he hadn't fired it when he had the chance.

The man was lunging for her now, coming headlong through the air. Ellie saw the knife flash in his hand and she got her arms up just in time to lock on the hilt and keep the blade from piercing her throat.

Ellie knew she couldn't compete with the man's brute strength for long. She had to take a chance. So when he shoved down for her throat again, Ellie tried to pull his wrist away with her left hand as she angled her right elbow up for his face.

The pain came simultaneously for both of them. Ellie felt the sharp blade slice through her coat and nick her shoulder. She screamed as her elbow impacted and shattered the man's jaw and cheekbone.

He groaned in agony but somehow righted the knife into another strike. Ellie had no choice now. Whatever thoughts she might have entertained of interrogation were lost in her concern for survival.

She rolled out from under the man as he twisted the knife for her again. She found the hilt at the same time and drove it sideways and up. The blade penetrated his lower abdomen and made a neat slice all the way across to his small intestine. The man's body spasmed in agony as hot pulsing blood steamed from the gash. He collapsed with his face a frozen mask of terror, his feet twitching only once before death claimed him.

Breathing hard and grateful that none of his blood seemed to have splattered over her, Ellie turned the man over.

His hat had come free and she could see his long hair and beard of the same color. The tight distortion of death made his features virtually unrecognizable, but . . .

I know this man. I'm sure I know him.

Ellie stared at the face closer and felt a shudder surge through her. She knew this man all right. They had met twice before, once in Greece and once in Egypt. Not as rivals, though.

The man was Israeli.

He was Mossad.

CHAPTER 11

Elliana saw the subway entrance just up ahead. It had been an hour since she had killed her assailant and her route through the streets had been deliberately slow. She had to learn if there were more, if she was being followed. They might have been biding their time, waiting for her to leave an opening. With this in mind, Ellie had baited several traps, but so far no one had bitten. Just two of them, four including the soldiers . . . There should have been more.

She could not recall the name of the man she had killed. He was about her age, a skillful operative. She tried to tell herself that he had gone freelance, but it didn't wash. Only two people, Isser and Annatoly, knew she was coming to Prague. Since Annie had slipped her the gun, Ellie felt that she could rule her out as a suspect. That left Isser, chief of the Mossad. But if he had wanted her killed, there would have been no reason for him to wait until she reached Prague. No, he would have had plenty of other opportunities without the presence of so many random factors.

Someone else, then. But who? Obviously the party must have wanted Annatoly eliminated as well. And if it was Mossad, they would have known that two men would never have been enough to finish her, even with the help of the Czech security police pair.

Not Mossad, but some force that had infiltrated Mossad. . . .

Ellie cringed as she knelt in yet another alley waiting to make her move for the subway. *The Council of Ten*. If they had surfaced at last in an attempt to kill her, then she was finally closing on them and they were panicking. Annatoly's words about the transports gained new meaning. Yet, there was no one to whom she could take the news without considerable risk. How could she know how deep Mossad had been penetrated? More, what reason did Mossad have to listen to her now that she was an outsider? Contacting Isser directly was her only hope, but how could she know when he would be available?

So many questions and no answers she could find. . . .

Feeling it was finally safe, Elliana rose from her crouch and walked the rest of the way to the subway entrance. The steps descended into the bowels of Prague. The cold became less fierce, then vanished in the modest heat of the underground. She purchased a number of tokens and pushed through the turnstyle. The clock on the wall read two A.M. Ellie hadn't worn a watch because few Czech women did and she wanted to blend in. Two A.M. It would be virtually deserted in the subway, which was good and bad. Ellie made her way to the platform to wait for the next train.

It didn't matter where it was going. Anywhere would do. The key was to keep on the move and make a slow but direct path to Prague airport before the opposing forces had a chance to regroup. She reached the platform and found she was alone.

Then footsteps sounded behind her. Ellie swung, feeling instinctively for a pistol she didn't possess. A pair of teenage boys slid down the railing of the steps toward the platform. They were dressed almost identically in dark slacks and leather jackets. Both were smiling beneath their sandy-blond hair. They seemed drunk. Neither paid any attention to Ellie. She felt relieved.

Other people gathered slowly. A businessman, a pair of well made up women with tight skirts who might have been prostitutes, an older lady clutching her handbag tight, two younger men with caps tilted low toward their dark, slavic eyes. A group of strangers with nothing more in common than awaiting the next train. A Czech security policeman joined them on the platform as a train thundered down the tunnel. The teenage boys kept up their banter.

The Prague underground, like its cousin in Moscow, was

spankingly clean. No litter, no derelicts or bag ladies loitering about, and absolutely no graffiti.

The train lights flashed in the tunnel. The tile flooring shook slightly and now Ellie was especially careful. For the next few seconds, without her ears to warn her and all sounds of violence drowned out by the roar, she was especially vulnerable. She backed up against a cement beam and rested her shoulders against it, eyes sweeping from one direction to the other.

The train squealed to a slow halt. It was long, with many cars, but most were darkened and locked at this time. All those waiting stepped into a car directly before them. Ellie entered after the policeman. Somehow his presence made her feel safer, even though he could have been part of the opposition just as easily as the others, easier in fact. He wore a Kalishnikov assault rifle slung from his shoulder and his boots made him look considerably taller than he was.

Ellie had briefly considered waiting until all the others had entered the car to leave it and return to the platform. She had no way of knowing, however, when the next train would come or when more of her pursuers might show up at the station. This way at least she had the benefit of safety in numbers. No professional would act in the presence of so many witnesses, especially a Czech policeman with an ominous Kalishnikov draped around his shoulder.

The train rumbled away, picking up speed. Ellie chose a seat on a bench across from the businessman and probable prostitutes, and between the teenage boys and two young men. The older woman sat the farthest away against the wall, still clutching her handbag.

The train thundered on.

Ellie had no conception of when it was going to stop. Many stations would be skipped at this time of night. She shifted positions and a bolt of agony surged through the shoulder that the Mossad man's knife had nicked. The cold had numbed it so that she had forgotten about it. But the cold was gone now and she could feel a trickle of blood dripping down her arm. She grimaced but refused to reach up to the shoulder with a squeeze of comfort. She could handle the pain and the blood easily enough, but allowing herself a distraction was out of the question.

She reasoned that one of these people in the train was here to kill her, a pair if any of three duos were involved. Eight people besides herself were here, no, nine including the policeman. Who was it? Ellie had to make her determination before he or she or they made their move. Otherwise the advantage would be too great to overcome. Her best chance would probably be to place her trust in the Czech security man and exit the train when he did. That might be just what he was hoping for, however, and even if that wasn't the case, it wouldn't stop the real stalkers from leaving the train at the same time.

Madness! She had to know!

Without a weapon, she felt ridiculously vulnerable. Even all her training with creating a weapon where none existed was useless since she could make no move out of the ordinary here. Darkness was a possibility, of course, the absence of light a reliable ally when one was placed in an inferior position.

Ellie gazed around her. There were too many lights in the car to hope for darkness, even in the tunnels. It had to be something else. . . .

Her rotating stare caught the teenage boys in their path. The boys turned away quickly. Ellie's heart began to thump. Something was wrong. They shouldn't have turned away so fast. Looking at her would have been an expected response under the circumstances for a pair of boys. Unless . . .

Ellie buried her shudder by switching positions on the bench. What if they hadn't been looking at her? What if they had been looking at the two young men to her right?

Now Ellie gazed at the prostitutes. Their skirts showed barely a wrinkle, the soles of their shoes hardly wet from the soaking they should have taken in the slushy streets. Unless they were just going out to work, this couldn't be.

The train thundered through a darkened tunnel and Ellie held her breath. All the lights returned quickly. No eyes were on her.

It couldn't be! It couldn't be! Not one or two of them, but *all of them*!

The impossibility of the premise made it plausible. They would have taken her out on the platform or perhaps as soon as they were on the train, if it hadn't been for the untimely arrival of the security policeman, now standing in the center of the floor, gripping a ceiling rail with one hand and smoking a cigarette with the other.

Ellie's mind worked frantically. Eight against one—incredible odds, but it might well be the odds that had kept her alive this long. The hit team had no reason to rush. She had to make sure that situation continued, make sure she did nothing to give away the fact that she was on to them.

Eight against one . . . bad odds, yes, but there might be a way to equalize them, perhaps even tilt them in her favor. Ellie's eyes fixed briefly on the policeman's Kalishnikov. If she could somehow get it away from him and turn it on the hit team members, she could take them all by surprise.

The problem was timing. Grabbing the gun, stripping it from the security policeman, swinging around to fire—all of that would take many seconds. The hit team's weapons would be within easy reach; under a jacket, fastened to the thigh beneath a skirt, within a handbag. Ellie's strike would have to be more than fast; it would have to be immediate.

She could feel the killers trade glances again. The boys were laughing, joking, trying to provide cover. She pretended that the ploy worked. Then she was on her feet, moving so suddenly that she surprised even herself.

The policeman was still smoking his cigarette as she stepped up to him.

"Excuse me," she said in Czech. "Might I have one of those?"

"Da," he answered and started to reach inside his overcoat to his uniform jacket. To do so, he had to lower the Kalishnikov from his shoulder to his hand, and that was when Ellie acted.

She was on him, going for the gun before the policeman had located his cigarettes, before the others could respond. The problem for a team of killers is that often each will wait for another to make the first move. Such was the case here.

Ellie had gained control of the assault rifle and shoved the policeman out of the way to the floor before any of the team's weapons appeared. She fired the Kalishnikov in a semicircular arc, starting with the bench she had been seated on because it held four of the team members in a narrow space. The young men had their pistols out, but the boys were still reaching for theirs when the powerful assault bullets sliced into their heads and midsections.

Ellie kept her finger on the trigger as she swung the rifle around in the direction of the prostitutes and the businessman. All three had scattered, diving in separate directions, their responses professional. Ellie felt the heat of their bullets surge past her, shattering glass as she plunged and rolled, firing the Kalishnikov in midair, her aim remarkably on target. Both prostitutes fell victim to head shots, the businessman losing most of his throat to a single bullet that sent him rolling crazily across the floor, gasping and praying for death. Kneeling now, Ellie held her fire and twisted the Kalishnikov in the direction of the policeman and old woman.

The old woman was screaming, hiding her face.

The policeman had his pistol out and held it within a trembling hand.

"Don't!" Ellie ordered, Kalishnikov barrel leveled toward him.

The policeman let the pistol drop to the floor and raised his arms in surrender from his half-prone position in the center of the car. Ellie could hear the train's brakes being applied now. The next station stop was approaching.

Its clip exhausted, the Kalishnikov slid from her grip, and Ellie quickly grabbed the policeman's discarded pistol. It was a miracle that he had survived the barrage. His fallen hat revealed blond hair and a surprisingly young face. There was no reason to kill him, and Ellie walked by without even exchanging a glance.

"No!" the old woman pleaded. "Don't kill me! Don't! I've done you no harm!"

Ellie turned away from her as the subway train ground to a halt. The exit doors slid open. She started to step out. She was halfway out the door when the security policeman saw her swing back around and aim the pistol in his direction. He screamed once, but the gun was already roaring, three times at least, and he looked up to discover he was surprisingly still alive. He gazed behind him.

Three neat holes had been carved in the midsection of the old woman, her eyes fixed sightlessly forward. A small pistol clanged to the floor from her hand.

"Tell anyone who asks you the truth!" Ellie shouted at him. "Tell them they made me do it. I didn't have a choice. Do you understand?"

The guard nodded and watched the woman disappear into the station, as he fumbled for the walkie-talkie on his belt.

Elliana ran breathlessly, her chest burning but her mind clear. The Council of Ten was behind this terror-filled night, behind all the guns that had sent bullets toward her. But this time they had left a trail.

The town of Getaria in the Vizcaya province of Spain. A man named Lefleur.

Ellie was already on her way.

CHAPTER 12

"If you're ever in the area, stop by."

After realizing that his isolation had been compounded by his status as a fugitive, Drew had racked his brain trying to figure out what to do, where to go. Finally, he recalled Mace's open invitation, along with the fact that the man who was able to best him, and everyone else in mercenary camp for that matter, lived on Hibiscus Island in Miami Beach.

An hour after seeing himself on television, Drew was in a cab heading onto the McArthur Causeway. The driver swung right onto the private drive leading to Hibiscus and Drew shrank low in the backseat at the sight of a uniformed guard keeping the mechanical rail down until she had a chance to note the cab's license plate.

Drew blessed the fact that he remembered Mace's address. The house turned out to be a brown ranch of typical southern Florida design. He paid the driver, stepped up to the front door, and was about to hit the bell when he heard a splash coming from the backyard. He circled around the side beneath a carport harboring the cloaked, sleek shape of Mace's latest sports car. Drew moved onto the grass and breathed easier when he saw Mace doing laps in the pool. For all he knew, Mace could have been in South America, a possibility Drew had not let himself consider.

The pool was small and it took Mace only a few strokes to cover its length. Drew moved forward, uneasy about disturbing his routine, suddenly feeling like a stranger. The backyard bordered Biscayne Bay and several motorboats pulling skiers rolled close enough to kick spray onto Mace's property.

Mace caught Drew's presence on his next lap back. He looked up with no small degree of surprise, shaking the water from his face and hair.

"Hi," said Drew lamely.

Mace looked at him as if struggling for words. "If we were back playing the game in Georgia, I'd say you'd finally beaten me."

"It's no game."

Mace started to pull himself from the pool. "Decided to drop in?"

"Not exactly."

Mace was on his feet now heading toward a chaise longue containing a floral beach towel. His shoulder and back muscles rippled with each step. Drew followed behind tentatively. Mace dried himself and looked Drew over.

"I'm in trouble," he said, trying not to break down.

"Pull up a lounge and tell me all about it."

Drew slid one closer and sat on its edge. Mace toweled his hair.

"I killed someone," Drew said because he could think of no better place to start.

"You *what*? For real? No game out in the woods?"

"For real. In a restaurant called Too-Jay's."

Mace expressed a flash of recognition. "Trelana . . . Christ, that was you?"

"No! I didn't kill Trelana. I had planned to, but I couldn't and someone else did who then tried to kill me. It was that man I shot."

"Wait a minute, slow down. . . ."

"I wasn't alone. A man helped me, set everything up. I thought he was from the DEA. I *made* him help me. I thought I could do it, but when the time came, I—"

"Hold on. Did you say DEA, as in Drug Enforcement Agency?"

"Because of the *letter*!" Drew's face sank into his hands. "God, I was such a fool to—"

"What letter?"

"I thought it was from my grandmother. But it was just bait to lure me into the setup. You see my grandmother died and . . ."

Drew's voice was breaking by the time he finished telling the story. "It makes no sense to me even as I tell it. So damn elaborate, too elaborate to work, to risk so much on."

"Not really," Mace said, seeming to grasp more essence from the story than Drew himself. "Shiteaters did their homework on you, that's all. They wanted Trelana dead and you were the perfect pigeon to do it. Course, you needed motivation and a little help, which they were more than happy to provide once you bought their scam."

"But it didn't turn out to be enough to make me finish the job," Drew said almost dejectedly.

"So they had that shiteater standing by just in case you fucked up. If you don't fuck up, he kills you in the confusion after you're finished and walks out. Like magic. No trace left. End of story."

"You sound so sure."

"Comes with the territory. Trouble was you surprised them. You killed their iceman and took off. When they couldn't find you easily, they decided to enlist the cops to help them."

"But I didn't kill Trelana!"

"Doesn't matter. They merely extended the plan a bit. These shiteaters got power coming out the asshole. Reality's what they make it. That's how they suckered you into this in the first place."

"And if the cops catch me . . ."

"You tell your story, which sounds like the biggest crock of shit ever. They'll have proof you're guilty and witnesses to back up the shiteaters' side of the story. In plain English, you'd be fucked." A pause. "If they let you talk at all, that is."

"What do you mean?"

"You don't know squat, kid, but you know too much as far as whoever's behind this setup is concerned. Right now I haven't got the foggiest as to why the shiteaters needed to use you to ice Trelana, but they musta had their reasons to go through such an elaborate setup."

"So, what can I do about it?"

It was mercenary camp all over again; teacher to student, master to pupil.

Mace whipped his sun-dried hair off his forehead. "Okay. We've got plenty of advantages over them now, but we've gotta make them count. So, lesson number one is we make up our own rules. . . ."

"Fine. Where do we start?"

"You didn't let me finish. We make up our own rules based on the ones we figure the enemy will be using, to counter him. Like your enemy in this case can't afford to have you circulating. Too much risk involved there to the shiteaters. So, they leaked your name. And on the chance the police don't find you and make life easy for them, they will have retained a killer to take you out."

"He'd have to find me first, too."

"This man would also be a hunter. Like me back in the woods. It's what *I* do, what their person does. So, our first rule is that after today you stay on the move."

"But I've got nowhere else to go!" Drew protested.

"You'll go where I tell you, do what I say. You should be safe enough here for the rest of the day. Rest up. Grab some chow. But stay inside. By ten tonight you'll have made your way to the Marriot Marina on Biscayne Bay. There's a boat there called *Jude the Obscure*. I'll see you in the cabin at ten sharp."

"What about until then? What will you be doing?"

"Hitting the road to see a few people. Miami's really a small town. Not much goes down plenty don't know about. Our second rule: find them before they find us."

"Us?"

"Just like the woods, only this time we're on the same side." Mace slapped Drew's shoulder. "Hey, against that even the fuckin' Timber Wolf would have his work cut out for him."

"Maybe," Drew said with a shrug. "But it's not like I thought it would be. I wanted to kill Trelana more than anything in the world. I even had the gun out, but I couldn't do it. You told me reality sucks. I didn't believe you."

"You got out of there alive, kid, and that's all that counts."

The night belonged to Selinas because it belonged to death. He preferred working in it because it never betrayed shape or motion. The fact that it was the enemy of most made it his friend.

Maybe it was the ease with which he walked through the darkness outside the Biscayne Bay Marriot en route to the marina that made him vulnerable. It was inconceivable that another could take him within darkness, especially at close range, so when the shape whirled before him, a glimmer of steel preceding it, Selinas hesitated.

If it had been a normal, hand-held weapon, he still would have had a chance. But it was something else, something much different wielded by a huge shape that nudged against him as its weapon sliced forward.

Selinas felt it first as a hard smack to his chest, followed by a tearing sound he dimly realized was his own guts being spilled as he searched for the air needed to scream. The blood was already filling his mouth when he crumbled, coughing it out, dying then, almost dead as he began to drag himself forward.

Drew waited in the cabin of *Jude the Obscure,* the night waves softly lapping against the side of the boat. Beyond that sound there was only the loud din coming from a disco called Tugboat Annie's, which overlooked the marina from the first level of a condominium complex.

Mace was twenty minutes late. Under the circumstances that was something he would never do. Unless something had gone wrong. Drew moved to the window that contained a view of the dock and, if he strained hard enough, the disco. He swung around only when the cabin door creaked open.

And Mace fell on him with his stomach falling out.

"Looks like I lost this time."

Mace virtually coughed the words out, almost matter of factly. Blood followed after several of them.

Drew held part of him in his lap. Mace was trembling everywhere as his body clutched for life. Drew trembled, too, words denied him from the shock.

"Worse than I thought," Mace said. "Worse than *you* thought. Different. Shiteaters used me. Wanted—" A hefty swallow, which brought him some air. "—me to kill you, too. Never would have. Would . . . have found you . . . and warned you off." Mace's eyes flashed life briefly and found Drew's. "Want you to know that,'' he said grasping Drew's forearm tightly, each syllable becoming a chore for him.

"Not you," Drew moaned. "No! You couldn't be a part of this!"

"Not me. Selinas. Facade created by me. I'm not a . . . mercenary. I'm an . . . assassin. Money was better. Accepted this assignment so they wouldn't give it to someone else. Would have found you . . . but you found me." Mace seemed to smile and blood rushed out from between his lips. He grasped Drew's forearm even tighter, as if it were his own life he was fighting to hold onto. "No time to explain who. They're . . . too . . . close. Run. Get out." He heaved for air. "The Timber Wolf . . ."

"A part of this, too?" Drew cringed.

"Not yet. Get to him. Tell him everything that's . . . happened. Give him—" Mace's words were lost as he spasmed.

"The Timber Wolf's here? In Miami?"

Mace managed the semblance of a nod. "My right pants pocket. A . . . list. He'll know what it means. He'll know what to . . . do. . . ." He had spat out an address when a final spasm overtook him and his eyes locked open.

Holding his breath, Drew reached into his dead friend's pocket and withdrew two sheets of paper, wrinkled and bloodied. He started to back away, terrified.

Mace was dead.

Mace, the man who had taken him easily at the mercenary camp three times running, had been killed by men who were close, by men who were—

Footsteps pounded the dock, then slowed. Drew heard voices whispering, exchanging information.

They were here.

The footsteps picked up again. The killers had found the trail of Mace's blood they had been searching for.

Drew tried to make sense of it as he pressed his back against the wall. The bastards had tried to hire Mace, in the guise of a killer named Selinas, to kill him. But Mace had turned the tables and gone after his employers. Only he hadn't been good enough.

What chance do I have against them?

The question made Drew shudder. Mace was the best and they had got him.

The men were approaching the boat now, easing closer by the

111

second in the bloody trail. As far as they knew, though, they were seeking only Mace. So, Drew would have his chance, the opportunity to take the men by surprise just as they must have done to his friend.

The pool of blood was spreading under Mace's corpse.

A weapon, he needed a weapon! A quick strike to stun and disable and then he could make his escape.

Drew's eyes locked on the large fire extinguisher bracketed into the wall. He ripped it free as the first of the killers dropped onto the deck. Drew brought the fire extinguisher up over his shoulder, testing its weight. Heavier than he had expected. His strike would have to be perfect.

He could hear what sounded to him like two men approaching the cabin door.

A four-step descent separated the cabin from the deck. Drew would strike while the killers came down in single file, one after the other. He jammed his back against the wall adjacent to the steps and held the extinguisher by its nozzle and neck, something like a baseball bat.

The door opened slowly. The men would see Mace's body immediately and focus all their attention on it. At least that was what Drew was counting on, for if they so much as gazed to their left his presence would be forfeit.

The killers started down the steps. Neither of them looked his way. Drew held his breath.

He struck when the first man was halfway down the final step and the second had another two stairs to go. Drew leaped out, angling his body for the best possible strike, and swung the extinguisher hard. There was a thud as it struck the lead man square in the chest, forcing him backward against the second. Both men gasped and tumbled. Drew hurdled up the steps and onto the deck.

A third man was leaping down from the dock, gun in hand. Drew crashed into him before his balance was firm. A *whoooosh* of air poured from the man's mouth at impact and his pistol clamored to the deck. Then Drew was lunging from the gunwale up to the wharf, sprinting at full speed for the head of the marina where boats and jetskis were rented by a company called Sunsplash.

There was a spit followed by concrete exploding around him as he pulled himself onto the cement that connected the marina to the condominium complex and entrance to Tugboat Annie's disco. He never looked back; there was no reason to. The disco was his only hope for survival now, his only sure way to escape the killers' bullets. There was no one checking IDs at the door of the disco, so Drew passed right through unhindered into the crowd, determined to lose himself while keeping a sharp eye on the door.

It was only seconds later when two of the men appeared. Drew had not gotten a clear look at either of them on the boat, but he realized who they were immediately. They were substantially older than the rest of the patrons and were breathing hard, faces tautly determined as they surveyed those around them and began shouldering their way through the packed disco.

Drew turned away and shrank into the mass, heading for the dance floor. He needed a rear or side exit, and then saw the red flash of a sign across the floor to his right. Halfway there he veered from it and pushed toward the bar. He had seen only two men enter the disco. What about the third? Drew realized the third killer must have been left outside to watch the other exits.

Drew was effectively trapped inside. A boy who couldn't have been more than seventeen turned awkwardly from the bar and sprayed him with beer, muttering an apology. The Timber Wolf's address was not twenty minutes from here on one of the Bay Harbor islands. But to reach it, Drew had to escape.

And to escape he needed to create a diversion. Drew's eyes swept the dance floor and focused on the white-suited DJ atop a raised dais who had just flipped a switch to "create some atmosphere," releasing a thick, foglike substance from beneath the dance floor. The effect was gained simply by exposing dry ice to water. But if all the switches were flipped at once, the entire stuffy room would probably be enveloped by the fake smoke in seconds. People would be forced out. He would have his cover. Yes, that was it!

Drew pushed his way toward the DJ, slanting across the far edge of the dance floor to better his angle. He hoped the killers were unsure enough of what he looked like to allow him to cover the distance without being noticed. Everything rested on what he was about to do. He climbed the steps to the dais from the rear, the way a patron with a request might.

"Hey," the DJ started, "what are—"

Drew yanked him aside and flipped all five switches with

"smoke" stenciled under them into position. A slight hissing sound followed, and clouds of white started pouring from beneath the dance floor, remaining thick as they climbed and spread.

The DJ was trying to grab him now. Drew twisted from his grip and knocked him away, lunging from the dais. The smoke was still rising, pooling, more like fog, and the patrons of Tugboat Alley's were holding their ground uncertainly, flapping their hands to clear the air immediately before them. Many shoved their way toward the front door and Drew shoved with them. Halfway there, he started coughing from the slightly noxious fumes. A crowd had emerged through the main door before he did. Once outside he swung left, hoping to make his escape into the Marriot directly across from the disco. Then he saw a group of men running from behind the hotel toward Tugboat Annie's. Another escape route was obviously mandated, but all three directions were blocked one way or another, and the fourth was Biscayne Bay.

Drew looked down at the docks. Three jetskis owned by Sunsplash rentals had been lined up on the dock immediately beneath him. A trio of people were hovering over them, obviously having arranged for a night rental. A fourth, the proprietor perhaps, was working one of the jetskis forward into the water.

Drew threw himself into motion, leaping down to the dock and rushing for the jetskis. The proprietor had just gotten the first into the water when Drew shoved him aside and jumped in near it. Seconds later he had climbed atop the jetski and was feeling for the starter. He twisted it and the engine caught immediately as the proprietor struggled to his feet and his customers cursed at Drew. It had been years since he had ridden one of these surprisingly fast and easily maneuverable water scooters. Nothing to it at slow speeds, but fast took a bit of skill.

Drew let out the throttle all the way from the start, splashing water in his wake as he surged through the marina area. From the Port of Miami, cabin lights in the huge cruise liners seemed to flicker, as if to laugh at his flight.

He was swinging out of the marina when a glance to the rear revealed the killers rushing down the dock, guns ready. Drew started to weave, cutting across his own wakes with the tip of the jetski rising like a bucking horse. Bullets smacked water about him, farther and farther off the mark as he drove the jetski into Biscayne Bay, taking from the small engine all it could give.

A small island dotted the sea before him, and Drew turned right toward the collection of bridges that linked Miami Beach to the rest of civilization.

CHAPTER 13

DREW LOOKED UP AT THE INTERCOM BUZZER ONCE AGAIN, BUT HE didn't press it. The black iron fence surrounding the home on West Broadview Drive in Bay Harbor intimidated him, seemed to warn him not to request entry from its occupant.

From Peter Wayman . . . the Timber Wolf.

The night before Drew had ridden the jetski to the Miami Yacht Club and ditched it there. His clothes drenched, he climbed back on land and considered briefly returning to his room at the Ocean Palm. The men who had killed Mace, however, might have tracked him there by now. If he showed his face in the vicinity, he could be walking into a trap. Instead, he had spent the night on the move, letting the warm air dry his clothes as he sat beneath trees and finally on the beach off Fifth Street where he dozed until the first of the morning's sunbathers arrived on the scene.

His money, fortunately, had dried as well, which allowed him to breakfast on a pair of hotdogs and a Coke purchased from a beach vendor. The morning was comfortably cool and he walked a ways in the hope of steaming the wrinkles from his clothes before grabbing a bus that ran the length of Collins Avenue. He climbed out at 96th Street, stiff again, and loosened up by walking the last few miles onto Bay Harbor toward West Broadview, which he reached drenched in hot sweat.

He knew the walking was just an excuse, an excuse to put off his approach to the Timber Wolf, a stranger who had no reason to believe and even less to help him. But Drew clung to the hope that he would because he *was* the Timber Wolf, a true champion of the innocent, a man beside whom even Mace had paled by comparison.

The little that Drew actually knew about the Timber Wolf had been pried out of Mace during quiet night hours in the mercenary camp. His real name was Peter Wayman, proclaimed the Timber Wolf for his ability to stalk and kill those who had taken innocent American lives abroad. The Timber Wolf's skills were purely retaliatory. Never was he summoned until an atrocity had been committed. Mace claimed that he had once been the most feared man in the world by the terror network, and, all things considered, the most deadly, dangerous man anywhere.

Once . . .

Then he had quit, dropped out. It was just after Corsica, one of the landmarks of his career, which had seen him at his legendary best. No one knew why, not even Mace. His services were still requested but no longer offered. The best had taken himself out of the game for reasons only he knew.

But he remained the Timber Wolf. Mace had sent Drew here because he must have known that, known that Wayman was the one man alive who might be able to get him out of this with the help of Mace's bloodied sheets of paper, which contained thirty addresses scattered all over the country.

Drew started to raise his finger for the buzzer.

The house beyond the gate was brown wood with inlays of brick, modern in structure with a large carport in place of a garage. A Mercedes was parked beneath it, shining and bright. The yard was not large but well sculptured.

Drew steeled his courage and pressed the buzzer. Seconds passed and it seemed no one was going to answer, so he buzzed again and then a third time.

"Yes?" came a voice out of the intercom speaker. A man's voice. It had to be the Timber Wolf.

Drew swallowed hard. "Mr. Wayman?"

"Who is this?"

"You don't know me. A friend of yours sent me."

"I asked who you were."

"My name is Drew Jordan. I don't expect that to mean anything to you. That friend of yours sent me here for help."

"He sent you to the wrong place," the voice said coldly.

"No," Drew begged. "Please. That friend of yours, they killed him and now they're after me. Just let me come in and talk to you. You'll understand."

There was a pause, then a high-pitched buzz as the steel gate unlocked itself mechanically.

"Walk straight up the driveway," the voice instructed through the box. "Keep your hands where I can see them and don't so much as step one foot off the cement. Clear?"

"Yes. Thank you."

Drew stepped inside the gate and did exactly as he was told, approaching a small raised porch before the front door. He saw the door open slowly and kept walking until he was inside the house, feeling the refreshing cool of the air-conditioned atmosphere, embarrassed all at once by his sweat-soaked shirt. It was dark inside. His eyes were having trouble adjusting. He was barely a yard past the doorway.

Peter Wayman kicked the door closed but left the lights off. Drew swung quickly and saw the huge pistol in his hand.

"You shouldn't move that fast," the Timber Wolf warned him.

"I'm sorry. I mean, well, it's just that I've been through a lot. It's all crazy." Drew paused. "I don't know where to start."

"How about with the name of that friend of mine who sent you."

"His name is—was—Mace. He's dead. They killed him because he tried to help me." Drew eyed the Timber Wolf as best he could in the half light.

"I don't know anyone named Mace."

Drew felt like he'd been jabbed in the gut. "He said he worked with you. I've got something he told me to give you." Drew produced the pages but the Timber Wolf ignored them.

"Lots of people have worked with me through the years and a lot of them are dead. None of them were friends."

But Drew held fast. "There's this mercenary camp in Georgia. That's where I met Mace. He told me all kinds of stories about you, said thirty of us wouldn't have stood a chance against you."

"Yeah. A few years ago maybe." Wayman stepped forward. Just a little. Drew noted the large revolver in his hand again. The Timber Wolf's eyes were ice. "What'd you say your name was?"

"Drew Jordan."

"Well, Drew Jordan, you don't look much like a mercenary to me."

"No," Drew said, despite himself his voice almost a whine. "I'm not, not really. I went to the camp first to write a story about the experience. I went back a few times because I liked it." He gulped air. "Mace took me under his wing, taught me how to develop an edge. He sent me here because he thought you could help." Drew realized he was trembling, the sweat still coming in buckets. "I came here because I've got nowhere else to go. Mace isn't the only one who died. There are others, one from my hand and a few more they've tried to pin on me. But it wasn't my fault. I was set up and then—"

"Hold on. Slow down." Wayman seemed intrigued now as he sized up the young man before him. "I don't know why, Drew Jordan, but I'm going to listen to what you have to say. Believe me, it goes against my better nature."

"Thank you. You don't know how much I—"

"I know your clock's running and you'd better grab my interest fast. Here, let's go into the living room."

Wayman hit a light switch and the foyer was immediately aglow with soft light. He holstered his cannon-size pistol and instructed Drew toward the sunken living room just off to the left, keeping Drew in front of him and reasonably out of striking range at all times. Drew moved stiffly, his motions sluggish as if terrified of making one move too fast for the man behind him. Retired or not, the Timber Wolf remained a chilling figure, ominous not so much in appearance as aura. A feeling radiated from him like an animal in the moments before it lunges into an attack, an undercurrent of suppressed tension and strength. The two men faced each other from matching chairs set ten feet apart and Drew felt as if the pistol were still poised on him.

"I want it all," Wayman said. "From the beginning."

Drew's eyes sharpened as he obliged, starting with his grandmother's funeral and the letter given to him by Kornbloom. From there he went to his meeting with the man he thought was Masterson and the uneasy, or too easy, alliance forged between them. Finally he recounted the happening at Too-Jay's and its bizarre aftermath, which left him alone and isolated, and, lastly, his link with Mace, which culminated in the events of the previous night.

In the end Wayman looked somewhat confused but interested. Before speaking, he finally accepted the pages held in Drew's hands and returned to his seat. "So, what you're telling me is that Mace was originally hired by the people who killed him to kill you."

"Not exactly. Mace had another name, another identity. He told everyone in the camp he was a mercenary when he was really an assassin. Selinas or something."

"Selinas?"

"Yes. You know him?"

"Just of him. Selinas isn't just any assassin. He's one of the best. Absolute top of the fucking line."

"He ran into someone better," Drew said sadly.

"Someone you got away from."

"I was lucky."

"Luck's never enough, not in this business. You said Selinas, or Mace, killed several people for the employers he eventually turned on."

"I couldn't make out much of what he was saying by then." Drew shrugged. "There were a pair of brothers, Riv-something, and a man named—I think it was Landros."

The Timber Wolf's eyebrows flickered. "Or Lantos?"

"Maybe. Why?"

"Because there used to be a guy named Lantos who was quite an assassin himself. Got a bit old for the trade and moved into more mundane work. How he would be connected to Arthur Trelana and this drug business is beyond me, though."

"But he *is* connected. *Everything's* connected, including the grandmothers. I'm the one piece whoever is behind it all let slip away and how long that stays the case is probably up to you."

Drew's plea seemed to act like a leash on the Timber Wolf, pulling his interest back. His eyes dimmed. The intensity slid from his features, the indifferent chill back.

"You got yourself mixed up with the wrong people, Drew Jordan," he said finally. "Damn wonder you're still alive. You came here for my help and now I'm going to give it to you: put yourself in a cab and go to the Miami police. Tell them everything you told me. Take these pages to them."

Drew felt his whole insides sink. Dry disappointment filled his mouth. His mind wandered strangely back to high school, to the coach's announcement of the final cut and waiting for his name to be called among the team members. It never was, and now that parched, dull feeling had returned to his mouth, even a swallow denied him.

Wayman stood up impatiently. "Keep running, Drew Jordan, and you'll only dig yourself a deeper hole. At least now the trail of whatever's really happening here is still warm. You've got a chance of finding the right people to listen, maybe from the police, maybe from somewhere else. Stay on the lam and you'll just be giving your friend's killers more time to get you."

Drew wanted to stop him right there, stop him and say that this wasn't the way it was supposed to be. You're a hero. You're supposed to help me. Let's start all over from the time I hit your buzzer. But he just sat there in silence, gawking lamely ahead.

"You came to me for help," Wayman continued, starting to walk from the living room up toward the foyer. "I've done the best I can. I'm sorry."

"For what?" Drew said with the heaviness forced back. "I mean, if you've really done the best you can, what do you have to be sorry for?"

"For not being what you figured I would be. I'm sorry for not living up to whatever it was your friend Mace told you about me."

Drew was on his feet now, as much angry as disappointed. "He didn't tell me everything. He didn't tell me why you quit."

Wayman's features froze. "It doesn't matter. Why should you care?"

"Because it *does* matter, that's all." His eyes were on the holstered pistol now, not caring about it anymore. "I know about Corsica and the others. You were the best. No one else even came close. Then all of a sudden you just walked away. It doesn't figure."

"Drop it, kid. You don't know as much as you think you do. Maybe I figured I'd done everything I could. Maybe I figured my luck had run out. What's the difference?" He opened the front door. "This way, Drew Jordan. If it helps any, I really am sorry. You rang the bell expecting to find the Timber Wolf, and all you got was me."

Drew stepped up from the living room and stopped even with Wayman near the door. "I'll leave, but I don't plan on turning myself in and letting them kill me. I've got to keep on the move, that's the way I see it. I've got to find out who's behind this and get them before they get me. I figure I've got to do the best I can at making up my own rules because maybe the world you used to thrive in and this one aren't so different.'' And he started through the door.

''Jordan,'' the Timber Wolf called after him, a second call lost in midstream when it was obvious that the young man wasn't going to turn.

Drew walked on through the gate and made sure it latched tight behind him.

He didn't see the police cars until he was ten yards down West Broadview Drive still fronting Wayman's property.

They screeched to a halt from all directions, men lunging from them with guns drawn. Drew barely had time to throw his hands in the air before they were on him, shoving him viciously face first into Wayman's fence so his flesh kissed steel. One of the cops started reading him his rights. Others were talking, muttering, guns still drawn. He paid no attention, grimacing only when they yanked his hands together behind his back to fasten the handcuffs in place.

And inside the house the Timber Wolf turned away from the window in disgust.

What could I have done? he asked himself, squeezing the pair of bloodied pages Drew had neglected to retrieve from him. *What could I have done?*

PART FOUR:

NARCO-
TRAFFICANTÉ

CHAPTER 14

THE INTERROGATION ROOM WAS NOT DARK AND CRAMPED AS DREW had expected, but spacious and frighteningly stark, overly bright with too many fluorescent bulbs.

Lieutenant Wexler pulled a chair out from under the single table, swung it around, and straddled it with his arms folded over the back.

"Let's go over this from the beginning."

"Why don't you just listen to the tapes your buddies made?"

"I'd rather start fresh. Something might jar your memory. Can I get you a Coke or something?"

"Nope."

"Okay. You change your mind, you let me know." Wexler was probably a decade Drew's senior. His face was taut and serious, hardly compassionate. "Let's start with Arthur Trelana. A respected businessman, frequent giver to charities, sponsor of several southern Florida youth programs, and—"

"—an all-around nice guy. Gee whiz, being a major drug trafficker just worked wonders for him."

"How did you learn he was a drug trafficker?"

"You mean you didn't know? Sorry to enlighten you. . . ." And then, "From the letter."

"The one from your grandmother?"

"I *thought* it was from my grandmother."

"Right. The letter was a plant to make sure you would call a

DEA agent who turned out to be dead for two days so he would help you kill Arthur Trelana.''

"You *did* listen to the tapes. I'm impressed."

"So, with the help of this fake DEA agent, you went to Too-Jay's and proceeded to murder Arthur Trelana."

"No!" Drew broke in, his frustration peaking. "No! No! No! I *didn't* kill Trelana. The man I told the others about did."

"Yes. That's the one you *admit* to killing."

"Because I didn't have a choice."

"Then why have we positively identified the gun you ditched as the weapon that killed Trelana?"

"Talk to the people who were in there. They saw what happened. They had to."

"We have. All those who remember anything insist you killed everyone, including that innocent bystander who tried to intervene."

"*Innocent bystander?*" Drew shook his head in mock disbelief. "That fucker tried to kill me after he killed the others, damnit! I should have let him. Then at least you'd be out there looking for the real killer. Or am I giving you too much credit?"

"That doesn't explain the positive make we got on your gun."

"I only fired two goddamn—" Drew cut himself off. "They set that up, too."

"Who did?"

"The people behind all this."

"Of course. The mysterious force you keep alluding to." Wexler paused. "Now let's talk about Selinas."

"Mace," Drew corrected. "I never knew him as Selinas."

"Because as Selinas he was supposed to kill you, but as Mace he agreed to help you stay alive. Have I got that straight?"

"Close. Only you're missing the point. There's more going on here. If you'd open your eyes you'd see that. As Selinas, Mace killed other people connected with this. I already gave you their names. Check them out. There's a pattern present. Everything's connected and it starts with the grandmothers."

Wexler softened his features. "Look, Drew, somebody wants you nailed with this awfully bad. They called us *and* the newspeople and fed your name. You're alone, but you don't have to be. Tell us who else you were working with. Who set you up? Talk to us and we'll protect you."

"Even if I had anything more to tell you, it wouldn't help, not with what you're up against."

Wexler sat back down and straddled the chair once more. "Let's take it from the beginning again."

"I think I'll take that Coke now. . . ."

The footsteps woke Drew up the next morning. He had no idea what time it was and realized he was ravenously hungry, having not eaten since the hotdogs nearly twenty-four hours before. Then again, even if those footsteps did mean breakfast was being served, Drew would have to think twice before eating it in view of Mace's warning, which was still firm in his mind.

The problem turned out to be academic since it was an empty-handed guard who conferred with the one who had been posted outside his cell all night. It was that man who unlocked Drew's cell and swung the door open.

"Come with me," said the policeman who had just arrived.

"We eating out?"

"Just come along."

Drew had no idea what to expect as he followed the man through the bowels of Miami police headquarters toward the main levels. In his mind he could almost see the Timber Wolf waiting for him upstairs with a plan to find who was behind everything that had happened, having changed his mind and ready to plunge back into the world he had abandoned.

Upstairs he saw no one he recognized. They gave him back his watch and money and told him he was being released. Drew gazed at the clerks in shock as he signed a series of vouchers. A pair of policemen escorted him to the building lobby where a huge man in a light suit was waiting for him. Drew looked at the man, then at the officers poised at either elbow.

"So, this is how it ends," Drew said to no one in particular.

"Thank you," the big man said and the guards took their leave. "There's a car waiting for us outside," he told Drew.

"I don't suppose I have a choice of going for a ride or not, do I?"

The big man shook his head.

"Fine. I'm too tired to make any trouble for you and I'm too damn sick of running."

"Let's go," said the big man and he led Drew out into the sun toward a waiting limousine.

"At least I get to go in style," Drew muttered, searching himself for a smile.

It was about the time the limousine reached a small, isolated airfield somewhere north of Miami that Drew realized with considerable relief that they weren't going to kill him. A single Learjet sat warming its engines and the limo came right up to it. The big man led Drew up the five steps leading to the cabin. The driver stayed behind and drove the car off as the Lear's engines prepped for takeoff.

"You plan on telling me where we're headed?" Drew asked the big man. "No, I don't suppose you do. . . ."

"The *Islas del Rosario* off the coast of Colombia," the big man said suddenly. "There's someone who wants to see you."

The flight was longer than Drew had expected, his own confusion and anxiety lengthening it. The big man refused to answer any more of his questions and for Drew the mystery of what was happening to him was agonizing. Someone had rescued him, saved his life. But who? And why?

The answers lay in Colombia.

They landed in Cartagena where another stretch limousine was waiting for them on the tarmac. Again the big man guided him inside, his vigil constant. Drew knew the man hadn't slept during the flight, had barely closed his eyes. The limousine brought them to a dock where a cabin cruiser was waiting. Once more the big man ushered him aboard.

Drew was vaguely familiar with the *Islas del Rosario*, was aware that they composed a small chain of lavish islands two hours by boat from Cartagena. He tried to relax, but the hot sun bore into him and he found himself feeling weak and dizzy. After half an hour he went below to the cabin, accompanied by his huge escort, and drank ice water until his stomach ached. Then he returned to the deck and collapsed in a chair set in the shade.

The *Islas del Rosario* came into view an hour later. They were strikingly beautiful, lush green oases in the midst of a piercing blue sea. The water rolled upon the narrow beaches, seeming to fondle the sand. As the cabin cruiser drew nearer, Drew made out the large villas and smaller summer homes constructed on the larger members of the island chain. A few even boasted condominium complexes to rival the best that Miami and Palm Beach had to offer. Strange, he thought, how so many Colombians had made their way to America while numerous Americans had purchased property here.

Drew didn't need to be told that they were nearing their destination. The presence of two armed patrol launches suddenly before them revealed that much, followed by the sight of a series of huge white parapets, something like guard towers, rising out of the center of the next island. Whoever had sprung him from jail was certainly well protected.

Four men, all dressed in khaki and all armed, were waiting on the dock when the cabin cruiser pulled in. The deckhands joked with them in Spanish and together they tied the boat down. Drew was led off by his giant escort to a waiting jeep. The man's sole human move during the entire trip had been to strip off his suit jacket when they were about halfway to the islands.

This particular island was small and the massive villa Drew had caught glimpses of from the sea composed most of it. The ride by jeep was understandably short through the abundant flora, always with the sound of the sea not far away. The greenery cleared five minutes into the drive, allowing Drew to see one of the largest homes he had ever laid eyes on, something to rival the Post estate in Palm Beach. The enormous villa was three stories high and stretched into the forest for as far as Drew could see. A huge, cream-colored wall, the same shade as the villa itself, surrounded the entire complex. Two more guards swung open the main gate to allow the jeep to pass through.

Drew caught sight of three majestic marble pillars adorning the villa's front. The structure, he surmised, was fashioned after the gothic homes of Spanish royalty from centuries before. The windows were wide and long. The villa's exterior had an unfinished, stucco quality about it, adding to the rustic flavor.

There was yet another trio of guards waiting to greet the jeep when it pulled up before the massive entrance doors. Drew's escort climbed out and conferred briefly with one of them.

"This way," he instructed and led his charge down a flagstone walk that seemed to encircle the entire front. They passed through another guarded gate and headed toward a huge swimming pool enclosed by cabanas and small palm trees.

As they got closer, Drew could see a number of canopied tables placed around the pool. They were spaced well apart, some larger than others. Three figures sat at one, the middle figure with his back toward him.

The escort bid Drew to stop some fifteen yards from the table. The two men sitting on either side of the third said something to him and the man in the middle started to rise. He turned slowly and Drew figured at first that the sun was playing tricks on him and then he was certain that he had gone totally mad.

Because the man staring him in the face was no stranger at all.

It was Arthur Trelana.

CHAPTER 15

"I SAW YOU DIE," DREW MUTTERED, THE LAMENESS OF THE STATE-
ment never really occurring to him.

Trelana stepped forward, the breeze toying with his thick,
silvery hair. He spoke with only the barest traces of a Spanish
accent. "And then, from what I understand, you were given the
blame for my apparent murder. My death was an illusion I
created just as my being responsible for your grandmother's
death was an illusion fostered by those behind your rather desperate predicament."

"Then who was it I saw—"

Trelana came closer, flanked by his guards, and interrupted.
"The man in Too-Jay's was my double, a regrettable but necessary sacrifice to be explained in time. Come, let's sit in the
shade." Only then did Drew realize how much he was sweating.
Trelana let him catch up and they started walking, the bodyguards looming near. "I'll call you Drew if you don't mind,"
the drug lord continued. "I have children older than you, so I'm
sure you'll understand. First, let me apologize for bringing you
here in the manner I did. It was necessary, I assure you."

"I should be thanking you for posting my bail, especially
since I was in jail for *your* murder."

"Bail?" Trelana queried. "Oh, there was no bail to post. I
had to use other means to get you out. Again, necessary. You'll
understand why in good time." He gestured toward the canopied
table they had reached. "Please, sit down. We'll have a cold

drink. You must be famished. I'll send for something right away."

"Yes," Drew said thankfully. "Please."

Trelana joined him under the canopy at the wrought iron table and waved the two bodyguards away with a simple flap of his hand. They took up a silent vigil in the shade near the series of cabanas off to the side of the pool.

Drew, meanwhile, tried to form a fresh impression of Trelana. He looked considerably younger than his sixty-plus years, at least on the outside. His skin was bronzed and creased little by wrinkles. His eyes were a piercing shade of brown, almost black, missing nothing. But it was his eyes that gave away the fear that lurked within, the rapid shifting that indicates a man taken to looking constantly over his shoulder. The lines of his neck muscles were stretched and taut, his throat seeming to remain forever dry and uncomfortable despite the swallowing of ice water from a huge glass he drained and swiftly refilled.

A man dressed as a waiter approached the table and Trelana spoke briefly to him in Spanish.

"I find it best that the help know only their native language," he explained after the waiter had nodded and left. "I've just ordered you a substantial meal. But I'm sure you're hungering for more than merely food." His expression turned almost warm. "I suppose I'm partly responsible for the hell you have experienced. I'll explain it all as best I can, starting with what got you involved in the first place: your grandmother."

Drew flinched.

"She did work for me," Trelana continued after swallowing more ice water. "Her reasons, as I understand them, were based on her concern for you. Near the end of your college career, the money was drained that had formed your support. She sought a vehicle for earning more and I provided her with a lucrative one."

"You make it sound like a . . . business arrangement."

"Because that's what it was." Trelana sighed and stroked his glass. "I make no apologies for what I am and I refuse to engage in curt denials. There is a need for the services I oversee, a need for a central organization to coordinate certain facilities that people would find elsewhere anyway. Does that make sense?"

"I suppose it does to you, but I can't accept your business, no matter how you put it."

"Neither could your grandmother after a time, but I'm getting to that. The key to any successful smuggling chain is to use it sparingly, only when the need arises. That is how men like myself stay ahead of those in law enforcement, who formed our primary antagonists until recently. When was the last time your grandmother ventured down to Nassau?"

"About two weeks ago. She'd been back only three days when . . ." Drew let the statement tail off.

"I hadn't sent her down there in nearly a year. It was generally only once a year—sometimes less, but never more."

Drew stared at the drug lord, dumbfounded.

"Someone penetrated my organization, utilized the chain I created to bring in their own powder." Trelana's eyes sharpened. "You told the Miami police about your friend Mace. What were his last words to you?"

"That something different was going on. Something . . . worse."

"Indeed. I had come to the same realization myself but only recently. I am what is commonly referred to in my business as an overlord. And like any lord, I do not hold complete control over all my subjects, which explains how the truth of the penetration escaped me for so long. My suspicions began with the murder of a courier of mine named Lantos."

"By Selinas—Mace. Yes, he told me!"

"Lantos's role was to deliver money and instructions to the next link in the chain, a rather unsavory but efficient pair named the Rivero brothers."

"Rivero!" Drew almost shouted. "Mace told me their name, but I couldn't remember it."

"He was hired to eliminate the brothers, too, no doubt. The Riveros, keep in mind, were the ones responsible for distribution of the cocaine as per Lantos's instructions. You see where this is leading, Drew. You must."

Drew nodded uncertainly. "The instructions that the Riveros received for distribution weren't yours and neither was the cocaine they received through the grandmothers. Yes, I see what you mean by penetration. But then Mace, as Selinas, comes in."

"To wipe out the whole channel from the bottom up," Trelana

elaborated. "Anyone who had anything to do with this particular powder chain was killed. Control—I had lost it. I realized this in time to arrange for the double to take my place. It had been necessary for me to use him several times in the past, but never with so much certainty of what his fate would be. In fact, not only did I expect it, I hoped for it."

"You wanted them to go after you, I mean, him?"

Trelana nodded. "His death was the only way I could be assured of enough freedom to learn what was actually going on. When word reached me of the attack in Too-Jay's, all of my worst suspicions had been confirmed."

"But why would the force behind Selinas wipe out a chain that was working so well for them?"

Trelana eyed Drew warmly before responding. "We're about to come to the most painful part of the tale. It was your grandmother, Drew. She really did go to the DEA."

"My God, the letter . . ."

"All the facts in it were true, but she didn't write it. Perhaps she could have lived with the yearly trips I sent her on. But three, sometimes even four times a year became too much for her conscience. From what I gather, she went to the DEA before the last shipment. Selinas was hired to wipe out the chain so there would be no trace. The grandmothers had to be eliminated as well, along with four DEA agents and a supervisor who had no conception of the gravity of what they had stumbled upon."

"The real Masterson," Drew muttered. "But what had they stumbled upon?"

Trelana ignored his question. "I need you, Drew, and no matter what you might think of my profession I'm afraid you need me now, too." The drug lord's piercing eyes regarded him closely. "You were to be killed this morning. The breakfast eventually served in your cell would have been poisoned and if you failed to eat, several other contingencies had been made ready."

Drew shivered. "How could you know?"

"I have people in the police station. When word of their suspicions reached me, I arranged your release."

Drew was suddenly awe-struck by how far Trelana's power extended. "Then I owe you for saving my life, too—really something since I thought I almost took yours."

"It was that act that plunged us together," Trelana told him, "plunged us together to a point where we needed each other's help to survive."

"You seem to be doing pretty well on your own."

Trelana started to raise his water glass, then changed his mind. "I'm as much a prisoner here as you were in that jail. I can never leave, never show my face off this island . . . until the matter currently before us is resolved."

"When did you learn I was, well, that I was involved?"

"First came a report of the bizarre circumstances surrounding the hit itself. Then your name was conveniently plastered across television screens and newspapers. It was obvious to me even then that you had been set up by the same people behind the deaths of Lantos, the Riveros, and, yes, the grandmothers. All I lacked was the why and how, which later came into focus when tapes of your interrogation were played for me."

"But why did they use me in the first place? I still don't see how that fits since they had another gunman in Too-Jay's anyway."

Trelana hesitated. "You asked me before what it was that the DEA people had stumbled upon thanks to your grandmother, and I avoided it. The answer to that question has much to do with the answer to this one. Things tend to get complicated from here on. I'll explain as best I can."

At that moment the servant returned with a tray laid out like room service in the finest hotel. Drew watched eagerly as a plate of eggs, bacon, and toast were set down before him along with a huge glass of freshly squeezed orange juice and a pot of coffee. He began to eat immediately, gobbling up the huge portion of eggs in rapid mouthfuls.

"I'll continue as you eat," Trelana told him.

"Excuse my manners."

"As understandable as your actions in Florida. Let's talk now about the drug world. Last year it was roughly—and conservatively—estimated as having annual revenues exceeding half a trillion dollars. More money is spent annually on drugs than food worldwide. But I do not wish to discuss figures here so much as effects. No sphere of American life is untouched by the drug world and, despite claims to the contrary, it is growing in unheard of, immeasurable fashion. Any ideas as to why?"

"Supply and demand," Drew muttered between mouthfuls. "Just like you said before."

"The answer is a bit more complicated than that. The drug industry is not one that has sprouted from the bottom up, but from the top down. From governments, Drew, and that includes the government of the United States. Countries all over the world depend on their drug crops to assure an influx of dollars, that accounts for their very existence. Concurrently, the only hope powerful American banks have of recouping their vast loans to these countries in question rests in the continuance of the drug trade. During prohibition, a man named Kennedy is said to have made his fortune smuggling a drug of a different kind. There are many in America now, I fear, with sights on achieving that same kind of power with narcotics as the impetus instead of alcohol."

"Are you telling me that all this is about getting someone elected president?"

"Not yet, but someday it might well come to that as it already has in several other countries. The narcotics industry has become an expansionist brotherhood that courts vastly divergent interests from the public and private sectors. It represents an empire that holds resources any nation would be proud to boast. Its appetite for growth is insatiable and satisfied in any number of ways from the toppling of governments to the more subtle takeovers of major banks. All this may sound bad enough as is, but there is an even harsher scenario in which one *unified* force would control all the maneuverings. At this point, competing forces within the world of narcotics form its own worst enemy. Eliminate such factionalization and all checks and balances would be lifted, no telling how far such a force could go."

Drew looked up from his eggs. "But if you're a part of all this, why would they go after you?"

"Because I *am* a part," Trelana said, "but not a part of them. The reasons behind my so-called execution were simple. They want to create chaos among the overlords, the worst feature of all because it breaks down control. They don't want to wipe us out. They want to take us over. A multibillion-dollar industry and the immeasurable power that goes with it in the hands of one centralized and currently unknown dark force. Banks, industries, governments—this dark force is after them all."

"Through you?"

"And others like me. I can't be sure, but the indications are present. If I'm right about this, the ramifications are too terrible to contemplate. One force controlling the whole of worldwide drug supply and distribution is a thousand times more horrible than the system currently in place. You must believe that."

Drew pushed the last of his eggs onto a stray piece of toast. "Even if I did, that still doesn't explain what it has to do with your bringing me down here."

Trelana leaned back and sipped his water. "Stick a pin into a bag of white powder, Drew, and the powder will gradually, almost unnoticeably slip out, but in the end the bag will be empty. Such is the case with the cocaine channel that originated with the grandmothers in Nassau. Somewhere along the line is a leak in my own organization, which allowed the dark force to penetrate it. It's our only link to them, I'm afraid, our only means to uncover their identity."

"I asked you about me."

Trelana sighed. "I was too substantial a figure for them to erase through an ordinary hired gun. They needed a means that would freeze my organization, not mobilize it." Trelana paused. "You came complete with motive, one they cleverly arranged for you, but a motive nonetheless. You kill me for vengeance and die in the process. The story ends there. No one pursues it further because there is nothing to pursue. Only you crossed them up by surviving, and I crossed them up by taking you out of circulation. I don't exist anymore and neither do you—the perfect advantage for both of us."

"Advantage?"

"There is no one in my own organization I can send out to find the place in the bag where the pinprick made its mark," Trelana explained. "There's no telling how deep I've been penetrated, how many of my soldiers and couriers are known to them. The dark force used you because you were an outsider with no links to anyone and I want to use you for the same reason." Trelana held Drew's eyes as warmly as he could. "I want you to follow the trail of powder from its origins in Nassau, and then along the same line the grandmothers started."

"But it's been wiped out. You said so yourself."

"Not entirely. Bits and pieces are still in place and will respond if the proper cues are given. Within one of them must lie the point of penetration and we will follow it to its source. Don't you see? A man, an *unknown*, shows up to continue a channel that by all rights should have been cut off. Confusion will become our ally. Their purpose in using you was to *avoid* a mobilization on the part of my forces. My purpose in using you is to *force* their forces *to* mobilize. We must get them in the open where we can fight them on our terms. You will accomplish this by becoming a *narcotrafficanté*."

"Narco*what*?"

"*Trafficanté*. It means many things, but mostly it means drug lord."

"And if I refuse, I go straight back to the jail you sprung me from. Is that it?"

Trelana looked offended, hurt. "I find myself liking you, Drew, and I could never knowingly send a man I liked to his death, which is what a return to the States without protection would mean for you. I will get you out of this either way and do my best to protect both you and your girlfriend. But if you don't cooperate, you will only be running. Help us uncover the truth behind the dark force, though, and you will be living."

Drew hesitated, seeming to accept the drug lord's words because they made perfect sense, with one key exception. "Like you said, Mr. Trelana, I'm an outsider and even if I get lucky in Nassau I won't be able to get very far on my own."

"You will be furnished with a Miami contact number. Call it to make any arrangements you desire, request any help you need. I will be made aware of everything in minutes and will make sure whatever you request is provided."

Drew found himself almost smiling at the absurdity of it all. "So, first I'm set up to kill somebody and now I'm recruited to help the person I was originally set up to kill. . . ."

Trelana regarded him with a fatherly stare. "And in that madness lies your greatest reason for cooperating. You were willing to kill me partly because you were led to believe I killed your grandmother. I didn't. But somewhere along the trail you'll be following are the people who did. I ask you to remember that."

"I haven't forgotten," said Drew.

CHAPTER 16

ELLIANA STOOD IN THE SHADOWS, WAITING FOR THE MOMENT SHE was expecting to come. The air outside Lefleur's processing plant smelled of fish and oils even three hours past closing time. She kept her breaths to a minimum.

Ellie had arrived in the fishing village of Getaria along the Basque coast of Spain after a long and unsettling trip, employing many means of transportation to ensure she wasn't being followed. Such precautions seemed necessary after Prague. Events there had frightened as much as they had confused her. If the Council of Ten could penetrate the Mossad, they could penetrate anything. At no time could she allow herself to feel safe.

Getaria was a small, picturesque town perched right on the water, which relied on fishing for its day-to-day survival. Annatoly's last words had brought her here late Monday afternoon, at which point she followed a narrow breakwater road across to San Anton Island and an isolated rooming house she had learned of in town. The proprietor was a boisterous, flabby woman who loved to talk and Ellie was only too happy to listen, especially when she was able to turn the discussion toward Lefleur.

The woman made a spitting motion and went on to explain that the Frenchman operated the town's only fish cleaning, packing, and freezing plant. It was located right on the main pier and fishermen in for the day would drop their catch with him and be paid as poorly as the market allowed. Most of the fishermen knew no better and simply accepted. The few who rebelled were not long for Getaria.

Lefleur's setup was perfect, Ellie reckoned. He had set himself up in this isolated fishing village as a sort of godfather. The sea gave him easy routes for shipping without the bother of major ports, so he was able to move whatever products he desired without undue scrutiny. Annatoly's description of him led Ellie to believe that Lefleur was a black market smuggler, the transport planes being one of several projects underway at this time.

But one that might ultimately lead her to the Council of Ten.

She spent the early part of Tuesday out on the docks in the damp mist, playing the part of an interested tourist over for a brief stop. Lefleur showed himself on the waterfront promptly at ten, wearing a yellow rain slicker to guard his bulky frame. He was a heavy-boned man with strangely sallow cheeks and a face caught in a perpetual grimace. There was something dirty and repelling about him. Ellie knew he lived directly over his processing plant and wondered how he could stand the constant smell of fish.

Shortly after Lefleur made his appearance, a woman emerged from a separate area of the plant. She was scantily clad in a thin dress, her jacket equally as thin and more suited for a warm night than a cool, misty morning. The innkeeper had said Lefleur was constantly seen in the company of "dirty women," her term for prostitutes, and now Ellie smiled at the fact that she had found her means to gain access to him.

Ellie spent the last minutes she could allow herself there that morning checking out the plant's layout, careful not to get in anyone's way. The front section was devoted to cleaning, peeling, and filleting. Rows of men and women, villagers all, stood over metal tables working with knives and other instruments. When finished with a fish, they would drop it in a tray, which once full was picked up by another worker and taken to the processing machines in the rear of the plant. One was used to press and flatten certain brands for shipment to various packaging plants. Another strange-looking apparatus instantly froze huge slabs of the day's catch to be sold somewhere else as fresh.

All the workers were garbed in rubber body aprons, boots, and gloves. A few wore earmuffs to block out the piercing sounds of the machines. To this Ellie would have added nose plugs to block out the pungent fish odor that all these workers must have somehow gotten used to.

Ellie started back for San Anton Island, only to return at nightfall to take up her vigil. She had been in the shadows for three hours now, hidden between two discarded, burned out shells of former ships where no eyes could find her. She was beginning to wonder if she might have to spend the whole night there when the dim lights of a taxi strained through the dark.

Lefleur's guard responded to the door after the third soft knock. The woman outside, holding a thin jacket over her head to shield it from the rain, looked to be a bit better than his employer's usual fare. She smiled at him seductively, bright lips dancing. The man grunted and beckoned her to enter.

Elliana stepped through the door with her eyes never leaving the man. Keep your eyes on someone, she knew, and they will see you for just what they expect you to be without further scrutiny. Her entire plan had been based on the hope that Lefleur received a prostitute every night, proven right when a colorfully dressed woman in high heels had slid from the backseat of the taxi just minutes before.

As the whore passed by her hiding place in the shadows, Ellie sprang and gripped her from behind, jamming her right thumb into the soft flesh beneath the woman's chin. The effect was to cause her intense pain but, more importantly, to silence her long enough for Ellie to locate her carotid artery and squeeze for forty seconds, denying the brain its oxygen supply. The whore was out after twenty, but Ellie maintained the pressure for twice that to make sure her sleep would last well into the night. Risky, for permanent brain damage could result, but nonetheless necessary. Then she took the whore's place on the walk and continued around the building to the front door.

Her eyes continued to tease the guard as he preceded her toward the steps leading hopefully to Lefleur's bedroom. A second guard stood at the top, a giant twin of the first, but with dark hair. These two were certain to cause problems for her. Yesterday's whore had spent the entire night, probably the common practice. How, then, could she leave the building without drawing attention after completing her business with Lefleur?

She would cross that bridge later. The thing now was to get Lefleur to talk.

"You new?" the dark-haired guard at the top of the stairs asked her, eyes wary.

"First time here," Ellie returned in the same Spanish dialect, doing her best to imitate the local accent. "But I'm hardly new."

"I have to search you."

Ellie winked and tossed him a smile. "Get your jollies, eh?"

She dropped her handbag and raised her arms. The flimsy dress she had bought that afternoon clung to her breasts and sides. The guard patted her up and down with surprising tenderness. His hands lingered for a second on her well-formed breasts.

"The boss will like these," he quipped.

"Finished?" Ellie asked him, tossing her head so her thick auburn hair flipped back.

The guard ruffled through her handbag and then angled his hand toward the nearest door. "Go right in. I'll hold on to this for you."

Ellie did as she was told. The handbag had been meant as a distraction; there was nothing inside she had intended to make use of. The guard closed the door behind her and the smell of the room assaulted her immediately—stale fish and oils mixing with perspiration. Lefleur lay face-up on a huge bed in the rear of the room, naked to the waist. His midsection was huge and misshapen, lifting upward with each breath. He pressed out a cigarette and sat up.

"Right on time," he smiled. "I like that."

Ellie tilted her lips seductively but didn't speak.

Lefleur pushed himself from the bed. His eyes widened as he looked her over.

"Do I know you?"

Ellie opened her blouse. Her large breasts came free.

"Would you like to?" she asked.

Lefleur moved toward her. He was barefoot. Ellie couldn't tell if the awful smells were from the room or if they came from him. She fought not to be sick. The man revolted her, hairy everywhere.

He grasped her shoulders and squeezed as if to size her up. He nodded, apparently satisfied. Then his mouth was coming forward and Ellie maneuvered hers to join it. She focused on other thoughts, like the questions she would soon be asking him, fighting to keep her mind from what she was doing.

Lefleur's tongue swept about her mouth like a snake. She used her own against it for self-defense more than anything. His hands cupped her breasts, squeezing them to the point of pain.

She separated herself forcefully.

"Don't be rough," she giggled, teasing him with another smile.

She took his hand and led him to the bed. Lefleur followed along like a willing puppy, yapping at her every move. It was so easy to manipulate weak men with sex. They were so vulnerable, especially to women who had been trained to use it as a weapon. Mossad female operatives received routine courses in such areas. When your life or the lives of others were at stake, nothing could be spared. You did what you had to. Anything.

Lefleur was on top of her now, his head buried in her chest, his tongue alternately licking at each nipple. She had to have him totally distracted; she couldn't risk a sudden scream from his mouth when she acted. Her hands slid across his hairy belly for the snap and zipper of his trousers. Taking a deep breath to steel herself, she grasped him and began to fondle and stroke. First with both hands, then with just one.

Lefleur moaned and sank his head deeper against her. The pressure hurt. His arms squeezed her tight from behind, nails digging into her skin.

Ellie kept fondling, the flesh in her hand hard and pulsing. She could feel him submit totally to her. Her free hand roamed to her hair and removed a small three-inch blade as sharp as a scalpel.

It was time.

Her hand moved for his testicles and she squeezed just hard enough to make him gasp, as she brought her body up and around. With that, he was suddenly beneath her, their positions switched, his face contorted in pain but missing the air needed to cry out.

Elliana made sure he saw the blade as she drew it up against his throat.

"I'm going to release your balls now," she said coldly. "Scream and I'll cut your throat."

Lefleur didn't scream. His erection had gone limp, but he was too terrified to notice.

Ellie was about to speak when he did.

"They sent you, didn't they?"

"Who?"

"Don't play dumb. They must want something. Otherwise I'd already be dead."

"Shut up!"

"No," he wheezed from the pressure of the blade against his throat. "I did what I was told. I followed through with all of the shipments just as instructed."

Lefleur met Ellie's eyes and his lips trembled when he grasped their puzzlement.

"My God, they didn't send you. . . ."

"What shipments?" Ellie demanded, seizing the advantage.

"Where are you from? Why are you here?"

She drew a speck of blood from the tip of the blade. "What shipments?"

"I can't tell you. I'll be killed if I do."

"You'll be killed if you don't." Ellie applied more pressure on the knife and a steady trickle began to slide from the wound.

"N-No, wait! I'll talk. There were fourteen shipments made, maybe fifteen."

"Which?"

"I'm not sure. Years, they happened over years."

"How many?"

"Four-and-a-half, almost five."

Ellie found herself intrigued. This was not the information she had come for, but clearly it was important, possibly even connected to the greater picture.

"What did the shipments contain?"

"I don't know. I swear I don't," Lefleur pleaded. "I never examined them. Those were the orders, not to be violated under any circumstances. Just check their weights for the manifest and send them on their way. Two hundred pounds always, almost exactly."

"How were they shipped?"

"By boat, always by boat. Instructions again."

"To where?"

"The Bahamas. Various ports. Never the same one twice."

Ellie realized she was breathing hard. "Very good. Keep this up and I might let you live."

Lefleur was breathing even harder, in short rapid heaves as if afraid too great a breath would force the blade through his throat.

"Now let's talk about the transport planes. How many of those have you obtained?"

Lefleur looked up at her strangely, as if confused by the track of her questions.

"Answer!"

"One hundred with a request for twenty more."

"A hundred and twenty transport planes? For what?"

"I don't know. I swear it!"

"Men like you never go into anything blind." And once again Ellie increased the pressure on the blade's edge.

"All right. All right. Many people are being moved at the same time. To America."

"With hostile intentions?"

Lefleur would have nodded if not for the knife. "The indications are there."

"A hundred and twenty planes are going to drop hostile troops in for an invasion *past all of America's defenses*?" Ellie posed disbelievingly.

"No," Lefleur rasped. "The defenses will be down. They will no longer pose a problem."

"We're talking about billions of dollars worth of surveillance and defensive systems. Thousands of personnel on duty always."

Lefleur's eyes were pleading. "I'm telling you what I know, what I've gathered. It's the truth!"

"How?"

"I don't know. I didn't want to."

Something occurred to Ellie. "Those shipments to the Bahamas, were they connected in any way to the transports?"

"No. Of course not. How could they?" Lefleur's eyes gazed downward.

"They were! I can tell. Lie again and you die!"

"It isn't much," Lefleur relented. "Please, my air—I can't breathe. The blade, move it away a little." After Ellie obliged, he continued. "The shipments were all sent by private courier from the town of Berga in the Catalonian province. The name of the street was Farguell, sixteen or eighteen, I'm not sure which."

"So?"

"The calls requesting progress reports on the transports often originated in Berga. I traced them. Only as far as the town, though. The individual exchanges were impossible to obtain."

Ellie barely heard him, so great was the thudding of realization in her mind. Lefleur had provided her with a concrete location for the Council, a small town in Spain where contact had been made. And the transport planes. Annatoly had suspected a strike against America was planned, an invasion even. Now this had been confirmed, along with the fact that America's defenses would be down to permit it. But how could the strategic armaments of such a power all be lowered at the same time? Might it have something to do with those shipments Lefleur made to the Bahamas? Too many questions . . .

"You're going to lead me out of here now," Ellie told him, yanking his huge frame from the bed with the knife still pressed against his throat.

"There's no need for th-th-that," Lefleur stammered. "I swear."

Ellie acted as if she hadn't heard him. She dragged the Frenchman across the floor to the door and stopped.

"Once we're in the corridor, one word to your guards to do anything but stay back and I'll cut your throat. Understand?"

Lefleur nodded fearfully. Ellie reached for the knob.

Maybe it was the fact that she had underestimated the Frenchman. Maybe it was the fact that his move was timed perfectly while both of her hands were occupied. Either way, Ellie felt him yank away and go for her knife hand at the same time. She knew in that extended instant that she would not be able to kill him and chose a strike to wound instead. The razor edge dug into his cheek, making a neat slash, but Lefleur screamed and shoved his bulk into Ellie as they both lunged through the door.

Ellie stumbled. Lefleur pulled from her grasp and staggered backward.

"Kill her! Kill her!" he screamed down the steps.

One of his guards, the dark-haired one, charged at her from below. He was fast for a big man and as he reached for her with his powerful hands, Ellie twisted away, striking with her blade. He had stolen enough of her balance, however, to force the blow off and the knife lodged in the fleshy part of his shoulder. He wailed but kept his grip on Ellie as their struggle took them toward the staircase.

The light-haired guard was hurtling up the steps, and Ellie timed her next move perfectly, forcing Dark Hair into him. Dark Hair screamed again from the wrenching impact upon the blade still wedged in his shoulder.

Ellie started down the steps. A hand reached out from the darkness behind and tripped her up. She felt herself falling and knew she was powerless to do anything but brace for impact. When it came at the bottom of the flight, she tried to jump back to her feet immediately, but she had been too stunned. Her eyes glazed and the room's meager light flirted with darkness. Somehow she righted herself and started on when Light Hair grasped her from behind in a choke hold.

She lashed her right arm up and around, taking control away from him and trying for a counter, which would lead to a broken neck for her attacker. He was equal to the task, however, and she was still slowed, so when she went for his chin to execute the move, he backed away enough to throw off her timing. Ellie felt her control flutter away, lost as it had been gained for an instant. She turned to break his hold, but he had already let go, and she saw the crunching blow too late to dodge or twist.

It struck her in the right temple. A bright flash erupted before her eyes and suddenly the floor was pulled out from under her. Another dizzying blow struck before she landed, but she barely felt it. Everything was numb. Strangely, she never lost consciousness totally, maintaining enough of it to hear Lefleur's words shouted from the base of the steps.

"Take her into the plant," he ordered, "and feed her to the grinder."

CHAPTER 17

"SORRY I'M LATE, PETER."

The Timber Wolf had not noticed the woman approaching until she was almost upon him. He cursed himself silently for allowing distraction as he rose to greet her in Washington's Fort Dupont Park. They embraced briefly, Wayman more interested in the manila folders protruding from the woman's handbag.

"You got it," he said in what had started out as a question.

"And then some," she returned tautly. "What in hell are you onto here?"

"Tell me what you learned and maybe I'll know."

For reasons he was just beginning to understand, yesterday the Timber Wolf had gone to the police station determined to aid Drew Jordan. He had not been able to put out of his mind the sight of the police piling the young man into a squad car. At the station, however, he had learned not only that Jordan was missing, but that all traces of his ever being there had been erased. Wayman bit his own lip to punish himself. Drew Jordan had been the victim of professionals all along and they weren't finished with him yet. Now he had been made to disappear, and one way or another it was the Timber Wolf's fault.

Because he had refused to get involved.

Because he didn't want to get his hands dirty anymore.

Because he couldn't be the person Drew Jordan expected him to be.

So, yesterday he had called Jilly. Years before she had been part of the same network as he. She was a courier then and a good one. Their love affair had been silent and subdued, nothing that might attract the attention of their superiors. She left the network shortly before he did and that was the end of their relationship. Business had dictated the rules, and without the business there were none to follow. Jilly went to work for a private intelligence firm known as Beta Group. Free from congressional restrictions, Beta Group was widely known as the finest organization of its kind in the world, providing information-channeling services that Wayman had found himself sorely in need of.

Because she was headquartered in Washington, D.C., Wayman felt it best that he fly up there to meet her. Jilly had chosen Fort Dupont Park for the meet and he approved. The park was spacious and wide. The leaves had begun to change, and Wayman could almost picture the beauty cast over the scene by the winter's first snow as he sat back down on the bench next to Jilly. The breeze grabbed the long black hair from her face and tossed it off.

"Where do you want me to start?" she asked him.

Wayman recalled that Drew Jordan had asked him a similar question two days before. "With the grandmothers," he told Jilly.

She pulled the folders from her bag and opened the top one. "Your crystal ball's retained its sharpness, Peter. The times of increased financial activity you told me to look for correspond directly to the weeks immediately following their returns from those vacations in the Bahamas."

Wayman nodded, not surprised. He had felt that Drew Jordan had been right from the beginning. "Any links you could draw between the ladies and Trelana?"

"Not directly, but that doesn't mean a thing, not in the drug world." She opened another manila folder. "Speaking of which, you seem to have stumbled on an entire distribution chain that is—or was—quite successful. The details are all in these. I'll just give you the highlights. Lantos was one of Trelana's couriers, all right, along with a very deadly—now very dead—woman named Sabrina. And those brothers you asked me about are the Riveros. The most feared pair of coke traffickers in Miami until someone knocked them off last week." She closed the folder, her features stiffening. "Your interest in this is all very strange, unless you're planning to seize the opportunity to move into a new line of work."

"No, just get back into my old one."

Jilly arched her eyebrows. "Did I hear that right?"

Wayman just looked at her. "See, there was this kid, well, young man, who turned up on my doorstep with an incredible story, knowing all sorts of names he shouldn't have, which could only mean he had stumbled onto something way out of his league. His grandmother was one of the ladies who got killed and I think I believed what he was saying and I still didn't do anything to help. He was the kind of person I used to fight for, lay my life on the line for. Nobody special, just a poor bastard who'd had the living shit kicked out of him by society's under-layers. Hell, I didn't even know the people I fought for back then. They'd been hurt by the fuckers I hunted and that was enough for me."

"It was more than enough. It was too much."

"Is that what you think?"

"I think it ate you up, burned you out. I think that's why you quit. After Corsica—"

"Forget Corsica."

"I can't and neither can you," she said accusingly. "It marked the end because all of a sudden you couldn't live up to your own standards anymore. But it was impossible to start with because nobody could live up to those standards. They were too damn high, and as the years and the missions went on they got higher. You expected too much of the network, me, and most of all yourself."

"How can you expect too much? We were fighting for a cause, damnit!"

"That's the problem. You *became* the cause, Peter, and when you found out you couldn't win by yourself, that you were prone to mistakes like the rest of humanity, you got out. It took Corbano to finally show you the truth."

"Fuck Corbano. All he showed me were the bodies of all those kids who died because I fucked up."

Jilly's voice softened. "Nobody blamed you."

Wayman's expression was placid to the point of being stonelike. "But the trouble was *I* blamed me. You knew me better than anyone back then and most of what you said is right on the mark. The only thing you left out was the fear. After Corsica, I got scared of making a mistake, of not being able to live up to my own legend. I quit because I figured I could run away from those standards you say I set for myself." His features sharpened and with them his voice. "But I couldn't. And a couple days ago when I turned that young man away, I violated every standard I'd ever set for myself. I tried to tell myself that the code didn't matter anymore, that I'd lived without it so long what was the life of one more poor bastard anyway?" He paused. "Plenty, Jilly. Standard number one. And if I violate it, if I don't help this guy and keep my back turned, then everything I thought I'd accomplished will be meaningless because I'll be no better than those fuckers I spent all those years hunting."

For a while neither spoke but then, almost reluctantly, Jilly produced another manila folder from the bag. "This may be what you need, Peter. I ran those thirty addresses you gave me and came up with a direct link with the Riveros—their distribution points no doubt, and the periods of activity correspond directly to the return of those grandmothers from Nassau. But what does it mean?"

"Plenty, Jilly," the Timber Wolf said. "Plenty."

It was the ear-blasting whirl of the plant machinery that snapped Elliana all the way awake. It sounded even louder in the night with none of the workers to help absorb it. Her head pounded and throbbed. She forced herself to think, to plan.

Light Hair was dragging her across the floor in the direction of the pressing machine that reduced fish parts to pulp. Since Dark Hair was maintaining an even pace behind them with gun drawn and free hand clutching his wounded shoulder, that meant Lefleur had to be the one who switched on the machines. So, it was three against one, not to mention the machines. Lousy odds.

Ellie kept her eyes drooping and let her feet continue to drag. It was her only chance. The strike to her temple had opened a gash that looked much worse than it was. The blood would serve as a disguise. She could see the pressing machine, what Lefleur had called the grinder, now.

It was a huge apparatus, its opening up a ramp perhaps eight feet off the floor. Feed the fish in and out come the pressed parts ready for freezing or shipment as is. To facilitate large loads, the opening was easily wide enough to handle a human body.

Ellie tried not to think about what a body would look like when it emerged on the lower level conveyor belt en route to the freezing station. God . . .

The grinder was humming loudly. She smelled grease. Footsteps hurried to catch up with them, no doubt belonging to Lefleur who would want to witness the grisly killing. They had reached the ramp. Light Hair began to drag her up, and she could hear him breathing loudly from the strain. To lift and dump her into the machine was a task she didn't expect him to be able to handle alone.

At least that was what she was counting on.

They reached the top of the ramp and Ellie's eyes were now staring straight down into the grinder's teeth, huge steel bands actually, which formed the start of the pressing process. Her stomach fluttered.

Light Hair started to lift her from the ramp.

Wait! she urged herself. *Be patient! React now and the other one will have a clear shot at you.*

Ellie felt her feet being raised just a bit off the ramp and she concentrated on making herself as heavy as possible.

"Give me a hand with her, will ya?" Light Hair called to Dark, who started up the ramp.

Ellie blessed her fortune. With both of them occupied with her, she would have a chance. She hoped. Surprise would be on her side. If successful, she would have only Lefleur to deal with.

Patience . . .

Dark Hair lowered his one good arm to her legs while Light Hair fumbled about her upper body, both searching for the best angle to drop her down into the grinder's mouth. The teeth moved back and forth, back and forth, back and forth . . .

"Now," one of them said, and Ellie took that as her signal.

At the instant they began their final heave, Ellie twisted from Light Hair's grasp and launched a kick into Dark Hair's face. Still twisting, she angled her body to the side and crashed an elbow into Light Hair's midsection because he was closest to her. The blow sent him pitching backward down the ramp.

Dark Hair came in for her fast and hard, reaching with both hands now, forgetting about his shoulder wound as blood gushed from his nose. As he reached out, however, Ellie entered into the force of his strength, joining it and grasping him with both hands. He was off balance, all his weight going in one direction. Ellie kept it going.

Toward the grinder.

He entered head first, a brief, horrible scream replaced swiftly by a mashing, grating sound like a garbage disposal with something wedged in its works. Blood coughed upward, splattered flesh and pulverized bone spraying against the nearest wall and almost reaching the ceiling.

Light Hair was back on his feet, gun drawn, but the awful whining of the grinder unsettled him. He fired three shots, all errant, and by then Ellie was upon him. He kept his focus solely on the gun, struggling to use it. But in close his pistol was virtually useless, too easily jammed against his body, which was exactly what Elliana did. Her free hand rose up in a half fist and swished down into the flesh and cartilage of his throat. She felt it crack and knew he was dying even before he crumbled to the floor.

Behind her, she heard a scrape and a whirling sound. Ellie ducked instinctively.

Lefleur's angry scream rose over even the roar of his machines, as he pulled the six-foot fish spear back for another attack. Ellie leaped over Light Hair's corpse, as Lefleur came in with a thrust this time. But he aimed too high, for her throat instead of her midsection and she was able to avoid the blow easily. She might have finished him then, but she felt he was just out of her range and she lurched to her feet instead.

They faced off against each other, Lefleur with the spear, Ellie with her hands. He was breathing wildly, his face contorted. Although he had pulled up the zipper of his trousers, they were still unsnapped and sagged low past his hips. He was still naked above the waist.

Ellie looked frighteningly calm. She moved with him step for step, waiting for him to strike again. She could take no chances. This weapon was deadly even when wielded by an amateur. Ellie's right eye was filling with blood from the blow to her temple. She was vulnerable from that side, but Lefleur seemed unaware or unable to take advantage of it.

Ellie squared her midsection to him and offered it as a target.

Lefleur took the bait and lunged out with a vicious thrust, putting all his vast bulk behind it, his torn cheeks dripping with blood.

Ellie grasped the spear palms down on the hilt as she stepped sideways to avoid it. Turning suddenly and twisting the spear they now both held forced Lefleur into an off-balance stagger backward. The floor was slippery with fish oils and he flew into the air when he tried to right himself.

He landed hard on the conveyor belt leading from the grinder to the freezing machine, atop parts of Dark Hair that were still emerging. Dazed, he nonetheless realized what he was heading for and with a yard yet to go might have leaped off had not one of his feet been caught in the tread.

His scream as he passed into the machine was not as loud as Dark Hair's had been, but it rang in Ellie's ears and she raised her hands to cover them as the remains of Lefleur passed through the various stations of the freezing machine.

She did not wait to see what emerged on the other side. She headed for the first exit door she saw and, smelling the thick sea air, ran into the night.

The white-haired man closed his eyes and turned his face back to the sun.

"This whole business surrounding Jordan disturbs me," he said to the giant hovering over him. "No sign of him you say?"

Teeg grunted. "Not since he vanished from the jail."

"He vanished because someone wanted him to. But who? And why? The task could not have been easily accomplished, which means we may be facing a new enemy of dangerous potential."

Teeg grunted again and curled his hook inward. For as long as he could remember, he had been ugly. Before he even knew what the word meant, other kids teased him with it. He was bigger than they were, clumsy and awkward. For a time, they called him Frankenstein and then Lurch after the Adams Family butler.

Then something happened. Teeg kept growing, but he was no longer clumsy and awkward. In seventh grade, a boy called him a name and Teeg calmly knocked all his front teeth out with a single punch he didn't even throw hard. He became a feared force and could have ruled the school, but he chose instead to remain isolated and a loner. Teeg cared little for his appearance and did nothing to change it, not that he could have. Every adolescent pimple he ever received left a scar, and he gave up on acne creams after three tubes failed to help.

What he later came to view as his greatest blessing occurred one dismal night when a jack gave way while he was changing a tire and the wheel crushed his hand. They cut it off at a local hospital, and a few days later a doctor arrived with a catalogue detailing Teeg's choices for prosthetic devices.

Teeg said he wanted a hook.

He had used it many times since to good advantage. It had become his trademark in the select world of the hired assassin. Add to this a hugely muscled frame that towered just three inches under seven feet, and the result was what many referred to as a human monster. Teeg's reputation spread and began to precede him. He was far too recognizable and not very subtle, the hook being his favorite means of dispatch. He had begun to fear that his services were no longer required by anyone when he first met up with the white-haired man.

They had been together off and on ever since, seven years now, Teeg being summoned whenever his skills were required. That turned out to be frequent enough to suit both of them and Teeg was allowed to work any way he chose. The white-haired man knew Teeg better than anyone alive, but Teeg figured it cut the other way as well. The man's white hair gave the illusion of age, but Teeg knew it was due to some sort of chromosomal deficiency, the same one that had made the man's flesh retain its ghostly tint no matter how many hours he sat in the sun.

Still, he tried. Every day when he was in a warm climate, the white-haired man would sit out in the sun, although the effects of its rays on his pallor were minimal at best. He was a big man compared to most and well muscled, although to Teeg, few others seemed either large or strong. He would never dare cross the white-haired man, though, for reasons other than his reputation. Teeg hated the way the man's eyes digested him, analyzing his every motion and action as his mind deciphered whatever report Teeg had come to give. They were deep-set eyes, almost sunken, very light, and somewhat almond-shaped. Eyes, Teeg had often heard, formed the mirror of the soul. If that were the case, he tried not to imagine what lay within the white-haired man, although he was certain that whatever it was held the basis for their fond association.

Today he blessed the fact that the white-haired man's sunglasses were hiding his milky lenses.

"Did Selinas have much time with Jordan?" he asked Teeg suddenly.

"From what I'm told, no. And even if he did, he had uncovered nothing that could harm us."

The white-haired man smiled. "I'm glad I had you make sure the bastard died slow. He betrayed us. Death in itself was not sufficient punishment. He had to suffer."

Teeg flexed his hook. "He suffered."

A cloud rolled before the sun and the white-haired man stripped off his sunglasses. "So, between the time he escaped from the marina and the time he was arrested, we have no idea of Jordan's whereabouts or who he might have spoken with."

"He could not possibly have hurt us."

"What was he doing in Bay Harbor when the police finally found him? That, too, disturbs me. But it is his escape we must concern ourselves with now and the parties behind it. We must proceed on the assumption that he has inherited a guardian angel and we—a fresh enemy."

"Have you informed Europe?" Teeg raised, hoping for the sun's return so the white-haired man would put his glasses back on.

"I will inform them when this Jordan matter is finished and not before. He must be dispatched with all due haste. Our mistakes must be rectified, even if that means the identity of his guardian angel remains a secret." He paused. "Jordan will go to Nassau. He knows that's where it began for his grandmother and thus where it must begin for him." Milky eyes were boring into Teeg's. "And end."

The sun peeked out from the corner of a cloud and shone off the giant's hook. "Consider it done."

Corbano smiled.

CHAPTER 18

DREW ARRIVED IN NASSAU EARLY THURSDAY AFTERNOON. THE rest of his stay in Colombia had been spent with Trelana's people rehearsing the part he was going to play. As *narcotrafficanté* Adam Balazar seeking to continue a thought-to-be discontinued drug smuggling chain, there were things he could and could not do, say and not say.

Drew's cover required the use of commercial flights that seemed forever off schedule. He finally arrived more than six hours late and took a cab from Nassau Airport to the Cable Beach Hotel and Casino. The complex's expanse amazed him. His grandmother's postcards could not do justice to the twin wings containing almost 400 rooms each. Nor could they accurately display the ultramodern sports complex located across the street from the hotel whose facilities could be freely enjoyed by guests. A brief walk of barely fifty yards would place him on the beautiful white-sand beach bordering the hotel, and, of course, its casino was renowned the world over.

It was the pool area, however, that held the greatest interest for Drew, and he planned to head down to it as soon as he had checked in and changed. His pocket held a gold coin that Trelana had instructed him to hand over to the pool attendant as a signal that would set the links in the chain back in place. It was the same signal used by his grandmother in her excursions here. He would be following many of the procedures she had, leading ultimately to the penetration in the

157

line, Trelana's prick in the bag of white powder, that had cost her life.

Drew was given a room on the third floor with a spectacular view of the crisp blue ocean. The corridor was exceptionally long and he passed at least fifty other rooms en route to his own. He noted that such a length might be a problem if a quick exit from the hotel was mandated, but he would have to live with it. Twenty minutes later he stepped out into the pool area, which was only sparsely inhabited. This was not prime season in the Bahamas. Had it been, all chaise longues would have been taken hours earlier.

A tall, thin pool attendant bearing an armful of towels approached with a smile.

"May I pick you out a choice spot, sir?"

Drew fished into the rear pocket of his bathing trunks for the gold coin. "Yes, thank you." And he handed the coin over.

The attendant's eyes widened briefly, then regarded Drew. As fast as it had vanished, his smile returned.

"Right this way," he offered and Drew followed.

The attendant arranged his chaise longue to make sure it was facing the sun and draped a huge towel over it. He handed another to Drew and started to take his leave.

"If there is anything else I can do . . ."

Drew thanked him and sat down. He was all by himself in the back left-hand corner of the pool area. The spot itself was obviously some sort of signal to alert someone to his presence. It was just a question of waiting.

Fortunately, among the supplies Trelana had obtained for him back in Colombia was a tube of suntan cream, which Drew smeared over his face and body. The last thing he could afford now was a sunburn, and he had no idea how long he would have to wait here under the burning sky before someone made contact with him. At last, he settled back and closed his eyes, squeezing his arms against the lounge armrests and trying to look the part of the contented tourist.

He actually dozed off for a while and might have fallen into the deep sleep that had eluded him last night, if a shadow hadn't suddenly blocked out the sun. Drew sat upright quickly, his eyes squinting against the brightness.

A waiter in a white jacket hovered over him holding a tray.

"Sorry to disturb you, sir. But I have your drink." And Drew noticed the frosty Piña Colada perched on his tray.

"But I didn't order one."

"Yes, you did, sir," the waiter told him gently. "The order was called in some minutes ago."

Drew realized he had been stupid not to play along from the beginning. "Yes. I'm sorry. I forgot."

The waiter set the tall drink down on a small wrought iron table within Drew's reach, placing a napkin down first.

"If you'll just sign here, sir."

Drew did and the waiter departed. He realized he was frightfully thirsty and the Piña Colada looked like the perfect solution, in addition to being connected somehow to his eventual contact. Sipping its thick contents through a straw, he noticed the napkin had writing on it; not on the top or bottom, but on one of the inner folds. Drew reached for the napkin and unfolded it. Its message was simple: *Potters Cay. Sunset tonight.*

Drew dabbed at his mouth with the napkin and went back to his drink. Potters Cay was another landmark he remembered his grandmother speaking of frequently. It was one of the must-see attractions of Nassau, a lively, colorful, open-air market located beneath the Paradise Island Bridge. Fresh fruit, fish, and vegetables were available on the Cay in a wide selection. Midday, if the wind was right, the fresh smells passed inland for miles. The Cay was packed with shoppers daily, natives as well as tourists, who came to watch the local fishermen go about their daily ritual of shelling conch. Potters Cay ran perpendicular to the bridge, perhaps a half mile long or a little less. Almost all the shops closed before sunset. It would be emptying out by the time Drew arrived tonight.

He leaned back and finished his drink. There would be no more rest for him now; his mind was at work again. The note on the napkin didn't specify a particular shop on the Cay. That indicated the people he would be meeting already knew what he looked like, who he was. That bothered him. Everywhere he went, someone had the advantage over him. He had to resign himself to that, he supposed. This was their world, after all, not his.

But he was a *narcotrafficanté* and that made him a member.

This time of year, the sun in the Bahamas didn't set until nearly eight o'clock. Drew took a cool shower in his room, trying to reduce the effects of the sun's heat, and dressed casually before heading for Potters Cay. The walk to the Paradise Island Bridge was short, but he wasn't in the mood for it, so he spotted a cab in front of the hotel and had it deposit him near the start.

The lights of Potters Cay loomed beneath the bridge, but not many people were walking it now and few shops were open to serve them. The stands of various sizes were still in place, but their contents had been boxed up and taken away by the proprietors until tomorrow. A few of the more vigorous merchants continued to push their wares, announcing specials in a variety of languages.

Potters Cay, a long, thin island itself, was accessible from the bridge by a dual set of wide steps running down from either side. The steps were often so packed with people they resembled a midtown Manhattan traffic jam, but at this time of day that was hardly the case. Drew strolled to the center of the bridge and descended alone.

The lingering smells of fish, fruit, and vegetables found his nostrils immediately. It was a fresh scent that sent hunger pangs surging through him. With no sure destination in mind, he planned to simply keep on the move. Those who had contacted him by the pool would spot him before too long. Staying on the move made him less conspicuous.

Drew walked up the Cay. Several people moved by him, mostly blacks, which made them natives either closing up shop or coming to make offers for the day's leftover perishables. There were only a few tourists left. The bustling, hectic atmosphere of the Cay during daylight hours vanished once the sun went down. It was almost eerie now and sinister, lined with dark shadows and crevices.

Drew stepped up his pace. Ahead lay a large conch shop where the daily catch was still being sold and a few fishermen continued the process of shelling their mussels. He stood and watched them work, their hands scarred from years of toil with jabbed nets, turning a strangely curved, razor-sharp blade into the conch shell and emerging with a chunk of meat.

Suddenly a black man in a white shirt was standing next to him.

"You enjoy the drink I sent you by the pool this afternoon, captain?" he asked, his eyes never leaving the shelling.

Drew swung and held fast to his calm. "It was refreshing. I owe you one."

"My pleasure, captain."

"I always pay my debts."

The man turned toward him for the first time. The whites of his eyes were yellowy.

"We better talk, captain. I got a place back on the mainland." He hesitated. "That agreeable?"

"Why not?" Drew returned and together they moved to one of the staircases that led up to the bridge.

The man led him back across but then away from Nassau center where his hotel was located to an area dominated by cheaper motels interspersed with shanties occupied by locals. There were several small shops on the streets as well and the man took Drew up to the front door of one.

"In here, captain," he announced, opening the door and leading the way through a darkened gift shop toward another door in the rear.

The man unlocked that door as well to reveal a sparsely furnished apartment. He turned up the wick on a standing kerosene lamp. Obviously the luxury of electricity had not reached this part of Nassau yet, at least for locals.

"My home is yours, captain," the man offered nonetheless and Drew stepped in just after him.

He heard something shuffling to his right an instant before a powerful set of arms that felt like bulging steel bands grabbed him from behind and choked off his air.

"Best not to move, captain," the man said with a smile.

CHAPTER 19

DREW STARTED TO STRUGGLE BUT QUICKLY ABANDONED THE EFFORT. His captor was a good head taller than he and seemed incredibly strong. Escape this way was impossible. And being held at the throat meant every forced motion stole more of his breath away.

The man with the yellow eyes turned up the flame of a second kerosene lamp on what looked like a kitchen table. Two more blacks rose from it and moved to the sides.

"Bring him over here," the yellow-eyed leader instructed.

His captor half dragged, half carried Drew toward the table and plopped him down in a chair. Drew was free for an instant before the giant clamped his head back and held him by the hair. He caught a glimpse of a massive bald dome and shiny white teeth. The giant was obviously enjoying himself, shifting his huge hands laced with scar tissue under Drew's chin and over his head to keep him from moving.

The leader pulled a shelling knife from his pocket. "What you want here, captain?"

Drew detected a note of fear in his voice and seized the advantage. "This is going to cost you," he said as sharply as he could manage.

The leader's yellowy eyes wavered, uncertain. "Who sent you?" he rasped.

Drew stayed silent. Obviously the man was as frightened as he was, but for altogether different reasons. Perhaps with the violent closing of the chain in Florida, he feared for his own life.

162

But a man sent to dispose of him would never have initiated contact with the gold coin. Clearly there was more involved here.

The leader came closer and flashed the shelling knife before him. "I slice you up piece by piece less you talk, captain," he threatened, fear still in his voice. "Who sent you?"

"I used the gold coin; that's all you need to know."

The leader turned up the kerosene lamp on the table beneath him. He pulled it closer to Drew so the light danced madly against the blade he was fondling. "I grew up here as a sheller, captain. Got to the point where I could shell the mussel without even disturbing its overskin. Bet I could do a pretty good job shelling you, less, of course, you start answerin' me straight. What'd they send you down here for?"

It was the leader's use of "they" that formed Drew's response. "Shouldn't I be the one asking the questions?"

The man's features flared and in an instant the blade was pressed against Drew's throat. "I done nothin' wrong! You tell 'em that. I do what I'm supposed to. No need they send you down here. I think maybe I send you back in a box, captain. I think maybe that'll teach 'em good."

"All right, all right," Drew stalled, realizing he would die here unless he found a way out fast. The man was obviously hiding something; his fear proved that much. But Drew would have to uncover what it was later. For now escape was the issue. He needed a weapon. Mercenary camp had taught him that there was always something to be made of nothing. His eyes wandered to the kerosene lamp, his mind flashing like a computer. "I think we've got a misunderstanding," he resumed, feigning submission. "Look, I'll tell you whatever you want, but a drink, I need a drink first. . . ."

The leader motioned to one of the two men who'd been seated at the kitchen table. The man moved to a cupboard and pulled out a bottle and a glass. As he approached the table, Drew saw that it was cheap rum. The man set the bottle and glass down near the leader.

"Drink and then talk, eh, captain?" the leader said, opening the bottle and filling the glass.

Drew nodded and accepted the glass with both hands, not because he needed them but because the motion forced the giant holding him from behind to slacken his grip. He started to sip the rum, eyes sweeping from the bottle to the kerosene lamp and back again. He would have to act fast, incredibly fast.

The head man was smiling again. Drew took a final breath.

His first motion was deceptively simple. A sudden flick with both his wrists covered the bald man behind him with rum, stinging his eyes. By the time the leader grasped what had happened, Drew had kicked out with both feet, spilling the rest of the bottle all over the table. Almost simultaneously, he slapped outward with a now free arm against the kerosene lamp. It keeled over, contents mixing with the rum. Flames leaped outward immediately. A few caught the leader in the chest as he reached to restrain Drew. He fell backward into the table and took it with him to the floor.

But the giant had his bearings again. Drew reached down for the lamp now on the floor and wrapped his fingers around its burning hot handle, then swung it in a narrow arc. Glass cracked against the bald giant's head. Fire spread over his bald dome.

The big man toppled over screaming, colliding with the leader who was fighting to rise after successfully putting out the flames that had caught on his shirt along with the tablecloth. The other two men were in motion now, but the advantage belonged to Drew. One had a gun out, but the confusion rendered it useless and Drew crashed into him without fear. The other tried to trip Drew up as he made for the door, but Drew kicked backward and mashed his nose. Then he was flying back into the night.

Drew knew his escape could easily be short-lived and he didn't bother to celebrate it. His first thought was to make a dash back to his hotel. But the sounds of men setting off in pursuit quickly made him realize that he'd never make it. He was halfway to the Paradise Island Bridge by that point and so he simply continued for it.

Running, he reached the bridge in under two minutes. The pedestrian walkway was deserted and the only light came from a fairly constant stream of crossing cars. He tried for a sprint down the walkway, but his burning chest and lungs denied him the pace he needed. He was almost to the center when the shots crackled through the air, soft pops in the night.

Drew glanced behind him to see the leader and two of his henchmen in pursuit. His foot caught in a loose board and it sent him flying. He hit the wooden walkway hard and nearly lost his wind. Bullets chewed the rails above him. The steps leading down to Potters Cay were just up ahead, his only hope.

Drew kept low to reduce himself as a target. More bullets sailed through the air, all way off. Finally, he reached the steps and charged down to the Cay.

At the bottom he searched frantically for a weapon. His eyes found a nearby decrepit stand on the Cay, its wood rotting. Drew rushed to it and ripped a board free.

Above him footsteps pounded the bridge walkway.

Drew moved back toward the steps, not hesitating. He heard shoes thundering down and raised the board. A face appeared. Drew swung the wood like a baseball bat. It impacted with a thud, followed by a grunt from the already unconscious attacker.

More footsteps slammed down the stairs on the Cay's other side. Drew was already lunging for the downed man's discarded gun when the first shots from the second man pounded his ears. The second attacker was charging toward him now, steadying his aim.

Drew brought the gun up and fired. The first shot was errant and the second merely slowed the man down. Drew fired again. And again. He emptied the whole cylinder, in fact, before the man finally crumbled, firing his last two rounds harmlessly upward.

That left only the leader. Drew swung fast, first left and then right. No sign. Drew started down the center of the Cay.

The yellow-eyed leader would be waiting for him somewhere, the advantage obviously his. Now, however, it was one on one instead of four on one, an unexpected turn. Nor would he have expected Drew to proceed directly down the center of the Cay. This would confuse him, make him hesitate. Another lesson from the weeks spent at the mercenary camp: always do the unexpected.

Drew kept walking, heart lunging forward in his tired chest.

He reached one of the shelling booths and stopped. It was deserted now along with the rest of the Cay, but one of the fishermen had left his shelling knife behind, the mussel oil glinting off the blade in the moonlight. Taking it in his hand, Drew headed on. He could feel the leader close by now. The man must be scared, cursing himself for underestimating his captive. He had to be sure of the kill now, and he would not act until he was. Rashness had cost him already.

Drew came to a break between two of the booths and ducked between them, lowering himself to his knees. He wanted to force the leader to act suddenly, to give himself away.

Headlights coming down the bridge caught the shimmer of something metallic three booths down. The leader's pistol was stainless steel, but the shimmer could have come from any metal object, not necessarily a gun. More headlights flashed. The shimmer was gone, indicating that it must have come from an object that had been moved—very likely the gun. The leader must have been changing his position.

Staying on his knees, Drew crept into the aisle that ran behind the booths and began to crawl with his head low. This denied him inspection of whatever it was he would be facing and created the dreadful possibility that the leader would spot him first.

Drew willed his limbs and joints to stay silent and smooth. He had learned all about the importance of silence at the camp. Silence could make up for various other shortcomings, including inferior position and weapon. A man could only accurately shoot what he could see and not when it was already upon him.

Drew crawled on, almost to the spot of the shimmer.

He was one booth away when he heard one irregular sound and then another. Shoes brushing against dirt perhaps, or a change in a man's breathing cadence. He would have to move blindly. He could not risk returning the advantage to the yellow-eyed leader by trying to better his vantage point.

Drew saw the scuffed heels on a pair of work boots and he knew he had guessed right. He rose and lunged in the same motion, the conch knife tight in his hand.

The leader's turn came much too late. Drew saw the gun coming around and locked his hand on the wrist holding it as he pounded the man's face with an elbow. The man groaned but still tried to fight back, concentrating all his efforts on freeing his gun, which allowed Drew to smash his face with three more hard strikes, rendering him to near unconsciousness. A quick knee to his wrist separated the leader from his gun altogether and then Drew's knife was pressed against his throat just as he had practiced a hundred times.

"Now it's my turn to ask the questions," Drew charged, making sure the man saw the handle of the conch knife. "I don't have to tell you what this is. You're the expert."

The man's yellowy eyes bulged in fear but not surprise, as if he suspected that this was what Drew had come to Nassau for in the first place.

"Doesn't feel too good, does it?" Drew spit out. "It'll get a lot worse unless you talk. I need to get my facts straight. Let's start with the gold coin."

"The women used it, just like you, whenever they came down."

"*Old* women. They hand the gold coin over and then you supply them with cocaine."

The man looked puzzled. "Don't you—"

"Answer my question!"

"Yes, captain, yes. Sixteen shipments, but they weren't all cocaine."

"*What?*"

"Only four, five times maybe they were cocaine all right, but the rest . . ."

"What about the rest?" Drew demanded.

"Those times a few days before the old women arrived, a shipment made it here from Spain. Always by water but never to the same port twice." He hesitated. "It was powder, captain, but it wasn't cocaine."

"How could you know?"

"I . . . kept some two shipments back," the man confessed. "Just a small bag. Never thought it'd be missed. Never meant to—"

"How'd you know it wasn't cocaine?"

The man swallowed hard. "Sold some, captain. Watched a man snort a line right in front of me. Watched him die. Horrible it was, captain, like he exploded from the inside."

Drew looked down at him, confused. *The white powder that wasn't Trelana's also wasn't cocaine.* What was going on? What had his grandmother gotten herself involved in?

"I figured they'd send someone sooner or later, captain. I knew I made a mistake, but there wasn't nothin' I could do about it 'sides hope the bag wasn't missed. Then, when I got word 'bout the gold coin today . . ."

No wonder the man had been terrified of him back in the apartment, Drew reasoned.

"This bag," he started, "do you still have it?"

The man did his best to nod. "Figured I could return it in trade for my life if it came to that. Hid it back in the apartment under the center floor boards lined up with the kitchen table. Let me live and I'll take you to it."

"The grandmothers didn't know there was any . . . difference in the shipments, did they?"

"I didn't tell 'em, captain. I just made delivery when the signal came through all those times. I got no idea what they knew or didn't know."

"Then why—"

It was sudden fear in the man's bulging yellow eyes that made Drew stop and twist in the direction of their gaze. The motion saved his life. A hook flashed by his face and imbedded in the man's midsection. His blood-curdling scream gave way to a gurgling rasp as blood streamed from his mouth.

Drew jumped back. The hook was in motion toward him again.

At first he thought the attacker was wielding it as a hand-held weapon. Then he saw the hook *was* his hand. He dodged to the left and the hook sliced clear through a wooden counter on the Cay.

Teeg yanked his arm upward and swung to stalk his target.

Drew backpedaled, eyes focused on the huge figure before him. He'd thought the man back at the shack was big, but this one was mammoth. The darkness made his features indistinct. There was only the hook.

Teeg lunged forward again, sweeping the hook in a crosscut.

Drew jumped back, but the pointed edge caught his shirt and tore it. A thin line of blood appeared on his flesh and began to widen.

Teeg sensed the kill.

Drew watched the giant raise the hook mightily again before he sent it into a blurring descent. This time Drew ducked to the inside to avoid it, realizing at that instant that he still held the conch knife in his hand. He swung it up quickly, arm climbing at a virtual ninety-degree angle to find the monster's throat.

Teeg caught the flash of motion and whirled his hook upward

in an uncharacteristic move of defense. He was going for the target's wrist, but the soft clang told him he had miscalculated slightly and had clapped his hook against the knife itself.

Drew's wrist stung and he lurched backward. A set of crates tripped him up and he tumbled over them. He looked up to see the hook descending for his throat, and he wrenched his head to the side. The hook imbedded in the floor surface of the Cay.

Drew grabbed for the arm it was attached to with both hands, and in desperation he snapped a foot out at the pitted face leaning over him. The move staggered the monster enough to buy him time to regain his feet. Drew nearly tripped on another crate and grasped it as the huge attacker rushed him once more.

Teeg bellowed as he raised the hook over his head.

Drew tossed the crate into his face.

There was one crash and then another, but Drew didn't let himself turn to see the giant topple. Instead, he ran down the center of Potter's Cay at the best speed he could manage toward the staircases. His plan of escape yet unclear, he nonetheless knew that the Cay offered him nothing but death. He reached the stairs and took them quickly.

Another scream sounded behind him as he neared the top. He felt the hook slice through his shoe and yanked his foot out of it, crawling the rest of the way up to the bridge. He heard the hook clang against steel as he lunged to his feet and raced down the walkway. Immediately the sounds of heavy footsteps reached him. He glanced back and saw the enraged giant coming fast, hook raised and ready. There was no way to escape him on foot. Just one move left to make.

Drew grasped the bridge railing and began to hoist himself over. He heard himself scream when the monster rose over him, hook already into its descent. The hook sliced through his shirt and made a thin tear down his back, but not enough to stop his leap. His wail of agony came as he was airborne, unable now to adjust his position in relation to the water. He smacked it hard, teeth gnashing together, but consciousness thankfully staying with him.

Dazed, he began to paddle his arms in the semblance of a stroke, tense against the knowledge that another *plop* in the water would mean the monster was following and he was finished.

He could see the giant coming up on him from below, like a

hungry shark. But the plop never came and nothing rose from the dark depths. Drew's strokes settled and he turned in the direction of the mainland. Gazing up, he saw that the bridge was deserted. He kept his mind focused on the task before him, but something else tugged at his thoughts: If the white powder the grandmothers had been smuggling wasn't cocaine, then what was it?

PART FIVE:

WHITE POWDER

CHAPTER 20

THE CALL CAME INTO THE TEL AVIV BUILDING AT NOON ON A CLOSED channel that rang directly in Isser's office. The sudden chiming startled the Mossad chief and he reached the receiver.

"Yes?"

"It's Elliana, Isser."

"Ellie, this number, how did you—"

"It doesn't matter. In your office last week you asked me for proof, Isser, proof that the Council of Ten exists. I think I have it."

"Where are you?"

"That doesn't matter either. And I don't plan on staying on this line long enough for anyone to find out. Nothing's safe, Isser, not even where you are. Two men tried to kill me in Prague. They were Mossad."

"What?"

"I don't recall their names. One was bearded. Worked with me on the Libyan rescue. It's all in the files. You'll find that he's disappeared."

"Ellie, you're not making sense."

"Aren't I? Mossad's been infiltrated, Isser. Even our hallowed halls are no longer safe. I'm getting too close to the Council for comfort, so they mobilized. Trace the bearded man's background, his past. There'll be a clue there, some shred that must link him to the Council."

"Then your proof is a rogue agent who tried to kill you. He could just as easily have been sent by me."

"In which case you would have had no reason to let me reach Prague in the first place. But the Council needed my contact there out of the way as well. They had to wait."

"Then come in. Stay under guard while I check this out."

"No, Isser, I'd be playing right into their hands. There's no telling how deep they've penetrated us. I'm safer out here on my own." She paused. "I don't expect you to believe me yet, but check out what I'm saying. Follow the threads. And, for God's sake, do it on your own. Trust no one."

"If I find something, we will back you one hundred percent. But if I don't I will have a dead agent killed admittedly by you. You know what that will mean."

"It won't matter by that time. Believe me, it won't."

Ellie hung up the phone. She had made the call from a post office near Berga the day after leaving Getaria. She knew little about Berga other than the fact that, like many other towns in the northeast of Spain near the French border, it was dominated by the textile industry. Most of the town's 14,000 residents drew their living from the industry in one form or another, and factories of varying sizes and modernity filled out the main streets.

Berga lay at the foot of a mountain landscape known as Queralt Sierra, a steep, multifaced landmark that provided the town with what little fame it enjoyed thanks mostly to the *Nuestra Senora de Queralt*, or Our Lady of Queralt Chapel. The chapel was a huge structure built centuries before and run by nuns. It was constructed more than two-thirds of a mile up the mountain and its backside featured a panoramic view looking down over a wall of rock that even the best climbers claimed made an impossible scale.

Elliana was not interested in such landmarks, however, only in the address Lefleur had provided her back in Getaria. She finally located it in town but well off the main drags. She found it with a mixture of surprise and disappointment.

It was an old textile factory, abandoned and boarded up. She checked the address three times to be sure.

Had Lefleur lied to her about the address those strange shipments had arrived from? No, he had no reason to. Of course, this building could easily have served as a front and nothing more.

Ellie moved to the front door, which was secured by a single sturdy padlock. She fished in her pocket for the proper picks and had the door open in less than thirty seconds. It squeaked loudly as she pushed it to the inside, propping it ajar since the doorway would supply her sole source of light other than what rays were able to sneak through the covered windows.

There wasn't much to see in any case. Empty crates and boxes lay strewn randomly about. There was no machinery, but Ellie could tell from the impressions on the floor and the sagging in certain areas that not too long ago a textile business with all its heavy lathes and other machines had indeed been housed here. Past tense. Her trail stopped at this apparent dead end. The shipments Lefleur had received might have originated here, but, as she had feared, the building was only a front, nothing more than an address.

No, wait. There was something else. *The building, stick with the building*, Ellie urged herself. *The clues lay there.* . . . She paced about the wide factory floor, once manned with workers who sweated and ached for pennies a day. She stepped in and out of the offices where the employers spent the days before whirling fans. A few of the desks were still there, but their drawers contained nothing.

Ellie kept walking about the interior, letting her thoughts roam. Enough light filtered through the boards nailed over the windows to allow for a careful search.

Wait! The windows! Her heart began to beat faster. She was on to something and she knew it. Her memory had stirred. She made a mental photograph of the interior layout of the building and hurried back outside, matching one picture to the other.

There was another forty feet of building *beyond* where the last window seemed to indicate the building ended from the inside. Forty feet hidden behind a false wall and lacking windows. Ellie rushed back inside.

The offices were lined up against what must have been the false wall, and she tried two before the third yielded what she was after. The rear wall was discolored in the shape of a door that a simple shove from her shoulder sent swinging inward.

The smell assaulted Ellie first, a smell of must and mold and rot and gloom from an airless building within a building. There was light, however, from a pair of skylights Ellie hadn't spotted from the outside, and it was more than sufficient to allow for an inspection. She stepped slowly into the inner structure and felt her heart racing with the excitement of discovery.

This part, too, was empty and abandoned. Her eyes adjusted to the dimness and she noticed that this section had been partitioned. The main floor took up the bulk of space, but several smaller quarters of varying sizes had been constructed.

The second smell she noticed as she walked forward made her nose wrinkle slightly. It was a chemical scent for sure, strongest around the partitioned sections, which were complete with counters and supply closets.

What had she discovered? Something else must have been produced here besides textiles or why bother to hide it?

Ellie gazed up at the ceiling and felt her heart pick up even more. Suspended from the rafters were two huge filtration and air-conditioning devices. Ellie had seen them before in large commercial factories and chemical plants, their role being to continually purify the air of toxic gases.

She walked about. If not textiles, then what? Something had been produced in secret, its manufacturers wanting no one to know of its origin or existence. Whatever it was had then been shipped from here to Lefleur in Getaria for transfer to the Bahamas. But what was it? Ellie didn't have a hint. She continued to walk, surveying all that lay around her.

There wasn't much, nothing in fact. She made herself calm, trying to feel with her senses what had been produced here. The strong chemical smell continued to assault her. The room was large, 3,000 square feet perhaps. The possibilities were endless. Anything could have been made within these walls.

No, Ellie thought to herself, not anything. Something to do with chemicals produced and shipped over a long period of time. Lefleur said the shipments had been coming regularly for over four years. And he had indicated clearly that they weren't very large. Why so many shipments spread over such a long period? Moreover, what of their ultimate destination? Ellie felt certain that the Bahamas were just a midpoint, as Getaria had been. The direction, then, was west.

Toward the United States.

Ellie felt frustration nip at her. Those shipments were the key to uncovering the Council of Ten and learning what they were up to. She was so close, yet—

The rustle of the hidden door opening again froze her thoughts. She spun, going for her pistol, but her eyes found the dark figure in the shadows before she could whip it out. The figure raised what must have been a shotgun and steadied itself before her.

"Move and I'll kill you," the figure warned.

The voice was female.

"I know you've got a gun," the woman in the shadows said. "Take it out and drop it on the floor. Slowly. Do it now! I know how to use this."

Elliana started to do just as she was told. She knew this woman was not a professional; no professional had to announce their proficiency. In the darkness from this range, she felt certain that she could quickly gain the advantage. But she sensed there was something she could learn from this woman if she remained calm and did not act rashly.

Her pistol clanged to the floor.

The woman stepped farther into the glimmer provided by the skylights. She held the shotgun tight before her, hands steady.

"I knew you'd come back. I knew they'd send someone," she said.

Ellie saw there was more than rage in her eyes; there was hate. Still she said nothing.

"You've got to make sure no one returns," the woman continued. "You've got to be certain there are no more problems."

She moved forward until she was almost eye-to-eye with Ellie, separated by little more than the barrel length of the shotgun. For an instant, Ellie thought both its chambers were going to be emptied into her midsection.

"I waited for you!" the woman ranted. "I prayed I'd get this chance!"

The fury was plain on her face. Ellie was certain she was going to pull the trigger now, certain enough to force herself into action. The shotgun was her biggest concern and she grasped its double barrels with both hands, forcing it away from her as she lunged toward its bearer. The woman tried to pull it back, which made her midsection an open target and Ellie slammed it with an elbow. The woman groaned, her grip on the shotgun slack enough for Ellie to pull it from her grasp as she ducked behind the woman and knocked her to the floor. She aimed the shotgun right for her face so the woman would make no sudden moves. Fear replaced rage in her eyes.

"Listen to me," Ellie began with surprising calm. "If I were one of those people you speak of, I'd kill you, wouldn't I?"

The woman beneath her made no motion to nod or speak. The answer was obvious.

"I'm not the one you think I am," Ellie continued. "I don't work for whomever it is you think I do." In an instant she had tossed the shotgun aside and jammed her fingers into the woman's throat in a way that made movement agonizing. "I'm not going to kill or hurt you. We're not enemies, do you understand that? I'm going to ease the pressure off your throat now. I have questions for you and I'll answer yours as well."

Without waiting for a response, Ellie released her fingers. The woman made no move to resist further.

"Who did you think I worked for?" Ellie asked her.

"The owners."

"Of the factory?"

The woman shook her head and gazed around her. "No. This."

"The owners were different?"

"It doesn't matter. The factory was just a front."

Ellie noticed the chemical smell again. "For what went on back here, of course. But what was it?"

"I don't know."

"Yet you wanted to kill me," Ellie said. "Why?"

"For revenge." The woman's eyes glazed over with tears. "For my mother."

"She worked here?"

"Yes! Yes!"

"How many others?"

"It fluctuated. Around twenty I'd say, always from this region. But there were others. They looked different, acted different, never spoke with the locals."

"Listen to me," Ellie said gently. "I'm being hunted by the same people who are behind whatever was happening here. My only chance to stay alive is to find them first. You've got no reason to trust me, but I beg you to."

The woman looked up at her.

"I need your help. I've got to find out everything that went on

178

in this building. Much more is at stake here than a few lives. Believe me. Please, is there anything else you know?"

"I've told you everything *I* know. But my mother, she can tell you much more."

"She's still alive?"

The woman nodded. "She lives up on the Queralt Sierra. She was lucky. She only lost her eyes."

CHAPTER 21

QUERALT SIERRA WAS A DECEPTIVE MOUNTAIN. NOT OVERLY HIGH, and flush with lavish greenery, it seemed an ideal place for a leisurely stroll. But the trails were treacherous and difficult to follow for anyone not familiar with the area. A few were set aside for tourists, and there was a single, narrow road that wound its way up to Our Lady of Queralt Chapel.

None of these, however, would be helpful in reaching the old woman's small cabin.

"I'm not even sure she'll speak with you," her daughter warned Ellie. "We may be doing this for nothing."

The daughter's name was Teresa Carvera, but she preferred the American version of Terry, more appropriate since her stylishly short dark hair and softly angled face made her look more like a visitor from the West than a native. She had spent a year in the States as an exchange student, she explained, and planned to return there someday to settle. Her mother's name was Maria and she had spent her entire life in this region. Terry's father had run off when she was an infant, and she had only vague memories of the grandfather who was taken to prison for speaking out against the government a few days short of her sixth birthday and was never seen again.

Ellie's car brought them to the foot of Queralt Sierra and from there it would be a three-hour hike to Maria Carvera's cabin. It was inaccessible from the regular trails, Terry explained. By necessity.

The going was tough right from the start and the night complicated matters even more. Darkness fell while they still had a thousand yards of hard upward ground to cover and neither had brought along a flashlight. The grade was steep and Ellie found herself grasping hold of tree branches to aid her climb. Terry was in the lead and Ellie followed her steps as close as she could. They reached a ridge lined with thick brush and punctuated by sudden gulleys, which made for excellent natural defenses. The uphill grade was less steep but the walking more dangerous with sudden drops into fathomless abysses to be negotiated.

At last Ellie followed Terry's finger to a clearing nestled on a plateau up one last steep grade of rocks. A series of surprisingly tall trees rimmed the plateau beyond which Ellie could make out a small shack all but camouflaged by the underbrush enclosing it. The clearing, moderate as it was, extended straight back forty yards or so, its back resting against the start of another steep incline and its sides bordered by ominous gulleys. They stopped at the edge of the trees before they gave way to the underbrush.

"I will speak to my mother," Terry said and approached the house.

Elliana wrapped her arms about herself. The mountain air was chilly, laced with a brisk wind. She had only a thin jacket, which did little to shield her. To distract herself, she focused on the cabin. It was made of stone and wood, obviously old. But it was well constructed, one floor with a chimney protruding from the roof and gray smoke the color the night had been an hour before sliding from within it.

Terry emerged from the front door slowly. The shotgun she had worn slung by a strap around her shoulders had been discarded.

"My mother will see you," she said. "But she is tired and old and she speaks a Spanish dialect you might not be familiar with. I can translate her words for you, if you wish, or repeat sections you are unable to grasp. Her mind wanders. We will have to put things together as best we can. Come."

Elliana followed Terry inside the cabin. The things she saw first were the dogs; bull mastiffs by the look of them, huge animals with a bite that could sever steel. There were two of them, one on either side of the door, and both eyed her warily as

181

she entered behind Terry. Maria Carvera sat in a wooden chair in the corner close to the fire's warmth. Her frame was withered and frail, thin arms grasping the chair as if to hold onto it for dear life. Her white hair was thin and tied neatly in a bun atop her head.

Elliana moved closer and cringed. The old woman's eyelids were layered with scar tissue and sunken. She didn't try to guess what had been done to her and didn't want to know. The old woman raised her head as if to look at her.

"Bring her here," Maria ordered her daughter in a guttural Spanish that Ellie could follow well enough. "I want to be close to a person not long for this earth."

Terry nodded and Elliana moved to within arm's distance of the old woman.

"You've come about the lab," the old woman said suddenly. "I knew that even before Teresa told me."

"How?"

"Because it was only a matter of time before someone had to come." The old woman turned her head up as if to gaze into Ellie's eyes with her empty sockets. "It'll mean your death, you know."

Ellie turned away from the nonexistent stare. "The laboratory behind the factory, you worked there."

The old woman nodded. "For two of the six years it was in operation, the last two. The pay was very good, best in the area, and I was one of the few with credentials."

"Credentials?"

"In nursing. I understood chemicals, sterile procedures."

"You worked with chemicals?"

"We all did. There were several stations. I learned three different ones in the two years I was there. Why does this interest you?"

"Because I've got to find out what was produced there."

Maria Carvera suddenly thrust her arm out and grabbed Ellie's wrist in a bony grip. "You're strong, I can feel that. But I can also feel your fear."

"And I yours."

"It's old age you feel, girl. Brittle bones ready to give up. But they weren't brittle until four months ago when they did this to me."

"When *who* did this to you?"

"A force more powerful than it wished anyone to know. But I saw, I knew. So they had to take my eyes. I swore revenge on them. I came up here and prayed, knowing that the Lord would send someone to be my salvation." The old woman grasped Ellie's wrist tighter. "You are that salvation."

"Tell me about this force."

The old woman's grizzled features squeezed together. "Ask too many questions and the same fate awaits you. Or a worse one. They meant to kill me, you see. It was two weeks after the factory closed, two weeks after I saw *him* again. I had gone back to work as a volunteer in a hospital near Barcelona. Two men jumped me inside one night. One held me while another pulled out a syringe. I struggled and almost got away. One of them grabbed a bottle of acid from the shelf. I closed my eyes but not in time. . . ." The old woman's voice trailed off, then picked up again. "They did what they could for me, and as soon as I was fit I had someone I could trust take me here. I haven't left the cabin since. How long has it been, four months—five?"

"My God," sighed Ellie.

"He was never present in the lab, girl," Maria Carvera followed. "It was the work of the devil we did, I see that now, the work of the devil himself that cost me my eyes."

"Tell me about the work," Ellie requested.

"We thought it was harmless, ordinary. They told us we were producing a new material that would make fabrics more resistant to stains. It made sense. We had no reason to question."

"And the material?"

"It took a long time to produce, painfully long. Many steps had to be followed, a number of safety precautions observed. Sixty pounds a month produced when we were lucky."

"Sixty pounds of what?"

"Powder. White powder."

"Describe it."

The old woman pulled her hand from Ellie's wrist and ran her fingers together as if she was sifting something through them. "Fine. Granular."

"Like sugar?"

"No, finer. More powdery. Smaller granules. That was one of our purposes, to make the powder fit very precise specifications."

"Whose specifications?"

"The supervisors."

Elliana turned to Terry who spoke before she had a chance to voice her question. "They're nowhere to be found. Believe me, I've tried."

Ellie looked back down at the old woman. "So, you produced this powder and ground it into a specified, consistent form. What went into it?"

"We were never drilled on the chemicals we were working with, only the procedures. The more technical work went on in the smaller rooms. We were never allowed in them."

"And after the powder was completed?"

"It was packaged and shipped out, for testing we were told, though few of us bothered to ask. The process was constant every month. Finish one batch and go to work on another."

Ellie calculated in her head. Sixty pounds or so a month made in the area of seven hundred pounds per year, which made somewhere around three thousand pounds since the lab was in operation. A ton-and-a-half of white powder produced in Berga, then transferred to Getaria for shipment to the Bahamas. What was the Council up to? And where did those transport planes come in, not to mention an apparent invasion?

"We were dismissed six months ago, seven maybe," the old woman was saying. "We were told that the laboratory was being shut down and we were given bonuses. Everything was friendly." She paused and took a deep breath to steady herself. "That's when I saw him again."

"Saw who?"

"A ghost from the past. A man I remember from World War II. A Nazi."

Elliana grew cold as she waited for Maria Carvera to continue.

"So many years ago . . . I was young, barely out of my teens but still a war-trained field nurse. This man was about my same age but already a captain, the boy wonder they called him. He led an offensive against an allied stronghold. The troops fled, leaving their wounded behind for our medical corps." Another deep breath. "The bastard had them all shot."

Ellie tried to put together the old woman's words. She had just linked an ex-Nazi to the white powder produced in Berga and thus, perhaps, to the Council.

"What was his name?" she asked.

"Back then I never knew. Now . . ." The old woman motioned Terry to bring her something from an old chest of drawers. Seconds later, her daughter placed a tattered news clipping in Maria Carvera's lap. "This is from a newspaper I used to read when I had eyes. His picture was on the front page five months ago, a few weeks after I saw him in the back of a car at the lab. He had changed just as I have, but I could not forget his face, not ever!"

The old woman thrust her clipping out at Ellie. She inspected the photograph first and then the caption: Heinrich Goltz, defense minister on the present West German government. An ex-Nazi, somehow in league with the Council of Ten. Incredible!

"You're sure this is the same man?"

"The same face," said Maria Carvera, "but not the same man. He escaped the trials and became someone else. In his seventies by now. Who else might still recognize him? No one. It was left for me to bring him to justice. I went to people. Days later the men came to the hospital."

Ellie gazed at the picture again. The man was smiling, shaking hands in a posed shot. His dome was bald and his light eyes shone even in the black-and-white photo. Heinrich Goltz . . .

"Mrs. Carvera, how many times did you—"

Ellie stopped when the dogs rose to their feet growling, hair standing straight up on their backs. The old woman motioned her to be silent with a sweep of a finger across her parched lips.

"Someone's coming," she whispered.

"I'll go," offered Terry, already starting for the door with shotgun in hand.

Elliana moved to block her path. "No. This is my kind of work, not yours. Stay with your mother. Let me handle it. Besides, I think it was me that drew them here."

"What? How can you know that?"

"It doesn't matter. Just stay here. If I'm right, there'll be several of them. You know these woods well. Once you hear shots, get out. Take your mother and the dogs to the best hiding place you can find. It's your best chance."

"But—"

"I'm going. They won't be expecting an assault right on

them. The element of surprise will work against them. That's *my* best chance.''

Ellie continued toward the door and pulled her pistol from her belt. One clip loaded and other in her pocket—only sixteen shots in all, additional ammunition left in her car at the foot of the mountain. She would have to make the approaching men scatter, that's all. Create confusion in which the troops might fire at each other, and escape using the shots as distraction.

She stepped outside into the cold mountain air and closed the door tight behind her. The night was pitch-black and there was no moon. Good. Darkness would work well as her ally. Ellie lowered her legs into a crouch as she moved, keeping her head even with the level of brush while she approached the trees rimming the lip of the plateau.

Twenty feet later she heard the first footsteps. Two men who were probably mere scouts were coming, bait for her to snap at and reveal her position in the process. The other killers would have as many shots at her as they wanted. No, she would have to take these first two out silently and then rush straight at the rest, maintaining surprise as her greatest ally.

Ellie pulled a long hunting knife from a sheath fastened to her left calf. Hunching behind a thick nest of bushes, she settled to wait. The path up the final incline was narrow, which would force the approaching scouts to walk close to each other. She would need that if her plan was to work.

The footsteps grew louder. Ellie thought of Terry and her mother back in the shack. They would probably be dead, too, if she failed. She wondered how many other deaths had already occurred to protect the secret of the Berga laboratory.

A pair of men emerged on the plateau, pulling themselves up by exposed tree roots. They held automatic weapons and were, as expected, pressed close together. A strategic error. They should have known better. Ellie elected to wait until they passed before she sprang. She figured they would either have to duck or use a free hand to part the branches where she had positioned herself.

The men passed by her, each raising a hand to keep the stubborn wood from their eyes.

Elliana lunged, the men never hearing her. She went for the one closest to her first, looping an arm around his throat to shut off his wind as he crouched slightly. The other man swung and responded just as she had expected. Instead of using his gun right away, he came forward first, enough for Ellie to thrust her knife hard into his midsection with her free hand. As he crumbled, gasping, Ellie joined her second arm to the other man's neck and twisted violently.

The snap seemed as loud as a gunshot. The man stiffened in her grasp and she let him drop to the ground, already in motion to grab the knifed man's machine gun, which was lying on the ground. Scooping it up, she headed off the path and into the brush, keeping low and cutting diagonally across the thick woods toward one of the gulleys. She could probably escape now if she chose such a perilous descent, but that would leave Terry and the old woman totally vulnerable, and this she could not accept.

The rest of the troops appeared over the lip quicker than she had expected. Their precise number was impossible to gauge in the darkness, but there were at least ten and they were well spread out. She could never hope to get all of them with a single burst from her machine gun. Possibly from the rear, though, she would have a chance. Kill them all and then flee down the mountain, eventually to Germany and Heinrich Goltz.

A sudden drop-off on the jagged ground stripped her of her balance. As she was falling, the noise that she created frightened her most of all. Suddenly gunshots split the night air. Orders were shouted, then more shots, closing on her now. *Damn!*

Ellie rolled onto her stomach and fired a burst in the direction of the loudest concentration of rushing footsteps. Screams and thuds sounded as some of her bullets found their mark. But movement was the key now. She had to keep her position a mystery to them, never staying in the same place long enough for them to find her.

Ellie pulled herself back to her feet. One of her ankles, twisted and sore, started to give way and she bit her lip against the pain. The lack of mobility was the last thing she could afford. The fast motions certain to be required of her would now be impossible. In the darkness she had no way of telling how many her initial burst had felled. Probably two at most. That left at least eight, probably more.

Bullets cascaded into a tree just above her head. Ellie ducked and felt her back showered with bark. She ducked behind the trunk and fired a blind series. Again came the sounds of groans and thuds. The night was her ally, always had been. Years ago, so much of her training had been concerned with firing at sounds, rather than sights. It was paying off.

There was a burst of pain to her shoulder and Ellie gasped in agony as she hit the dirt and rolled. More bullets chewed up the ground around her, coming from the side of the tree behind which she had taken refuge. They had her surrounded, boxed in. Her shoulder burned with agony, already stiffening, her fingers soon to be useless. She fired a quick barrage in the direction she was facing. But the shots were errant, one arm not enough to control the gun's powerful kick. She fired another burst behind her and heard the hammer click on an empty chamber.

Then she was in motion, a combination of crawling, running, and dragging herself along through the darkness as the enemy bullets struggled for a bead on her. The pistol was grasped in her hand now, but she didn't dare use it for fear of giving her position away.

It didn't matter. A pair of black boots flashed before her as a man lunged with rifle in hand. She tried to roll, trying for a shot she knew was hopeless, when an ear-wrenching blast stung the night. The black boots were thrust backward through the air. Another man rushed her and before Ellie could get her gun up, his midsection ruptured with another blast and he, too, was airborne.

Ellie swung to her rear. Terry was standing between a pair of trees, shotgun snapped open. Their eyes met and Terry fumbled for another pair of shells to load in the chambers.

Ellie saw the shape appear behind the woman who had saved her life and raised her gun. A bullet stung her wrist from another direction and she watched her pistol go flying as Terry stumbled forward with shots pounding her back, making scarlet exit wounds through her chest and stomach. She pitched over finally as Maria Carvera's dogs rushed into the brush and attacked the man who had killed her.

Elliana felt her wrist join her shoulder in numbness and did her best to flee. She had no gun now and looking for it in the darkness was futile. Escape was her only concern.

There were more shots and horrible wails as the killers descended on the dogs, and still more as another set found the old woman's shack. Ellie had underestimated their number. There were probably dozens more spread through the woods, circling in on her and making escape impossible.

Undaunted, fueled by the incredible reserves called upon by desperation, Ellie found her legs and ran. She kept her head as low as she could, but speed was of the essence now. She would have to rely on the darkness to shield her.

Bullets split the air, tracing her flight, trying to angle themselves with her pace. Ellie changed to a zigzag, confusing the shooters and buying herself as much time as she could.

Suddenly her feet went out from under her. She felt herself falling, realizing she had lost track of her position and the gulley had claimed her. She braced but there was no hard impact, just a continuous roll as she plummeted downward. Pain racked her body and she felt consciousness struggling from her as she finally came to a halt, sprawled on her back beneath the night sky, unable to move.

A pair of twin figures in black appeared over her and Ellie closed her dimming eyes, resigned to death now and just hoping it would come fast.

Then hands were reaching down, probing, as the darkness enveloped her and she submitted to it.

CHAPTER 22

THE TIMBER WOLF WAS BAFFLED. THROUGH THE RIVEROS, THE GRAND-mothers' cocaine had been distributed literally all over the country, thirty different drop points from coast to coast. Such a precise, repetitive pattern could be nothing else but by design, which meant that the powder brought in by the grandmothers received totally different treatment from the rest of Trelana's vast supplies. Apparently, a complete network had been set up just to handle it, with Lantos and the Riveros as key elements.

Yet, none of the points, or few anyway, would normally be associated with cocaine trafficking. Many of the drops were located in small, out-of-the-way towns, which didn't fit the expected profile in the least. The points were so randomly spread across the country that it didn't seem to matter at which one he started. Wayman purchased a portable road atlas and circled all thirty of the drop points on the respective state maps, finding the geographic distribution to be incredible. Something stuck in his head, something that held all thirty together through a common thread, but what was it? He stored the question temporarily and turned his attention to Wapello, Iowa, which he had chosen as his starting point mostly because it seemed the least appropriate of all the ones circled. He headed for Des Moines on Wednesday where he picked up a rental car to take him the rest of the way into Wapello, and hopefully some answers.

The trip was comforting only in that it felt good to be active again, to have purpose. Nagging at him always, though, was the final sequence of events that had set into motion his inevitable withdrawal from the field.

Corbano . . . the White Snake, one of the most successful terrorists for hire anywhere. A man with no delusions of patriotism, cause, or morality whatsoever. He was simply a hired hand. Corbano's trademark was that he was always at the scene of the violent deeds he perpetrated, never trusting the work to subordinates. He was also one of the most elusive men in the world.

The Timber Wolf had followed a string of leads and had traced Corbano to Corsica, specifically to a small inn nestled in the Corsican hills overlooking the sea. He made base at a nearby hotel and waited for his opportunity to get close enough to complete the assignment. He had ample time to call for a backup strike force, but he wanted the White Snake for himself.

It took the Timber Wolf a day and a half to figure out that Corbano was in Corsica to meet with a radical cell of the Red Brigades. That meant something big was being planned and a lot of innocent people would die if it were carried out. The principals met regularly in a cabin located farther up the mountains. Since the Timber Wolf would be working alone, outnumbered, he would have to strike at night.

Wiring the cabin with explosives was not feasible without risking exposure. But going in at night would allow the Timber Wolf to use a portable rocket launcher to obliterate the cabin. Of course, there would be guards posted around the perimeter, and he dispatched four neatly without fuss.

Everything was going like clockwork. The Timber Wolf had been after Corbano for years and savored the moment of releasing the first rocket. He hit the trigger and the rocket sped out from the launcher's barrel with a great *whoooooosssssssh*. As it turned out, the second rocket was not needed, but he fired it anyway. Chips of wood splattered everywhere and flames engulfed what was left of the cabin.

The Timber Wolf knew something was wrong right away. There had been no screams, no flaming bodies projected outward. His heart thudding with uncertainty, he approached the clearing.

The bullets were at once everywhere. The Timber Wolf hit the ground, grasping his Uzi. He sprayed it in the direction of the enemy fire but kept moving. He realized he'd been had, tricked, fallen into a trap like a novice. It was all a setup. Corbano had lured him here. The cabin obviously had a tunnel beneath it that led back into the woods somewhere.

The Timber Wolf had never fought better. Calling upon every skill he knew and plenty he didn't kept him alive against odds that should have been insurmountable. By all reports twenty men had surrounded him—Red Brigades or Corbano's, it didn't matter. It was one of the most incredible battles of its kind ever, adding to and confirming his legend. But the legend didn't mention that it occurred after the fact, meaningless in and of itself.

Wounded and battered, Wayman made it back to his hotel an hour before dawn, collapsing with his wounds until a knock on the door came several hours later. The desk clerk handed him a just-delivered letter. Its contents were simple: *Al Forno school in Rome. Nine this morning. Fuck you, Corbano.*

Wayman had checked his watch. It was nine on the button. Frantically he rushed for the phone, his call reaching Rome seconds too late. The Al Forno School had been leveled to the ground with the ringing of the nine o'clock first period bell. Three hundred students, none over fourteen years of age, would die. Another five hundred injured.

All because he had played right into Corbano's hands, let something become personal when by all definitions it couldn't be. The White Snake had used him from the beginning, used him to keep other authorities off the job because the Timber Wolf was on it, while he planned his latest atrocity.

So, the Timber Wolf pulled out, resigned two weeks later. His blunder had cost too much, and it should have cost him his life as well. Wayman did not feel fortunate to be alive. Everything he was, everything he had been, was over. He knew it wasn't just the one incident, not just Corsica. It was a culmination of all the years he had fought the enemy on his own terms. He had only asked all along that he be allowed to know when he couldn't cut it anymore, limits of the body easily compensated for but limits of the mind not so swiftly made up. It had become personal for him, and the personal was a sign of weakness that created other weaknesses, like predictability, and this he could not afford. So, he withdrew to Florida and did his best to forget that the Timber Wolf ever existed.

But time had caught up with him. *He* had caught up with himself. The legend of Corsica, Wayman reflected. Things were seldom as they seemed.

There was little traffic on the interstate leading from Des Moines to Wapello and the only scenery along the way was rows and fields of grain ripe for harvest. Wapello itself was a small town carved out of simple Americana with three main roads forming a small business center on the outskirts of a classic Iowa farming community, which boasted corn as its major crop.

Wayman picked up a local map at the small post office and followed Route 61 for ten miles before turning west onto a nameless, numberless road that would lead him to the drop address. He was in deep farm country now, even deeper as he turned off onto a dirt road. His car kicked clouds of dust up thick enough almost to obscure the mailbox with the address in question stenciled on it beneath a single name: TUMBLEFIG. The name of the farm's owner obviously. Wayman pulled his car over to the side. There was a white farmhouse set back a bit and beyond it lay a modest farm, six hundred acres perhaps lined with what Wayman judged to be corn. A pair of tractors and other heavy farm machinery were parked before a barn. Cows grazed in the fields beyond.

The Timber Wolf climbed out of the car to stretch. His back ached and his muscles felt stiff.

As he stretched, Wayman looked down and noticed the huge ruts carved into the dirt and rock road. A lot of heavy machinery had been down here for quite a while and not too long ago either. Certainly these impressions were too deep to be explained by the inventory of farm equipment present in the yard, the treadmarks obviously those of massive front loaders and back-hoes. But what would so much heavy machinery be doing in farm country?

His thoughts were interrupted by the emergence of a husky man in denim overalls from the house. A screen door slammed behind him. He was wearing a straw hat and made straight for the largest of the two tractors. Tumblefig, Wayman assumed, ready for his afternoon chores.

The tractor's frame sagged as Tumblefig settled into the seat and gunned the engine, backing up a bit to angle the machine for a direct approach to his fields, plow teeth at the rear ready to be lowered and churned. Wayman kept watching, following the tractor's progress. On two occasions it swerved to avoid something rising out of the ground. Without binoculars Wayman couldn't tell exactly what the things were, but his eyes were sharp enough to identify steel extensions, something like baffles.

His mind registered the incongruity with a slight increase of his pulse. He had been looking for something out of place, something that didn't fit. Perhaps this was it. Clearly he needed a closer look.

Wayman waited until Tumblefig's tractor was a safe distance away before venturing stealthily out onto the farm. He made it easily to the rear of the barn and then covered the distance to the first of the steel extensions from the ground with a quick dash.

It was indeed some sort of baffle, used in either the intake or jettisoning of air, a steel grating over it to guard against unwarranted entry. *But why here?* Such a baffle implied the existence of some sort of underground shelter. It made no sense.

Staying low, using the baffle for cover, Wayman gazed around him. There were at least three more baffles spread over regular intervals across the fields he could see along with something else; something less distinguishable in the dirt and grass but present nonetheless. Wayman was attracted to its presence by the reflecting sun. Still hunching, he made a quick dash for it.

It was a steel hatch, similar to the kind found on submarines! Again, *why here?* Wayman's heart picked up its pace. Yes, there had to be some sort of underground shelter contained beneath this farm. But what could this possibly have to do with the cocaine distributed along Trelana's channel? The answers lay underground.

Wayman pulled a file from his jacket pocket. He knew that such a hatch was constructed under the same principles as a standard door lock, secured by tumblers. He worked the file around the outside until he located the tumblers and then maneuvered it against them, manipulating until the bolt came free. He grabbed the single handhold and lifted, starting to lower himself down before the hatch was all the way up.

Down in the darkness his feet found a ladder and he began to descend, closing and sealing the hatch again. Beneath him was bright, antiseptic light. His feet touched a tile floor. Confused and disoriented, he took about ten steps forward with his back pressed against the wall and reached a huge white corridor that jutted off in two different directions at a right angle.

The air around him should have smelled of damp earth, but instead it was clinically fresh and scented. Obviously this underground structure had its own air supply or at least sophisticated filtration devices; that made sense considering the baffles above. He recalled the prints of the huge construction machinery from the dirt road in front of Tumblefig's land as he started down the empty corridor before him. The scope of what they had undertaken and accomplished was amazing. But for what purpose? What exactly had he uncovered here?

Wayman heard the echoing of his own footsteps against the tile. No other sounds met his ears. A few more yards and he noticed the doors. They were spaced regularly, equidistant. The scope of this construction job amazed and fascinated him. It must have taken years. An underground bunker beneath a simple Iowa farm. He recalled the layout of Tumblefig's land. It was isolated and apart, probably the only farm for miles. Yes, they could have pulled it off.

But that didn't tell him *why*.

Wayman noticed the main corridor was intersected in several places by other hallways, neither as long nor as wide. He was coming up on one when the shuffle of footsteps forced him to backtrack. With nowhere else to go, he tried one of the doors. It gave and the Timber Wolf ducked inside, closing it behind him.

The darkness was total. Wayman waited until the sound of footsteps had passed and then eased the door open to allow light in so he might view the contents of the room he had entered. He frowned in confusion. It was a dormitory of some kind, unmade cots lined one after the other with little room in between. What had he stumbled on here? There were forty beds at least and it seemed reasonable to suspect many more were contained behind the other doors. Yes, he had suspected all along that more than simple cocaine trafficking was involved here, but this? The cocaine was involved somehow, though as merely a part of something much greater. He had to look at it from a different angle to see.

Facilities to house hundreds of people underground. A private air supply. What did it all mean?

The Timber Wolf crept back into the corridor. If answers were going to be found, he had to get out of here. There was no reason to check any more of the doors. Wayman suspected more of the dormitories would lie behind most of them, probably supplies of food and water behind others. The whole place had the feel of a giant, fortified fallout shelter. He shivered at the thought, then dismissed it. Nuclear weapons had nothing to do with what he had uncovered here. They didn't fit the scenario that somehow involved Trelana's cocaine. But something else was clearly involved of potentially comparable catastrophic ramifications. And someone was getting ready to protect themselves from whatever these were.

Which meant someone was preparing to implement . . . *something*.

He had seen enough; he had to get out. A feeling of dread fear filled him. Wayman didn't rush, however. He knew that hatches similar to the one through which he had entered would be scattered throughout the structure.

A sign marked Portal Three with an arrow after it made him swing left down one of the intersecting corridors. He was halfway down it when the soft echo of footsteps found him, coming from the opposite direction. A shadow appeared and then a shape. Wayman froze. If he ran, he'd be made for sure.

He started walking in the opposite direction, ears primed to any change in the cadence of the footsteps behind him.

"Hey!" The shout came before the footsteps had a chance to pick up. "Hey!"

Wayman kept walking at the same pace, walking as if lost in concentration.

"You, stop!"

Footsteps were coming fast now, pounding tile, almost upon him.

"What the hell do you think you're—"

The man had grasped the Timber Wolf at the shoulder and started to yank him around. Wayman went with the motion and entered into it, cracking the guard under the chin as he did. The man's head slammed backward into the wall. The Timber Wolf held his chin still and rammed his skull twice more backward. The guard's eyes glazed and closed.

"Intruder in the bunker! Intruder in the bunker! Sound the alarm!"

The guard halfway down the adjoining corridor had dropped his walkie-talkie and was starting for his rifle when Wayman went into his rush. At the start his plight seemed impossible and was no better when, with the gun sighting on him, he went into a legs-first leap. The resulting collision forced the rifle barrel up as the guard squeezed the trigger and a jagged design of bullets dug chasms out of the ceiling. Wayman landed atop the dazed guard and stripped what remained of his consciousness away with an elbow.

A piercing alarm had begun to sound. The Timber Wolf was back on his feet and charging toward Portal Three. Echoes of footsteps were everywhere when he reached the ladder and started climbing, swinging the hatch open easily when he reached the top.

The grinding sound bubbled his ears. The tractor was coming straight for him, too late for him to duck back down. Wayman pulled himself all the way out from the hatch and rolled, unaware till the last whether he would be crushed or not. The smell of freshly groomed fields and gasoline filled his nostrils. One of the huge tires grazed his shoe. Tumblefig started to bring his tractor around again.

The Timber Wolf had already leaped on the plow attached to the rear, lunging forward onto the main tractor frame. Tumblefig turned just as Wayman cracked him with a kick to the ribs. The farmer was built like iron. The tractor wobbled as the husky farmer turned to meet the assault, a pipe wrench in his hand.

He swung it overhead, but Wayman twisted aside, ramming a rock-hard fist into the big man's soft ribs. A gush of air fled Tumblefig's mouth as he grimaced in pain, flailing out wildly with the pipe wrench.

The tractor was rolling awkwardly toward the woods bordering the farmer's property. The Timber Wolf avoided all his strikes deftly, exchanging each for a slicing punch combination to Tumblefig's face, afraid to take the time needed to draw his gun. The farmer took a half dozen combos before he crumbled over the tractor wheel as it rolled straight for a tree. Wayman heard the collision when he was airborne, the sickening thud of crunching metal forcing his teeth to grind together. He rolled free into the forest as the bullets started up behind him, chewing tree bark as he scampered into the cover of the trees.

In seconds he was sprinting through the woods away from the farmer's land. His car, parked on Tumblefig's private road, was useless to him now. Replacing it wouldn't be a problem, but leaving it, unfortunately, posed an unavoidable one. The road atlas he had marked was hidden beneath the front seat and the men from the shelter would be in possession of it before long. The enemy would then be made aware that he was on to at least a portion of their plan. Other sites like this one would be altered. People would be warned to expect him.

The other distribution points were stored in his memory. Another road atlas in his hand and he'd resume his search for the pattern he knew existed, albeit with much new to consider. Thirty locations scattered across the country from coast to coast. Wayman cringed at the thought that each held an underground shelter like the one he had just left. Who would be taking refuge in them? And, more importantly, what would they be taking refuge from?

The answers, perhaps, would be at his next stop. Bullets still marking him from the rear, the Timber Wolf churned his legs faster through the woods.

CHAPTER 23

"IN PREPARATION FOR OUR LANDING IN MIAMI, PLEASE EXTINGUISH all smoking materials and make sure all seatbacks and tray tables are in their upright, locked positions. . . ."

The view of the night lights surrounding Miami International created a brief surge of security through Drew. He had made it this far. Yet, it meant nothing, for there was still so far to go if the killers of his grandmother were to be brought to justice.

He stowed the small airline bag under the seat before him reluctantly after clutching it close through the duration of the flight, never letting it leave his lap. Inside was the bag of white powder he'd extracted from the apartment in downtown Nassau.

The final minutes prior to landing brought it all back to him, everything since his leap off Paradise Island Bridge had led to a chilling swim to Cable Beach. He reached the sand cold and uncomfortable, shivering from fear as much as the night waters. First, the natives had tried to kill him, then the giant with the hook for a hand. In both cases he had narrowly escaped death. Having time to consider that reality made the fear even worse. He had walked down Cable Beach toward his hotel, longing only for a hot shower and relief from the deep scratches along his back and chest inflicted by the hook. Then reason broke in, the practical considerations of the situation at once before him.

On Potters Cay the yellow-eyed leader had told him that a bag of the white powder was located in the kitchen of his apartment under a set of false floorboards. By tomorrow the apartment

199

would certainly be under watch. He had to act now while the opposition was in disarray if he wanted to obtain the mysterious powder. And the powder had to be the key, he saw that now, the key to everything both he and Trelana were after. There was more than drugs involved here; there had been all along.

Steeling himself to the task, he returned to the run down section of Nassau where the apartment was located. His memory eluded him for a time, but it came back well before panic set in. He located the small shop that formed the apartment front, but waited several minutes before entering, worried that more of the local men, like the bald-headed big one, might be inside. At last he entered with his breath held to find the apartment deserted. It took only a few moments to locate the false floorboards and the bag of powder beneath them.

Of course, the problem then became one of getting off the island. The enemy knew him and where he was staying. They would be watching for him, waiting for him to leave an opening in his strategy they could seize. He needed a plan, a means of safe flight.

The answer came to him with surprising ease. The enemy's only means of picking him up again was waiting for his return to the hotel so, quite simply, he wouldn't go back. He found an all-night shop in downtown Nassau where he purchased a change of shirt, a pair of sandals to replace the shoes useless to him since he'd lost one, bandages and antiseptic for his wounds, and a tote bag to store his white powder. From there he checked into the smallest motel he had passed and left a call for seven A.M.

He called Trelana's contact number before retiring to report that he would be coming in the next day. His instructions were to call again upon arriving in Miami. Plans would be detailed to help him reach safety. The white powder, whatever it was, was not mentioned.

Drew similarly figured that the airports would be under close watch, so he ruled out planes as a means of exit—at least planes that departed from Nassau. Freeport was another matter. The next morning a taxi deposited him at the main Nassau pier where boats were chartered. By eight-thirty A.M. he was settled beneath the hot sun on a pleasure yacht with nine other people bound for Freeport.

It was a long trip but a safe one, and Drew reached Freeport only to make straight for the airport and the next available flight to Miami. It took off just before eight P.M. Finally, he was on his way, his suitcases abandoned at the Cable Beach Hotel since there was no way to safely retrieve them or have them forwarded. He was running short of the cash Trelana had provided him and he hoped that wouldn't begin causing problems as well.

He would be arriving at Miami Airport at a busy enough time to have plenty of other travelers to use for camouflage. In any case there was no way the enemy could watch every flight from every terminal. The first pay phone he saw would be used to reach Trelana's people and then he would be home free.

The flight had proved to be a difficult one. Even though he was physically exhausted, sleep eluded him. He should have felt happy, triumphant. Instead, all he could think of was his grandmother taking a similar flight dozens of times, believing on each of them that her suitcase was full of cocaine when in reality it had been something else that in the end had cost her life. Also haunting him was the fact that he had killed again in Nassau, pumped four bullets into one of the men on Potters Cay. The problem was that it didn't bother him this time, and he felt that it should have. There had been no question of remorse after he killed the man in Too-Jay's; that man had been trying to kill him. The same had been true in Nassau, except that Drew felt nothing for yet another man dead by his hand. Something was changing in him. He could feel it, but he couldn't quite identify it.

Drew passed into the terminal building using the crowd of other passengers to shield him. Many broke off to head for those who had come to greet them and, smiling, Drew pretended to do the same. He never looked back as he followed the arrows directing him toward the baggage claim area and ground transportation. There was a bank of phones up ahead. All the way, he kept his gaze down, afraid to meet the stares of anyone he passed for fear of what their eyes might tell him.

At last he reached the phones. He slid the coins into the proper slots with his flight bag still clutched tight.

"Hello," said a male voice. He wasn't sure if it was the same one he had spoken to from the motel last night or not. The connection then had been poor.

"It's Jordan."

"We've been waiting for your call. Everything's all set. We'll meet you in one hour. Greynolds Park in North Miami. Do you know it?"

"No."

"Then listen. As you enter there's a pond to the right and a straight road leading down to a building. Walk halfway down the road. Across the way, beyond a median and another road, there are woods. We'll have a car parked just within them. It will flash its lights twice. Got that?"

"Sure."

"That's the signal that it's safe to approach. If the lights don't flash, stay away. That's key."

"What about Mr. Trelana? I'd like to speak with him."

The speaker hesitated. "You'll be talking to him from a phone in the car in an hour. It's the best we can do."

Let's hope it's enough, Drew almost said.

The ride to Greynolds Park by cab took longer than expected, at least ten minutes over the alloted hour, with those final minutes nagging at Drew to the point of desperation. What if Trelana's people left the park when he was late? How could he know what to expect from them?

With that question in mind, he had left his flight bag containing the white powder in a locker at Miami International. If all went well, it would be no problem to retrieve it. If all didn't go well . . .

He had the cab leave him at the entrance and strolled past the park name plate inside. The park was built on a downhill grade and Drew was immediately conscious of his shoes making too much noise atop the road, so he moved out onto the center grade of grass. The park was lit by only a few sporadically placed lamps, but the full moon more than made up for that. He could see the stone fence off to his right, which looked out over the pond. To his left beyond another road and large plane of grass lay the woods where Trelana's people, he hoped, still lay in wait. Drew kept walking.

Footsteps somewhere around him made him dive and hug the ground, stilling even his breathing. A figure dressed in dark clothes, features indistinguishable, was walking across the median, head swinging from side to side, obviously looking for something or somebody. Drew stayed as he was, frozen, unsure of what his next move could or should be if the figure spotted him. He could jump up now and signal for help from the car. If they could get to him before the figure— No, that was too risky. Better to bide his time silently.

The figure had reached the other side of the median strip now, halfway between Drew and the expected location of Trelana's car. Damn! But wait. One of the few lights caught the figure's face. It was a boy, late teens probably, in the park for who knew what reason. He was looking for someone, yes, but obviously not Drew. And he was no professional, or he wouldn't have given himself away so easily. Drew relaxed, raised himself into a crouch en route to regaining his feet.

The boy was still walking, across the parallel road into the grass plane fronting the woods. Drew was walking again now, too.

A pair of headlights flashed twice, drawing Drew's attention. The boy saw them and turned toward them, shielding his eyes from their sudden brightness. Still approaching, Drew heard the whine of car doors opening. *They think he's me*, he realized, and picked up his pace.

Then the gunfire began, a pair of staccato bursts accompanied by a series of loud individual reports. Drew froze in his steps. Before him, the boy's body was pitched backward as bullets slammed into him again and again. The body spasmed, jerked.

Drew started to back away as, high beams still on, a limousine came forward out of the trees flanked by gun-toting men on either side. Their handiwork needed to be checked. The muscles in Drew's stomach knotted. One look at the corpse and they would know they had shot the wrong person.

Shot? These were Trelana's men. They were supposed to be on his side. What had gone wrong?

Don't run. Get low and move slow!

Drew turned and obeyed his own command. The limo's high beams found him at the same moment that the gun-wielding men realized their error. There was a shout and the gunfire started up again, this time aimed at him.

Drew turned and ran, all thoughts of a concealed escape vanquished. Car doors slammed and the limo screeched forward with high beams locking on him and guns clacking continuously.

Drew's eyes focused on the stone fence that lay up a grade of turf before him. Beyond it lay the pond and potential safety. No other chance he could see. At least this way the limo couldn't follow him even if the bullets of the men within it could.

The big car was breathing down his neck when he hit the upward grade. The sudden narrowing of the gap must have thrown the shooters' aim off because their bullets came no closer even at this distance. The stone fence was almost within reach.

I'm going to make it, Drew thought.

Then his feet slipped out from under him. He went down and started to slide, the limo roaring closer, just over him, an angry beast ready to pounce.

Drew found his feet, reached up to grab the stone fence, and threw his legs forward in the same instant. The limo's engine shook his ears, revving high and sprewing gas fumes, lunging for him at the last as it raced up the final stretch of the grade.

Drew was airborne an instant before its grill smacked into the stone fence, compressing its front end and sending its passengers hurling about the inside. Pieces of rock spewed outward, plopping into the water even before Drew landed with a splash. The water was shallow, but he managed to avoid injury upon impact with the bottom, more shaken than anything but still possessing enough control to begin a quiet swim toward the other side, doing his best to stay underwater and fighting against the temptation to gaze back.

If any of the gunmen from the limo saw him, he was dead. No sense, then, in considering anything but the warm, murky water before him.

Drew kept swimming.

CHAPTER 24

ELLIANA AWOKE SLOWLY TO THE THROBBING OF HER HEAD. HER mind lagged and she struggled for control over her thoughts and memories.

Men had been chasing her. She'd been shot, had plunged down a deep gulley, and come face to face with her pursuers.

I must be dead, she thought.

But then her eyes cleared and she found a figure robed in black and white standing before the bed in which she rested.

"We were starting to worry about you," said the female figure in Spanish.

"Where am I?"

"Nuestra Senora de Queralt," the figure told her. "Our Lady of Queralt Chapel."

Ellie gazed around her. The walls of the small room were barren. A single table holding a lamp and water dish rested near the bed. A crucifix lay suspended over the heavy oak door. The woman at the foot of the bed was a nun.

"In the woods," Ellie started, forcing the words through her parched mouth. "I remember. I fell and when I looked up, I saw you."

"Not me," the sister corrected. "Three others from our order. I am Sister Catrina. Who are you?"

"Trust me when I say it's better you don't know. You've already endangered yourselves by helping me. That's enough."

"God is with us, child. Our walls serve as sanctuary. Everyone is safe here."

"No, you don't understand. No one is safe, not anywhere. Not from them."

Sister Catrina moved to the night table and began squeezing water from a cold compress. "You've had a terrible experience. You've lost blood and you've suffered a slight concussion. Rest. Relax." And she settled the compress across Ellie's forehead.

"How did the others find me?"

"They were out walking when they heard the shots."

"And they didn't run immediately back here to the chapel?"

"Someone might have been in need, child. Helping those in trouble is the essence of our order."

"Well," said Elliana, "I certainly fit there. What about my wounds?"

"We have all had training as nurses. A bullet passed straight through your shoulder. We've packed and bandaged it. The loss of blood worried us and you're still very pale. Besides numerous cuts and lacerations and bruises, the worst of your injuries was to your ankle—a sprain, we think. We've kept it packed in ice."

"Wait a minute, how long have I been here?"

"Since Thursday night. Today is Saturday."

Ellie sat up quickly and the compress slid down to her chest. "My God, I've lost a whole day. I've got to get out of here."

Sister Catrina restrained her at the shoulders. "Easy, child. You're in no condition to travel."

"They'll know I'm here by now. They could attack any time."

"Attack? Here? Child, what are you saying?"

"You're all in grave danger because of *me*. You've got to get me out of here and erase any evidence of my presence. Please trust me, Sister."

"This is a chapel. Our walls are holy, sacred."

"And soon to be splattered with blood if I'm not out of here quickly. Just get me some clothes. And my gun if you were able to find it."

Sister Catrina seemed unmoved. "If these men are as strong as you say, what chance would you stand against them?"

"I've gotten this far."

"With two good legs and two firm shoulders." Then, "Who are these men?"

"An order, Sister, based in evil instead of holiness. The only deity they worhsip is power and they won't stop until all of it belongs to them."

Sister Catrina looked at her. "You can't make it alone."

"You've done enough for me already. I can't endanger you further."

"We've worked too hard keeping you alive to let you foolishy sacrifice yourself. You must let us help you."

"I suppose you've got a plan worked out as well."

Sister Catrina smiled for the first time. "As a matter of fact, I might."

The scrambled transatlantic phone line could not hide the displeasure in the voice of the leader of the Council of Ten or prevent Corbano from being chilled by its intent.

"Mistakes are not tolerated by us, Mr. Corbano, and you have made far too many."

"Things have happened I couldn't have foreseen."

"None of which could have anything to do with your failure to dispose of Jordan in the park last night."

"I explained that. My men mistook another figure for him. He ran, escaped. But his routes are limited and we are watching them."

"Perhaps that is the same reason you failed to report Jordan's presence in Nassau to us."

"I had no idea he would make contact with your men there. Matters were under control."

"Apparently not. Not then, and not now. I find myself growing tired of your assurances. Meanwhile, Jordan has caught on to the truth of the powder as a result. We believe he is now in possession of a sample of it."

"He knows only what it isn't, not what it is, and only because one of your men in Nassau kept a sample." Corbano paused. "None of us are immune to mistakes. We are limited by the people we retain."

"And I, it seems, am limited to you. After learning that one of those old women had talked and the DEA was going to follow the chain, I decided to wipe it out. That task I gave to you while

I worked on moving up the timetable for Powderkeg. Now, though, I learn that not only is Jordan still at large, but so is the man it was his role to kill.''

"Too-Jay's went off without a hitch."

"Except your man there must have killed a double, leaving Trelana at large. I've listened to the tape of Jordan's phone call last night on the line you placed an override on. He asked about Trelana specifically. Obviously the drug lord is the one who sprung him from jail and sent him to Nassau in the first place."

"They're cut off from each other."

"Only for now. I am concerned over the potential damage a man with Trelana's power could do us even at this juncture."

"I'll get Trelana."

"No, Mr. Corbano, *we'll* get Trelana. You seem to have your hands full with Jordan." The leader paused. "Not to mention this added complication I have just become aware of. A stranger paid a visit to one of our shelters yesterday. He fits the description of one Peter Wayman, better known as the Timber Wolf."

Corbano cringed. "Impossible!"

"Ah, I see you recall the name. An old friend of yours from what I've been told. And also, apparently, a friend of Jordan's."

"When? How?"

"Miami, probably, before the police picked the young man up. It doesn't matter. The point is that the Timber Wolf is involved and has uncovered yet another aspect of Powderkeg. The harm a man of his abilities could do us is immeasurable."

"No, he's just a shell, a shadow. I know. I made him that way."

"Not according to my reports, which indicate he is at the top of his game. Our people are looking for him now, but his involvement in this must be regarded as another failure on your part."

Corbano squeezed his eyes shut. He was not used to reprimand, even less so to the kind of fear that the leader's unwavering voice could generate. His teeth gnashed together. He found himself speechless.

"I am willing to forget about your oversights concerning Trelana and the Timber Wolf," the leader continued. "But only if Jordan is apprehended before further damage can be done. If our efforts to locate Trelana fail, he may be the only one who can help us.''

"I'll get him," promised Corbano.

Drew had gone straight back to Miami Airport after fleeing Greynolds Park. The warm night air dried his clothes well enough to get by and he booked a seat on the next flight bound for Washington, leaving himself barely enough time to retrieve the flight bag containing the white powder from a locker before departure.

With Trelana's forces no longer accessible, he had to reach Pam. She was a biochemist. She could find out for him what the white powder really was. Of course, the FBI or a similar agency could perform this task equally well, but Drew recalled the words of Trelana warning him that the enemy's reach was everywhere; what had happened to the drug lord's own organization proved that much.

Drew was safe only so long as he stayed on the move. He still had no conception of what was really going on, no story anyone would believe, and until he did there was no sense in approaching legitimate authorities of justice. The powder was the key. Learn what it was and he would have a place to start, the evidence to back up his story.

Drew arrived in Washington in the cold hours of Saturday and checked into the Hilton Hotel close to the airport to consider his next move. Pam was only a phone call or short cab ride away, but neither was possible. He had seen enough this past week to be sure that she would be under constant watch with her line tapped. Whatever means he employed to reach Pam could not place her in any danger. That was priority number one. She was the one person left he loved and trusted. He knew her schedule thoroughly and this being Saturday she would spend the day working on her thesis in the George Washington Library. Under watch all the time. Impossible to approach without someone noticing him. There had to be a way. Disguise, perhaps. Ridiculous. They'd make him in a second. Or maybe he could hire a messenger. No again. Too many questions, too much time to prepare, and mostly anywhere he sent Pam to meet him, her tails would not be far behind.

Drew lay atop the covers in the darkness, occasionally passing into an uneasy, brief sleep. He could never remember being so tired, but sleep refused to come. His body ached and throbbed everywhere, twists and turns painful for him. His head pounded. His mind, though, refused to shut down, continuing to ponder, running the same options over and over, inevitably rejecting them.

Pam would arrive at the library, book bag in tow, by ten A.M. What if Drew waited inside for her, in an elevator perhaps, or near her carrel?

He sat up suddenly, mind racing. The carrel Pam worked out of, that was the key! George Washington University reserved a special section in its library for graduate students with carrels set aside to allow them to leave the dozens of necessary books within them. Drew could arrive early, leave a note in Pam's carrel, and be gone long before she arrived. Contact would be initiated. But so much more was required, so much he had to explain to her. Directing her to a phone or a meeting would be to defeat the whole purpose. Any change in her routine, anything that looked out of place would alert the enemy to his presence. Everything had to fit in context.

The answer came to him quickly. It wouldn't be easy to pull off, but it was all he had. The men watching Pam would never know the difference.

Pam saw the envelope as soon as she sat down. It was wedged between two books in her carrel, hidden and yet meant to be seen. Pulling it out, she noticed her name scribbled across the front of the envelope and recognized the handwriting as Drew's, noting that the envelope was part of a local hotel's stationery. She lifted the single sheet of paper and read as quickly as her mind would let her, breath held and eyes widening.

Pam—
There's lots to explain and I can't possibly put it all down here. The whole world seems to be coming apart. We've got to talk, but I'm sure you're being watched and I can't contact you directly. Don't react to what you're reading. Pretend it's just some stray notes. All of this is my fault. I've put you in danger, but I think I can get us both out. Come to my house tonight at eight o'clock. Turn on the

computer and plug in the phone modem. I'll contact you from another terminal and explain everything as best I can. I'd meet you in the house, but I'm sure they're watching that, too. In the meantime, don't do anything out of the ordinary. They're watching you even now. You'll never be able to see them, but they'll see you. I love you.

Drew

As calmly as she could manage, Pam placed the letter on her carrel desk and made some notes on it, pretending it was just a bit of research she had picked up on where she left off. Involuntarily, her eyes wandered to the front and sides. Other graduate students were busy at work, none interested in her. Any of them could be watching, though. She had to keep Drew's warning in mind.

My God, she thought, what does it mean? She had been so worried about him since he had left for Florida. And then the police had come with their questions, informing her that Drew was a murderer. It had been so hard to keep her mind on her work, but it was her only outlet until sense could be made of whatever was going on. Now at least Drew had returned, obviously in desperate trouble.

Pam read the letter again. None of it made any sense, but she was terrified nonetheless. Only Drew could reduce her fear.

And she was the only one who could help Drew.

Elliana had never worn a nun's robes before, so she wasn't sure what they were supposed to fit like. Sister Catrina assured her that she would blend with the others well enough for their weekly descent down the mountain into the village.

Our Lady of Queralt was located at the top of a long winding road. All windows within the ancient building provided a magnificent panorama of the surrounding hills and the town of Berga below, especially from the side of the chapel that opened over a solid wall of rock. In fact, from below the chapel looked to be teetering precariously on the edge of the precipice, in danger of plummeting downward at any instant. Ellie shuddered at the thought that America's plight might well be no different, with the Council of Ten behind it to lend the final shove.

"I don't know how to thank you," Ellie said to Sister Catrina as they moved together into the courtyard.

"Go with God, child. That will be thanks enough."

Ellie found herself shaking her head. "I've committed enough sins for any ten people. Don't waste your prayers on me. I'm not worth God's help."

"Why not let Him decide that?" Sister Catrina returned calmly.

Minutes later, Ellie, in her robes, was flowing in step with a group of a dozen sisters out the huge gate fronting the courtyard and onto the winding road that would lead them to the village. Under Sister Catrina's careful instructions, the nuns made sure Ellie was always in the center of them so her slight limp and pained walk would be virtually unnoticeable. Ellie found herself amazed at how the older sisters were the ones who set the pace, the oldest of all being the spriest. The peaceful existence these women enjoyed provided a marked contrast with her own. To live for so long and be happy, at least content. . . . As they continued their silent trek down the mountain, Ellie thought of how wonderful it would have been to have spent a normal life with David, building a house, raising a family, traveling in peace. All that was gone now, in its place a trail of pained vengeance that marked her pursuit of the men forming the organization that had taken her husband's life. She was close to the Council now, but she felt no satisfaction, only apprehension of where the next step might take her.

Heinrich Goltz, presently a cabinet minister in West Germany, was identified by Maria Carvera as a Nazi. A man with a past he wanted to hide. And a present. Goltz was the strongest connection anyone had ever made to the Council. She had to reach him, interrogate him. She would find a way where none seemed to exist. There were questions that had to be answered. The Council was surfacing. That could only mean their predestined, manifest strike was close. The chain she had followed proved that.

And somehow the white powder was the key. Goltz would tell her how.

Ellie's ankle was a mass of fiery pain by the time they reached the village. Her shoulder hung limply by her side. Moving it in the slightest sent waves of agony through her, but she bit them back, not wanting to attract attention to herself from those she was certain were still watching for her.

Saturday was by far the biggest shopping day in the town of Berga. All the shops along the main streets were crowded with patrons out to buy, or just out. The second stop took the sisters into a clothing store. Following Sister Catrina's plan, Ellie slipped away into one of the dressing rooms and slid out of her robes to reveal a casual dress beneath. A few tosses of her hair and she looked enough like a local to pass at first glance. The sisters who had found her had not retrieved her gun, so the journey would have to be made weaponless.

The bus was due any minute now. It would stop directly in front of the clothing store and Ellie waited inside right up to the instant it squealed to a halt. She slid with a crowd toward it and climbed aboard the bus bound for Cardona.

From there for her it would be Bonn. And Heinrich Goltz.

The Castle of the Moors, *Castello dos Mouros*, had seen much life since its construction in the seventh century. It had also seen much death. Located in the hills of Sintra, a short drive from Lisbon in Portugal, the castle itself was thought to be dead for years. The overgrowth of brambles formed its coffin and the soupy coastal fogs its shroud. The slightest step upon them would force the ancient stone steps to crumble, the castle's only residents seeming to be the birds nesting in the once proud battlements. It was a gloomy place, eerie, avoided by villagers for the haunting sounds of the winds swirling through its ramparts and by tourists for its pervading sense of doom.

The Council of Ten had changed little of this when they decided to make the castle their headquarters. The exterior of the castle had to remain the same so as not to draw attention from the curious. To further assure this, the legend of the ghost of the moors was created. A pair of young lovers seeking to spend a night on the ancient grounds to the castle were never heard from again. So, too, a young boy who had gone up on a dare. And an old man who had simply lost his way. Word spread among the locals that death itself resided in the *Castello dos Mouros*, and being a superstitious lot, the castle ceased to exist for them.

Which was just the way the leader of the Council wanted it.

At nightfall the fogs would roll in, hiding the structure from all sight even under the brightest moon. Occasionally lights were known to flash in one window or another. Few paid attention. No one investigated.

For anyone brave enough to try, the Council had also constructed a number of booby trap and trip devices, a labyrinth of possible death promised at almost every step from every approach. The precautions were necessary. The castle held the base of operations for the most ambitious plans for world domination since the time of Alexander the Great.

A plan known only to the prime Council members as Powderkeg.

All major construction within the castle had been undertaken underground in huge chambers once used as dungeons, torture cells, and prisons. The work had been started a generation before by the original revivers of the Council of Ten, ambitious men who lacked the facilities and resources to attain what they regarded as their destiny. Time passed and in the natural order of things, these men were replaced by others, always forcefully and often violently. For years, the Council found itself plagued by the same problems besetting more legitimate orders.

Until Powderkeg and the man who found it.

The leader of the Council of Ten sat now at the head of a conference table deep within the bowels of the great castle. His chair, he liked to say, was an ancient relic once owned by Alexander himself. Although this could not be confirmed, neither could it be denied. The story held.

Extraordinarily few could grasp the scope of his power or the intricate means he had used to obtain it. Yes, Powderkeg would be the final catalyst that would propel the Council to the genuine status of a world power, but it was the steps leading up to the plan where the true accomplishment, the true genius, lay. The 1960s and 1970s—much of the 1980s as well—had been filled with many groups and men with an obsessive desire to change the system. Mostly they took the role of terrorists, revolutionaries, anarchists fighting small wars they lacked both the capacity and the vision to win. Occasionally small strides would be made. Mostly, however, for every foot they gained, there was a yard lost.

The leader of the Council of Ten had watched such quests with keen interest, especially when a belated and insincere attempt at unity resulted in something amorphously titled the

International Terror Network, something that for all intents existed only in name. Yes, the terrorists had the right idea; they just lacked the resources to carry it out. Still, the attempt awakened thoughts in the Council's leader. In the end what had destroyed the terror network and others like it was a collection of individuals whose own vested interests far outweighed their desire for community. The problem became one of convincing enough men who stood apart but stood with many, that, although they had reason to hate each other, they had even more reason to hate the powers governing the world. Eliminate the chasms of race, culture, and perceived destiny to forge a common goal of achievable ultimate power. Men chosen not so much for whom they led as *that* they led. Men with incredible resources and followings who nonetheless alone could never hope to achieve the sweeping changes mandated for the world and their followers. Link those resources and central organizations together and all obstacles could be overcome. It became a matter of forgetting hostilities long enough to remember ambitions.

On paper it all looked good, ingenious, terrifying. Yet, it still remained for one to bring it all together, one man whose own conviction might overcome collective hate and doubt and channel raw ambition into tangible ends.

The leader of the Council of Ten leaned back in the cold of the castle and smiled. The entire brain center lay around him, and yet none of the other Council members at present had ever even been here. Five days from now they would meet together for the first time, just as Powderkeg was dawning at a time when such petty distractions as their differences might easily be shoved aside. Since they had never met, there had been no time or opportunity for bickering, second guessing, or the type of politics that doomed the terror network before it started. There had merely been individual roles to fill and duties to carry out, all leading toward a whole that was far greater than the sum of those individual parts.

The leader had offered the destruction of the country they loathed the most as their first project. America was the one thing that stood in all their ways, but now out of its ashes the true Council of Ten would rise. The inevitability of that had forged tungsten links out of tenuous ones. Together the

Council of Ten would accomplish what alone its members could only dream of.

The end of America. The birth of a new world power.

All starting in five days.

CHAPTER 25

PAM SWITCHED ON DREW'S APPLE IIe JUST BEFORE EIGHT P.M. Saturday night. She hooked up the telephone modem, fit the telephone receiver into its slot, and sat back to wait. Soon he would make contact with her from another terminal. She would stay here poised before the screen for as long as it took.

Using the computer in his condo was a regular procedure for her, three nights a week at least, so there was no reason to expect undue attention from the men Drew insisted were following her. Additionally, if they had the phones tapped as well, a conversation held by computer would remain undetected. Unless they knew exactly what to watch for, they'd never even know the phone was in use.

Pam wondered what words Drew would send dancing across the black void of her terminal. She had so many questions for him, a horrible sense of dread shadowing them all.

Come on, Drew, make contact!

The Georgetown computer center was a familiar building to Drew. It had changed little since he had left the university, and thankfully the security procedures remained lax. His old college ID, which he had never taken from his wallet, gained him entry past a student security guard and he headed immediately for one of the banks of terminals, specifically the one equipped with telephone modem jacks. The modems provided access to other computers scattered across the university community. Theoretically, without a complex access code it was impossible to contact a computer outside of the loop. But there were ways around this, especially if the call was local in destination. No matter how many fail-safe measures programmers attempted to plug in, it wasn't hard to plug them out.

Saturday night was traditionally slow in the computer center and the terminals equipped with modems were all deserted. Drew sat down behind one, switched the machine on, and punched in the proper access codes. The computer screen sprang to life. A few buttons later and he had initiated the modem procedure. The machine told him it was ready to achieve interface.

Drew dialed his own number into the keyboard.

Pam watched the green letters streak across the terminal board, centering themselves.

DOING ANYTHING SPECIAL TONIGHT, PRETTY LADY?

And she typed:

YES. WORRYING MY ASS OFF. ARE YOU ALL RIGHT?

Drew's answer was immediate.

I'VE BEEN BETTER BUT THINGS COULD BE WORSE.

WHAT HAPPENED IN FLORIDA?

Drew hesitated and ran his hands briefly over his face. Even over computer, there was no simple way to explain it.
He typed:

I CAN'T TELL YOU EVERYTHING NOW. MOST OF IT CENTERS AROUND MY GRANDMOTHER. THEY KILLED HER.

WHO?

LONG STORY.

Drew's screen held those words for ten long seconds until Pam's next question flashed across it.

DID YOU KILL THOSE MEN?

No hesitation:

JUST ONE OF THEM AND ONLY BECAUSE HE TRIED TO KILL ME.

WHAT ABOUT TRELANA?

TRELANA'S NOT DEAD. THE MURDERED MAN WAS A DOUBLE. I'VE MET WITH THE REAL TRELANA. WE'RE ON THE SAME SIDE.

I DON'T UNDERSTAND.

Drew could feel Pam's anxiety even over the line.

WHAT DO THEY SAY TRELANA DOES FOR A LIVING?

REAL ESTATE AND CONSTRUCTION.

NO. HE IS A DRUG LORD. COCAINE MOSTLY.

WHAT DOES THAT HAVE TO DO WITH YOUR GRANDMOTHER?

SHE SMUGGLED FOR HIM. HER AND THREE OTHER OLD LADIES. I WAS MADE TO BELIEVE TRELANA KILLED HER. BUT HE DIDN'T. SOMEONE ELSE DID. THE SAME PEOPLE WHO ARE WATCHING YOU NOW.

A pause and then:

THAT'S CRAZY.

NO. IT MAKES PERFECT SENSE. EXCEPT IT WASN'T REALLY COCAINE THE GRANDMOTHERS WERE SMUGGLING. BUT THAT'S WHAT EVERYONE CON-

CERNED THOUGHT IT WAS, INCLUDING TRELANA HIMSELF.

I'M CONFUSED.

SO AM I. I'VE THOUGHT THIS THING OUT A THOU-SAND TIMES AND I STILL CAN'T MAKE SENSE OF IT. BUT I'VE GOT SOME OF THE WHITE POWDER THAT THE GRANDMOTHERS THOUGHT WAS CO-CAINE. I'VE GOT TO FIND OUT WHAT IT IS. IT'S THE KEY.

KEY TO WHAT?

Now it was Drew's turn to hesitate.

MOSTLY TO FINDING MY GRANDMOTHER'S KILL-ERS BUT ALSO TO KEEPING US ALIVE. SHE WAS USED. I WAS USED. TRELANA WAS USED. LOTS OF OTHERS TOO.

WHY NOT GO TO THE POLICE?

IT'S NOT SAFE. THE ENEMY IS EVERYWHERE. THEY TRIED TO KILL ME IN NASSAU.

WHAT WERE YOU DOING IN NASSAU?

FOLLOWING THE POWDER'S TRAIL. EVERYONE WHO'S TOUCHED IT SEEMS TO BE DEAD. A POW-ERFUL FORCE IS BEHIND ALL THIS AND THE POW-DER IS OUR ONLY WAY TO FIND OUT WHO THEY ARE AND WHAT'S GOING ON.

OUR???????????????????

I NEED YOUR HELP TO ANALYZE IT.

DIFFICULT SINCE WE CAN'T MEET.

I CAN GET YOU THE POWDER. THERE'S A WAY.

YOU SAID THERE WERE MEN WATCHING ME.

ALL THE TIME. PROFESSIONALS FOR SURE.

THEN HOW?

I'VE GOT IT FIGURED. WHAT IS THE BUSIEST TIME IN THE LIBRARY TOMORROW?

EARLY AFTERNOON.

ONE O'CLOCK?

YES.

GOOD. GET THERE MUCH EARLIER. MAKE SURE YOU STEP INTO THE LEFT-HAND ELEVATOR BE-TWEEN 12:59 AND 1:00 EXACTLY. UNDERSTAND?

YES. WHY?

THE TIMING IS CRUCIAL. YOU'LL SEE WHY TOMOR-ROW.

I GUESS WE SHOULD SYNCHRONIZE OUR WATCHES.

Pam tried to quip, but humor traveled poorly over computer lines.

NOT A BAD IDEA.

YOU'LL BRING ME THE POWDER.

ONLY IF YOU'RE SURE YOU STAND A CHANCE OF FIGURING OUT WHAT IT IS.

WITH AN M.A. IN CHEMISTRY, I'VE WASTED A LOT OF MONEY IF I CAN'T.

Total silence filled the small cubicle in which he was perched, and Drew found himself missing the click-clack of the terminal keys. He waited for Pam to say something, mostly because he could think of nothing else to say himself.

She typed: I LOVE YOU, DREW.

I LOVE YOU TOO.

The hours of sitting before her carrel Sunday morning proved agonizing for Pam. There was no way she could concentrate on her work, and yet she had to appear to be doing so to make sure the men watching her did not become suspicious. She gazed at open books mindlessly, turning pages and jotting down senseless notes at regular enough intervals.

Finally, 12:30 came. Less than a half hour to go, but these minutes promised to be the most agonizing of all. They passed with dreadful slowness, each second on her digital watch seeming to take a minute. At last it was 12:55, her instructions from Drew explicitly directing her to enter the left-hand elevator within five minutes. Soon he would hand over the mysterious white powder. They would have time to talk, he promised, thanks to distraction.

What distraction?

Pam **started** for the elevator bank. She had timed the walk from her carrel precisely upon arriving that morning. Not too fast and not too slow. Do nothing that makes them suspicious. . . .

She pressed the down arrow with her left hand, book bag held tightly in her right.

Wait for the left-hand compartment.

The one on the right opened. She ignored it, pretending to drop her book bag. She bent to retrieve its contents as the elevator's doors closed. Rising, she pressed the down arrow again and stole a glance at her watch: 12:59 and thirty seconds.

Oh God, hurry!

A bell toned and the down arrow flashed over the left-hand compartment. The door slid open and Pam stepped in. The doors had only closed halfway again when she noticed Drew pressed up against the front with his frame covering the number board. A finger was perched across his lips—silence. The elevator began its descent.

Suddenly there was a grind and a squeal. The compartment throbbed to a halt, shaking Pam against the wall. The lights died. One red bulb flashed on, providing the illumination.

"Drew!" she gasped.

He found her and held her. "Don't worry," he whispered. "It's all right. This is my distraction."

"What?"

"I paid someone to cut power to the elevators at exactly one o'clock. We've only got three minutes."

Pam gazed into Drew's eyes through the dull red light and hugged him tight.

"I'm so damned scared."

"So am I." And he eased her gently away from him. "We haven't got much time."

Drew stepped back and reached into his flight bag, extracting a thick clear plastic bag packed with fine white powder.

"Cocaine," Pam muttered.

"That's only what it's supposed to be. Like I said. Can you get into the lab tonight?"

"Sure. I've got my entry card. I go there lots of nights."

"Perfect," he said, squeezing the package into her book bag. "Make sure you don't get caught with this," he added with a smile. "Might be hard to explain."

Despite herself, Pam smiled, too. "God, I've missed you."

"It's almost over. Once we know what the powder is, the authorities will have to listen to me, to *everything* I say. It's my insurance policy against—" He stopped abruptly.

"Against what?"

"We haven't got time."

"Answer my question."

Drew sighed. "They tried to kill me in Miami after I got in from the Bahamas."

"Oh God . . . Drew, let's take the powder to the police. *Please.*"

"No, you don't understand. They can get to me there. I'd be a sitting duck. That was the plan when I was in Miami the first time. Trelana told me so."

"You're not making sense!"

"It's the best I can do." He hesitated, easing his hands back over her shoulders. "I'm going to give you a telephone number. You'll have to memorize it. When you've figured out what the powder is, call the number from the lab. I'll be waiting all night."

"Then what?"

"I'll meet you inside to get the powder back."

"But how will you get in?"

"There's a rear service entrance that leads into a cellar. Always locked but easily picked. I know the building. I studied it this morning."

"Christ . . ."

"We'll need a code," Drew continued. "A way you can warn me you're in trouble when you call."

"Something I say, you mean?"

"No, something you *don't* say. Added words would only raise the suspicions of whoever's watching or listening." He thought briefly. "If everything's okay and it's safe for me to come, say 'I love you' at the end. If it's not safe, leave it out."

"Simple enough."

"One more thing, whatever this stuff is, I've got a pretty good idea that it's dangerous. Use extreme caution."

"Our isolation lab's one of the best in the country. And I'll use the Hands." She looked at him closely, red emergency lighting giving his face a strange tinge. "Drew, you . . ."

Pam stopped because she didn't know what to say. She wanted to tell him that he had changed, that he wasn't the same person who had left for Florida what seemed such a short time before. Yes, he'd been through a lot and looked ragged because of it. But Pam felt sleep and rest could do little to ease the problem, for it extended much deeper.

"Hold me," she said.

And Drew did. Then the lights flashed on again and the compartment jolted back into its descent. The lights, however, made little difference. Pam still felt as if she were held in the arms of a stranger.

"An elevator, you say?" Teeg rasped, stroking his chin with his hook.

Corbano nodded. It was cloudy in Miami and these were the days he hated most of all. A biting wind had come up and rain was in the forecast. Nevertheless, he had stubbornly spent the day out by the pool, hoping to coax whatever rays he could through the clouds.

"As near as we can figure," he told Teeg. "Presumably Jordan used the opportunity to slip his girl friend the powder. Convenient that she's working on her doctorate in chemistry."

"For Jordan as well as us," added Teeg. "More for us."

"We might have had Jordan in the library, but he must have emerged on a different floor than the girl. We didn't have enough people there to cover everything. Of course, we could move on the girl now, but that would net us only the powder.

We must have Jordan, too, and she's our best chance to get him.'' Corbano's eyes said the rest for him.

Teeg rose from the lounge chair. ''I'll call you from Washington.''

CHAPTER 26

PAM APPROACHED THE CHEMISTRY BUILDING JUST AFTER ELEVEN o'clock Sunday night. Officially at such an hour the building was closed, even graduate students prohibited from entry. But for those with a rare electronic access card, entry could not be denied no matter what the time. Careful not to appear interested in the sights and sounds around her, Pam climbed the steps and inserted her card into the slot. A red light flashed and the front glass door swung mechanically open. Book bag in hand, Pam closed it behind her and headed for the main laboratory.

The lighting in the corridors was minimal, and she didn't want to attract undue attention from George Washington security by flicking switches needlessly. She knew this building well enough for the lighting to suit her. The silence was deadliest of all, broken only by the clicking of her boot heels against the hard floor.

Pam repeated the card insertion process when she reached the main laboratory and waited until the door was safely closed behind her before she activated the main overhead lighting. Since the lab had no windows, there was no reason to fear that her actions would be noticed from the outside.

The fluorescents illuminated a huge display of dials and gauges, of computer terminals and controls, centered primarily against the wall directly across from the entrance. The other walls were lined with various monitors, CRTs, and ever-whirling memory banks. Since the sensitive experiments carried out here often employed a large risk factor, the main lab was actually composed of two rooms linked electronically and visually. Pam approached the main console in the control room and flicked a switch.

The wall before her parted like curtains to reveal a ten-foot-high window of foot-thick glass looking into the inner lab where the experiments were actually carried out. The glass ran from waist level to within a foot of the ceiling to permit ample visual access of all that was about to transpire. Another two switches and the lighting within the inner lab sprang to life.

The inner lab at first glance looked far more simple than the control room. A series of white lab tables were scattered throughout, the largest directly in the center. The far wall contained neatly stacked shelves of various chemicals more commonly associated with such a lab, while the left side wall was lined with covered cubicles housing a variety of lab animals. Pam hated using animals for her experiments, avoided it at all costs, but tonight was an exception. Her only consolation was that whatever happened within, the airtight seal would keep her safe in the outer lab.

The inner lab was accessible from the control room in only two ways. The first and most obvious was a heavy, steel-reenforced door eight feet to the left of the control board. The second was a small slot just to her right built into the console. She opened the slot and drew out a drawer that once closed was accessible only from the inner lab. Next, with calm reserve, she lifted the plastic bag full of the mysterious white powder and placed it in the drawer, slid the drawer inward, and finally made sure the slot was locked firmly in place.

Next she turned back to the control board and activated the Hands. The soft whirl of machines was comforting. Her CRT screen flashed the word READY, and inside the inner lab the Hands sprang to life. They were part of an incredibly complex piece of machinery, the Hands themselves (pincers actually) being the simplest mechanism to understand. They were extended from arms made from steel bands, which were surprisingly supple thanks to sockets modeled after human joints. They were maneuverable as well due to long, similarly agile attachments extending from the ceiling, which permitted the Hands range of the entire lab.

Using the central joystick, Pam lowered the mechanism to the proper height over the white experiment table and twisted a second, smaller joystick about so that the right Hand slid out in the direction of the drawer in which she had placed the powder. Of all the abilities of the Hands, perhaps their greatest was the range of being able to exert tremendous pressure when called upon while being agile enough to handle a single grain of sand.

Pam had been sorely uncomfortable using them at first. The precise maneuvers made to look simple by experts defied her for months. She had realized on her own what the problem was: she had been trying to work the Hands instead of considering them an extension of herself. Relax and just make them a part of you. . . .

Within weeks, the Hands became her specialty. The men she had once sought advice from were coming to her for it.

Pam moved her right hand under the table and fit it into what felt like a glove, which served as control for the pincers. Other mechanisms had been employed, but never with any success. People seemed to manipulate artificial hands best when using their own as guides. Pam opened the pincers, used the joystick to ease the arm forward in line with the bag, and closed the pincers gently over the top of the bag without disturbing the powder. Wasting no time, she had the pincers lift the bag from the drawer and place it gently on the main table five yards back. She held it there as she switched control over to the left pincer, easing it to the top of the bag. She let up the pressure inside the glove for more supple control and opened the seal. Both pincers were in position now and both her hands were inserted into the gloves to control them.

The extension process had truly begun.

As the left Hand retreated for a lab slide, the right gently pried the bag open, poked inside, and came out with a small sample of the powder, which was then agilely placed on the slide. Pam maneuvered the left pincer to the slot running to the electron microscope, treated the slide upon it properly with the right, and then moved both pincers away. She turned her attention at that point to the computer terminal on the main console, ordering up the proper program for a chemical analysis of the material.

Seconds later, a model of the material's molecular structure appeared on the screen. Within the helix, the computer analyzed and properly broke down the chemical composition of the powder. Pam felt her neck stiffen as she leaned forward to read.

The powder's base was a simple paste ground into its present form. The active chemical ingredients puzzled her for their simplicity. She had seen all of them before but never in such a bizarre combination. She searched her broad academic mind for a reasonable match out of a textbook, but nothing came to her. Then she asked the computer to check if such a chemical composition was on record anywhere.

NEGATIVE. SORRY.

She told the computer next to speculate on what such a formula might be utilized for.

INSUFFICIENT DATA. SORRY AGAIN.

A few keys later and she had instructed the machine to crossmatch this composition as closely as possible with any currently known or in production. She was trying to get a feel for what she was dealing with, perhaps uncover a clue as to how best to proceed. A few seconds passed. A good sign. At last the computer sprang to life again, its green message darting across the terminal screen.

MATCH FOUND. LIKENESS 3.5%. CHEMICAL FOR-MULA COMPOSING HELON. NO OTHER LIKENESS MATCH FOUND OF MEASURABLE PERCENTAGE.

Pam asked the computer to tell her what Helon was. The terminal spit out line after line, but only the last few were of interest to her.

SUCCESSFULLY DEVELOPED FOR USE IN FOAM FORMS OF CHEMICAL FIRE FIGHTING AGENTS. NOTED FOR SUCCESSFULLY INTERRUPTING CHAIN OF BURNING PROCESS.

Pam leaned back, confused. A match likeness so small as this meant little, in this case simply that both compositions had something to do with air and oxygen. It could have been anything, but the business about interrupting the chain of burning disturbed her. Clearly, though, easy identification by the computer had been denied. That meant it was time to identify the powder by characteristics instead of compositions. The battery of tests was standard, an order she had followed a thousand times.

She started to turn back to the Hands when something else occurred to her. Drew had warned her that the powder might be dangerous to work with. Maybe the computer could help her yet. She swung again toward the terminal.

REQUEST INFORMATION ON TOXICITY LEVEL OF COMPOSITION X.

In her mind she could hear the computer tapes whirling. The answer came quickly.

COMPOSITION UNKNOWN.

SPECULATE.

Pam knew the computer could respond only to specific commands.

TOXICITY LEVEL OF COMPOSITION X 98%.

Pam's eyes widened. A chill crept up her spine. The powder was pure poison, incredibly potent. But how? It didn't seem possible. With a toxicity level of ninety-eight percent, a cheap plastic bag could have done little to contain its properties. Unless . . .

Pam went back to the terminal, fighting to still the slight trembling in her fingers.

Wanting to know if the formula was toxic to the touch, taste, breath, or what, Pam told the machine:

SPECIFY TOXICITY.

INSUFFICIENT DATA.

SPECULATE.

INSUFFICIENT DATA.

The lack of an answer actually provided one. If the powder's toxicity could not be specified in its present state, then it had to be mixed with something else before the toxic properties were attained. Again, there was a procedure to follow, especially since the evidence already pointed to toxic transmission by air.

Pam moved to the Hands once more after depositing the slide in an isolation drawer. She maneuvered them back to the main table, reaching under it with one for a glass case about the size of a shoe box. After placing it on the table, she manipulated the other Hand to a darkened wall where the strike of a light switch revealed a selection of laboratory animals. Using the right Hand, Ellie opened one of the cages and withdrew a glass case containing a rat. She rested the case atop the table and fitted a plastic tubing into it through a tailored slot, attaching the other side into the now empty "shoe box" glass case.

She paused for a second to mop her brow and then extracted a small sample of the powder with the left Hand holding a scoop. She slid the glass cover into place and snapped a smaller plastic tube through a hole in its top. This tube connected to a vacuum tank the Hands were fitted for whereby substances could be induced through the tube into the glass case without releasing anything into the air. This was crucial, especially in experiments with potentially toxic or unknown substances, whose potency was unknown.

Such was the case here and Pam could afford to take no chances. Again procedure. Her eyes found the rat scratching at his glass walls and sniffing furiously, obviously agitated. She used the left Hand to open the passageway into his home so that the air contained in the second glass case could travel into his. Then she hit the proper sequence on the computer terminal, so the screen would display exactly what the rat was feeling through a CAT scan-like monitor. The technology of it all never ceased to amaze her.

Pam waited, alternating her eyes between the rat and its

outline dancing across the computer screen. Nothing. Her suspicions were confirmed. In its natural state, the white powder was harmless. The problem now became one of identifying what additive turned the powder hostile, a process that could take weeks or months, never mind a night.

In the end it took hardly any time at all.

The true scientist sticks to established procedure and when searching for the proper additive, established procedure was precise on where to start. Pam turned her attention to the right Hand, which was still inserted into the vacuum tank, and used it to pour an amount of a colorless liquid down the tubing. Almost immediately, the liquid joined with a portion of the white powder, diluting it.

The inner lab's microphone broadcast a slight hissing sound. Pam gazed at the video display on the monitor to her left, but she saw nothing where she expected to see a gas forming.

The computer began to beep, alerting her to the action unfolding on the terminal screen. Pam looked at it, eyes incredulous, bulging at what the screen revealed. She shifted her stare to the rat, back to the terminal, then to the rat once more.

The animal was dying horribly, eyes bulging as its nails scratched futilely at the glass encasing it. Seconds later it lay dead on its side.

Shuddering, Pam made herself watch three different, graphically enhanced computer analyses of the rat's death, each making her grow progressively colder. The third was the most terrifying because it visually depicted the *exact* process that had led to the rat's death.

No! Impossible! No substance could—

She ran the analysis again. The rat had indeed suffocated, died for lack of oxygen to breathe within its glass tomb. The oxygen had been swallowed up by the white powder in gaseous form once she had dissolved it with the most common element of all: water.

The computer had drawn a probability likeness to the chemical helon, used in fighting fires because of a chemical structure that interrupted the chain of the burning process. Now she knew why.

What Drew had stumbled upon here was worse than anything he could have imagined. How much of this powder had his grandmother and the other women smuggled into the country? She tried to estimate the figure in her mind, gave up, and turned to the computer.

SPECULATE ON PERIMETERS OF TOXICITY SPREAD OF CURRENT ACTIVE SAMPLE OF COMPOSITION X.

A fifth of a gram, she reminded herself, as the computer searched for a response. At last it came, terrifying in its simplicity.

26.5 SQUARE MILES.

From only a fifth of a gram! Pam felt she might pass out. She had to call Drew. Yes, they would meet here and go straight to the FBI, State Department, even the White House if that's what it took. She had the proof he needed to support his incredible story. And more.

Pam reached for the phone, searching her mind for the number she was supposed to dial, and began pressing out the digits.

The cold steel found her throat at the same time a huge hand stripped the receiver from her. She swung quickly, a scream starting in her throat only to be choked off by the steel against it, and looked up into the most hideous face she had ever seen.

Teeg smiled.

The pay phone rang finally just after two A.M. Drew grabbed it before the first ring was even complete.

"Pam!"

"It's me."

"Are you finished? Did you find anything out?"

"Yes. Plenty."

"Hang on. I'll be right over."

"Hurry, Drew. I'm scared. Oh God, I'm scared."

"But you're all right."

"I don't want to be here alone. Hurry, please hurry!"

"I'm not far away. Just give me a few minutes."

"Hurry," Pam said and the line went dead.

She had found the answer. The mystery of the white powder

his grandmother had spent nearly five years smuggling was about to be solved.

Drew felt relieved, elated. And then the elation vanished.

Pam hadn't said "I love you."

She thought at first that the giant was holding a strangely shaped knife at her throat. Then she realized it was actually his *hand* or, more accurately, what he wore in place of it.

"You were very good," Teeg told her.

Two other men, both smaller and neither as ugly, had entered the lab and were carefully planting what must have been explosives.

"After we're finished with the two of you, it will look like an accident," the giant told her, fingering a black detonator.

Drew reached the door through which he planned to enter the building out of breath and far too noisily. It didn't matter.

Pam was all that mattered.

He had met her enough in this building to be familiar with its layout, right up to the location of the main lab within. The problem was entry into that lab. There must be just one door and no windows. Almost certainly there were ventilation shafts he could use, but he didn't have the time to search for them, and neither did Pam.

The rear service entrance to the building was just as he had left it that morning. They had taught him how to pick most any lock during his stays at the mercenary camp, neither a complicated nor difficult practice if one had the right tools. The darkness lengthened it a bit, but he was inside within two minutes, making a rapid pace down the long angular corridors in the dim light, stopping only once at the door with the familiar logo denoting hazardous materials etched on it.

Pam was their bait. They couldn't risk killing her until they had him. This gave Drew reason for hope, although not much. His only weapon now was a glass bottle gripped in his right hand. It would work nicely on one man, but he fully expected to find more than that within the lab.

He swung onto the corridor leading to the main lab. He had to know she was all right, had to be sure. A little farther on, he stopped.

"Pam," he called out softly. "I'm lost. Am I getting close?"

"Three doors down on the right. I left the door open for you."

Drew swallowed hard. He was almost surely walking to his death unless he could find more than just a single glass jar to use as a weapon. His eyes swept the corridor and locked with something on the wall. Taking as much air in as he could force down, he moved toward it.

With the giant's hook pressed firmly against her throat, Pam could hear the echo of Drew's steps growing louder. She wanted to shout a warning, but reason kept her words down. She had given him the proper signal over the phone. He knew what he was walking into and even if he didn't, to scream now would be to guarantee her own death and his as well. She had to trust him, biting her lip to make sure she stayed silent.

His footsteps slowed, almost to the door.

"God, I had an awful night," she heard him sigh. If only she could warn him about the giant's two henchmen poised on opposite sides of the lab with their guns drawn.

Drew's shadow crossed into the room. Pam opened her mouth to scream with all her restraint gone.

Then suddenly she was blinded by a white haze that filled the room and blotted out all vision.

Drew had pictured her exact location from her voice and aimed the ultrapowerful fire extinguisher in that direction because that was where he expected her captors to be. Because chemical fires are the most difficult to put out, the building was equipped with a number of extinguishers that produced white foamy jets of incredible range and scope.

Teeg was blinded by the first assault as Drew continued his sweep. He knew immediately that Pam's other captors were spaced apart and swung the extinguisher around, hoping its jets would move faster than their bullets. A barrage of automatic fire from the right was wild and Drew knew the foam had done its job there. He felt its last spurt emerge as he swung to the left and felt something hot burn into his side and spin him around. The spin was fortunate in a way, for it saved him from the bullet that otherwise would have struck him squarely in the forehead. He felt a graze that singed his side, desperation the only thing that kept him from losing consciousness.

His assailant charged at him, angling his pistol for a better shot. The empty extinguisher rolled awkwardly across the floor, and Drew yanked the bottle of clear liquid from his belt and popped the cork top off, flinging the contents forward as the man steadied his gun.

The bullet flew hopelessly errant as the acid compound burned into the man's face and eyes. He staggered backward, wailing horribly and clutching his burning face.

But the issue seemed only delayed, because a giant whom Drew recognized as the man with the hook in Nassau was charging him, and out of the corner of his eye Drew saw the foam-covered man steadying his machine gun once more.

There was a flash of motion and Drew realized it was Pam charging into the gun-wielding man just as he was about to fire. His burst cut a jagged line across the room, punching holes in the computer data banks, smoke and sparks rising with the smell of burnt wires.

The man tried to right his aim, but Pam was all over him. She was big for a girl and always a great athlete. She screamed as she tore at him, clubbing, striking, and scratching, forgetting about the machine gun for now.

Teeg rushed at Drew with his hook raised. Drew saw it start into its descent and twisted sideways from its path. He then came in under the giant, trying to knock him off balance with as much of a blow as he could muster. The best he was able to manage was to send both of them reeling headlong toward the heavy door leading into the inner lab.

The black detonator slid across the floor of the outer lab.

The force of Teeg's bulk snapped the latch from its grasp and the door pounded inward. Teeg and Drew stumbled inside, Drew holding on with both his hands to the giant's hook.

Pam continued to struggle with the other man, but he found her face with an elbow and pummeled it twice. Pam had never been struck violently before and the sudden pain and flow of blood from her nostrils nearly stripped her consciousness away. But the man she was battling had neglected his machine gun just as she had, and now Pam was able to gain control over it an instant ahead of him. She twisted the barrel around so it was square on his midsection as her finger closed on the trigger.

The machine gun clicked on an empty chamber. Pam freed one hand and did one of the few moves she recalled from her limited martial arts training, pounding the heel of her hand with all her might into the man's throat.

She wasn't sure if she killed him or not, but suddenly his face went purple and he was gasping for air. His grip on the empty rifle let go and both hands clutched for his throat.

Pam lunged to her feet.

In the inner lab, the struggle had taken to the floor with Teeg hovering on top, the final death bite of his steel hook stopped only by Drew's hands locked on the base. He was aware of his own screaming and the pain within him that seemed everywhere at once.

Pam rushed to the door and tried the latch. It was jammed from the inside where the hook was just inches away from Drew's throat.

Driven to despair, Pam realized Drew's last hope lay with her, and she rushed back to the console. Wasting no time, she jammed both her hands into the gloves controlling the Hands and went to work.

Teeg smiled as he readied the hook for its final plunge.

Drew wailed in agony, the last of his strength ebbing.

And with that, one of the pincers suddenly descended and latched onto Teeg's hook. The giant felt a jolt and was powerless to stop the pressure from pulling him to his feet.

Pam worked the mechanism feverishly, joining the second Hand to the giant's opposite shoulder and rotating the joystick so that the Hands worked together to yank him away from Drew. Free, Drew rolled once, then tried unsuccessfully to climb back to his feet.

The giant struggled against the hold of the Hands, tearing his shoulder free of the grasp and the flesh with it, held only by the lock on his hook now.

Pam struggled to bring the now free Hand back down for purchase, shouting into the microphone at the same time.

"Drew, get out! Get out!"

Drew gazed up at the window and pushed himself on, crawling for the door. At last he reached up for the knob. Even that proved an enormous effort. His body was racked with pain, the feeling of burning coals singeing his flesh in the areas where he'd been wounded.

Teeg flailed at him with a bloodied but freed arm, still fighting to loosen his hook from the grasp of the left Hand. Finally, with an ear-wrenching scream, he tore it free and rushed forward.

Drew made it into the outer lab just in time and slammed the door behind him.

It wouldn't catch. Somehow the crash of bodies into it had knocked out the alignment. From the inside, Teeg began to pull. Drew kept it shut, but it took all his strength, which was failing rapidly.

Pam had started to lunge from her chair to help when her eyes fell back on the glass case containing the undissolved powder and still holding the gas that had killed the rat. It would have remained active; it could wipe out 26.5 square miles the computer had told her.

Drew grimaced in pain, hands locked on the door handle to hold firm. The door began to buckle.

Now, Pam realized, *it had to be now!*

And she twisted the right Hand back over the experiment table directly in line above the glass case. Without hesitating she brought the pincer down hard. The glass shattered.

The gas escaped.

"Seal the door, Drew!" she screamed. "For God's sake, seal it!"

Drew could feel the slackening in the giant's efforts as he did. Teeg staggered backward into his line of vision through the observation glass. He reeled about the inner lab, crashing into one wall and then another, clutching for his throat. Bottles and jars fell to the floor. The giant's features were scarlet, his face that of a drowning man with no hope of reaching the surface in time. Saliva frothed at the corners of his mouth.

"My God," muttered Drew, easing himself toward Pam. "What the hell is happening?"

In the inner lab Teeg crumbled to the floor, retching and writhing, holding to life with the last of his reserves.

"That powder, it's some sort of poison!" Pam said frantically, not able to watch the rest. "Mix it with water and it drains the air of oxygen, swallows it up incredibly fast. Right now there's not one molecule of oxygen left in there."

"What about us, out here?"

"The seals are all airtight. We're safe."

In the inner lab the giant had ceased his struggling. He lay on his back, parts of his body twitching spasmodically.

The man against the far wall, one eye clear enough to see, had located Teeg's black detonator, which had been separated from the giant during the struggle. He reached for it with a trembling hand.

Drew's legs were going wobbly. He swung to right himself and caught the hint of motion. He registered what the man was doing in an instant and pushed himself into motion.

Too late.

In one eternal second, the man pressed down on a button.

It seemed to Drew as if his ears had been ripped out. The blast rocketed him into the air. He landed hard on the floor with a bitter sulphur smell heavy on his nostrils as flames were suddenly everywhere. He shook himself alert and grabbed hold of his bearings. He had been blown halfway to the door. Before him the entire front wall was a mass of smoke and flames, the inner lab thankfully unscathed.

"*Pam!*"

He crawled forward into the crackling heat to reach her.

"*Pam!*"

No reply. Drew crawled on, taking in scorched breaths that made him feel like hot coals were swishing about his mouth, as the crackling flames spread through the entire room.

He found Pam near the console, blown out of her chair, face black and charred. Her eyes were closed and Drew couldn't let himself consider that she might be dead. He suddenly found himself on his feet, carrying her.

"Ahhhhhhhhhhhhhhh!"

With that scream, he propelled himself forward through the flames. When he reached the corridor only his pant leg was on fire. He smothered it against the floor as he started to lay Pam down, collapsing over her as he leaned down to check for a heartbeat.

There was another, secondary explosion and flames poured into the corridor. Drew shielded Pam with his body, then dragged both of them across the tile until the last of his strength gave out and the flames made a determined rush for him. Drew had nothing left to fight with. He closed his eyes.

Then he felt the hand grab him from behind and yank viciously. Drew felt himself being dragged and heard the scraping of his shoes against the floor. The air turned comfortably cool, the acrid stench of smoke and flames vanquished.

"Pam! Pam!"

"I've got her, boy," came a voice struggling to stay calm.

And the last sight Drew recorded before consciousness fled him was the face of Jabba the Hutt.

PART SIX:

BONN

CHAPTER 27

THE TIMBER WOLF LEFT FOR BONN EARLY SUNDAY MORNING ON an odyssey that would not see him reach Germany's capital until early on Monday. Anxiety nagged at him, frustration mixing with confusion. He had more pieces to the puzzle now, but the overall picture made no sense.

After escaping from Tumblefig's farm in Wapello, Iowa, he had headed to another of Trelana's distribution points by way of stolen cars, three to be exact, never staying in any one long enough to risk capture. Dearborn, Michigan, was a good choice, not only because of its reasonable proximity, but also since its profile was distinctly different. From farm country to a working class city—the range was incredible. But something held these two locales together besides being apparent centers for cocaine, and Wayman could only wonder whether another underground shelter would lie beneath 1812 Mohican Lane—the Dearborn drop.

He had arrived in the city late Thursday night but not too late to order up a huge meal from room service, which included the best bottle of port the house could offer. Twenty minutes after finishing the meal without bothering to savor the wine, he was sound asleep.

Wayman rose at ten the next morning and had a cab take him to the address in question; 1812 Mohican Lane turned out to be located in the southeast section of Dearborn off Miller Road. It had once been a huge factory laid out in the shape of a square with a formerly sturdy fence enclosing the combination parking lot-courtyard that fronted the complex. All that remained now was a shell with boards taking the place of windows and tired brick worn by poor treatment and the elements. The entire area, in fact, was desolate with the exception of a few kids churning by on their bicycles and a rare car, rusted and clanking, inching down the street as if looking for a place to expire.

A farm in Wapello, Iowa, and now this. Wayman knew he had to be careful. The incidents in Wapello would have forced an alert to be sent out to all other drop points to be on the lookout for him. That probability made a close, thorough inspection of the building too risky to contemplate. It was certainly large enough to accommodate an underground structure on the same scale as the one beneath Tumblefig's farm. But how could Wayman learn if one existed without making a careful search?

The answer came with surprising swiftness. He never even had to leave his car to see the iron sign posted off to the side of what used to be the building entrance. The letters were rusted over from long years, but its triangular logo was unmistakable.

It seemed that 1812 Mohican Lane housed a massive fallout shelter.

The connection with what he had stumbled upon in Wapello was undeniable. Wayman's heart was pounding as he entered Dearborn City Hall to check for the building's owner and thus a concrete lead. The land records were being refiled in a new computer system, so his search proved far more frustrating and arduous than should have been the case, mostly due to the time involved in getting distracted workers to lend assistance.

But in the end his patience paid off. The building and land designated as 1812 Mohican Lane had been purchased six years before by a group known as the American Workers Regime, better known as the American Nazi party.

Further research revealed that the local chief, almost certainly the man in charge of whatever was going on, was named Edgar Brown. He lived off Gulf View Drive in the city's plushest section and was by all accounts a very successful man. He was divorced, and his one son, aged thirteen, spent all weekends at his home. It took the Timber Wolf until Saturday night before the opportunity presented itself to approach Brown directly.

The local Nazi leader had just arrived home from a dinner at the Dearborn Country Club and stepped into his downstairs den to turn off the lights before retiring.

"Good evening, Mr. Brown," Wayman greeted him from a leather desk chair.

Brown felt along the wall for the panic button rigged into his alarm system.

"I wouldn't," the Timber Wolf warned, "at least not until you check your son upstairs."

Brown bolted up the stairs only to return breathless seconds later.

"What have you done with him?" he demanded.

"He's safe," Wayman assured. "But how long he stays that way depends solely on you."

Brown was shaking. "How much do you want?"

The Timber Wolf rose from behind the desk. "Money? None. I'm here for information. Answer my questions truthfully and completely and your son will be returned to you safe and sound. Lie or withold information just once and he dies. Very simple. Don't you agree?"

"Yes. Oh God, yes. Anything!"

"Good. Tell me about 1812 Mohican Lane."

"What? It's, it's just an abandoned factory."

"I'm talking about the shelter beneath it."

Brown's face paled at that. "Christ, who sent you?" he managed.

"It might as well have been Christ for all it matters to you. Now the shelter. It's been renovated, updated, hasn't it?"

"Yes."

"I want the specifics."

Brown fought to compose himself. "The walls and ceilings had to be relined to make sure they were totally airtight. Generators were installed along with refrigeration systems for food and water. A huge air system was the biggest job, similar to the kind used on submarines, only much larger. Enough air in the tanks to last at least a week, maybe longer, probably longer."

Wayman's mind was working feverishly. Brown might have been describing the structure beneath the farm in Wapello.

"Are these tanks in place now?" he asked.

"They have been for months."

"Then there must be plans for people to flee down there. What's going to happen? Who's behind it?"

Brown interlaced his fingers before him as if to pray. "I don't know the answer to either. I swear it!"

"But you're in charge of the shelter, aren't you?"

Brown nodded. "Only from an organizational standpoint, though."

"What kind of organization?"

"To signal the people when it's time to go down and to take charge once we're down there."

"You don't know what's going to happen, but you'll know when to contact them . . ."

"No!" Brown shrieked. "I'm to be contacted first. The people all listen to a certain radio station at certain times of the day. If a specific message, an advertisement, comes over the air, they know it's time. I don't know when or why. I just have my orders."

"From whom?"

Brown squeezed his lips together defiantly.

The Timber Wolf walked out from behind the desk. "Listen, your people are going to be running down there to escape something horrible going on above. Don't tell me you haven't figured that much out. If you haven't, let me tell you it means lots of people on the surface are going to die and if you think the life of you or your son matters to me when measured against that, you're— "

"All right, I'll tell you what I know, but I'm signing my own death warrant."

"Your son's is made out as well."

Brown took a swallow of air. "My orders come from Heinrich Goltz."

"The West German cabinet minister?"

"The man who has remained ever true to the Nazi cause. He recruited me because I had come to loathe everything this country has come to stand for. We've become a land of the weak. Goltz promised me that was going to change. There was a plan, he said, and I was a part of it."

"That was all he said?"

"That and the assignment to reconstruct the Mohican Lane fallout shelter to meet his specifications. That was almost six years ago."

"And you've met with him regularly since?"

"No, only his contact."

"What contact?"

"I never knew his name. I didn't want to. He scared me. So goddamn white. . . ."

The Timber Wolf felt a rush of blood to his cheeks. "What? Did you say white?"

"Yes. Features almost like an albino."

"Was he old?"

"Not particularly. He just looked it. His hair was ash-white, too."

The heat turned to ice and Wayman felt cold everywhere. Corbano! No other man fit Brown's description. But how did the White Snake fit into all this?

"This man relayed Goltz's instructions to you," Wayman said finally.

"In part. But his major concern was the powder."

Wayman's eyes bulged. At last, everything was coming together.

"Cocaine?" he asked.

"I don't know. I never examined it. What about my son?"

"Keep talking."

"The powder came regularly every six months, sometimes nine, over the last four-and-a-half years or so. I was always there to pick it up at the very same place. Never had my hands on it for more than an hour, though. The instructions were precise as to where and how to get rid of it."

"How much powder?"

Brown stopped to calculate. "It varied between thirty and forty pounds per shipment. Say a couple hundred in all."

"And you have no idea what happened to it after you turned the stuff over?"

"Not a clue. I wouldn't lie. My son . . . *please!*"

Wayman found himself speechless. Too much information had come in all at once and he tried to assimilate it into some sort of context.

"I've told you everything!" Brown pleaded. "Now tell me where I can find my son. Please, God. You promised!"

"Upstairs," Wayman said simply.

"I checked!"

"Only his room. Not your own. He's safe."

Now, as the plane neared Bonn, the Timber Wolf was still assimilating. Clearly this white powder, whatever it was, was connected to the shelters and ultimately what would force a select group of people into them. Drew Jordan's grandmother and the other women had smuggled it into the country under the guise of cocaine, where it ended up with the Riveros who waited for Lantos to arrive with payment and specific instructions as to shipping. To Wapello, or Dearborn, or one of twenty-eight other drop points. All he was missing now was the why. Find the answer to that and the problem of what the powder really was would be solved in turn.

Wayman expected Goltz to shed a great deal of light on the picture, although not reveal it totally. Goltz, too, was part of something much greater, and whatever it was America's fate was now hanging in the balance thanks to it.

Wayman spent the last minutes of the flight staring blankly at the fresh map of the United States on which he had placed Xs on all the distribution points in search of some sort of pattern. Maybe because he wasn't trying, a point of connection at last came to him. He wasn't sure what he had, but it had to be something. He checked again.

All but one of the drop points were located next to a large body of water.

From Spain, Elliana proceeded slowly to Bonn. There was no need to rush; it would be impossible to gain access to Goltz until Monday, even if she were able to do so then.

Here she got lucky. Old sources, nearly forgotten, informed her that the defense minister reserved an hour every day from ten to eleven in the morning for interviews with the press. Further, the sources were able to pinpoint for her which particular periodical was on the docket for that Monday since, thankfully, Goltz *was* in the city.

At eight-thirty Monday morning she called the minister's office and requested that the scheduled interview be moved back to nine. His secretary was happy to comply since Goltz's schedule was extremely tight in the later morning.

Since the interview involved a foreign periodical, Ellie did not expect that her face would be known within defense ministry headquarters. Trying to pass herself off as a reporter from a West German daily or newsmagazine would have been fraught with risk. She had nearly forgotten to ask her source whether the actual reporter was a man or a woman, and was relieved to find that it was the latter. Otherwise, her plans would have been delayed.

Bonn, the most modern of Germany's cities, stands as a paradox. The capital is actually very old indeed, with plenty of buildings left intact from World War II still standing in the historic district. Around this, ultramodern buildings have been constructed in uneasy contrast, steel and glass being too ugly and functional to mix well with the wood, stone, and concrete from years before. The government buildings lie, also functionally, in the heart of the new construction, one indiscernible from the next.

The Ministry of Defense complex was no exception, and Ellie's head was pounding as she approached it from across a square on Monday morning. The long days were finally starting to take their toll. She felt tired and sluggish and could afford neither. Her body, far from recovered from the wounds suffered on the mountain, rebelled against the demands being made on it. Ellie knew her limitations well enough to know she had exceeded them. Yet, she knew she must stay sharp and alert, for Goltz was not about to answer her questions of his own volition. With the Council on to her, she felt sure he would recognize her almost immediately. She would have to move fast, but once she reached him, the rest would take care of itself.

She patted her handbag to assure herself that the black pouch was still inside.

Bringing in a weapon such as a pistol had been out of the question since she fully expected the most thorough of searches and a gun seldom lasted beyond even the most cursory of frisks. She entered the Ministry of Defense building and announced herself at the guard table. A phone call later she was told she was free to go up to the fourth floor where Goltz's office was located. She was expected. It was exactly nine o'clock.

She was actually searched twice: first before stepping onto the elevator and again at a guard station down the hall from Heinrich Goltz's office on the fourth floor. She was escorted the rest of the way by one of the guards and waited as a receptionist informed Goltz of her arrival and then smiled up at her to go right in.

Heinrich Goltz had risen from behind his desk to greet her as she entered. Ellie closed the door behind her, shielding as much of her face as she could, before stepping forward.

Goltz's expression changed immediately, first to apprehension and then to fear. He felt for something beneath his desk.

Ellie covered the distance in an instant. She plunged one hand into the defense minister's throat to shut off a possible scream and used her other to yank his right arm to her. Using her upper arm to hold it in place, she fumbled for the loaded syringe stored within the handbag now dangling from the arm she was using to keep Goltz pinned silently to his chair. Grasping it firmly, she lifted the syringe out and jammed it through the sleeve of his jacket into his forearm. Goltz's eyes bulged with terror, then glazed over as his entire frame went limp with the serum's immediate effects.

Sodium Amytal, the truth serum Ellie was using, was basically a very strong sedative, which in this dosage numbed the inhibiters deep within the mind in order to break down will. For a man of Goltz's years, the amount surging through his system could easily cause death if the battle between his subdued conscious will and activated subconscious response caused the kind of agitation Ellie expected. Still she had no choice. A lesser dosage might keep him alive but would go nowhere toward gaining her the answers she so sorely required.

"What is your name?" Elliana asked the minister.

"Heinrich Goltz."

"And before that?"

"Johann Krieg."

"You were a Nazi?"

"I *am* a Nazi."

Ellie passed her hand in front of Goltz's eyes. They didn't respond. The serum had achieved its full effect.

"Does the Council of Ten exist?" she asked, holding her breath.

Goltz resisted briefly. "Yes."

"And are you a member?" Ellie raised next, trembling slightly, confirmation of something she had always known finally obtained.

"Yes."

"A strike against America is about to be initiated, correct?"

Goltz's lips trembled. "Yes. It's called Powderkeg."

Ellie felt a shudder of realization. "That has something to do with a white powder compound produced in Spain, doesn't it?"

"Yes."

"And the powder was transferred to Getaria for shipment to the Bahamas and then to America. Why such an elaborate chain?"

"Exposure had to be avoided at all costs. Too much risk."

"After the powder reaches America, what happens?"

"Distribution. Everywhere across country."

"Toward what end?"

"Destruction. Total."

"Of America?" Ellie posed disbelievingly.

Goltz bit his lip, trying with all his will to hold back against the serum. Again he failed. "Ninety percent of America's population is going to be killed."

The statement smacked Ellie like a blow to the stomach. "How?" she managed, fighting for breath.

"When mixed with water, the powder creates a gas that drains oxygen from the air."

Ellie shivered. "The procedure, tell me the procedure!"

Goltz resisted harder. Veins sprang out from his temples. His face reddened. "Thirty drop points scattered strategically across the nation, each close to a major body of water. Each has accumulated a storehouse of powder over the years to be dumped into the water to create a cloud, which will gain size and strength as it spreads, growing geometrically and eventually linking up with—*ahhhhhhhhhhhh*!"

Goltz's head collapsed to his desk. Ellie grabbed the little hair remaining on his dome and yanked it back up.

"The timetable, what is it?"

Goltz was shuddering now. "It begins Thursday with the East Coast to eliminate those centers crucial to emergency response. The rest will follow simultaneously on Friday. The deaths will begin immediately. In three days the entire country will be covered."

"Ninety percent of America's population will be dead in three days?" Ellie fought to stay calm. "What about the hundred transports you requisitioned?"

"Our people will be flown in on them after the death clouds have dissipated thanks to exposure to ultraviolet rays within seven days after release. They have been well chosen, the select of our various movements. Only America's people will be dead. Her country will belong to us."

Ellie could not help but shudder. The army she had first gained an inkling of in Prague was an occupation force, not an invasion one!

Goltz, meanwhile, seemed to be on the verge of a seizure. His teeth ground together. The struggle with the serum was beginning to tell on him. Stroke, heart attack, seizure—any were possible. Ellie knew she didn't have much longer with him, none to use to dig into the who and why behind David's death. There was something far more important she had to learn.

"Where is the Council headquarters?" she demanded.

"I . . . don't know."

"You must!"

"Location secret from . . . even me until . . ."

"Until what?"

"Wednesday," Goltz said with teeth clenched as if to hold back his own words. "All of us . . . meeting there . . . for first time . . . Wednesday. Address in Lisbon. I'll be picked up, taken to . . . headquarters."

Yes, Ellie reasoned, that fit the Council's methodology perfectly. The ultimate security since none of its members could betray that which they did not know. They could reach Council headquarters only under escort with activation of this plan Powderkeg a mere hours away.

"The Lisbon address," Ellie demanded. "Give it to me!"

White foam puckered from between Goltz's lips, turning pinkish as blood flowing from his torn tongue and mouth joined it. He was struggling for air.

Ellie shook him. "Give me the address!"

Goltz gurgled it out as his head lopped forward. Ellie memorized it.

The intercom buzzed.

Goltz gazed dimly at her, face pulsating madly. His mouth dropped, but no words emerged.

The intercom buzzed again.

Suddlenly Goltz's entire frame spasmed and locked. His eyes bulged and his face turned purple. Ellie tried to steady him, but his mad hands clawed out at her and she recoiled in pain. Goltz's body slid to the floor, writhing there as his heart pumped a final stream of blood through his body before giving up the struggle. Ellie approached and turned him over.

The office door opened and the secretary started to enter.

"I'm sorry to inter—"

The woman screamed at the sight of her employer, West Germany's Minister of Defense, shaking on the floor.

"He's had a heart attack!" Ellie screamed. "Get a doctor!"

The loyal secretary had no choice but to obey. An alarm sounded. In seconds men were rushing into the room to find Ellie feigning CPR.

"Somebody's got to massage his heart!" she barked, knowing the muscle had burst beyond repair.

The building paramedics arrived a minute later and took over the process. The others just looked on, dumbstruck and terrified. Ellie slipped to the back of them, then rushed to the door with a purpose apparently in mind.

"Miss, wait a moment, please," a security guard called after her in German. "Miss!"

But Ellie was already sprinting down the corridor. Chaos surrounded her and she became a part of it. She heard the pounding of the guard's feet after her. He had abandoned shouting at her and was concentrating solely on the chase. Ellie ducked into a door marked Exit and took a flight of stairs quickly, huddling against the wall when she heard the door burst open again.

The guard took the stairs even faster than she had. He was actually past her when she lashed out with a hammer fist to the back of his head. There was a grunt and then the guard was tumbling down the steps, landing unconscious. Ellie stopped to retrieve his pistol and then continued down as fast she she dared.

Another flight and she emerged on the ground floor and headed calmly for the lobby. The activity there was chaos, bedlam, just as she expected it would be. What she didn't expect were armed guards posted at the inside of the doors, denying exit to anyone who sought it and permitting entry only to those with official papers.

The Ministry of Defense building had been sealed off.

She was trapped.

CHAPTER 28

THE OFFICIAL VEHICLES, SIRENS WAILING SLOWLY DOWN, WERE STILL arriving when Wayman reached the Ministry of Defense. Gaining access was a simple matter of rushing forward and joining a surge of official bodies through the door. In the confusion no one noticed, the guards being more concerned with those trying to leave than enter.

Staying reasonably detached from a group of security police and medical personnel, he made it to the fourth floor and the office of Heinrich Goltz. The Timber Wolf really had no idea of how he was going to approach the Defense Minister, but now that problem was academic. Goltz was dead. Information was sketchy, but it seemed that a heart attack had originally been blamed until an alert paramedic noticed a small trickle of blood drying on the minister's left forearm. A bit more investigation yielded a needle hole. Goltz had apparently been injected with something. Assassination was now suspected, the perpetrator being a woman who had come in the guise of a reporter and was inside the office for at least ten minutes. Furthermore, a security guard had been found unconscious in a stairwell after giving chase to this same fake reporter. The building had been immediately sealed off, guards posted at each exit.

The Timber Wolf backed away from the crowd and headed down the corridor. He knew it would not be long before he was identified as an intruder, which would lead to a series of uncomfortable questions. So, he stayed on the move as he put together both what he knew and what he could safely assume.

An assassin would never have used a needle as a weapon. Needles were too difficult and clumsy to handle. They required the unnecessary risk of getting very close to the victim. It was more likely that the woman had injected some sort of truth serum into Goltz to force him to reveal whatever was requested, and eventually the strain had killed him. The maneuver was bold, rife with risk; the actions of a professional, probably acting in desperation, who had exhausted all other options. A professional who knew, like Wayman, that Heinrich Goltz was not what he seemed.

A professional who was a woman. And his ally.

Goltz must have talked. Ten minutes inside the office was plenty of time to produce lots of information. And if the woman's questions mirrored the ones he would have posed, then she was now the only one in possession of the answers. The Timber Wolf had to find her.

He felt fairly certain that she had not escaped the rapid dragnet thrown over the building, which meant she was trapped somewhere without benefit of mobility.

Wayman placed himself in her position. After fending off the guard, she would have headed straight for the lobby to escape. With this route closed off and forces converging from above, only that which lay below was left open to her. And in this building below would be a cellar layered with pipes and lined with box after box of documents from the premicrofilm days.

The Timber Wolf turned into a stairwell and headed down.

Elliana huddled in a warm corner of the cellar contemplating her next move. It had been just an hour since she had fled Goltz's office, and already two sweeps had been made by the guards with a third promised soon. She had the gun containing a clip of nine bullets but little else to aid her among the discarded files.

They had massed an army upstairs by now.

Death was something she had long learned to accept. In the event all else failed, in fact, Mossad agents had been outfitted with a false filling in a rear molar. An agile working of the tongue to free and ready it and then a heavy chomp down on what was actually a capsule would release a stream of fast-acting cyanide into the mouth. But there could be no suicide for her now, no death by any means. The Council of Ten had surfaced at last, its plan to destroy the United States and then occupy it. The preparations had undoubtedly been in the works for years. People had been chosen, a new order of control over the entire world ultimately. No wonder they had killed David. He must have latched onto the plot six years before.

But they could still be stopped. Goltz had said Lisbon. Ellie had to find a way to make that work for her.

Escape first, however. She had run to the cellar because there had been no other choice. Yet, now she regretted that decision. She had trapped herself. The concentration of troops above her was staggering. Since no one reported seeing her leave, the assumption would be she was still in the building. Their numbers would not be broken off until she was found.

Ellie held her breath suddenly. The sound of heavy boots making a soft, careful stride caught her ears. How many of them she didn't know. But they were close. And they were coming.

She yanked her revolver free.

It was not easy for Wayman to reach the cellar since all doors had been locked to keep the suspect pinned down. He managed to slip stealthily behind a group of eight or ten armed guards into the stairwell and then to keep the door from slamming closed after they passed in. He gave it a few seconds and then entered the basement after them, hanging back as they began their sweep down the aisles between the shelved boxes of buried material. Somewhere among them, he felt certain the woman was hiding.

Wayman lagged behind the guards, keeping his frame hidden and studying the layout of the basement for possible later use. Not much to make note of besides the many boxes and serpentine structure of pipes just beneath the ceiling.

Twenty yards away, Ellie found the police search to be careful but not precise. They were looking for her without any expectation of being successful and were thus not as sharp as they should have been. She began to edge away from her corner hiding place, using the shelved boxes as cover. Her steps were cloaked in silence, but her pistol was held ready on the chance that one of the men was alerted to them.

The Timber Wolf heard the shuffling and held his ground. He drew a rapid fix on the figure's angle of approach and determined immediately that it could not be one of the police officers. The soft slide indicated the steps of a woman and he tried to calculate the best route of safe approach to her. Hands held in the air was always a possibility, although the cellar was dark and there was no guarantee that she would notice the gesture. A man was a man and all of them were after her. Approach from the rear, then, seemed his best shot. He would have to incapacitate her before she could respond. The impetus of persuasion lay with him.

Wayman crept from aisle to aisle as the officers up ahead continued their wide search of the basement. His plan was to pass the woman going the other way and then double back in order to take her from behind after cutting down one of the aisles.

Their paths converged seconds later, although at different ends of the aisle. Wayman stayed pressed against the shelves, but the woman turned briefly and he caught a glimpse of her face in the near blackness.

The shock of recognition widened Wayman's eyes. Elliana Hirsch! Here now, a part of this. One of the Mossad's top field agents. *God* . . .

To think that she was the one responsible for Goltz's interrogation and eventual death. Thoughts raced through the Timber Wolf's mind. Clearly the two of them were pursuing . . . something that made them allies. But what was Elliana's stake in this? What exactly had she risked her life to ask Goltz?

His plan of approach and incapacitation would have to be reworked. Ellie was too good to take by such crude means. But they had worked together twice before, and if he could silently grab her attention, somehow alert her to his presence, perhaps that would be enough.

Wayman stepped up his pace down the aisle, the woman three aisles ahead of him by the time he reached the other end.

Elliana swung when barely ten yards separated them, swung because of a soft scraping not far to her rear. Her gun came up as all the tensions within her unspooled. She recognized the figure instantly, saw that it was the famed Timber Wolf, and was not surprised at all that the Council of Ten would have employed such a hunter to finish her once and for all!

Wayman saw the fury in Ellie's eyes in time to dive to the side before her pistol began to spit death. The bullets chewed through a rusted-out pipe above him. Steam sprayed outward. Wayman rolled and a second bullet ricocheted off the floor.

"Ellie, no!" he tried to shout, but he couldn't be sure if the words had emerged.

Then feet trampled forward in their direction, police officers alerted by the shots and probably certain that one of their number had been cut down. Elliana rushed off, boot heels clicking against the cement floor. Wayman rose to follow her, but first the police had to be neutralized. Not by shooting, though. They were innocent men here only to do their job.

The echo of gunshots stung his ears as the officers fired wildly at the fleeing Ellie. The Timber Wolf stayed low and waited until they passed him before making his move. He had twelve bullets in his nine-millimeter Beretta and he used eight of them to rip chasms in the heating pipes strung across the ceiling. Water sprayed in all directions, gushing out in fast jets. Steam followed almost immediately and enveloped the front section of the basement in a hot gray cloud that seared everything it touched while temporarily blinding those within it.

Wayman heard the screams as he bolted forward with a handkerchief ready to cover his eyes. Orders were being shouted by some, pleas of help by others who writhed painfully on the floor. A few lucky officers missed the assault of steam and rushed through the stairwell on Ellie's trail. Wayman thought he saw two, but in the darkness he couldn't be sure. He crashed through the door and turned the locking bolt as he slammed it shut and followed the pounding steps up the stairs.

He took them quickly, the loudest concentration of activity almost two flights above him. A single shot rang out, ricocheting, and he pictured Ellie waiting ahead in the alcove where one staircase gave way to another, lunging out when the guards rushed near. One of them had gotten a shot off, harmless probably, before Ellie had dealt with both.

The Timber Wolf kept climbing. He saw her just up ahead now, between the fourth and fifth floors. As he rushed toward her, she fired a single shot, which went wild. When she turned to better her aim, he lunged on her, forcing her wrist down and stripping her of her balance. The gun's bore flashed orange. They tumbled together down to the fourth floor landing.

At impact, the Timber Wolf raised his free arm to strike her but Ellie deflected the blow and rammed a half fist into the soft flesh between his lower ribs. Wayman grasped and tried to power her backward, but she was too seasoned to be taken by simple bull strength and used his own momentum to slam him face first into the wall.

He felt her gun wrist stripped from his grasp and felt the hard steel pound him in the back of his neck. A numbness grasped his head. He slumped to the floor, never feeling impact, and gazed up at the hatefully determined look on Elliana Hirsch's face, her pistol aimed straight for his face.

"You should have killed me in the cellar when you had the chance," she snapped, finger ready on the trigger.

Doors slammed closed above and below them. Guards were massing from both angles, ready to converge.

"We're on the same side, damnit!" Wayman heard himself say. "Don't ask me why or how. I came here for Goltz, too!" Footsteps were hurdling up and down the steps toward them now. "We've got to get away from them. There's a way, but we've got to move. Keep your gun on me. If you're not convinced we're on the same side in five minutes, you can blow my fucking brains out. Come on!"

With the footsteps almost on them, Wayman grabbed Ellie's wrist in a sudden motion and yanked her through the fourth floor entry door, the very floor on which Goltz had died.

"You're mad!" she said as Wayman forced the door closed behind them.

"Been that way for lots of years. Now let's find someplace to hide."

Consciousness skipped and darted from Drew Jordan. He was aware of pain and numbness and of the dull haze that encircled his eyes every time he was able to open them. He saw no distinct figures, just shapes and outlines. Occasionally words were thrust at him, but they sounded slurred, unintelligible. A few times he tried to speak himself only to find that his mouth was a stranger to him, a foreign part of his body he had no control over. Night and day meant nothing to him. One hour swirled into the next.

His longest grasp on consciousness came Monday night when he awoke with his mouth parched and dry. A huge shape hovered over him, still just a shape, although the face held its context long enough for him to recognize the bulbous features of Jabba the Hutt holding a water glass complete with straw down to his lips.

"Jabba," he muttered.

"Drink this."

"Where am I?"

"Safe."

Drew sipped at the straw gratefully and took in as much water as his stomach would let him. He felt better immediately. Fragments of memory returned to him like selected shots off a movie trailer too fast to make sense of.

"You've got to go back to sleep now," Drew thought he heard Jabba say.

"The fire! Oh God, the fire!"

He tried to sit up and Jabba held him down by the shoulders.

"It's over."

"No! No! I've got to save Pam! I've got to save her! She's burning! *Burning!*"

"Sleep, Drew, sleep."

"But Pam, what about Pam?"

Jabba the Hutt pulled the water glass away and patted Drew's forehead.

"Sleep."

Wayman yanked Ellie through the door of a supply closet down the hall and around the corner from Goltz's office not far from the checkpoint where she had been searched a second time. In the darkness, they felt their way to the rear and huddled behind two large crates. Wayman felt Ellie's gun still close to him and possessed no illusions that the darkness might inhibit her aim.

"This is crazy," Ellie said. "Goltz's office is right around the corner."

"Precisely why it's the last place they'll look for you—us

now. The scene of the crime is always the best place to hide out until things cool off. Now put that damn gun down.''

"I haven't decided whether to trust you or not.''

"Damnit, Ellie, if I wanted you dead, they'd be carrying you out of the building by now. You know that.''

"I don't know anything anymore.''

"Then listen. Reach over to my left hip and pull out my pistol. If I'd been sent to kill you, I could have already used it while you were distracted.''

"I knew it was there. I was waiting for you to use it.''

"What do I have to do to convince you?''

"You can't.''

"What about Goltz? I'm telling you *I* came for him, too. Only you beat me to him.''

"It's more than just Goltz. He is—was—just a small part of it.''

"A part of what?''

"If you don't know that, then you've got no business here in Bonn.''

"What I know is that all of a sudden somebody's been building underground shelters all over the United States that can house thousands, tens of thousands of people. Goltz was behind the construction of at least one and that's what brought me here. He—or this thing he's a part of—is preparing for a catastrophe only they seem to know about, which means they're behind it.''

In the darkness Wayman could feel Ellie stiffen. The crack under the door provided just enough light for their eyes to use and he saw her lower the gun.

"That means something to you,'' he said. "Tell me.''

"It's the one thing I didn't ask Goltz about,'' she muttered more to herself. "Those who were a part of the plan in America would have to be protected once the powder was released.''

"Powder? *White* powder?''

"What does the color matter?''

"Just tell me if it's white!''

"Yes. Now tell me why that's important.''

"Because, my Israeli counterpart, it was supposed to look like cocaine. That's been the cover from the start.''

"Cover . . . '' Ellie's voice came up slightly. "Yes, that fits!

It fits! The powder was produced in Berga, Spain, and then transferred to Getaria for shipment to the Bahamas.''

"Nassau? Freeport?" asked the Timber Wolf.

"I suppose so."

"Oh my God . . ."

"What is it?"

"Everything makes sense now. That's why the grandmothers had to die."

"Grandmothers? You've lost me."

"This powder, just tell me about it. What is it really?"

Footsteps sounded just outside their closet along with voices too muffled to make out. When they departed, Ellie told Wayman the truth about the white powder and the transports as related by Heinrich Goltz.

"*Ninety percent of the population asphyxiated because there's no air left to breathe. . . .*"

"No," Ellie corrected. "The air will still be there, but drained of oxygen."

"It's the same damn thing with 200 million deaths any way you describe it. America will crumble, be reduced to ashes."

"Not quite. The shelters, remember? Their people will survive and re-emerge organized and ready to take over with the help of the thousands arriving on the transports. Yes, it would take such a plan to explain them surfacing at last."

"You keep speaking in the plural."

"With good reason. The force behind this rivals any government in the world—the Council of Ten."

"The Council of what?"

"Ten. Don't tell me the great Timber Wolf has never heard of them."

"Unless you want me to lie . . ."

"They're an international cabal composed of outcast leaders from around the world, if I'm reading my cards right."

"Goltz," Wayman noted, "a former Nazi who still keeps links with revivalist parties of the Reich."

"Yes, he perfectly fits the pattern of what I would expect the Council members to be: desperate, fanatical, ruthless, and all with large followings of their own. It all goes back to the time of Alexander the Great. His plan to rule the world was to divide his conquered lands into ten nations or territories, each ruled by a minister directly responsible to Alexander. To prevent revolution and rebellion, along with possible wars among the separate nations of wholly divergent peoples and cultures, a system of laws, decrees, and policies would be laid down for each to follow loyally—to be determined by the ministers meeting together under Alexander as a . . . council of ten.''

"So, Goltz and these others have picked up where he left off.''

"More accurately, they've succeeded where he failed.'' Ellie's tone turned eerily contemplative. "I know. I've tracked them for five years. They killed my husband.''

"David Hirsch,'' Wayman recalled. "He was murdered shortly after being forced to resign from the Israeli cabinet.''

"His killers were never found because the Council of Ten never leaves anything that might lead back to them or even suggest their existence. Their work is carried out invariably by intermediaries who know only what they have to. The chain is long and complex, roundabout in many areas, but such precautions are everything to them.''

"Yes,'' the Timber Wolf said knowingly. "I've seen that. The grandmothers, Trelana, the whole drug chain.''

"That's twice you've mentioned grandmothers. What does it mean?''

"Hold onto your hat, Ellie, because here's where my story starts to get good. . . .''

And the Timber Wolf proceeded to relay the story told him by Drew Jordan and later confirmed by his Washington contact after his guilt over the young man's incarceration and subsequent disappearance led him to investigate the affairs of Trelana. Wayman explained how this investigation had turned up a trail of distribution points all over the country, each apparently housing an underground shelter of the type found in Wapello or Dearborn. He finished by rehashing his interrogation of Edgar Brown, which had led here to Bonn and Heinrich Goltz along with alerting him to Corbano's involvement in the chaos.

"The White Snake,'' Ellie reflected at the end. "I've met up with him before.''

"Haven't we all?'' Wayman shook his head in mock disbelief. "Even telling the story as it's happened doesn't make it any easier to believe for me. This Council seems to have gone through a pretty elaborate scenario just to get a few tons of white powder into America. They could just as easily have disguised it as sugar.''

"Not necessarily," Ellie countered. "It's like I told you—everything comes down to control. The Council had to be aware of the powder's exact status every step of the way. Even shipping Federal Express doesn't ensure that. Utilizing Trelana's network was elaborate all right. But since it was already in place, the strategy was actually the safest.'' She thought briefly. "Brown told you he received an allocation every six or nine months. That leads me to believe that the shipments of powder brought in by the grandmothers were distributed by lot regionally. Thus, the importance of that man Lantos delivering *specific* shipping instructions each time to the Riveros.''

"Along with the need to eliminate the entire chain thanks to Drew Jordan's grandmother.''

"The Council leaves nothing to chance," Ellie acknowledged.

"Okay, so we've got to nail this Council at the source," noted Wayman grudgingly. "Did Goltz tell you where they could be found?''

Ellie shrugged. "The Council never leaves traces, remember? They haven't met together yet, the ultimate in security precautions. And when they do rendezvous, this coming Wednesday, they will be escorted to the Council's headquarters from contact points throughout Lisbon, if I'm reading my cards right.''

"That narrows it down a bit.''

"Not enough. But I've got an idea how we can make it work for us. It's a long shot and we can't put all our faith in it, but I don't see we have much—''

More footsteps raced past their hiding place. They grew silent and still, hardly daring to breathe. A hand twisting the knob had them both rigid and ready to spring, but the door never opened.

"The distribution points for the powder," Elliana whispered when the hall was quiet again, "you know them all?''

"I memorized them.''

"Iowa, then Michigan. Where would you suggest we head next?''

Wayman's eyebrows flickered at Ellie's use of *we*. "An address in the back country of Georgia.''

"Why?"

"Because it's the only one on the list *not* near a body of water."

"Corbano's headquarters?" Ellie raised.

"And maybe the means to find the Council's."

They gazed at each other in the darkness.

PART SEVEN:

BACK COUNTRY

CHAPTER 29

"HOW MUCH DO YOU REMEMBER?"

Drew sat huddled before the fire, shivering slightly in spite of the blanket wrapped about his shoulders.

"Everything. I think." He steadied his coffee cup with both hands as he raised it to his lips. "Tell me about Pam again."

Jabba eased his bulbous frame forward. "She's resting as comfortably as can be expected just a few miles from where we are now at a rather discreet hospital being treated by a team of rather discreet doctors who still, incredibly, make house calls."

"On me?"

"On you. You're quite lucky, my boy. A deep slice out of your side and a graze to your head is about the size of it. Virtually no burns whatsoever." Jabba hesitated. "Pam suffered several, enough to cause severe trauma. She hasn't regained consciousness yet, but there's reason for optimism I'm told."

Drew gazed out the living room window at the open spaces of land around them, filled with trees shedding their autumn leaves, which he couldn't see now that night had fallen.

"Where did you say we were, Jabba?"

"Virginia. In the country about a hundred miles west of Arlington."

"Safe?"

"No guards outside, if that's what you mean. But I've got the best electronic surveillance system you can lay your hands on."

His gaze turned toward a pair of monitors flashing atop a nearby desk. "Designed by experts to be used by fools."

Drew almost smiled. "Who are you, Jabba?"

"You asked me that once before, my boy, and I gave you a selection of answers. Which one would you prefer today?"

"The truth."

"I told you weeks ago that myths create their own truth. In this case it was a matter of truth creating its own myth. The rumors about me, my boy, were suprisingly close to the mark. My days before holding court at Clyde's were spent with a secret subdivision of the CIA. The details don't matter. Suffice it to say that I was damn good at what I did until the pressure closed in and the brandy bottles started opening up."

"CIA," Drew muttered. "If only the gang could hear you now."

"They wouldn't like it. I made a much better pompous ass drunk than I did a spy. The company eased me out to avoid embarrassment for both of us and took care of me financially, but couldn't do much about my life, which wasn't much of a life at all." Jabba cleared his throat, sending waves of flesh rolling along his jowls. "Let's talk more specifically about your health now."

"No," Drew told him, "my health can wait. If you left the CIA, what am I doing here? How did you find me?"

The fat man's voice lowered. "I owed you, my boy, long before and for much more than just your rescue of me from those ruffians weeks ago. Jabba always pays his debts, always did. The news of your exploits in Florida was easily attainable in these parts. Add to that a plea from Pam that I send down a lawyer or something of that sort. She knew we were friends, thought I might be able to reach you."

"And how did you end up learning I came back to town?"

"By tapping your phone line . . . and Pam's. The monitoring took me away from Clyde's for a while, but it was for the best. I knew sooner or later you'd make contact in a deceptive, clever way based on your lessons from the soldier camp. But your use of the computer surprised even me. . . ."

"Wait. The bad guys must have had my line tapped, too, but they couldn't have caught on."

"Correct. But there are several ways to tap a phone, several devices to choose from. Mine relied on electronic signals passing through the line; theirs was voice-activated. I was actually able to play back your entire computerized conversation over my terminal by decoding the electronic signals. Fascinating, my boy, and brilliant.''

"And then?"

"I tried to locate you at the library, of course, and when I failed I simply followed Pam to the lab and waited for you to show. Alas, I neglected to consider that I am not the locksmith you are. I wasn't inside until that awful blast sounded.''

Drew shuddered at the memory.

"If I had been earlier," Jabba said guiltily, "if my damn hands could work without trembling . . .''

Drew cut him off. "You saved my life, Jabba. Mine and Pam's. That's enough.''

"No, my boy, it's not. I hid myself at Clyde's so I'd be left alone. Retire quietly and you're never left alone, not by your former enemies or friends. But become a public joke who drowns himself in brandy and people leave you alone." He paused. "Yet you, Drew, always treated me with dignity. I wasn't a joke to you no matter how hard I tried to be one, and you don't know how much I've appreciated that. Saving you at the lab was not enough to repay that debt. Keeping you alive might be. It's a wretched business you've gotten yourself in, my boy. Indications are that you infringed badly on someone's private property, someone with a rather low regard for human life. I need to know everything. From the beginning.''

Drew told him and Jabba regarded his story with varying degrees of shock and fear through its course, stopping him occasionally for questions and then reclining back in a trance at the conclusion.

"Incredible," he muttered dimly. "Far worse than anything I could have imagined. The intent of this powder in all its volume is obviously an attack on the United States. My God, all these trips your grandmother made to Nassau . . .''

"A lot of powder, Jabba. I saw it work. Millions will die, everyone maybe.''

Jabba stood up, face staunch as if he were trying hard to be someone else. "No, we can stop them. I still have contacts. People will be mobilized. Yes! Yes!''

And he started for the phone, stopping when a steady beep on one of the alarm monitors started up. He lumbered over to it and adjusted a few dials. Another series of beeps followed.

"Probably just dogs, or kids maybe," he muttered unconvincingly, grabbing for the phone off a nearby end table and raising the receiver to his ear.

Jabba's huge face paled. Drew didn't have to ask because he knew—a dead telephone line.

Suddenly the second monitor flashed its warning signal. Drew hovered over Jabba's shoulder.

"They're here," the fat man said helplessly. "We've got to get—"

He was interrupted by a continuous squeal that sounded like birds chirping from a third monitor poised on the mantel. The intruders had passed the last perimeter alarms and were closing on the house. Just seconds away now.

Jabba steadied himself with a deep breath. "What matters is that one of us makes it out of here. The authorities must be alerted. We must pray there's still time to stop this force you've described." He grabbed Drew's shoulders and lowered him to the floor as shapes flashed in the narrowing distance through the window. "I'll give you names, numbers, people to contact. They'll know what to do. I can hold them for a while," Jabba promised. "Long enough to give you the time you need."

"No, I can't do it! I can't get through them!"

Shapes flashed outside the windows. Jabba scribbled several lines of writing on a note page grabbed from his desk, tore it off, and thrust it in Drew's pocket.

Which was when the largest of the windows exploded in a hail of gunfire. Jabba pulled Drew with him all the way to the floor. Impact sent waves of pain through his racked body. Lights faded and the room was suddenly drenched in darkness.

"Listen to me," Jabba whispered quickly into his ear. "There's a cellar beneath us with a door at the rear leading into a tunnel. The tunnel will take you into the surrounding woods. You'll be safe."

More gunfire peppered the walls as they crept toward the entrance to the cellar.

"I'll hold them off as long as I can," Jabba said when they reached it. "Call those numbers I gave you. The men on the other end will take it from there." He opened the door. "Go! Now! Quickly!"

And Drew pushed himself down the stairs into a dank basement lit by a single emergency light. He tried to stand three steps from the bottom and ended up tumbling to the floor. The pain that engulfed his body made him want to vomit as he hurried across the tile toward the escape door that would take him into the tunnel.

Above him the gun blasts came more frequently, mostly in rapid spurts indicating automatic fire. A new series, individual reports that were the loudest yet, started up and Drew could tell they came from within the house instead of out. Jabba was trying to buy him the time he needed.

Drew tripped over a crate and crawled the rest of the way to the tunnel door, throwing it open from his knees. The tunnel was totally black, not even the slightest spill of light to break the emptiness. It was narrow, too, and short. Drew hunched at the back and knees as he forced himself through, using the walls as his only guide, his eyes useless. A few times corners and turns confused him and he went sprawling, the pain so great at impact that even a scream was denied him. Always he regained his footing and pressed on; his clothes filthy, flesh on his hands raw and bleeding from breaking his many falls.

Above him the blasts had stopped. Jabba's resistance had ended, indicating that he was now on his own, left only with the hope that his head start in the tunnel would be sufficient.

Drew lost track of how much ground he had covered and distracted himself with reviewing the passage of time. It was Wednesday morning now, a few hours before sunrise. He had been at Jabba's since Sunday night, had changed into the clothes that the fat man had brought him late Tuesday.

Suddenly, the dirt path curved steeply upward. *I'm almost out!* Drew thought, thirsting for the moonlight about to welcome him. Get to a phone and call the numbers stuffed in his pocket. Tell whoever answers everything. Yes, he could do it! He rushed up the last of the steep incline and nearly collided head first with a wooden trapdoor.

It took all the strength his shoulders could muster to force the door open. He pulled himself back to the surface with his raw, scraped hands.

Three flashlights blinded him immediately. Through the glare he made out a single man standing ahead of several others, made him out because of the startling whiteness of his hair and skin that seemed no different than the shade of his suit.

"We've been waiting for you," said Corbano.

CHAPTER 30

"IT'S IMPOSSIBLE," SAID ELLIANA, RETURNING THE BINOCULARS to the Timber Wolf.

"Drew's inside, Ellie. I've got to get him out."

And Wayman gazed back into the binoculars so he wouldn't have to meet her disapproving stare. Before him stood a twenty-room, three-story fortress in the middle of Eastman, Georgia, fronted by a four-foot stone fence that effectively formed a huge courtyard presently lined with guards.

It was midafternoon on Wednesday. Flying first from Germany to the United States and then making their way into Georgia's back country had proved difficult on all accounts, an agonizing journey that saw them at the whims of the weather, twisted airline schedules, and ill-functioning rental cars. At each turn more and more of the precautions deemed necessary to keep the Council of Ten from catching them were abandoned in the more pressing interests of time.

The only luxury Ellie insisted on was a phone call to Tel Aviv.

"Isser, thank God I reached you!"

Isser's voice emerged in a dull monotone. "You have no reason to thank Him, Ellie. I can't confirm your version of what happened in Prague. That agent you said tried to kill you has been off our active list for months and has disappeared."

"That doesn't matter anymore! Just listen to me. The Council's ready to make its ultimate move. Tomorrow, Isser, it's going to start tomorrow!''

"What's going to start?"

"The worst horror you can imagine. A total realignment of the world as it's known. I can't explain everything. I don't believe it all myself.''

"And you expect me to?"

"Yes, because you have to. I'm not going to worry about the length of this call because if you don't believe me my fate won't matter. I have information that can stop them, but I can't follow it up alone. You have nothing to lose by helping me.''

"Ellie—"

"Stop it, Isser. How many years did I lay my life on the line for you? How many bullets did I narrowly avoid? I was the best, *am* the best. This is all real, no illusion. Thursday will mark the beginning of a new kind of world. No one will be safe, especially Israel. Trust me, you have to!'' She paused, seizing the offensive again when he made no response. "The Council's headquarters is somewhere near Lisbon. It doesn't matter how I know. What does matter is that sometime tomorrow a number of exceptionally powerful men are going to be arriving in the city. If you could catch onto one, follow him . . .''

"Ellie, what you're asking, it's impossible."

But she could feel him giving. "No! I've headed up similar operations before. With full intelligence mobilization even on short notice, you can pull it off. You *have* to pull it off. There's too much at stake.''

"Lisbon," Isser muttered, and she knew she had him.

Twenty-four hours later Ellie and the Timber Wolf had arrived in Eastman. They followed ten miles of dirt-paved roads and then abandoned the car. Camouflaging it with brush, they covered the rest of the distance through the woods on foot, hoping not to attract attention. The trek was longer than estimated and took a solid forty minutes before they reached the break in the forest beyond which lay the fenced-in compound. A few minutes later a black car mired with dirt and scratches wound down the narrow, private road. A heavy chain was pulled aside to let it pass. Wayman and Ellie watched its occupants with interest as all four doors opened together.

The first one they saw was Corbano, a dapper white suit over his muscular frame, his milky white features giving him the air of a corpse. The coloring he was cursed with made him a fearful sight, deadly and cold.

Two of his men emerged next dragging a figure whom Ellie didn't recognize but who took the Timber Wolf's breath away.

"That's Drew Jordan," he muttered in shock over seeing the young man still alive. "My God, he's— What's he doing here? What's Corbano want with him?"

"The point," said Ellie, "is that he's alive."

"Not for long, unless we do something."

"Any ideas?"

The Timber Wolf turned his attention to the binoculars and began to think. There were at least a dozen guards outside and probably a similar number within the house where Drew Jordan had been led.

"I've got to get him out," Wayman said for the second time minutes later despite Ellie's admonition.

"I agree," she relented. "So long as we get Corbano as well. He's the key to the operation. Powderkeg is scheduled to start tomorrow on the East Coast. He's the only chance we've got to stop it."

"Maybe. But the Council's pulling his strings. They don't impress me as the sort who'd give up any more control than they absolutely had to. That means the signals will come from their headquarters, not here."

"Interesting point. Except we don't know where their headquarters is, and Corbano must. We've got to get to him."

"Nightfall," the Timber Wolf said suddenly, his thoughts seeming to jell.

"We've got your pistol and mine. Hardly enough firepower."

"Then we'll have to get some more."

"Now? How?"

"You stay here," Wayman told her, moving to his feet.

"Where are you going?"

"Shopping."

"How good to see you awake," the all-white man told Drew as he finally came around. His eyes struggled to focus. His head pounded.

"Yes," the man went on, "you're probably uncomfortable.

We gave you something to make the ride down here from Virginia easier.'' Corbano stood up and moved between Drew and a raging fire that one of several men in the room with them had lit and was now tending. "Is there anything I can get you?"

"Water," Drew managed.

"Yes, of course."

Corbano motioned for a glass to be brought to him immediately. Another of the men handed it to him. Corbano stepped forward and started to offer it to Drew, pulling back at the last instant and tossing the contents into his face.

"Oh, I am sorry. How clumsy of me. . . ."

Drew licked at his face to find as much stray moisture as he could.

Across the floor, the flames in the fireplace roared higher.

"Unusually cold for fall in the back country," Corbano said to no one in particular. "A splendid night to sit by the fire." Then, to Drew, "You know all about fire, don't you? Sunday night that laboratory was destroyed by fire. I understand your girl friend was burned rather badly and you narrowly escaped the same fate. What a shame, she was such a pretty girl. . . ."

Drew felt himself tremble with rage. He looked up hatefully at the all-white man.

"You should have died then," Corbano told him. "Now you've gone and complicated things for yourself . . . and me." He paused. "It was not hard for us to trace your fat friend's hideout. He died alone, Drew, just like you're going to."

Drew gritted his teeth.

"You will answer my questions, won't you?"

Drew just looked up at him.

"I could give you truth serum and in your present condition it would almost certainly kill you by the time we'd finished. But then you wouldn't feel enough pain and we can't have that now, can we?"

Corbano motioned to one of the men behind him by the fire. The man pulled a poker from the hearth and brought it forward, holding it high for safety. Its tip glowed fiery orange. Corbano grasped it at the handle and waved it before Drew's face.

"What's happened to the powder?" he asked.

"Left, left in the lab," Drew replied.

"Then you found out what it was, found out what it can do?"

Drew looked away.

Corbano grabbed his chin and forced it back forward. "And you told your friend in Virginia about it, didn't you?"

"You already know the answer to that."

"But I don't know if *he* told anyone."

"The president. He should be arriving here any minute."

Corbano smiled. He patted Drew's cheek tenderly but made sure he could see the poker.

"I should ask you where the fat man took your girl friend. No, that would take too long to get out of you and I can probably find her quite easily by myself." Corbano knelt into a crouch. "You'd like that, Drew, wouldn't you? You'd like me to bring her here so you can be together."

"Fuck you," Drew said, more out of anger than bravado.

"No, it's her you'd like to fuck. Just say the word and I'll arrange it. Or perhaps you would prefer a trade. Tell me where we can find Trelana and I won't bother looking for her."

"I don't know."

"Where is Trelana?"

"I was blindfolded!" Drew lied. "I never knew where I was when we met."

Corbano smiled and shook his head. "I'm going to ask you one more time. Where can we find Arthur Trelana?"

"*I don't know!*"

"Suit yourself," said Corbano.

And drove the hot poker straight for Drew's face.

The Timber Wolf returned an hour before nightfall, a pair of shopping bags in his arms.

"We've got to hurry," he said, placing the bags down between himself and Ellie.

"What did you—"

"Napalm, grenades, tear gas, and a few assorted extras."

"In the *general store?*"

Wayman nodded and emptied the varied contents of the bags on the ground, explaining as he did. "Ammonia and bleach. Seal the bleach in a baby food jar and seal that in a larger jar filled with ammonia. When they shatter and the liquids mix, you've got homemade tear gas." Next, he pulled out a bag of kitty litter and a two-gallon drum of gasoline. "Napalm." The largest assortment came out last and included galvanized plastic piping, black powder, nails, candles, and assorted ropes, cloth, and jars. "These grenades will pack quite a wallop."

"If we don't blow ourselves up making them."

"I've had plenty of experience. Many of my assignments years ago required that I enter a country without any weapons," he told her. "I learned how to make them from scratch after arriving. I could even whip us up some pretty good nitro given the time."

"We might need some to penetrate Corbano's defenses."

"This will come close enough."

For the next ninety minutes, Ellie followed Wayman's instructions precisely, mixing compounds in exact measures in the bowls he had provided. The most dangerous work he saved for himself, and occasionally she drew far enough ahead to watch the sweat pouring from his brow as he sealed exceptionally volatile contents within ordinary glass jars. They both hurried through their work as night began to fall, knowing that darkness would signal the definitive end to their labors. Still, they continued well past the point when sufficient light had faded from the sky and their eyes began to deceive them.

The Timber Wolf was dividing their homemade arsenal into piles of pipe bombs, nail grenades made from Coke bottles, large napalm jars, and smaller tear gas ones—when the scream came. It pierced the night with an agonizing shrill that forced both him and Ellie to shudder.

"We've got to move," he told her.

"It's not dark yet."

"It's dark enough."

Drew lay on the cot motionless, hovering in different stages of consciousness. He was awake enough to think but not awake enough to move no matter how much he coaxed his muscles. He remembered the red-tipped poker coming at him, an involuntary shift of his head, and then the pain.

Oh God, the pain . . .

When the scream came, he was already detached from himself, so it seemed that he could hear it even as the sound left him on his breath.

The poker had missed his eye and pierced the flesh over his

cheekbone. He remembered the sizzling hiss and thought even as he screamed of steaks barbecuing over an open grill. He would have vomited if his stomach had anything in it. The eye had swollen shut immediately and hadn't reopened since. The body had worked fast to numb the incredible agony, which returned now one throb at a time as he lay on the cot hearing himself breathe as if it were someone else.

He wanted to die. When you came right down to it, there was nothing else to hope for. Jabba was dead, his grandmother was dead, and who knew about Pam. There was no one left to turn to, no one left to save him. Strangely, death no longer scared him, but seemed a welcome alternative to the further pain promised at the hands of the all-white man.

Drew inhaled deeply and prayed for sleep.

"We each have three pipe bombs, two nail grenades, and three containers each of napalm and tear gas," the Timber Wolf told Ellie. "Be careful with the napalm and tear gas. They're useful to us only from a distance."

"What about matches?"

Wayman reached into his pocket and produced two lighters. "One for each of us, but in this wind they might not prove reliable, so I also brought some cigarettes. The best way to light the fuses is to light a cigarette first and then hold it up to them. The wind's no problem that way. Takes a little longer, though."

Ellie looked satisfied.

They had dragged their arsenal to the very edge of the clearing. Rising would bring them into the range of the complex's heavy duty lighting, in addition to the guards' rifles. There was no other choice at this point. They would have to rely on darkness and distraction to shield them.

The Timber Wolf held a lighter to a cigarette, handed it over to Ellie, and then lit one for himself.

"We'll start with the nail grenades and pipe bombs," he explained. "Those should draw their attention and force the troops out where the napalm and tear gas will be most effective. The idea is to forge a tunnel for ourselves right through their ranks direct for the front door."

He held the cigarette up to the first of his pipe bombs, letting the fuse burn down.

"Go!" he instructed.

Ellie touched her cigarette to the first of her nail grenades and hurled it, already lighting the second as Wayman's toss exploded an instant before hers. The resulting explosions achieved even more than their desired effects. The guards scattered directly into the paths of the second grenades they each hurled. Two tosses later, the chaos total, the Timber Wolf started with the napalm.

The makeshift construction didn't work as well as he had hoped; the fireballs were not potent enough to link up and create the wall of flame he had been expecting. Yet, several of the infernos captured someone within them. The victims' screams punctured the night as they rolled hopelessly on the ground, catching the dirt aflame, too.

More lights flooded the courtyard. An alarm began to shriek. Ellie tossed another grenade and then a nail bomb. There were screams and more men fell. Others with rifles and machine guns were rushing from the house now, an instinctive reaction and the worst one since it played right into their enemy's hands. Confusion became Wayman and Ellie's ally, the troops unable to ascertain where the attack was coming from. It was time for the tear gas. They each hurled two of their jars, the clear liquid sloshing about. All four crashed open on impact and sent the guards closest to them clawing for their eyes and throats immediately, gagging. The gas spread quickly, forcing the others to stagger away shielding their eyes and mouths.

"Now!"

Ellie followed him. Each had their pistols out, Ellie holding another pipe bomb in her hand with a last stored in her pocket. For his part, Wayman carried several of the homemade weapons in his inside jacket pockets, including a final container of the tear gas compound that he could only hope a quick dive to the ground would not shatter under him.

They hurdled over the fence and rushed down the funnel that their blasts had created between the perimeter guards. Some of the guards had recovered enough to level guns at the intruders charging boldly into the light. Ellie's and Wayman's pistols clacked as they ran, at least half their shots being hits.

Even though they moved quickly, they could feel the effects of the tear gas. Ellie felt a dryness in her mouth and the start of burning down her throat. Wayman's eyes were watering heavily, obscuring his vision. As they neared the front door, each touched a lighter to a pipe bomb and lobbed it through a window. Screams followed the blasts. Smoke and flames coughed out from the shattered glass.

The Timber Wolf reached the porch and ducked as a hail of fire bore down on him from an upstairs window. Ellie tried to return it with her pistol, but the same gunman quickly had her pinned down as well. Corbano's men inside had reacted better than expected. The second-level windows made the most defensible positions of all and Wayman had feared their use more than anything. He crouched with Ellie in the cover of the high stairs and porch.

"Damn," he muttered.

Another second-floor window showed a gun, and automatic fire cut through what was left of the windows on the first floor, seeking their position. Meanwhile, the remaining functional guards along the perimeter had regrouped and were firing from beyond the cover of trees in the yard, effectively pinning Ellie and Wayman where they were.

"Trapped," she muttered.

"Handle the outside shooters," he told her, as rifle fire coughed wood splinters over them.

Ellie snapped another clip home. "I've only got one more after this."

"Use your last pipe bomb. Use anything! Just distract them!"

Ellie struck her lighter to the fuse of her final pipe bomb and hurled it toward the largest congestion of fire. In the instant after it struck, the Timber Wolf was on his feet challenging the fire from the windows on both floors as he hurled a pipe bomb through the first level and a napalm jar through the second. The screams on the ground floor came first as the last of the windows were blown out. On the second floor there were only screams and the bright orange glow of a room on fire.

The front door crashed open and two men with machine guns charged them. Their rapid spray forced Wayman into a spin that stripped him of his balance and he went down hoping the padding of his jacket would cushion his final container of tear gas.

He struck the ground as softly as he could, Ellie gasping at the sight while she fired at the men whose machine guns were still blaring. Miraculously, the tear gas jar remained whole and Wayman added his fire to Ellie's immediately. Both men crumbled. Wayman and Ellie sprang to their feet.

"The door!" she shouted.

Their only threat came now from the men firing from the cover of the trees. They'd have to chance it. The Timber Wolf lobbed his last pipe bomb and napalm jar through the open door and rushed in after them into a pool of dust, splinters, and flames.

He had just reached the staircase, Ellie right behind and gunfire tracing them, when the pipe bomb ignited. Men scattered, diving for cover, as more deadly fragments flew everywhere. Ellie and Wayman fired at the men who moved, fired at anything that moved as the spreading flames tried to follow them up the staircase.

Corbano had been in the master bedroom when the napalm thrown from below had set it afire. His sleeve was caught and he made it into the corridor and rolled upon the floor just before the fire reached his flesh. Although his burns were slight, the pain was intense. His white skin and hair were blackened by soot and smoke and he felt blood running down his face from a piece of glass. He had caught enough of a glimpse of the attackers outside to know the Timber Wolf was among them and that fact, along with the realization that the house itself had been penetrated, sent an uneasy combination of fear and hate surging through him.

Corbano rushed up to the third floor where a closet held the remains of his arsenal. There had been two dozen men with him at the house. How many remained he had no way of knowing, and it didn't matter to him.

What mattered was that he had the perfect means to kill the invaders himself.

At first Drew thought the explosions were products of his nightmare. Only the fact that his good eye was open and working reasonably well told him they were real.

Confusion blurred his thoughts. Obviously a battle was taking place, but between whom? Had another force attacked the fortress? Were they somehow his unwitting allies? If so, he had to reach them, at least alert them to his presence.

It took all his will to stir his frame from the cot and lower himself to the floor. He tried to brace with his feet, but they slipped out and he hit the wood hard. Pain surged through him in waves of anguish. He was dizzy and his head pounded. He lifted both hands to the cot and pulled himself up, trying to stand but crumbling again, this time to a sitting position.

He slid across the cot toward the wall and leaned against it as he finally rose to his feet. He stayed there for a few seconds to catch his breath and then pulled himself along the plaster toward the door.

He smelled smoke, then saw it sneaking under the door in thick blankets.

The effect of the flames on the dry upholstery and carpeting was dramatic and immediate. The entire downstairs had caught fire by the time Ellie and Wayman reached the second landing. There would be no pursuit coming at them from below now.

But there would be no escape in that direction either.

The smoke on the second floor hallway was soupy gray, drawn from the flames rising from below. They kept their frames pressed against the hot walls as they followed them almost blindly. The concentration of guards was all below now, trapped by the flames and probably massing to consider their next move. Wayman tried each of the doors on the right side of the corridor, while Ellie tried those on the left. A quick jump inside each room with gun leveled yielded no results.

A figure appeared at the head of the hallway, a white flash in the grayness. Both Ellie and Wayman knew it was Corbano, knew the short fat object in his hand was a Laws rocket, in effect a disposable, miniature bazooka that could blow an entire wall out. They each fired, aim confused by the smoke, and thus errant. But the Laws rocket was rising, readying for a clear shot down the corridor.

Drew threw the door open and registered immediately the presence of the all-white man before him along with the crazy-looking gun in his hands. Instinctively, Drew lunged. The move was poorly timed and weak. But it forced Corbano off balance and he pulled the trigger while the Laws's barrel was moving, which sent a blast high across the corridor into the farthest wall, obliterating it.

Ellie and Wayman had hugged the floor for cover and fought to rise now as Corbano struck Drew hard under the chin with the Laws's butt and ran off in the opposite direction. This time Drew never lost consciousness. He was aware, though dimly, of two figures hovering over him.

"Drew, can you hear me?"

The voice belonged to the Timber Wolf! He had come to rescue him! He really had! Drew tried to find him, but his vision had blurred over.

Wayman lifted Drew to his feet and pressed him into Ellie's grasp. "Get him out of here," he ordered, eyes already searching the corridor in the direction the White Snake had vanished. "I'm going after Corbano."

The Timber Wolf took the staircase after Corbano, his heart thundering and lungs bursting for air. He reached the third floor, which was smoky from flames that would soon consume it along with the first two. The entire house was turning into an inferno.

There was a screech of heels turning quickly against wood, and suddenly Corbano appeared at the edge of the hallway. Wayman dove and rolled as the White Snake's automatic fire pounded the walls above him. The Timber Wolf stayed in motion, ahead of the rounds at each turn, firing single shots from his pistol in Corbano's general direction.

"Die, you fucker!" Corbano screamed, still shooting, coughing the smoke out of his lungs.

Wayman stayed low, using the smoke spreading through the third floor as camouflage. Rising suddenly around a bend in the corridor, he threw his shoulder into a door and crashed through it. A hail of automatic fire greeted him from down the hallway, followed by heavy footsteps as Corbano rushed toward him.

The White Snake came into the room with machine gun blazing, but the Timber Wolf spun out from behind the door and locked his hands upon the hot barrel. They grappled, neither giving, and the force of their struggle propelled them into a surge across the room.

The window came up fast out of the smoke-filled darkness. Together they crashed through it and rolled toward the edge of the roof.

*   *   *

Ellie had led Drew the other way on the third floor, down another hallway where the smoke was equally thick. She knew a house of this size would have a second stairway somewhere that might permit them escape to the outside, but how to find it?

It was more a question of it finding them.

They had just turned a corner, Ellie dragging Drew along when the sound of rapid, climbing footsteps forced her to slam them both against the wall, hoping the smoke clouds would shield them sufficiently. As it turned out, the last of Corbano's soldiers rushing up the staircase through the door never even looked back. She counted at least eight and waited to be sure no others were following before yanking Drew down it after her.

They were both coughing by the time the stairs ended, eyes watering so badly that it was several seconds after they emerged outside in the back of the house before they could make them work again. Drew moved as if in a daze. The woman was tugging at him, forcing him into a run parallel to the burning house, close enough to feel the heat of the raging flames that had begun to pour through the walls.

A huge green tarpaulin rose before them and the woman dragged him against it so they could catch their breath. Drew watched as, intrigued, she yanked part of the tarp aside.

He saw her smile.

The roof flattened out just before the edge, saving both Wayman and Corbano from a potential deadly plunge. Wayman had the advantage briefly, but they rolled again and with that the White Snake's fingers were digging into his throat. The Timber Wolf felt his head over the roof's edge and realized that Corbano was trying to shove the rest of him off as well.

Instead of increasing the pressure on Wayman's throat, Corbano mounted a savage thrust. The Timber Wolf found himself able to twist his body enough to strip the White Snake's balance and throw him aside. Wayman rolled free and regained his feet, just as Corbano found his.

The old rivals faced each other on the sloped roof.

Corbano lunged first, screaming, with a kick that was poorly timed. The Timber Wolf blocked it out of midair and twisted the knee violently. Corbano bellowed in pain as Wayman toppled him face first to the surface, holding tight to continue his enemy's momentum off the roof.

Suddenly, shingles exploded by his feet. Armed men were pouring from the window one after the other. Wayman yanked the White Snake back to his feet and held him from behind by the throat, offering Corbano out as a helpless screen, making it obvious he could break his neck with the slightest motion.

The guards hesitated, unsure. Still, they fanned out in close ranks on the roof.

"Don't move!" Wayman screamed.

But they kept moving, coming at him.

"I'll kill him!"

But the threat only slowed them and the Timber Wolf realized that the stalemate belonged to them. He backed up to the very edge and felt for the last container of tear gas within his jacket. He searched for a way out, holding Corbano by the throat before him.

Then the grinding sound came. Wayman heard it an instant before he saw the massive yellow payloader, turned by tires six feet high with a shovel powerful enough to keep an entire river of mud from overrunning the house during the back country's rainy season, swing around from the side of the building. Ellie was behind the wheel and heading it for the front of the house where his heels teetered.

In that single instant, Wayman saw what he had to do and acted. He sent the final jar of tear gas crashing toward the men before him as he shoved Corbano away and leaped from the roof.

Part of the second story jutted out beneath him. He landed hard on its flat surface and wasted no time or motion as he rolled forward and dropped off toward ground level. Such a fall would have been deadly from three stories, but it was doable from a distance of barely twenty feet. The key was to reduce the initial impact by tucking into a roll as soon as the ground came up. He struck it hard enough to take his wind away, but he felt himself rolling and knew he was safe.

Ellie had spun the loader around so the cab was shielded by the raised shovel, effectively blocking out gunfire. Wayman's roll had stopped just two yards from the machine and he pulled himself into the high cab seconds later. It was built to hold one person, and three made for a tight squeeze.

Then they were moving in reverse, Ellie peering frantically behind her as bullets chimed off the loader's shovel. Wayman could hear Corbano shouting something to his men, but he couldn't make out the words above the roar. Ellie swung the loader around as they approached the stone fence, then lowered the shovel. The machine's pace wasn't even slowed as it crashed straight through and blazed a fresh path through the woods.

Wayman kept his eyes locked behind him, Ellie rotating hers as she struggled to control the yellow monster. Drew stirred and moaned, slumping against the right door. Bullets pounded the yellow frame as Corbano and his remaining men rushed through the woods giving chase, gaining slightly as Ellie did her best to maneuver among the trees. A volley of shots nearly found the gas tank, which reminded Waymen of something he had seen near Drew's feet when he pulled himself in. He shoved Drew's legs aside.

Yes, there it was! A gasoline can, full to the brim. He hoisted it upward and swung it hard against the rear window of the cab. The glass shattered outward. Wayman pulled the can back in and ripped off the top. Then he jammed his torso through the opening in the glass, gas can outstretched before him, feeling jagged shards slice through his shirt and find his skin.

The Timber Wolf steadied himself enough to tip the can downward and pour the contents onto the ground in the loader's wake, drawing a steady line behind them in the path it plowed through the woods. A narrow path, narrow enough for the plan to work.

Bullets whizzed by Wayman's head. He shook the rest of the gasoline from the can and tossed it aside. He pushed along the loader's backside to propel himself back inside the cab.

"Hurry!" Elliana urged, realizing his intention as a thick branch smashed into the windshield.

The Timber Wolf already had his pistol out.

Thirty yards back, Corbano was steadying another Laws rocket.

"Christ," Wayman muttered and pulled the trigger of his pistol.

The gasoline-fueled flames caught and ran directly up the line

Wayman had drawn on the ground. The gun-wielding men peeled off the path into the woods.

Corbano had moved to the side before them. He watched the wall of flames race by him as he squeezed the trigger of his Laws.

The rocket shot out.

The payloader went up in an orange fireball, which seemed to join the fiery path already plowed through the woods. Corbano lunged to the ground and covered his head from the possible falling debris. When he finally looked up, the shell of the payloader was resting on its side, one stubborn tire spinning slowly and turning flames with it. There wouldn't be much left of the bodies after such a blast, Corbano figured.

Nothing left at all.

CHAPTER 31

"YOU'RE SURE YOU GOT THEM THIS TIME?"

The Council leader's voice was laced with uncharacteristic concern.

"No one could have survived a blast like that," Corbano reported, the scorched side of his milk-white face covered with bandages. "We searched the woods to make sure. Nothing. Their meager attempt at disruption has been squashed."

"An interesting analysis considering the casualties encountered on our side."

"Soldiers, nothing more. Easily replaced."

"Eighteen men were killed or wounded."

"By two who were experts in their trade. The ratio is not so hard to believe as it seems. Place the resources of the Timber Wolf and the Jew bitch together and instantly their individual abilities become magnified . . . not that it gained them anything. All operations can move ahead as scheduled. By six P.M. tomorrow, Powderkeg will have begun to spread across the eastern seaboard. Washington, New York, Boston, Philadelphia—all will have ceased to exist by midnight."

"That would maintain the timetable. We are in contact from the castle with the other twenty-eight distribution points. They are waiting for their signal. When it comes, twelve to eighteen hours after your strike has been initiated, they will begin their drops."

"And the shelters?"

"The signals have gone out. Arrivals will begin just after dawn tomorrow as planned. Our people are ready."

"So are we."

Darkness.

That was all Drew could remember from the instant of the blast. The Timber Wolf had seen what was coming in time to leap from the still-moving payloader, yanking Drew out behind him. Elliana jumped out the other side. The flames that followed the blast shielded their escape by forming a wall of fire between them and immediate pursuit.

They had met up moments later and trudged long and hard through the woods. Most of the way Wayman supported Drew although his own condition seemed little better. Ellie hung back ten yards or so to serve as a buffer against possible attack from the rear. All three were hopelessly exhausted, the primary goal now just to find the car camouflaged miles back from the cabin, miles themselves lost in the darkness.

It was over an hour before they finally found it. Ellie drove, eyes constantly darting to the rearview mirror on the chance that Corbano's men had picked up their trail. Drew had no conception of how long or far they traveled through the night. He fell into a state of semiconsciousness, mind as battered as his body.

At last they came to the roadside motel with a pair of letters burned out on its neon sign. Drew accepted Wayman's help in getting inside where he collapsed on one of the beds. The woman swabbed and bandaged his wounds. His eye was open again, but his wounded cheek remained swollen, part of the flesh tinted gray. He tried to speak, but still there were no words. Finally, he felt himself slip off to sleep, a shallow slumber in which conversation between Wayman and the woman called Ellie was sometimes clear to him.

"Do you think Corbano knows we're still alive?" Ellie asked the Timber Wolf.

"I don't think it matters. Either way, there's a timetable they'll have to stick to. You said the eastern seaboard phase of the operation is scheduled to start tomorrow, followed by the rest of the country on Friday. That means people must already be arriving at the shelters. The Council can't risk letting that lead to questions."

"So, we know the East Coast is the first to go, but from which drop point?"

"There's only one that fits the bill geographically—Prudence Island."

Ellie stood by the window, peering out through a crack in the drawn curtain. Wayman sat on the second bed with his shoulders supported by the headboard. She turned toward him.

"Island?"

"Yes. Off the coast of Rhode Island in Narragansett Bay. Can't tell you much about it, beside the fact that's the only place Corbano, and the first phase of Powderkeg, can be stopped."

"Which would still leave twenty-eight drop points uncovered," Ellie reminded him glumly. "The drop points will be awaiting a uniform go-signal before proceeding, which must be coming direct from Council headquarters." She checked her watch. "It's time I made a phone call."

"Ellie, I don't know what to say. . . ."

But Isser's apologetic tone said more than enough. "What have you found, Isser?"

The head of the Mossad told her. It was all Elliana could do to keep her trembling hand steady on the receiver.

"My God," she said when Isser had finished. His report did not surprise her, but somehow the shock of the truth was no less great.

"He won't be at the Castle of the Moors," Isser went on, "but we will be. The operation's yours. How soon can you be in Lisbon?"

It was closing in on midnight where they were now. Ellie tried to calculate. "Twelve to fourteen hours," she said optimistically.

"A full strike team is being assembled. We're taking an awful chance here, Ellie."

"It's the only chance we have," she told him.

"It all fits," Ellie told Wayman twenty minutes later, eager to start her journey for Lisbon. "The Council would need a command center where Powderkeg could be controlled and monitored without scrutiny from the outside. The castle is perfect. That's where the go-signal will come from. And now with the Mossad I can stop it!''

''So long as they're not expecting you. And even if they're not, their perimeter defenses may be impenetrable.''

''Nothing's impenetrable.''

''It's a castle, goddamnit, full of chambers and catacombs. Seems like pounding the shit out of it with an air strike would be a whole lot more effective.''

''No,'' Ellie insisted, ''we've got to be sure the Council members, especially its leader, are killed. Otherwise, it could start up all over again.''

''That's only part of it,'' the Timber Wolf said knowingly. ''It's become personal for you.''

''No, Timber Wolf, it's *always* been personal and why shouldn't it be? I've been waiting too long for this day. They killed David, in case you've forgotten.''

''I haven't, but you might be better off if you did.'' His tone turned reflective. ''I know what happens when this kind of game becomes personal. People such as you and me can't afford that.''

''But we still call it a game, don't we? And is your desire to go after Corbano at Prudence Island any different? Can you sit there and tell me Corsica's been pushed out of your memory?''

''No. But I know what Corsica did to me in the first place and I can promise it won't happen again. I've got a job to do. That's where it starts and ends this time. It's the castle itself that concerns me.''

''And what about the open seas where you'll be searching for Corbano? I wouldn't trade you even up, and so what? You and I, Timber Wolf, have spent our lifetimes fighting the odds and the percentages, beating them more often than we had a right to expect to. No one ever cried for us before, so let's not go and shed any tears for our desperate plights.'' A look of grim determination crossed her face. ''They killed David. For five years I've struggled and searched, always knowing that if I ever found them it would mean my death. So, I'm used to the idea. Every minute I live now that I'm finally onto them is a bonus because it'll bring me that much closer. And if I get enough of those minutes I just might get them before they get me. Is it really any different for you? The East Coast operation, Prudence Island, is separate from the rest of Powderkeg. It's got to be stopped at its own source: You against Corbano just like old times, no matter how you want to describe it. Only you won't have a strike force backing you up as I will.''

"Not necessarily," said Drew, suddenly stirring.

"What do you mean Trelana *wasn't* killed at Too-Jay's?"

Drew was fumbling with the receiver. "It was a double who got shot. Trelana wanted to *appear* dead. But if I can reach him now, he'll help us. God knows he's got the reason and the resources." He pressed out the contact number. "Damn, it's been disconnected!"

"Who exactly are you calling?" Wayman asked him.

Drew related a frantic summary of the events from his jailing, to Colombia, to Nassau, Miami, and then Washington.

"My God," Ellie said at the end, "the powder. . . . Somehow I was hoping it might not work after all."

"Forget it," Drew told her. "I was there. My girl friend analyzed it." Then, to Wayman, "Why would Trelana disconnect the contact number he gave me?"

"Because he's probably given you up for dead. Or, worse, figures that you sold him out."

"Then if I can find another way to contact him, he still might help us. I saw a phone in his villa. We've got to get the number."

Wayman thought briefly. "Leave that to me."

Ellie had left by the time Wayman put in a call to Jilly's home number. A proper series of codes and signals drawn from their days in the network alerted her to potential danger, while he passed along the exchange at which he could be reached. She was to find a safe line and call back as soon as possible, which turned out to be thirty minutes later.

"Peter, what in hell's happening?"

"Whether I get the opportunity to explain or not depends on you. I need a phone number in Colombia, specifically the *Islas del Rosario* off the coast of Cartagena."

"All this for a number?"

"Belonging to Arthur Trelana's private villa."

"But he's dead."

"The reports, as they say, were greatly exaggerated."

"What are *you* saying? Have you found that fellow?"

Wayman's eyes fell on Drew who was watching eagerly. "Long story to both questions. Can you get me the number?"

"Give me an hour," Jilly said with a sigh.

Wayman left briefly in search of a map of New England at a nearby gas station. When he returned Drew was staring blindly at the wall, not even seeming to register his presence.

Wayman sat down next to him in silence for a time before choosing his moment to speak. "I'll get you out of this," he said. "I promise."

"That's not what I was thinking about. Besides, I'm already in it."

"What were you thinking about?"

Drew felt along the swollen, charred area on his cheek. "Everything, right from the start. It's almost funny."

"You're not laughing."

"I said almost."

Wayman thought for a few moments. "Look, I know people. I can make arrangements for you . . . and your girl friend. Keep you both safe."

Drew shook his head slowly, guiltily realizing that he hadn't thought about Pam at all since they had reached the motel. "No, I can't accept that. If you fail, I'm dead anyway along with the rest of the country. The difference is that I know what's coming. You can't expect me to sit back and wait."

"This is my game, Drew, not yours."

A slight smile lit Drew's face. "That's a line from *Shane*, you know. Alan Ladd says it to Van Heflin just before he rides into town to face the Ryker brothers, and especially Jack Palance as Wilson the gunfighter."

The Timber Wolf smiled with him. "I know the movie."

"All the times I've seen it, I always wanted Shane to take the kid with him in the end."

"As I remember it, the kid wanted Shane to stay."

"I know. But I always figured that if the kid knew he'd never see Shane again, he would rather have gone with him than stayed home. Only Shane couldn't take him cause the kid had all those chores and Jean Arthur to go back to." Drew paused. "I don't have anything to go back to."

"Do yourself a favor, Drew. Let me get you to Virginia where you can wait this thing out at your girl friend's bedside, keeping your fingers crossed that you'll be alive come Friday morning."

Drew waved him off staunchly. "Save your breath, Timber Wolf."

"It's not my breath I'm worried about."

The phone rang.

"The rest is up to you now, kid," Wayman told him, handing the receiver to Drew as he punched out the number Jilly had provided for Arthur Trelana. "Just remember everything I told you."

"I'll try."

The phone rang six times before it was answered.

"Yes?" greeted a deep, male voice.

"Mr. Trelana please."

"I'm afraid he's unavailable."

"Tell him it's Drew Jordan."

The man hesitated. "How did you get this number?"

"It doesn't matter. Look, I found what Mr. Trelana sent me to find. I know what's going on here and I can help him, but I need his help first. You've got to let me talk to him. I'll give you the number where I can be reached. Trace it if you want. Send men out here to kill me. It doesn't matter. Believe me it doesn't."

The man hesitated again. "I'll pass on the message, but I'm not promising anything."

The phone rang after an agonizing twenty minutes.

"This conversation was supposed to have taken place considerably earlier," Trelana said by way of greeting, sounding tired and nasal.

"It would have. But someone 'borrowed' the line you set up for me. I walked into a trap."

"I suspected as much," Trelana told him. "Someone's closing in on me, but they still haven't pinned me to this island. If you had talked, the battle would already be raging."

Drew swallowed hard. "I found what you sent me to find. It's got everything to do with power like you thought, with someone after total control. But it's got nothing to do with drugs."

"You've lost me, Drew."

"The powder that started with the grandmothers wasn't cocaine at all. It's some sort of compound that when mixed with water absorbs oxygen from the air. Behind it is a group calling itself the Council of Ten that plans to use the powder to destroy America. I've seen it in action. *Believe* me, it works."

The line filled with Trelana's labored breathing. "My resources are drained, Drew. I'm not sure there'll be anything I can do to help. But I'll listen. Tell me everything."

PART EIGHT:

PRUDENCE ISLAND AND THE CASTLE OF THE MOORS

CHAPTER 32

ELLIE WOULD BE MEETING THE MOSSAD LIAISON WHO WOULD LINK her up with the strike force at the Quinta Restaurant atop the hillside village of the Bairro Alto. From Lisbon proper she took the lift built by Eiffel himself, a hulking ironwork structure linking one world with another. The footbridge on top afforded a magnificent view and as Ellie paused outside the Quinta, she almost imagined she could see the Castle of the Moors. Her contact was waiting at the table as planned.

He didn't rise when she took the chair across from his. "We received your revised orders," he whispered nervously. "They have been carried out." He was a curly-haired dark man dressed in ill-fitting clothes.

Ellie felt a numbness pass through her. "What revised orders?"

The man looked confused. "The strike force has been recalled."

"*What?* I never—"

Ellie stopped herself. There was no point in going on, no point in chastising the man before her. The Council of Ten was to blame here, no one else. As discreetly as possible, she lifted her pistol from her handbag. If they knew about the operation, then they knew . . .

"Is something wrong?" the contact asked.

"If you want to live, listen to me. We're in danger. Don't make any move that stands out. They could be watching. I've got to think this out."

Ellie checked her watch; nearly five o'clock. Time for her to

301

reach the castle but not enough to wait for reinforcements from Mossad. If the Timber Wolf was successful, the Council might well activate the main portion of their plan ahead of schedule. So, it was just her. She'd be dead already if the Council wanted her to be.

"There are a few things I need," she told the contact, recalling her knowledge of castles in the Lisbon countryside, even then wondering what it was that was keeping her alive.

"When does the ferry reach the island?" Wayman asked the captain anxiously.

"When it docks, friend," the crusty man replied with a snide wink, "and that much you can count on." Then, after a short pause, "We should be in about three-thirty, way I figure it."

The Timber Wolf thanked the man and descended from the bridge back toward the sparse group of people making their way across Narragansett Bay's east passage to Prudence Island. Drew was standing alone by the railing.

"Well?" he asked.

"It's going to be close," Wayman told him.

It had been such the whole day. Drew had told his tale rapidly to Trelana hours earlier, slurring the words and events together. The drug lord grasped enough of the context to pose numerous questions of a technical nature, his own voice quivering. Ultimately, Trelana promised to do his best to get plenty of men and boats to Prudence Island prior to high tide at five-fifteen, which was the expected drop time for Corbano's powder to assure optimum spread thanks to favorable wind conditions. He made no promises, though. The hours might prove too short to accomplish so much with the drug lord's resources severely taxed. Drew was to carry some sort of flare with him and use it to signal Trelana's fleet to attack if they ever did show up.

From the motel, Drew and Wayman reached Atlanta Airport by stolen car where they boarded a nonstop flight for Boston. Then a rental car blazing along Route 95 into Rhode Island eventually brought them to the town of Bristol, where they just caught the two o'clock ferry shuttle on the *Prudence II*. They had no way of knowing whether Trelana's men would make it to the island in time. All they knew was that Corbano would unquestionably be there.

Elliana would have reached Lisbon by now as well. The Council of Ten would soon be in her sights. Even if she destroyed their stronghold at the Castle of the Moors, she could do nothing about Corbano since he was on his own. He belonged to Drew and the Timber Wolf, and if they failed, the upper East Coast would be wiped out.

The autumn waters were choppy, a stiff wind forcing Drew to wrap his arms about himself. The air was dank and gray, but he savored each breath as the mist played with his mouth, aware suddenly of just how precious even the damp wind was. The Timber Wolf leaned against the railing by his side.

"What do we do once we get there?" Drew asked him.

"Find a pier where we can rent a decent boat complete with flare pistol. There's no sense looking for Corbano on land. He'll be on the water by now."

It was closing in on quarter to four when the *Prudence II* angled itself for docking on a rickety pier that would take them onto the island. The scene looked desolate and dreary in the autumn gray, hardly a picturesque island paradise, which was just the way the one hundred and six full-time residents preferred it. They'd had enough of summer people rolling in and out with their shiny new Volvos, driving property values too high and ruining the season. The locals constantly bemoaned the fact that Prudence had been discovered by the summer tourists, who went as far as to frighten away the near-domesticated deer and darkened the landscape with sprawling antennas and satellite dishes. Let the tourists have the summer, the locals accepted grudgingly, so long as the other three seasons belonged to them.

The *Prudence II*'s single mate tied the ferry down against the dock and slid part of the railing out of the way to permit the seven passengers to exit. The wooden pier was bent and wharped. Wayman and Drew hurried ahead of the others, Drew feeling every step in his tortured bones and muscles. His wounds were too numerous to categorize, but his anger and determination gave him the strength to keep going. They headed toward a small dockside store featuring a pay phone and a single gas pump. A fiftyish woman wearing faded, baggy jeans and sporting pigtails sat on a bench by the entrance watching the two strangers approach.

"I help either of ya any?" she wondered suspiciously.

"We need a boat," Wayman told her.

"This time of year? Selection ain't exactly favorable."

"Anything with an engine will do."

She stood up and pointed to the right. "Walk that way about a third of a mile. That's the major pier, called Potter's Wharf. Not much to choose from these days, though. Find Captain Jack."

"How will we know him?"

"He'll be the only one around."

Captain Jack turned out to be a grizzled, partly toothless sort who smelled of the morning's fish catch. He was filleting the latest selection for the local market when Wayman and Drew found him in a shack.

"I do somethin' for ya city boys?" he asked when he saw them, pulling off his thick rubber gloves but leaving his ruddy rubber apron in place.

Wayman stepped toward him, Drew looking at Captain Jack with vague recognition probably because the man might have been a twin of the crusty shark hunter from the film *Jaws*.

"We need to rent a boat," the Timber Wolf told him.

Captain Jack slapped his hands together. "Well, you come to the right place. Plannin' to do some night fishin'?"

"Sort of."

"Got a few coves I can recommend. Trouble is, on account of we don't get much business this time of year, I got most of my boats pulled out of the water. Should be able to fix ya up good enough, though."

They followed the captain out of the shack and down a pier where the boards seemed to move at whim. They stopped before five boats in various stages of disrepair, the best of the lot being a small cabin cruiser with attached dinghy.

"Any of these'll do just fine," Captain Jack told them.

"We'll take that one," Wayman said, pointing to the cabin cruiser. "How much?"

"Hundred bucks a day."

"Sign outside said fifty."

"I'm the only game in town, friend," Captain Jack said, smiling. "Take it or leave it."

*   *   *

After they had cast off, Drew stood in the cruiser's stern. Other than a few fishing boats, they had the bay to themselves.

"Anything?" Drew asked.

Wayman let the binoculars dangle at his chest. He had given the fishing boats only a cursory glance.

"Corbano will need something bigger with lots more power," he explained.

Wayman returned to the wheel and headed the cruiser around the island farther out into the bay. It handled sluggishly, sputtering and nearly stalling when he asked for more speed. The dinghy clacked up against the side as the waves picked up in the deeper water. The seas around them were virtually deserted. Perhaps Corbano had been here already and set farther out to sea. It was possible, although Wayman expected him to hug the coastline as close as possible to assure a quick and maximum spread of the death cloud created by the powder being dumped into the sea.

Wayman's eyes contined to scan as he steered the boat through the currents. They would become increasingly difficult to negotiate as high tide approached, forty-five minutes away now.

The tach needle jumped crazily, then flopped to zero. The engine sputtered and died. Wayman turned the key. There was a slight cough, then nothing.

"Damn!"

"What happened?" Drew wondered.

Wayman was climbing down from the bridge. "Know anything about boat engines?"

"Not a thing."

"Likewise. Without being too pessimistic, I'd say we were stuck."

They hadn't had time to consider the prospects of that when a Coast Guard cutter appeared on the horizon circling the bay on routine patrol.

"At last, a break," the Timber Wolf mumbled.

"You going to contact them?"

"In person, kid. Don't see that we've got much choice. We'll drop anchor here and I'll go over in the dinghy. I'll make up a good story that'll convince them they have to help us. This may even turn out to be a blessing," he continued. "The cutter will have radar and whatever Corbano's on won't be able to hide from it."

"What about Trelana?"

"If he's not here yet, he's not coming. You'll be safe until I get back. Now give me a hand with the dinghy. . . ."

Wayman fought the small dinghy through the strengthening currents, reminding him that high tide was fast approaching. He cut a diagonal path across to the cutter so it would not run him down. It was truly a majestic sight at this point, its twenty-five-man crew and several guns surely a match for anything Corbano had brought with him. Only convincing the captain to use the ship's firepower remained. . . .

Wayman saw activity on the cutter's main deck and knew he had been spotted. He waved to indicate he was coming in and saw hand signals flashed in return to beckon him on. He continued steering the dinghy for the cutter's side, wondering what story might go the furthest with the captain. The truth, perhaps? The large boat had slowed to drifting speed and a rope ladder had been hurled down for him to climb up to the deck.

The hands kept directing him forward. Wayman's path was angular and he timed the approach with near perfection, grazing the thick steel of the cutter only slightly as he reached out and grabbed the rope ladder. After making the dinghy fast, he began to climb.

"Am I glad to see you," he told the host of uniformed faces as he neared the top. The Timber Wolf reached the gunwale and felt hands stretching to help him over. "I was trying to—"

He cut his words off when the familiar clicking of automatic rifle bolts sent a shiver up his spine. He turned right and then left and saw he was enclosed on both sides by Coast Guardsmen grasping guns.

"There must be some mistake," was all he could manage.

"I don't think so," a voice countered, and Wayman swung toward it, realizing already the mistake had been his.

"Welcome aboard," Corbano added.

Her contact had proved most cooperative and helpful, although Elliana couldn't help but wonder if both their efforts were for naught. She was about to go up against an incredibly well fortified castle alone instead of with a Mossad strike force. Instead of bemoaning that fact, she had to make it work for her, and her contact had helped by providing certain indispensable supplies. The Council of Ten would never have expected an attack by an individual. All their defenses would be geared for much larger assaults, and there lay Ellie's only advantage and the basis of her entire plan.

It was nine-thirty P.M. Lisbon time when she finally arrived on a hillside looking down over the Castle of the Moors. Her plan hung on several assumptions: First and foremost, since the Council could not risk lighting the supposedly deserted castle, the base of their operations had to be contained beneath it. More, for similar reasons regular patrols of guards were out of the question, although sophisticated electronic surveillance systems and carefully hidden trip wires would make a direct ground approach suicide. This left her with approach by air, with her options severely limited. Her first thought was to utilize a hang glider as she had several times in the past. But obtaining one on such short notice proved impossible and left her with the next best thing, currently stored in the second of her two packs.

The first pack contained eight slabs of exceptionally potent plastic explosives, along with several grenades of both the fragmentary variety for destruction and smoke for camouflage. In addition, her contact had supplied her with flashlights, a pair of handguns, and an Uzi complete with five spare clips.

Three hundred yards away the Castle of the Moors made a fearsome, imposing sight. Its natural stone ramparts were all but swallowed by the slithering night fog, the entire structure absorbed by it at times. A slight wind poured through the empty cisterns, sounding like wild cries of warning not to approach.

Elliana had already resolved not to heed them. Breathing heavy, both packs and the Uzi slung over her shoulders, she started moving again. For her plan of entry to work, she needed to get another hundred yards closer to the castle while remaining no less than one hundred feet higher than its battlements. She moved down the hillside, walking horizontally at the same time with eyes already searching out her first requirement.

She found it at as close to a perfect position as she could have hoped for: a huge tree stump growing out of the steep hillside looking down over the Castle of the Moors. It was near enough to two hundred yards in distance and at least one hundred feet in height away.

Ellie pulled both her packs from her shoulders and slid the contents out of the larger. First emerged a huge rolled packet of thick steel cable. She located its bracketed end and attached it to three separate driving spikes, which she hammered deep into the tree stump until only their ends protruded. Next she attached the other end of the steel cable to what looked like, and for all intents and purposes was, a short, squat version of an underwater spear with dual heads and a toggle bolt assembly in the front. Then she pulled out a riflelike object that might have been a hand-held mortar and snapped the spear mechanism with attached cable snugly into the slot tailored for it down the barrel.

Ellie checked her target first with her binoculars, focusing on the tallest of the castle's ominous battlements. The breeze was slight, a nonfactor, but the night had a way of playing tricks on your eyes, distorting distance and throwing aim off. She'd have to consider that. Ellie let the binoculars dangle and raised the firing mechanism to her shoulder. Its propellant was an air cannister, which would jet the spear forward at a speed approaching three hundred miles per hour. But after two hundred yards or so depending on the wind, the pace slowed and accuracy was lost. She could only hope for the best.

Ellie checked her aim a dozen more times before finally reaching for the trigger. There would be no second shots. This was it. She felt herself start to tremble and knew she had to fire now before hesitation stole her confidence. She squeezed one eye closed and sighted down the barrel, then squeezed the trigger.

The spear lunged out with a *poof*, the thick steel cable unspooling in its dark wake. As she watched it, Ellie realized with terror that in her haste she had neglected to make sure she was safe from the fleeting cable. Such a careless mistake could easily lead to decapitation at such a speed, but she had been lucky.

The cable would travel for barely five seconds, just enough time for her to raise the binoculars again to her eyes to focus once more on the battlement. The whining sound of the cable unspooling stopped just as she found her target in the lenses. The spear had sliced through the ancient stone with little problem at all, the tungsten toggle ends of both heads shooting out and sideways at impact to create a firm hold.

The zip line was in place.

The principle of the zip line was based in simple aerodynamics. Attach yourself by cylindrical hook onto the cable and jump off for the ride down. Of course, the key was that the center of the weighted cable had a natural sag to it, which had the effect of slowing the rider down and ensuring that the rest of the ride would be uphill to prevent what would otherwise have been an unavoidable collision at the other end. As of now, thirty yards of cable remained unspooled and she went about the chore of slicing off the extra, refitting the end, and then rebolting it into the stump using fresh holes. Before doing so she slid the bracket connected to the rope soon to be joined to her harness over the line and tested it for play.

Perfect. So far.

Next she climbed into her line harness and fastened it about her waist while inhaling to ensure a properly snug fit. Then she slung both packs and her Uzi back over her shoulders before bolting the bracketed rope into a pair of dual slots at her front. As she rose, the cable buckled slightly from her weight. The hillside lowered into a ninety-degree incline for a time just five yards away and Ellie dragged herself for it, on the very tips of her toes when she got there. There was no going back now, even if she had considered it.

Ellie leaped.

A shrill squeal from the steel bracket grazing the cable followed her descent. Ellie closed her eyes to the incredible pace she was making, opening them only when the expected sag came in the middle and she found herself sliding uphill. The most difficult part was coming up, for if she had not sufficient momentum left to last her, she would begin to slide back down the line toward the middle before reaching the end of the zip line at the battlement. Ellie pulled her knees up cannonball style, using her body as a rudder through the night air. It worked brilliantly. A few hefty shifts of her weight at the last brought her square to the battlement, and she managed to find a good enough ledge on it for foothold while she plotted her next move.

Access to the castle could be achieved only through one of its many windows, a misnomer of sorts since it had been constructed long before glass was in use, and thus the windows were either of wooden shutters or iron bars. She had hoped to find one sufficiently weathered through the years to provide easy access, but a quick inspection of those accessible from her vantage point showed rusted steel to be the best she could hope for.

Ellie resigned herself to the next task. Still balanced precariously on the ledge, she felt in one of her packs for the climbing rope. Working agilely with one arm, she was able to loop it over the cable and, shifting her body weight, succeeded with both hands in tying down a knot.

Rappelling was the next order of business, rappelling both down and to her left where the window ledge she had chosen as a target lay. She unbuckled the rope attaching her to the zip line and slid to the farthest edge of her perch before shoving gently off, controlling the flow of her descent with her feet against the castle's exterior. The zip line wavered under the pressure of her weight and nearly stripped her of balance on several occasions. But Ellie held fast and inside of thirty seconds found the window ledge with her feet. The steel bars forming a grate over the opening were set in enough from the outer structure to allow her crouched containment, preferable to another toehold perch at this point.

Ellie tried the steel bars with her hands. They gave slightly but nowhere near enough to hope that she might be able to free them by hand. Again her hand slid into her pack, this time emerging with an object that looked like a long, fat fountain pen. In reality it was a touch stick activated by pressure on its point, which then released a concentrated acid onto whatever it came in contact with. Ellie snapped off the protective cover and went to work.

A hissing sound and the sharp smell of melting metal followed her every move. Ellie only bothered with the edges of the steel bars where they were attached into the castle structure. But there were four of these on each side so the process became understandably nerve-racking, especially when the foul odor became too much for her nostrils. Still, Ellie forced herself to be patient until the last. She removed the bars one or two sections at a time and lowered them to the ledge near her in case ultrasonic security sensors were listening for an unexplainable and sudden clang.

She had to expect anything here. This was, after all, the Council of Ten she was dealing with.

Then why am I still alive?

Ellie had asked herself that question yet again, but she was saved further consideration of it when the last of the steel bars came free and she climbed softly into the Castle of the Moors.

CHAPTER 33

"SEARCH HIM!" CORBANO ORDERED, AND THE TIMBER WOLF WAS shoved brutally against a wall on the deck and frisked.

One of the men masquerading as a guardsman found his pistol and tossed it over the side. Wayman was then yanked harshly around where he could lock stares with Corbano.

"Going for a cruise?"

"Yes, Timber Wolf, a most comfortable one that will permit me to bring about the death of millions," he boasted, a twisted smile drawn over his face. Wayman could barely stand to look at it. The left side was its usual milky white, but the right was lined with bandages and puffy red flesh from exposure to the flames back at his Georgia fortress. "It would have been easier for you if you had died in the woods," he continued.

And Corbano came forward in his captain's uniform and laced a backhand across Wayman's face. A thin trickle of blood ran from one of the Timber Wolf's nostrils.

"I watched you in that damn boat, couldn't believe it was you. I was about to send a party out to greet you when you decided to make it easy for me. But rest assured," Corbano taunted. "Divers are preparing even now to take care of your young friend once and for all."

"You bastard!" Wayman raged without bothering to try pulling from the powerful grasps of the men restraining him.

"I think not, Timber Wolf. I'm doing the young man a favor. Either he dies quick . . . or slow like the rest of your nation. I've seen the powder in action. It's remarkable." A pause. "If you'd had something as effective in Corsica, this conversation would never have taken place.

This time Wayman did try to pull free and felt Corbano's fist slam into his solar plexus. He doubled over, gasping for breath.

"Back then, Timber Wolf, you never would have felt such a blow. But I suppose the signs were there even that night."

Wayman straightened up and looked into Corbano's mad, pale eyes.

"Bring him this way," the White Snake ordered, and the two uniformed giants dragged Wayman toward the gunwale. "It will be amusing to have you witness the beginning of our operation. In fifteen minutes all hands will be issued breathing apparatus and soon after we will begin to drop our allocation of powder. The winds are very favorable this time of the day from what I'm told, moving in a southwesterly direction."

"The cities," Wayman muttered.

"Yes, exactly. New York, Washington, and everything in between will be a mass graveyard by midnight tonight. Your country will be witnessing the onset of its downfall."

"And then your people will just move in and take over."

"They're not my people, Timber Wolf, not the members of this Council. I find that phase of their plan quite absurd. You see, it's the ultimate, inevitable chaos that I look forward to. I was made for such a world and at last I shall have it."

Another fake Coast Guardsman came forward and handed Corbano a portable radio. "Bridge wants you, sir."

Corbano held the radio to his lips. "Yes, what is it?"

"Sir, radar has picked up what appears to be a fleet of small boats heading our way."

"Fishermen?"

"The timing would be right, but we can't tell yet," the voice from the bridge returned. "We won't know until we achieve visual contact."

"Very well. Keep me informed."

Trelana, Wayman realized, it had to be! But how to signal him? How to alert his fleet to the fact that the cutter was their target? The signal was supposed to be a flare, but he had nothing like—

The Timber Wolf's eyes gazed over Corbano's shoulder and

saw a slot in the deck wall marked Emergency: Flare Gun. He had to reach it. Somehow. He needed time, both to think and to let Trelana's boats draw within firing range.

"Where's the powder?" he asked Corbano.

"Well protected, Timber Wolf, I assure you. We have constructed special devices to spread it once the time comes." He gazed out in the distance toward the shrinking shape of the cabin cruiser on which Drew was perched. "My divers should be getting to your young friend just about now. I should have liked to have had you watch his death, but well, we can't have everything, can we?" A demonic smile crossed the White Snake's pale lips. His ashen hair danced in the breeze.

Wayman made himself look angered, still focusing on the flare gun. Timing was the key now. He felt certain he could pull free of the guards' grasp long enough to get to the box. But to be sure of reaching it, he would have to make sure that Corbano was distracted as well. The radio still held in his hand provided the answer. Wait, he urged himself, patience. . . .

"Sir?" came the squawky call from the bridge.

"Yes," Corbano responded, mouthpiece to his lips again, his eyes held on Wayman.

"We have visual on those boats now. They're pleasure craft mostly, several speedboats, too. They're traveling too close to each other. Something's—"

It was at that precise moment that Corbano's attention turned totally to the radio and the Timber Wolf sprang into motion. The men holding him never could have expected a twist so violent and strong. Actually, it was just enough to upset them while he lowered his elbow and jammed it into the ribs of the man on his right, lifting a kick into the other man's groin. Corbano had dropped the radio and started forward when Wayman grabbed him under the chin and slammed him backward into the wall. He reached up for the flare gun with one hand, as he spun the White Snake into his converging guards with the other.

The gun was out and the flare loaded an instant later. A second flare skidded across the deck. Wayman dove after it as he fired the first flare into a group of rifle-wielding men charging from the opposite direction of the downed group. It burst into one man's midsection and he erupted into flames with a horrible wail as the others scattered long enough for Wayman to reach the second flare.

The Timber Wolf grasped it as he rolled, already aiming the smoking barrel upward when he snapped the second flare home and pulled the trigger.

The flare shot into the air and burst outward in the sky with an orange glow.

The fleet of Trelana's boats, their previous route generally aimless through the bay, swung for the cutter and spread into an attack pattern.

Corbano went for a gun that had fallen to the deck, but Wayman kicked it aside and pulled himself back to his feet.

"Kill him! Kill him!" Corbano screamed to his guards, who were only now regaining their bearings as he backed up out of their line of fire.

There was no time to think, only to act. The Timber Wolf did the last thing expected of him.

He charged straight into the onrushing group. The man closest tried for his trigger, but Wayman had the barrel grasped, bringing the butt upward under his chin. Immediately the automatic weapon was in his hands, spitting fire in a narrow arc at the rest of the men rushing him. Their bullets sprayed wildly as their bodies spilled to the deck. The rifle burned hot in Wayman's hands, exhausting itself finally. Without missing a beat, he grabbed the gun of the dead man closest to him.

A troop of guards charged him from the deck above, and Wayman felt the heat of their bullets slam into the nearby walls and gunwale. One grazed him in the side and spun him around with no cover to dive for. They had him in their sights and the best he could manage was a token volley aimed randomly upward.

They had him. It was over.

Until the new series of blasts sounded, just spits really, more like echoes on the sea winds. The lead ships of Trelana's fleet, featuring machine gunners lying prone on the bows, roared violently forward. Their fire cut a regular line across both the cutter's decks, spitting wood and metal splinters everywhere as the men who had almost been his killers rushed for cover.

"Battle stations! Battle stations! All crew members report to their battle stations! We are under attack! Repeat, we are under attack!"

The desperate words were followed by the regular screech of an alarm, adding to the chaos. Wayman made it work for him. He pulled one of Corbano's dead guards through a door leading into the guts of the cutter and stripped off the man's clothes. With no time to waste tearing off his own, he simply pulled the white uniform over his slacks and shirt. It would have to do well enough. All he needed was limited run of the ship.

To find Corbano.

And the powder.

He emerged back on the lower deck to find Corbano's men struggling to manipulate the cutter's main gun as Trelana's fleet continued their hail of fire. Their attack was surprisingly well coordinated given the circumstances, the fleet enclosing the cutter on both sides and the front to force the troops on board to fight a three-fronted war at sea. Trelana's bigger boats were swinging closer now, carrying larger explosives, which included bazookas and grenade launchers.

A shattering explosion from one blew out a section of wall just ahead of Wayman and forced him to the deck, covering his head. His target was now the bridge where Corbano would have retreated in order to direct his defenses. Wayman regained his feet and started running. Black smoke burned his eyes. He smelled oil and cordite along with the coppery scent of blood. The cutter was limping now, fighting to hold to its course. There were just twelve minutes to high tide.

He approached the ship's main gun and was nearly deafened by its sudden report. He collapsed to the deck holding his ears, as a pair of Trelana's lead boats exploded under the cannon's fire. Another boat featuring a grenade launcher prone on its bow roared close for a shot and perished similarly.

He had to knock out that gun!

The Timber Wolf pulled his hands from his ears and the constant clacking of fire assaulted them again. Screaming to shield the awful pounding more than anything else, he leaped to grasp the turret and used it to hoist himself up and over. He crashed into the pair of men handling the reloading chores and was feeling for his machine gun's trigger when a third man yanked him backward. Wayman went with the motion, slamming the butt behind him as he felt himself being pulled. There was a grunt and the Timber Wolf felt the pressure let up. He located the trigger as the first two men charged him and split their midsections open with a single burst.

He turned quickly at that point, free of the turret now, and the man who had been manning the cannon missed him with a swipe of his knife as Wayman backpedaled across the deck. He lashed the blade out again, but the Timber Wolf was ready, smashing a hard fist into the man's throat as he blocked his strike.

The front of the cutter was clear now. Trelana's fleet poured in with weapons ready to tear the ship to bits.

Wayman rushed into the spreading smoke in the direction of the bridge.

All in all, Drew considered the fleet containing all types of boats of varying sizes swinging into attack formation against the cutter to be one of the greatest sights he had ever laid eyes on. He had followed the proceedings up to that point through binoculars, saw the Timber Wolf be captured, then turn the tables, then be saved himself by the fleet.

From this distance, the scene held a texture similar to a film he had once seen of a pack of ants attacking a large spider. The spider seemed invincible, but the ants were able to wear it down and drain the larger creature's defenses.

They've got the bastards! he thought. *They've got them!*

Trelana's boats sped along as they fired, leaping over each other's wakes and narrowly avoiding collision after collision as they encircled the cutter with a constant barrage of fire. Smoke clouded most of the larger ship's bow, an occasional explosion sending a burst of flames toward the sky. The cutter seemed to be floundering, swinging around for land and much shallower water where its progress would almost certainly be arrested by the bay's hidden rises. But its deadly cargo, if released, could still do the damage promised to the same degree.

Drew peered tensely through the binoculars, searching for the Timber Wolf or Corbano and failing to spot either.

It was the sound of water dripping onto the deck that made him turn suddenly, just in time to see the black-suited scuba diver aim his spear gun. Drew dove as the spear shot out, missing the intended target of his midsection but digging deep into his thigh.

Drew screamed as he landed hard on the deck face first,

mouth filling with water. He coughed and tried to claw back to his feet, while another set of gloved hands appeared over the side and the first diver approached with an underwater knife drawn and raised. Drew twisted as the man lunged, feeling an incredible burst of pain in his torn leg that forced his arms back involuntarily. They closed on something round and wooden, and he brought it up and around without thinking.

The back end of the handle caught the first diver across the side of the face, staggering him. The second diver had leaped into the boat spear gun first and this time Drew had no way to move fast enough to avoid the shot.

He heard the *plunk* when the spear jetted out and screamed an instant before it passed through his life jacket and lodged in the fatty flesh of his left pectoral dangerously close to his heart. He lost his grip on the staff he had grasped before, realizing it had a hooked extension on the end used for drawing in fishing nets. The second diver was upon him as he tried to grab it. Drew felt a solid blow to his face, tasted blood, and then realized with terror that the man had grasped the spear shaft and was twisting and pushing the attached blade at the same time.

The pain was beyond anything Drew could have imagined. His eyes bulged as he screamed with all the air flooding from his body.

His agony allowed him to finally grasp the hooked staff. His next conscious thought was that the jagged end was rusty, as he brought it up with all the force he could muster.

The curved hook sliced into the diver's midsection as easily as butter. The man's body arched backward at an impossible angle as scarlet drained onto his black wet suit. He hung there suspended until an agonizing gurgle found Drew's ears and the man's mouth spilled purplish blood. The man kneeled over forward, driving the steel hook all the way through his back. It sliced through with a tearing sound and emerged coated with the dead man's flesh and spaghettilike intestines.

Drew found himself able to move only his head, and that was enough for him to see the first diver fighting to load a second spear in his gun with blood pouring down the side of his face. An underwater knife remained in the scuba belt of the dead man face-down by his side and Drew reached into the blood pooling under him to grasp it.

A horrible bolt of agony seared through him. He could feel fresh blood pumping from behind him and realized he was pinned, realized that the second diver's efforts had forced the sharp spear edge all the way through flesh and bone and into the wooden gunwale. He fought to angle himself to be able to reach the knife.

The other diver jammed his second spear home and started to bring it up from the deck while steadying it between a pair of trembling hands.

Drew strained forward as far as he could, but the hilt of the knife remained just beyond his reach.

He saw the gun coming all the way up now, saw the diver's hand closing on the trigger, and he knew the third spear would finish the job the first two had started.

His mind recorded those images between breaths, providing the panic he needed. Drew screamed as he pushed himself forward from the gunwale, flesh ripping and blood spurting behind him. The pain was so incredible that he felt only his fingers at the last grasping the hilt of the dead diver's knife and tearing it from his belt.

His eyes looked down the gun's barrel as the first diver started to pull the trigger. With another wail, Drew hurled the knife.

There was no real design to the move, only desperation. The blade split the air as the diver's finger jerked the heavy trigger. Drew closed his eyes after they seemed to record the knife flying hopelessly off target while the spear remained dead on his midsection.

They opened when the gasping sound found his ears. The first diver sat writhing before him on the deck, supported by the cabin wall with the hilt of the knife protruding from the center of his throat. Blood leaped from the wound. His hands flailed out as if to grasp something, then crumbled as blood poured from his mouth and nostrils, eyes locking open in a death stare.

I did it! Drew realized, exhaustion and pain robbing him of any feelings of elation he might have had. There could be no movement for him now. A feeling of deep repose came over him. His life jacket felt like a pillow and his head dropped for it, chin coming to rest with reasonable comfort. He felt cold everywhere, except where the blood was still running over his back and leg. The two spear shafts protruding outward made a sickening sight, but he was already used to it. In fact, Drew had just started to believe that he might live through this in spite of everything when the third diver hurled himself onto the deck.

Elliana stepped softly through the dark corridors of the Castle of the Moors, her path lit only by a flashlight as she inspected the ancient structure. Since the Council presence was nonexistent in the aboveground levels, as expected she had free passage of the halls so long as she maintained her stealth, careful to avoid the several trip wires and ultraviolet beams that would have betrayed her.

Ellie didn't know which floor she was on, third or fourth probably, but it didn't much matter. Her training had included extensive instruction on how to wire explosives to bring down a structure from *any* level. The trick was to place the charges at key structural and stress areas, especially in this instance to ensure that the ancient castle would crumble downward through the vast underground levels where the Council of Ten's headquarters undoubtedly lay. Six packs of her plastic explosives ought to do the job nicely, leaving her two for later if she needed them.

Into each of the plastic packs, Ellie jammed a miniature antenna, which stretched perhaps two inches above the mound. The antenna was homed in on a signal from a detonator that broadcast from a distance of a half mile. She had rigged the detonator into her watch so it would be near her at all times.

The safe thing to do would be to set the charges and detonate them from a safe distance outside the castle. But then she wouldn't be as sure of killing the Council members. She had to be certain they were here, which necessitated a foray into the deep bowels of the Castle of the Moors. Besides, after so much pursuit, so much blood and tears, she needed to kill David's murderers face-to-face.

Ellie set the final charge and moved slowly for a huge stone staircase that circled through the castle levels. The first floor was darker than any of the others and she moved down the hall with added caution. The problem now was to find an entrance to the underground chambers that the Council of Ten called home.

The dusty, cobweb-coated floor trembled slightly beneath her. Coupled with the night wind blowing hauntingly through the long-abandoned ramparts and cisterns, it should have been enough to make her flesh crawl. But Ellie shuddered only with a chill of recognition. The vibrations in the floor had to be caused by the whirl of heavy machinery almost directly beneath her. She was close now, very close. All she needed was a door to lead her to the underground levels, a door the Council would have no reason to guard since no one would ever have been expected to penetrate their perimeter defenses and get this far.

Ellie found the door built into a wall far along the corridor leading away from the huge rooms to the first floor. It was a monstrous door, made of thick wood and featuring a small trap that opened from the inside to identify those seeking entry. The door opened to the inside and had no knob. Ellie pushed on it gently. It didn't give, a latch obviously holding it in place from within.

She fished in the pockets of her fatigues for a long, slender knife. Holding it with a surgeon's skill, she fitted the blade between the wall and door and probed about for the latch. She worked quickly, twisting the blade until the latch came free and the door creaked inward. She eased it open all the way, shifting her flashlight to her other hand while holding tight to the door to prevent further sounds.

Her flashlight beam revealed a huge set of steps before her, angling to the left as it dropped into total darkness. Ellie stepped through and closed the door gently behind her. She began to descend one step at a time, careful to move softly enough to avoid echoes. The smell of rot, must, and mold caught her nostrils and nearly forced her to gag. She steeled herself against the odor and kept descending, finding a rhythm to her movements as she grew familiar with the layout.

By the time she reached the bottom after curving sharply to the left, the whirling of machinery was much closer. She made out the distant muffle of voices as well, along with footsteps. But sounds could travel a long way down these cold stone corridors. Flashlight tight in her hand, Ellie started on again.

The floor was made of dirt here and the smells that rose from it were putrid. Worse, she heard soft scuffling around her and aimed her beam down to find a host of rats skirting by, nothing to pass off lightly. If they were hungry enough and in sufficient numbers, rats would attack anything. Ellie picked up her pace.

The presence of the rats made her think. They were far too smart to make their home along a corridor that lacked any possible food supply. Obviously the ones that had passed her had come from somewhere else within this subterranean labyrinth, somewhere with far more activity and a potential food supply.

Or, perhaps they were heading for it now.

Elliana listened for the scuffling up ahead. When it ceased totally around a corner, she knew she was close even before she saw the slight shaft of light coming through what appeared to be a break in the wall at floor level. Sure enough, closer inspection with the help of her flashlight revealed some sort of tunnel running from one side of the labyrinth to the other. It was fronted by an ancient steel grate and was of ample size to permit her to crawl into and through.

The steel grating had weakened over the long years, and she had no trouble pulling it free and entering the tunnel, which, too, was made of dirt. She began pushing herself on her knees, focusing on the dim light at the other end and the increasing whirl of machinery. This was what she had come for; she could feel it.

Unfortunately, Ellie could feel something else even more plainly—the sensation of small animals dashing about and around her. She felt her heart lurch forward in fear that perhaps she had invaded the lair of the rats whose scouts had passed her back in the corridor. Immensely territorial, the animals would attack if that were the case.

She could feel more of them scurrying about her, seeming to mass, and stopped to develop some kind of defense. Retreat was a possibility, but not with the Council of Ten just yards away at long last.

More of the rats were gathering, scampering. Their enraged squealing intensified. Ellie saw the red eyes of one as it lashed out at her, taking a nibble at her hand. Ellie grimaced against the pain, thinking how easy it would be to grab her Uzi from behind her and finish these creatures quickly.

No, she realized, *there was another weapon she had, far more subtle and equally as effective.*

Ellie reached behind her into her pack and came out with a fistful of granola bars. Rising slightly, she tore off the wrappers and mashed the snacks up in her hand. Next she scattered the contents in piles behind her. This much accomplished, she turned around and lowered herself again.

The small, scampering creatures rushed over and by her, charging for the small dinner. Ravenous, their squealing hurt her ears as they fought against each other for mouthfuls of the suddenly available food. Ellie began to drag herself on again and eyed the grate just eight feet away now, reaching it at last to peer through into a nightmare.

What lay beyond the tunnel was a wonder of modern technology. Elliana's mind worked feverishly to catalogue the sights all at once. Besides the walls constructed of centuries-old rock, there were no traces of ancient times. The lighting was bright and fluorescent. Computer banks linked row after row of the main floor, all manned by technicians checking their stations carefully and wearing white lab coats. A host of computer terminals sat against the far wall, a man before each. Ellie counted over twenty and speculated that one had been reserved for each of the American drop points the Timber Wolf had discovered.

She noticed the many guards next, at least twenty-five standing at various strategic and possible points of entry, all well armed and dressed in khaki uniforms. They were the Council's soldiers, the final obstacle between her and those who had killed her husband.

Ellie strained in the tunnel to see out the grating to her left into the front of the huge room, which had probably once been a dungeon with a pair of twin staircases descending from the underground tunnels that Council personnel probably used to gain access. At last she found an angle that allowed her to view the proceedings at the front of the chamber where most of the activity seemed concentrated.

Two huge, aerial maps of the United States dominated large areas of the wall farthest away, enclosed in a glassed-off section lined within by machine after machine. At least a dozen technicians were moving about. One of the maps was highlighted with thirty or so blue lights, each indicating a drop point for the deadly powder probably, but only one was flashing now.

A small spot off the coast of New England. Prudence Island.

Within a matter of hours, the rest of the blips would be flashing as well and the spread of death would have begun over the rest of the country. Ellie's resolve strengthened.

The second map was a mass of sweeping and circling lines and angles, more than likely indicating current airflow and weather patterns across the entire country. Yes, such information would be crucial to the Council in their efforts to determine the timetable to maximize Powderkeg's effects. She imagined that all such information was fed continuously into the computers manned below by the army of technicians.

The command center was elevated over the rest of the chamber, and Ellie fixed her gaze on the occupants seated at a table within it, all watching the maps intently while talking among themselves.

Four of the Council of Ten. Isser had relayed their names, but somehow actually seeing them all gathered here deepened the nightmare even more.

There was Abu Salam, leader of a radical faction of the PLO and spokesman for all revolutionary Arab groups in general. Salam was generally considered to be the most dangerous man in the Middle East in addition to standing as the staunchest obstacle to peace. He was the one man capable of unifying the Shiite-Moslem forces with others in the Arab world, which made him the most powerful force in the Islamic underground.

There was the esteemed Russian, General Sergei Davetsky. In an order bent against the worshipping of heroes, Davetsky had become one. He was vehemently nationalistic and hated America with a passion of the gods. He had come up with at least a half dozen perfectly workable plans to overrun Western Europe and eventually cripple America, but each had been turned down. And with each failure, his own clandestine following grew, just waiting for the opportunity to usurp power from those who denied him. But the Council was behind him now.

There was Colonel Ismael Rouvella, ruler of a strategic Central American nation and envisioner of the eventual unification of all the countries in that region under a socialist regime, with him in place as the ultimate leader—a goal he saw squashed at every turn by the United States. Until now. Today.

There was Barton Hinkley Hunt, leader of a rising band of conservative-bordering-on-reactionary right-wingers in South Africa who saw the answer to his nation's problems not in terms of concession to apartheid, but in virtual extermination of the black race. Passed off as a fanatic for years, Hunt had recently been

credited with creating popular support for the latest police actions, which had wounded thousands and incarcerated thousands
more. He had become a rallying point for right-wing organizations all over the world. But in his own nation support was
denied him out of fear of further American sanctions. He was
like a general with an army of soldiers he couldn't use . . . as
long as America was in the way.

Ellie still couldn't believe her eyes. Four men linked together
by a common insatiable thirst for power that transcended culture
and politics. Add Nazi Heinrich Goltz to this group and it was a
nice package indeed. Liberals and conservatives, reactionaries
and revolutionaries—those dichotomies had been bridged by the
ambition to achieve a destiny and a place in history that only the
Council could provide. They would destroy America and turn it
into their own private domain where the plots of madmen could
be hatched and carried out without the kind of retribution that
had stymied their efforts till now. Men forced into the underlay-
ers of society to do their bidding suddenly carrying that bidding
out on the surface. How many millions might be moved to join
them? Revolution, anarchy, war—all would be welcomed, such
a world being made for men whose philosophies not only
accepted violence but depended upon it. A world that would
eventually belong all to them as their numbers increased until the
foretold number of ten for the Council was achieved.

But what of the leader?

Ellie noticed motion in the darkened corner of the glassed-in
command center. There was a man in the shadows, his features
indistinct, seated on what looked like some sort of throne.

Suddenly, activity in the command center became frantic. The
blue light flashing off the New England coast turned red. An
alarm sounded twice. Then a voice echoed through the entire
chamber.

*"All personnel report to emergency stations. Prudence Island
drop point is under attack! Prudence Island drop point is under
attack!"*

The Timber Wolf! she thought happily. Somehow the Timber
Wolf had found Corbano and was attacking!

Tears of joy slid from her eyes. A press of a button on her
watch face would reduce the Council headquarters to rubble, and

the Timber Wolf was filling his role equally well. Elliana felt elated.

Then she felt the agony as the rats, more ravenous than ever after gobbling up their snack, attacked her. The first bites sliced through her leather boots and dug into her legs. She could feel the creatures everywhere around her, clawing, scratching, pushing over each other, maddened by the smell of blood. She lunged forward to escape them.

The aged metal grating was forced outward when she struck it and plunged downward for the chamber floor.

Ellie saw it all unfold in slow motion, her Uzi already stripped from her shoulder when the echo of steel meeting tile caused all eyes to swing toward her. There was a moment of hesitation, uncertainty, and she seized it, leaping from the tunnel onto the floor with the Uzi blasting. She used her first spray to blow out the fluorescent ceiling lights, which plunged the chamber into near darkness.

The guards fired at her shape as she ran, but the advantage still belonged to Ellie. She ducked behind a row of computer memory banks and fired the last bursts from this clip into a group of converging guards. Even as they fell, she was reaching for the first of her gas grenades, which would help shield her rush to the glassed-in command center. Destroy it and Powderkeg would be stopped for certain, after which a press of her watch would destroy the Council forever.

"Intruder alert! Intruder alert!"

The warning echoed through her head as she ran into the smoke that her first two gas grenades had created, keeping her frame low and jamming another clip into the Uzi. She was a blur of constant motion to take advantage of the confusion caused by her surprise attack, necessitated by the untimely crashing of the grate to the floor.

Ellie was readying a third gas grenade when a pair of guards jumped out into the aisle before her and fired rapid bursts. Ellie hit the floor hard and returned their fire as she felt one bullet slice her shoulder and a second knife through her boot. The fiery pain flooded her senses, but she didn't let herself feel it as the men rolled against each other, dead.

Ellie yanked one of the fragmentary grenades from within her jacket and tossed it into the pooling smoke toward the largest congestion of pounding footsteps. Screams sounded with its explosion. She ran into the chaos where the guards not felled by the grenade tried to scatter, and she hit as many as she could with the Uzi, leaving her with barely half a clip.

Boot heels clicked behind her and she swung to fire a spray in that direction. Too much of the smoke had dissipated there and she ripped the pin from her final gas grenade with her teeth as she exhausted her second clip. The familiar *poof* sounded, and again the floor was drenched in thick gray smoke.

Then she was moving once more for the command center. She knew it held the facilities that would send the go-signal to the powder drop crews waiting across America. Destroy these facilities, then, and the signal could never be sent, even if the explosives above failed for any reason. But no bullets or grenades could penetrate the security glass. That would require at least one of her two remaining plastic explosives packs.

Ellie yanked the bolt of her Uzi back again and hurled a fragmentary grenade forward. This one impacted a major circuit board of the computer banks. Black smoke spilled outward, merging with the gray mist she had created to form even better camouflage as she charged for the command center, the Uzi spitting bullets forward.

Ellie felt a hot burst to her back and knew she'd been hit again. A numbness spread down her buttocks into her legs and she knew she was slowed now, fearing that her wound might be mortal but not giving it further thought. The glassed-in command center filled her mind, still ablaze with light and desperate activity, although the occupants surely considered themselves safe from her onslaught.

Ellie hurled another pair of grenades, one behind her toward another area of enemy fire and one to the front in the direction of the center to create enough distraction to clear a path for her.

It lasted long enough for her to slam her frame low into the five-foot section of wall running from the floor to the start of the glass wall. Already she had stripped one of her remaining plastic explosives packs from her bag and started to raise it toward the glass.

A bullet pounded her right side as she wedged it in firmly. The detonator slid from her hand. She fumbled for her final two grenades and hurled them randomly forward to buy herself the last seconds she needed. When they sounded, she had already recovered the miniature detonator and jammed it into the plastic. She grabbed the quick fuse and pulled, triggering a three-second delay. She then dragged her torn and bloodied body into a corner and covered herself as best she could. Her eyes sought out the occupants of the command center, who now realized in terror what was about to happen. The last thing she saw before the blast was the four Council members rushing for the escape door.

They never made it. The command center erupted in a single blast that flushed incredible heat through the front half of the chamber below. The thick glass had exploded inward mostly, turning those within into pincushions. Through the stench-filled smoke and flickering flames, Ellie could see no trace of anything even remotely alive.

She strained to rise and made it up far enough to see that all displays on the maps had died and the maps themselves were splintered and broken. Not a single control was left whole. Sparks and flames leaped from the shattered machines. All contact with America had been broken off. Powderkeg could no longer be triggered from this point.

Ellie's satisfaction was short. As she struggled to regain her feet, a volley of bullets slammed into her one after another. Numbness filled her legs an instant before she collapsed, tasting the blood thick in her mouth mixing with saliva. A final bullet shook her all the way to the floor as the last of the guards charged forward, guns first.

The watch! Push the button!

Ellie found the resolve, but not the strength. The guards in blood-stained khaki hovered around her, gun barrels aimed down as if deciding which of them would finally end her life.

"Hold your fire," a voice ordered from the gray-black shadows just beneath the command center.

Could someone from within it have survived the blast or escaped before it went off? Apparently so. Only the leader had been close enough to the escape exit. Ellie held to her last bit of life to stop her eyes from dimming. She turned them in the direction of the voice and saw first a pair of boots approaching, then a pistol held at waist level.

"I'll finish her," the leader told the guards, who separated to allow his approach.

He was close now, almost directly over her, and Ellie strained her neck to look at him. The motion forced more blood from between her lips. Ellie felt her breath desert her, and she gasped to get it back. Her eyes locked finally on the leader through the thinning smoke and haze of approaching death.

The sight made the blood left within her run cold.

She was looking at her husband—David.

CHAPTER 34

THE COMMUNICATIONS OFFICER ON THE BRIDGE OF THE COAST GUARD cutter turned behind him to Corbano.

"We've lost contact with the castle, sir."

"Try again!"

"I have. The signal's dead."

"Damn!" Corbano screamed, slamming his fist down against the control panel.

Just minutes ago everything was proceeding as planned without a hitch. Now the fury of the attacking fleet of boats continued to rage, turning the deck of the cutter into an inferno and scattering all but the hardiest of personnel toward the lifeboats. The attacking fleet continued to blast away at the cutter, more target practice than anything else at this point. And now, suddenly, contact had been broken off with Council headquarters across the ocean.

Elliana Hirsch at the castle, the Timber Wolf here . . . Somehow they had both managed to survive in Georgia, and now Powderkeg was falling to their efforts. Corbano had little regard for the Council members across the ocean. Their deaths wouldn't faze him in the least. But if these deaths prevented Powderkeg from being completed, then all he had worked for and envisioned these long years would be lost. The world he was meant to live in would never come to pass.

Corbano swore again.

But he wasn't beaten yet. There was still a chance to fulfill his vision. Fuck the damn Council. He still had his allotment of powder and if he dropped it now, the northern East Coast at the very least would be dead by morning. Washington, New York—America couldn't function without them. Mass chaos. A world gone mad. Corbano could still make it happen.

He rushed from the bridge.

The Timber Wolf had chosen an interior route to the bridge to stay out of the line of fire from the battle raging on the decks. The smoke had thickened even more and the fire alarm bells had begun to chime minutes ago. Trelana's forces were in total control; he was sure of that much. The attacking boats continued their zigzagging past each other while firing a constant barrage into the already crippled cutter. The drug lord's men had sustained casualties, but they continued to fight, obeying their orders to the letter. Corbano's troops were functioning in disarray, many already abandoning the effort along with the ship.

The entrance to the bridge appeared up ahead, and Wayman never hesitated. He crashed through the door firing at anyone who might have offered resistance. When he stopped a single man sat beneath a radio console with his hands in the air. Wayman reached down and yanked him out, a grimace of pain stretching across the Timber Wolf's face from the bullet wound in his side. He realized he was losing some blood and that a portion of it was soaking all the way through the white uniform he had donned over his own clothes.

"Where's Corbano?" the Timber Wolf demanded, sticking the rifle barrel against the man's chin. Out of control now, the cutter listed heavily to the left and began to flounder.

"I don't know! I don't know! He was here but—"

"But what? Talk or I'll kill you!"

"He left. Just before you came in, he ran out."

"To where?"

"I don't know!"

But Wayman did. "The powder, where's it stored?"

The man stayed silent, hesitating.

"Talk or you'll die. Last chance."

The man relented. "All right. Below deck. Storage hold number three. It's marked. Clearly."

"How do I get there?"

"Main stairs. You must have passed them on your way to the bridge. You can't miss them. Go down as far as you can, then turn right."

Wayman shoved the man to the floor. He had what he needed, but he didn't have Corbano. The White Snake had several minutes' head start on him now, plenty of time to begin the process of dumping the white powder overboard.

The Timber Wolf charged out through the door.

The third diver slipped in the pooling water as his flippers smacked the deck. He never went down all the way, but he lost his balance along with his grip on the spear gun. It slid to the deck and bounced once, ending up halfway between the diver and Drew.

Drew felt the agony tear through him as he tried for the weapon, fighting past all the pain to lunge forward with his leg dragging roughly behind him. He had almost reached the gun when the diver kicked it aside and cracked Drew's face with the same foot. Then he went for it himself, but Drew managed to trip him up and the man went sprawling hard to the deck.

Drew pushed himself back against the cabin and used leverage to hoist his frame up, as the diver struggled back to his feet feeling for the underwater knife sheathed on his calf. Drew pushed the door open and started to pull himself inside the cabin. He got the door closed and locked just as the diver stripped his blade free and started coming. Drew pulled himself along the musty inside, nearly falling, eyes in search of a weapon.

The door crashed inward and the diver came forward. He was breathing hard and transferring the knife from his left hand to his right.

Drew looked back at him, lost his balance, and reached up to a galley table.

The diver stalked forward, seeming to measure his pace, wary now.

Drew slipped back to the floor, dragging something from the galley table with him. It was a lamp, a kerosene lamp. The man was almost upon him and the knife was lowering in line with his throat.

Drew crashed the lamp upward against the man's chest. It smashed across his wet suit, splattering his face and shoulders with kerosene. The man screamed in agony and reeled backward. The knife slid from his hand.

Drew pulled himself up even with the table and grasped for a box of matches lying there. He struck three at once within a trembling hand and used them to set the entire box ablaze. The diver was charging him again now, bellowing with eyes red from the kerosene.

Drew hurled the flaming match box. The enraged diver rushed straight into it.

The flames swallowed his head and shoulders instantly, rapidly engulfing his entire torso. His shrill screams were the worst sounds Drew had ever heard, and the diver threw himself all about the cabin in a futile attempt to put out the flames that were killing him. Everything he struck, made of aged wood mostly, caught fire on contact, and by the time Drew pulled himself through the doorway, the entire cabin was drenched in flames.

He crawled across the deck and was halfway to the gunwale when the flames leaped out from below, licking at the spare gasoline cans they had purchased from Captain Jack. This last bit of desperation fueling him, Drew reached the gunwale and grasped it to pull himself over. His lower body weighed a ton, his legs useless. He had gotten his midsection up and over the side when the blast came.

Drew felt more than heard it. The heat pounded his back with a pressure that lifted him into the air toward the water. He struck it head first and went under as the boat exploded in a final burst of fiery orange that swallowed everything and spit back shards and splinters.

Beyond that, there were only the black depths opening their mouth to embrace him and Drew feeling himself drifting into it.

Corbano swung back the latch on the third storage hold and yanked open the door. Such holds on board a ship the size of a cutter were understandably small since the ship was seldom called upon to handle merchandise or cargo other than that confiscated at sea. The third hold was ten-by-twenty, constructed within the hull beneath sea level.

Corbano knew what he had to do.

The white powder was sealed in five specially designed bags, which were both air- and watertight for obvious reasons. He could feel the ship teetering now, swaying out of control at the mercy of the currents, and knew it was only a matter of minutes before she ran aground and was boarded.

Corbano rested the portable rocket launcher he had grabbed from the armory against the wall. Next he whipped out a knife and went to work on the bags containing the white powder, slicing them down the middle and pouring their contents onto the cold steel floor after making sure it was perfectly dry. Attached to his belt was an oxygen-supplied mask that he would don as soon as the final stage of his plan was ready. A power boat had been hidden in the cutter's stern for an emergency such as this and he would make his escape in it.

Once he was finished dumping the powder on the floor, Corbano planned to fire a rocket through the hull to allow floods of water to pour in and sweep the powder away with it. It would dissolve immediately and the deadly cloud would begin to form, the plan not in keeping with the original but a worthy improvisation. The East Coast would suffer just as it was supposed to and perhaps more of the country as well. America would fall rapidly, then the world. He would make his way back to Europe, prepared to seize the chaos for his own benefit.

Corbano had just finished dumping the contents of the third bag when the clicking of the door alerted him to danger. He reached for the pistol in his belt and spun fast.

The Timber Wolf lunged forward, managing to get one shot off just as Corbano did. They were upon each other quicker than either expected, each of their guns useless at such close range.

In fact, the initial collision separated the pistols from both and Corbano aimed a knee toward the Timber Wolf's groin. But Wayman managed to twist sideways, avoiding the strike as he grabbed Corbano's wrist in an iron lock and tugged viciously down and to the side.

They both heard the snap, but it was Corbano who wailed in pain from his cracked wrist. Wayman knew he had him now, what with the White Snake having only one hand to defend himself, and moved for the kill. His mistake was to concern himself only with Corbano's good side because the blow lashing toward him came from the bad, from the broken hand, in fact. At impact, it was hard to tell for whom the pain was greater.

Wayman was staggered, dazed. Blood ran from a nasty cut along the side of his head, making him dizzy.

Corbano crashed into him again, this time to the side with the bullet wound, and Wayman howled in agony as the White Snake shoved him backward against the bulkhead. Wayman felt all his wind desert him. Corbano pulled his good hand back for a killing blow to the throat, and the Timber Wolf managed to duck his head in time. Corbano's fist slammed steel and now it was his turn to scream.

Wayman tried to rush past him for the rocket launcher, not really sure what he was going to do with it, but Corbano tripped him up. Then, instead of continuing the assault, the White Snake charged for his stainless steel pistol, which shone in the dim light of the hold amidst the white powder.

The Timber Wolf registered this in time to rush for the door, half walking and half crawling. Corbano fired twice, heard a gasp, the signal that one of the bullets had found its mark, and moved cautiously to the doorway to complete the kill.

He emerged into the corridor good side first. It was deserted. No sign of the Timber Wolf. Corbano glanced down. A trail of blood was drawn neatly across the floor leading straight into storage hold number two. The door to it was still open, swaying slightly inward. The great Timber Wolf was probably looking for a quiet corner to die. Well, Corbano would just have to provide him with it. He lunged through the door leading with his pistol, eyes already searching out his target.

His mind had just registered that the hold was empty and that the trail of blood had ended *at* the door when an iron grip locked on his gun hand and stripped it from his grasp. The force spun him into the center of the hold, and he came around fast, rushing at little more than a shadow in the blackness. There was a flash before him and Corbano realized it was a gun bore in what seemed like an instant before the hot pain tore through his chest. The bore spit fire twice more and the White Snake found himself looking up from the floor without memory of falling to it. He knew he was dying, but he held life long enough to see a shadow pass over him.

"Almost like you did to me in Corsica," the Timber Wolf said calmly. "Remember? Fuck you."

And he fired three more times.

When he was sure Corbano was dead, Wayman rushed down the corridor to a storage bin where dozens of cans of emergency engine oil were kept. He figured two would do the job he had in mind and he carted them back to the hold containing the now scattered powder. He walked about the white granules, spreading the contents of the first can over them. When it was empty, he started with the second, finishing his sweep and then going over much of the floor a second time. He realized that the cutter's engines had ground to a halt and he knew he had very little time now to escape himself.

The Timber Wolf backed into the hallway and raised his gun, pumping the trigger once and then again. The heat of the bullets turned the oil to flames and the powder made perfect kindling for it. The flames swallowed it, hissing and forming an oil-black cloud that filled the entire hold.

Wayman left the door open to be sure that the fire would continue to burn unimpeded until there was nothing left for it to swallow. A sudden list to the left slammed him against the wall, and he heard a grating noise indicating that part of the ship had run aground and was tearing itself apart. It didn't matter because by the time water rushed into this part of the ship, no more of the powder would remain to loom as a threat. It was almost over.

But not quite. There was still escape to concern himself with, and Wayman yanked off his shoes to make sure that he brought none of the powder up to the deck with him. He could feel the heat of the steps right through his socks as he bounded up with as much speed as his wounds would allow. He turned onto a second staircase that would take him back to the main deck and a quick plunge over the side.

Upon reaching it, however, he found the smoke and flames had formed a barrier that was starting to extend down the steps he had just raced up. Wayman felt his breath flee as smoke filled his lungs and forced him to retch. He slammed against the bulkhead at the top of the stairs and started to slump.

No! Not now, not after this much!

The same incredible will to live, to survive, that had kept him alive so many times during the heyday of the Timber Wolf switched on again. He found the strength he needed to seize the only option he had left, which was to charge directly through the flames and hurl himself over the side. He tore off the white uniform shirt atop his own and covered his face with it. Then he was in motion.

It would seem later to him that there had been no flames, that a tunnel had opened up before him as he charged over the side. He felt wind and heat, but no fire.

He hit the water hard, feet first, going down deep into the cold and silent blackness, both welcome now. He rose to see the burning hulk that had been the Coast Guard cutter sitting dead in the water at a bizarre angle with the bow well below stern. A huge seagoing corpse giving up the last of her dead. Within her hull lay the last remains of a powder that would have claimed even more dead, an unimaginable number.

One of Trelana's speedboats was coming toward him and Wayman raised his arms in a gesture of surrender as he tread water with his legs. He thought of Drew Jordan for the first time in a while and gazed across the water to find the rubble that had been their boat. Through all his elation, the Timber Wolf felt his heart sink.

He could almost forget Corsica now, but not quite.

Ellie's first, fleeting impression was that she had died and that David had come to meet her. Then she thought her mind, resigned to the coming of death, had created an illusion to make the passage over easier.

But her eyes had not deceived her. The man above her *was* David Hirsch, the husband she had loved, a minister for the Israeli cabinet until he was forced to resign and later assassinated.

By the Council of Ten, she had thought.

"I'm sorry, Ellie," he told her softly, gun held low by his hip. "I truly am."

Ellie struggled for breath with which to speak. "The Council of Ten," she muttered, blood sliding from her mouth.

David Hirsch nodded knowingly. "Yes, Ellie, I am its leader, even before it became necessary for me to 'arrange' my own passing. I founded the Council as it exists now. I built it up from the raw foundation of another organization that possessed initiative but lacked sufficient vision. You see, the Council has existed in one form or another for thousands of years. But the time had come for a different order to take command, one that was of single mind when it came to purpose and would stop at nothing to achieve that purpose.''

"Why?" Ellie mouthed.

"You made it hard on yourself, Ellie," David Hirsch, leader of the Council of Ten, said instead of responding. "You had ample opportunities to die easily and swiftly, but you dragged things out and insisted on invading our very home. I could have had you killed this afternoon, should have probably, but something soft in me resisted. I wanted to see how far you could get, thought I might be able to persuade you to join us once you knew the truth. But all that was for naught." He leaned over close to her. "It all seems so futile now, Ellie, doesn't it? All the bullets, all the blood. Lying here with the certainty of your own death looming. Such is the price you must pay for your pursuits. Such is the price all must pay who come too close to us."

Ellie knew she was looking at and listening to a madman. It made the whole of her life seem so vacant. She was going to die, and everything was meaningless, nothing accomplished, all ideals wasted. Still she had to know.

"Why?" she repeated.

"So many questions they all had," David said, more to himself. "So many fronts I had to put up for all of them. Our marriage was a front, Ellie. The Israelis had to be satisfied. I was a mole for the Soviets. They helped me attain my position and then I doubled for the Americans and they helped me rise. But neither of these powers, nor Israel itself, was capable of running the world as it must be run. Dissatisfaction led me out on my own. I used my position to seek out others who felt as I did. Eventually, the Russians disowned me for my views, the Americans and Israelis, too. But I had the company of these other outcasts, powerful men and leaders all. I faked my own death, my *execution* because I had discovered the means they needed to link their causes together. We formed the Council and laid the groundwork for a new order to control the world."

"The destruction of America," Ellie rasped.

"Only of her people. The discovery of the white powder permitted us to spare her vast land and resources for ourselves. Don't you see? We will resettle the nation with the followers of our own causes. The transports will begin flying in a week and even now thousands of our American supporters are gathering in shelters that will keep them safe through the duration of Powderkeg. America's few other survivors will be enslaved to do our menial bidding. Peasants they will be, useless scum living off the memories of the world they once controlled, a world we will have taken over. America's missiles will be aimed at any country that dares stand against us, and if this is not enough, there is always the white powder to hold them in check. We will be in a position to hold all the world hostage as we ourselves have been held hostage through the years. Everything was functioning perfectly.''

David Hirsch's expression changed as he gazed up at the ruined command center. "I knew as soon as the trouble started that it was you and moved to a place of safety because I feared my troops could not stop you. Until today, I underestimated you, Ellie, underestimated your obsessive quest for vengeance against those you thought were my killers. I suppose I should have been grateful as I watched the folly of your pursuits. I never imagined you could get this far. And now, thanks to my error, a perfect plan has been disrupted. Just disrupted, Ellie, not destroyed. An inconvenience and nothing else. Where I found these outcast leaders, I can find hundreds more. And the powder is still out there, my people waiting across America for the signal to come. And it *will* come, Ellie. There is a backup system only I am aware of. Only *I*. You see I am the key, Ellie. It is I who hold the means with a clear vision of the end. You have failed by letting me survive. Take heart, for I failed by not killing you sooner. But America was to be home for the new Council of Ten and so it shall be someday soon. I will rebuild the Council to its predestined number to rule the world as we see fit. Destroy our headquarters, kill my underlings, but leave me to do what I must.''

Ellie's eyes dimmed, a curtain starting to draw before them. Out of the hopelessness of it all, she knew the madman before her had to be stopped. She had the means, but now, once again, she had found the desire and resolve to perform the final act of what suddenly seemed a meaningless life.

"I love you, David," she said weakly.

He just looked at her.

He nodded, satisfied, and kneeled down in her blood to move his pistol against her breast.

"Kiss me, David. Let me feel you one last time." And with that Ellie freed the cyanide capsule from her rear molar.

His mouth moved emotionlessly forward and met hers. She tried for passion amidst the blood still pumping from inside her. She could feel him starting to squeeze the trigger and bit down hard on the capsule now between her rear teeth. As the gas hissed out, she poured her breath into his mouth, feeling him pull back as the bitter almond taste reached his senses.

The gun slipped from his hand. David pulled away, gasping only once before he fell backward, horribly aware of his own death and seeking out his killer through fading eyes as guards rushed to his aid.

Ellie used her last bit of life to press the face to her watch. Above her the explosions sounded as sparks in unison, followed by a rumbling as the medieval castle began to crumble from above. She was dead long before the ceiling began to shower downward, covering the dead and soon-to-be-dead with the rubble of twelve centuries. But her face remained placid and calm, more at peace than it had been in life for years.

Meanwhile, the people of Sintra and the surrounding towns were awakened by what surely must have been an earthquake. The ground for miles seemed to tremble and the great rumbling disturbed both animals and sleeping infants. People poured out of their homes in fear and dread, desperate gazes locking on a shower of dust and debris, a thickening cloud that seemed to be rising out of the mist for the night sky. Only at sunrise would they understand what had happened. Only then would they see what had caused the rude and terrifying interruption of their sleep.

The Castle of the Moors was no more.

EPILOGUE

DREW DID NOT KNOW THE NAME OF THE ISLAND AND DIDN'T MUCH care. He knew only that it belonged to Arthur Trelana, and that was enough since in the end it had been Trelana who saved his life.

Mostly all he remembered was the pain. His sleep was interrupted constantly in the early days here by dreams of being trapped by walls of flame. He would wake up screaming, sweating, tearing the sheets off himself as the air conditioner hummed softly from the window.

Weeks had passed now, but Drew had lost too much track of time to know precisely how many. He measured its passing simply by the visits of his doctors, the increasing length between them telling him that he was getting better. Despite this the amount of pain was still enormous, along with an arm and leg that were basically useless. Pills had numbed it and him for quite some time, but now the pills were issued less frequently and Drew learned to expect the pain and tolerate it reasonably well. Slowly his mind began to clear and more memories returned.

Strangely, most came back in reverse order. He remembered waking one morning to find the Timber Wolf standing over him. He, too, was a mess, with a bandaged face, one arm in a sling, and a crutch held under his armpit. On another earlier occasion, Trelana himself had hovered over Drew's bedside with an explanation of where he was and an assurance that he was safe. Last he remembered the plunge into the frigid waters off Prudence

Island. He regained consciousness only after being lifted into one of Trelana's boats and placed in a cabin next to the Timber Wolf.

Trelana had returned this morning and informed him that it was exactly four weeks since that day. They sat together beneath the warm Caribbean sun, parting after Trelana announced that the Timber Wolf was due in that afternoon.

Actually, it was early evening when Wayman arrived at the villa, the sky darkening but still colored amber by the majestic glow of the setting sun. They sat on the veranda in chairs across from each other, neither speaking for a few minutes. The Timber Wolf had shed his bandages, but sudden motions brought a painful grimace to his face.

"You surprised them, Drew," he stated finally. "For a while nobody thought you were going to pull through."

Reflexively, Drew's hands swept across the still-bandaged areas of his thigh and chest. "Trelana was here today," he said.

"I know."

"Do you know what he came about?"

"He gave me a rough idea when I spoke with him this morning."

"Let me fill you in on the details." Drew eased himself forward. "He says he can arrange a new identity for me: new name, new social security number, a whole new lease on life. A fresh start, in other words, and he'll throw one in for Pam, too, once she gets better."

"I'm told her prognosis is favorable."

"Oh, she'll live all right, just like I will."

"I'm also told you've only spoken to her once."

Drew didn't respond right away, as if he were searching for an excuse. "The guy she loved and who loved her doesn't exist anymore. I can't go back to just being myself because he's gone, good as dead and there's this stranger in his place." Drew looked down, then up again. "Trelana's offering me a whole new lease on life," he repeated. "The problem is finding a reason to live."

"It's easier to find one not to die."

"Very profound."

"Just necessary."

Drew struggled up from his chair and moved to the veranda

railing. "It all comes down to hate, doesn't it, Peter? Back in mercenary camp, Mace told me that it was hate that kept you going, kept you alive. I didn't really understand what he meant until now. It's not so much hate as the absence of love. I just can't feel love anymore. I think back to the person I was before all this started and I don't even know him." Drew's tone became more businesslike. "Trelana said my future might depend on how much is left of the Council. He said to talk to you about what you found at the castle before I . . . make my decision. You found it, didn't you?"

The Timber Wolf nodded. "I found what was left of it. It's just rubble now with some parapets and towers lingering for effect."

"Elliana?"

Wayman shook his head sadly. "She knocked out the Council headquarters, which explains why the go-signal was never given for the rest of Powderkeg. She knocked it out so completely that she must have been trapped inside with the rest of them. A waste. She was the best."

"Including you?"

"Including anyone in this god-forsaken line of work. Things never stopped mattering to her. That made her special."

"Then she finished it. . . ."

The Timber Wolf rose and joined Drew at the railing. "Not quite. There are still twenty-eight drop points out there with their deadly supplies of powder ready and waiting. The Council's central command is gone and with it they've lost the number one thing they had going for them—organization. But they can get that back. Somebody will start the ball rolling again. It's inevitable." Wayman gazed out over the water. "I've been at this for more than fifteen years now. I've seen a dozen councils and a hundred Corbanos. All obsessed with power and all convinced they're the only ones who really know how the world should be run. Trouble is, to get it running that way lots of people have to die first—more each time."

"Then it's good that people like you . . . and Elliana . . . are out there to stop them."

Wayman smiled reflectively. "Save your praise, kid. We're not gunfighters saving the innocent farmers from the murderous ranchers. We're just hired hands caught in the middle. I gave up trying to figure out what was right a long time ago. All I know for sure is what's wrong." He hesitated. "Like Powderkeg."

"It's still out there, you said, still functional."

"But only temporarily. We've got the drop point locations, and Trelana's lending me the manpower I'll need to destroy them and all the powder."

Drew looked at the Timber Wolf closely before speaking. "What about me?"

"Walk away. Take Trelana's offer, pick up your girl friend, and build a new life. Forget all this crap about loving and hating—none of it means a thing. The world's not a very pleasant place, and it was your lot to find that out a little more blatantly than most. I used to think I tried to quit five years ago because my standards were too high. Truth was I realized there was no such thing as standards at all. It's a treadmill, Drew, and when the track speeds up you do your best to keep up with it. You survive—that's the object, the only object."

Drew shook his head. "I don't buy that. You're probably right about surviving, but I can't build a new life based on the person I used to be. My past started seven weeks ago and I don't have a present at all. All I've got is a future and I'm not really sure what's best for me, but I know a new name and social security number don't even come close."

"Drew—"

"No, let me finish. You're going to tell me to go back to Pam, that she needs me, but it's not like that, believe me it's not. If I take Trelana's offer, it won't be so much that I'm on a treadmill that's moving too fast as one that's not moving at all. I can't look back; I can only look ahead." His eyes became pleading. "But I need a target, something to focus on."

Wayman hesitated. "What does Pam say about all this?"

"We didn't quite . . . discuss it. We didn't discuss much of anything." Drew smiled sadly. "She did say she never could stomach my macho act in your typical Georgetown bar or my adventures at mercenary camp, but she was proud of what I've done these past few weeks when it was for real and lives depended on it."

"And what did *you* say?" When Drew stayed silent, Wayman seized the advantage. "You didn't say anything because it's your fault she's where she is. You got her involved. You don't want to face that so you turn your back on her. Get used to it, kid. In the world you're so determined to enter, people get hurt and you just block it out because otherwise it eats you up, tears you apart.''

"I've already entered, Peter, and nobody gave me much choice about it. I'd like to choose on my own to stay in.''

But Wayman wasn't giving up the fight yet. "No, it all comes down to what you just said, except you left something out. You can't look back because you're *afraid* to. But that's the way it always is in this business. You don't ever look back because there's too much pain there. It's called a one-dimensional existence. Hell, even Shane never looked back when the kid stood there on the edge of town screaming his name.''

"He was good at what he did. That got him through.''

Wayman moved forward and squeezed Drew's good shoulder tenderly. "I'll come back in two weeks. If you still feel this way, we'll talk. I owe you too much not to accept your decision, but I owe you too much not to make you think about it. Make sense?''

"Not really.''

"Get used to it.''

They stood together at the railing in silence. Wayman had expected Drew's request and planned for it. So had Trelana. He would spend much of the next two weeks praying the kid would change his mind, knowing all the time that he wouldn't.

They both gazed out over the sea where the fading light caught a tern swooning down from the sky to sweep up a fish that had wandered too close to the surface.

"Things don't change much, do they?'' Drew asked softly.

"No,'' the Timber Wolf said. "I suppose they don't.''

About the Author

Jon Land is also the author of THE DOOMSDAY SPIRAL, THE LUCIFER DIRECTIVE, VORTEX, LABYRINTH, and THE OMEGA COMMAND. He is thirty years old and lives in Providence, Rhode Island, where he is currently at work on a new novel.